Sliabh na mBan

Sliabh na mBan

MARY RYDER

FOUR SEASONS

FOUR SEASONS PUBLISHING
Baltinglass Wicklow

First published in Eire in 2005 by
FOUR SEASONS
Mount Carmel, Deerpark, Baltinglass
County Wicklow, Eire.

A CIP Catalogue record for this book
is available from The British Library

ISBN 0-9550127-0-8

Printed in Eire by:
Imperial Print & Design Co Ltd
Unit 12, Clonminam Business Park
Portlaoise, County Laois, Eire

Sliabh na mBan

Jet trails formed fluffy traces across the June sky. The brilliant rays of the sun played on the silvery aircraft, as it wove its way through the clouds, its distant drone reminding Jenny Anderson that it was time to pack her suitcases for New York. Soon she would sample life in the Big Apple, far from the beautiful valley of Sliabh na mBan, where she and her brother Mattie grew up.

Jenny patted Flan, her pony, and closed the paddock gate. Heading for the stable, she felt her green eyes becoming misty, while the soft breeze caught her titian hair. A pang of loneliness gripped her entire body, as she struggled to remove her riding boots and hang her hat on the peg. When, she wondered, would she get the opportunity to saddle Flan again?

Sighing heavily, she hung her jodhpurs and jacket in the cupboard, tears streaming down her cheeks. Grabbing a soft towel, she headed to the shower. If only the warm water could wash away her loneliness too. Such were her thoughts as she sensuously allowed the soothing spray to envelop her skinny five-foot eight-inch frame. Gingerly she stepped out on to the shaggy-pile mat and draped herself in the towel.

'Oh my goodness, you look a sight,' she remarked, catching a glimpse of her red eyes in the mirror. On closer scrutiny, she noticed her well-defined nose bore a scratch mark sustained from a thorn bush earlier. Carefully, she applied her make-up and glossed her rosebud lips. She brushed her titian hair and slipped on a pair of jeans and a sweater. Glancing at her watch, she realised she was running late. Quickly she made her way to the dinette where her grandma was waiting to serve coffee.

'It's good to be alive on such a beautiful morning,' Mary Anderson remarked to her grandchild while pouring coffee. 'Did you enjoy your ride on Flan?'

'More than usual,' Jenny replied, fighting hard not to break down. 'I really love that old pony, we've been partners for so long.'

Mary Anderson shook her head thoughtfully. 'I remember so well farm manager Tom Hanley leading him into the yard for your sixteenth birthday. You went wild with excitement and jumped on the poor animal bare backed.'

''Did I really, Grandma?' Jenny asked, between fits of laughter and tears. 'I'm sure the staff must have thought I was some sort of cowgirl about to enter a bareback Bronco riding competition or something.'

'They were all as excited as you were, Jenny, and even helped you to decide on the name Flan.'

'I hope Mattie will take good care of him while I'm away. I'd hate to think he was just left to roam around the pasture.'

'Never you fear, Jenny, he'll be groomed and exercised just as if you were around. Sure, you know I wouldn't have it any other way.' She reminded her that Tom Hanley's young daughters were taking a keen interest in horse riding just now, and would jump at the opportunity to go for a gallop on him.

'So I've noticed,' Jenny replied, staring through the window, her eyes fixed on the old Wendy house covered with rambling roses. She swallowed hard and a choking sensation filled her throat. Memories of her late parents playing with her and Mattie in the garden came flooding back.

'Are you okay, dear?' her grandma asked. You appear to be deep in thought.

'I'm just remembering certain things. I guess I'm going to miss everyone very much.'

'You'll soon settle into your new life and make new friends,' her grandma assured her. Just then, Tom Hanley knocked gently on the door before poking his head in.

'Ah! Good morning, Tom, what news do you have for us?' Mary Anderson asked, spotting the bundle of letters he was carrying.

'You ladies appear to be very popular this morning judging by this lot,' he remarked, handing her the mail. 'I'll leave you in peace to read it.'

'Bills, no doubt, Tom'. In any case, thanks for collecting it from the mailbox.' Mary placed the mail to one side for the moment. The commotion going on in the main farmhouse kitchen distracted them both. Cook Norah Leahy normally had things under control with one exception - Ben Breen. Ben, one of the farm hands had fancied Norah for years, and had tried every ploy to woo her, but to no avail. Undaunted by the fact that Norah was wielding a cleaver while she prepared to decapitate a salmon, Ben allowed his lecherous eyes to gaze at her well-shaped legs. Despite the precarious nature of the operation in hand, Norah spotted him, and narrowly missed the tip of her finger with the cleaver.

'I'll have you for harassment,' she screamed. 'Can't you get it into your thick skull for once and for all that I want nothing to do with you. Just because you've won the ploughing championship a few times doesn't mean you can win me over. Please take your eyes off my legs and my land. Understand?'

Ben gulped down his tea and stood up to leave. The O'Reilly twins were shaking with laughter, adding further to Norah's annoyance.

'Get back to work, you pair of scoundrels,' Tom Hanley thundered, trying hard to keep a straight face. The terrible twins had joined the farm staff for the summer to earn money for their college fees, though Norah Leahy didn't believe that yarn.

'Yes Mr Hanley, sorry Mr Hanley.' The twins couldn't wait to get outside the door to resume the laughter.

Luke Nolan, another old farm hand, was both deaf and indifferent. He had worked with the Andersons for years, and the shenanigans of Ben and Norah didn't bother him in the slightest.

'Praise be to God! What am I to do with Ben and Norah?' Mary Anderson whispered to Jenny.

'Ignore them, grandma,' she replied. 'Sure don't they provide a bit of entertainment if nothing else, to tell the truth, I'll miss them when I leave.'

Mary Anderson nodded, giving the impression that she was in agreement with Jenny. All the same, she knew Norah Leahy to be a feisty woman, and Ben Breen, though not intentionally, tended to get on her nerves, so perhaps a discreet word in both their ears might help.

'Take no notice of Norah gibbering on,' Ben said to Tom Hanley on their way to check the cattle. 'She's playing hard to get and I'm not one to give up easily.'

'I'd cool it if I were you Ben,' Tom advised. 'Norah doesn't seem to fancy you.'

'I have no intention of letting that fine woman slip through

4

my hands,' Ben spoke defiantly. 'A woman like Norah needs coaxing if you get my meaning,' he winked at Tom who simply shrugged his shoulders indifferently.

'Have it your own way, but don't say I didn't warn you,' said Tom.

Jenny and her grandma were opening the post when Mattie joined them.

'Anything for me in that pile?' he asked, lurching his bulky frame against the table.

Jenny handed him a large brown envelope. Mattie grabbed a sharp knife and ripped it open. 'More Department of Agriculture manure,' he remarked sarcastically, scanning the contents. 'Brussels this and Brussels that,' he mocked, running his fingers through his spiky hairstyle. 'Honestly, those bureaucrats think we have nothing else to do only answer stupid bloody questions.'

'Calm down, lad,' his grandma urged. 'Tom Hanley will give you a hand later. Anyway, we're part of Europe now, and we may as well get used to the idea.'

'I suppose so,' Mattie replied indifferently. 'Right now, I'm expecting the vet to check the cattle so I'd better be off.'

Mary Anderson handed Jenny her mail and proceeded to open her own. Having quickly read through the letter, she announced, 'My cousin, Tim Lucey, is coming home from Peru in August after spending ten years there.'

'What a pity I'll be in New York when he arrives. I'd dearly love to meet him again.' Jenny remembered him well when he came to the farm dressed in his black Dominican habit. When she told the teacher at school about her cousin, the priest, she had asked her to write an essay describing him and his work.

Father Tim had helped her to compile it, and even loaned her pictures of Lima to show the teacher and her classmates. She felt very important on that occasion, especially when the bishop's niece was mad jealous of her.

'Tell you what, Jenny, I'll write this very afternoon and tell him. I'll send a recent photograph he'll be amazed when he sees how you have changed. He may even decide to visit you there.'

'That would be lovely, I'm sure, Grandma, that is, if I ever get there.'

'What on earth do you mean? Of course you'll get to New York. What's got into you, all of a sudden?

'This short note from Doctor Ryan, that's what,' Jenny replied, passing the hastily written few lines from the doctor to her grandma.

She glanced at the note. 'So, Doctor Ryan wants to see you, what's all the panic about? If there was something really urgent, he would have phoned.'

'Thanks Grandma, I guess I'm over anxious at this stage. What in heaven's name would I do without you?'

Mary Anderson smiled sweetly. 'Run along and get ready for your appointment with Doctor Ryan and stop worrying, Jenny.' Mark my words, you're as healthy as a trout.'

'Trout or salmon, grandma, I hope you're right..'

Mary carried the elevenses tray through to the kitchen. Norah had just lifted a tray of currant buns out of the oven and was sucking her thumb. 'I'll never learn,' she remarked to Mary, who advised her to run the cold water on it. Norah laughed. 'It's not my thumb I'm talking about, it's Ben Breen'. Don't tell me you didn't hear me yelling at him earlier? I simply must learn to ignore him,' Norah continued.

'Would you like me to have a word with him?' Mary asked gently. A brief silence followed before she continued. 'I feel sorry for him in one way because I know that he is very fond of you.' Really, Norah, he is quite harmless. However, that doesn't give him the liberty to behave in an undesirable manner towards you.' I'll have a word after lunch, okay'?

'Thanks, Mrs Anderson, but I'd prefer if you didn't. I can handle Ben and I promise they'll be no more trouble between us. Like you say, he's harmless..'

'Very well, Norah, I'll say no more about the matter.'

'Thank you,' Norah replied, already practicing counting to ten.

Light entertainment was how Jenny had described the antics of Ben and Norah earlier perhaps she was right after all.

'I'll skip lunch if you don't mind, grandma,' Jenny remarked, zipping her handbag shut. 'I want to get this Doctor Ryan business over and done with, besides the walk will do me good, and help to clear my head.'

'Good luck, dear, and please give my love to the good doctor and his wife..'

The mile-long distance to the surgery was just perfect for Jenny to ponder her fate. Despite her grandma's reassurances, several things crossed her mind as she walked along. Suppose the X-ray had shown a shadow on the lung or, God forbid, both lungs.

Then there were the blood tests taken by Doctor Ryan two weeks previously. Anaemia, diabetes, peptic ulcer came to mind. Why had she suddenly broken into a cold sweat? Her head was spinning and she wished she could lie down.

'I want to go to New York so badly,' she shouted in a state of panic, please God don't let me hear bad news. Spotting the roof of the surgery through the trees, her step quickened. Nervously, she rang the doorbell. Doctor Ryan answered the door.

'Nice to see you, Jenny, please go through to the waiting room. I'll be with you in a tick.'

'Thank you, Doctor Ryan.'

Mercifully, the room was empty. She mopped the beads of perspiration from her forehead and tried desperately to compose herself. She could feel her knees knocking.

'Come through, Jenny,' Doctor Ryan called, leafing through a pile of freshly typed reports. 'Looking forward to New York?' he asked, still checking through the reports.

'Very much so,' she replied, trying to disguise her fears. The phone rang.

'Doctor Ryan's surgery.' He listened carefully to the caller, jotting down a few quick notes. 'Contractions every fifteen minutes you say. Well, I suggest you get Lynn to the hospital immediately. Tell her to do her breathing exercises and wish her luck. Thanks John!'

Suddenly Jenny felt relaxed. Doctor Ryan looked in her direction and smiled.

'The Reeds have been trying for a baby for ten years and this is a wonderful moment for all of us.' I feel a bit like God at this stage,' he remarked. 'I never stopped encouraging them to keep trying and it has paid off'.

'Jenny, when are you off to the States?' he enquired.

'In three weeks' time, if you give me the all clear today,' she replied.

'All the tests are perfect, you'll be glad to hear. But there's just one thing, you could flesh out a little, you're a bit under weight for your height.'

'I'm so relieved,' Jenny said. 'I was a bit scared when I got your note.'

'Marjorie and I are off on holidays,' he explained, 'and I want to leave everything up to date for the locum.' He stood up and shook her hand firmly. 'Best of luck for the future, Jenny, hope you'll be happy and successful. Remember me to your grandma.'

He watched her willowy figure as she walked smartly down the driveway and disappeared behind the grove of trees.

'You look very far away,' Marjorie Ryan remarked to her husband as she placed the afternoon tea tray on the table.

'Hmm, seeing Jenny Anderson just now brought that awful tragedy back to me again, as if it were only yesterday.' It is twelve years since her parents, John and Anne died, when their car skidded trying to avoid a pack of loose horses.

Marjorie poured the tea and added two slices of lemon for her husband.

'Drink this, Ken, and try not to dwell too much on that day.' He stood gazing through the window, the sad past obscuring the beauty of the multi-coloured roses, on a lovely June day. Marjorie noticed how tired he looked. He seemed older than his forty years. His shoulders drooped slightly, and a great shock of grey hair fell carelessly over his forehead.

He took a sip of tea. 'I felt so helpless that day, kneeling by them on the roadside, trying for a pulse that was no longer beating. Two children had been orphaned and I could do nothing.'

He shook his head at the hopelessness he felt. 'At least Father Rigney had the satisfaction of giving the Last Rites but I could do nothing.'

'Remember, Sliabh na mBan was your first appointment, Ken. It must be every doctor's biggest nightmare …'

'Oh Marjorie, I'm so sorry, I didn't mean to sound ungrateful for all the support you gave me then, and through the years. Just look at you wearing your new silk dress in readiness for our holiday. You're a picture of loveliness and I can't wait to fall in love with you all over again.'

Ken held Marjorie in his arms, reluctant to answer the phone. It was Marjorie who answered. 'John Reed wishes to speak to you, Ken.'

'We have a baby, Doctor Ryan, a beautiful bouncing boy arrived a few minutes ago and Lynn and I want to say thanks.'

'Congratulations to you both'. Marjorie sends her love too. This is great news, John, I'll call over when I get back from holidays.' Doctor Ryan replaced the receiver.

'Isn't that a nice note to start our holidays on?' Marjorie remarked to a very pleased Ken. He glanced at his watch. 'We better hurry, Marjorie, or we'll miss our plane.'

Jenny Anderson awoke bleary eyed after a restless night. Head cupped in hands, she surveyed the valley from a vantage point in her bedroom. Through the morning mist emerged Sliabh na mBan and, flowing from her breast, the glistening waters of the river Anner. Cattle, sheep and wildlife clung to her bosom or rested peacefully on her brow. Jenny's cousin, Mary Rafferty, once asked her what Sliabh na mBan meant in English. Although Mary's father Jack had explained, she wanted to hear Jenny's version. 'It means "Mountain Of Women", Jenny told her cousin from Boston.

The story goes that Fionn Mac Cumhail, a chief warrior of the Fianna and much sought after bachelor, challenged the women of Ireland to race to the top. The first woman to reach the top would win his hand in marriage. Grainne, the golden-haired daughter of King Cormac, won the race. However, she considered Fionn too old for her, and at a party given in their honour, she drugged the guest-cup effectively, causing Fionn and the other guests to fall into a deep slumber. This gave her the opportunity to elope with the much younger Diarmaid.

'It was good enough for the old fool,' Mary Rafferty drawled in her Boston accent and as youngsters they had rolled down the mountain in fits of laughter. 'I'd probably have done the same myself.'

'Good gracious, Jenny, are you not dressed yet?' her grandma's voice was as crisp as her neat white blouse. 'Have you forgotten the day that's in it? Come and help me with this tray. I don't want to spill anything on the newspaper.'

'Sorry, grandma, I didn't sleep very well. The thoughts of the exam results kept me awake.'

'You're bound to feel a bit anxious Jenny it's only to be expected. Exam results give everyone butterflies, but you have nothing to fear. Have some coffee and toast. The postman should be here in half an hour.'

Mary Anderson leafed quickly through the newspaper. 'It's a good shot of Mattie, I have to say, and Tan Bo looks well too. Here, take a look.'

'First prize, eh? Mattie kept that very quiet.' Jenny remarked, studying her brother and the bull. 'Sure, Tan Bo has won enough rosettes to fill the four walls of any room. There's not a more photographed or decorated bull in Ireland.'

'I'm sure you're right and Mattie knows that too, but he gets a great kick out of entering him and winning, and so do I, Jenny. An Anderson bull is always a fine pedigree animal and worth the money in breeding fees.' Mary folded the paper. Mattie hasn't seen it yet, she remarked. 'He'll be chuffed with it and, of course, your results.'

'Let's not crow about me just yet. I prefer to see my grades on official University headed paper before I say anything. Even then," Jenny continued 'I'll only think of it in terms of my work in America. God knows these past five years have been tough.'

'It'll be all worth it, Jenny. Soon you'll join Mary Rafferty in New York and carve out a good career for yourself as a social worker.'

Jenny dressed quickly when she spotted Luke O'Gorman's postal van wending its way up the avenue. Luke could have dropped the mail in the box at the gate but he was not one to miss out on a special occasion. He had earned himself the nickname X-Ray eyes for his uncanny knack of guessing correctly the contents of most envelopes and their origins. Today was no exception.

'Anyone at home?' he yelled, entering though the open kitchen door. He played an impatient rat-a-tat-tat on the kitchen table while he waited for Jenny to arrive. She ran down stairs to meet him. 'I'd be thinking this is the most important piece of mail in this pile' he said, leaving the rest on the kitchen dresser.

'I'd be inclined to agree with you, Luke,' she replied nervously, dithering a moment before opening it.

'For God's sake, open it, Jenny, and put us all out of our misery.' Luke pretended to read the newspaper while Jenny opened the envelope. Delighted with the contents, she danced a jig on the flagged floor, while Luke lilted an appropriate air.

'Well done,' he said, 'let me be the first to congratulate you.'

'Thank you, Luke, help yourself to some tea while I go and tell everyone.'

Mary Anderson had already gone to the farm office to show Mattie the photograph, and Norah Leahy was picking some parsley and thyme from the herb patch.

Breathless, Jenny arrived at the office door waving the envelope. A loud cheer came from the gathered assembly who had come to admire the photo. Soon Tan Bo lost his place in the pecking order and Jenny became the toast of Sliabh na mBan.

Luke sat at the pine table, his eyes fixed on the wedding photo of Anne and John Anderson. 'You'd be proud of her today,' he whispered, 'just listen to the chorus coming from the workmen.' Their radiant faces smiled back at him, almost ready to join in a verse of 'She lived beside the Anner.' That ballad, made famous by Charles Kickham in praise of an Irish colleen, seemed very appropriate.

Appropriate too was a celebratory drink, or so Tom Hanley thought, as he knocked the caps off some bottles of Guinness. 'Here's to Jenny,' Mattie announced. 'Cheers' came the response that seemed to ring through the valley and echo with the barking of dogs. The O'Reilly twins arrived late, puffing and panting. Tom Hanley couldn't say much to them as he stood there, glass in hand and creamy brew from ear to ear.

'Have we missed something?' the cheeky pair asked without as much as an apology.

'Yes, two hours' pay,' came the reply from Norah Leahy, only too happy to get her own back. To their disgust, Norah handed them two glasses of fizzy orange. 'Please toast Jenny who has just qualified in Social Science.'

'Cheers, Jenny, its well for you,' was the best they could do.

'That's the reward for hard work,' Norah pointed out. 'Spending the nights discoing and coming late for work isn't the way forward.' They tried hard not to giggle even though everyone else seemed amused.

'Right, men, the party is over,' Tom announced, 'it's back to the grindstone now and, you pair,' he looked the twins in the eye as he gave his orders, 'trim those hedges and mow the lawns, and properly this time, or else ....' He stormed off, leaving them to work out what the 'or else' bit meant.

'Fizzy orange, work hard, did you ever hear the likes of it? Nigel remarked to his brother, Con. 'That Norah Leahy is full of her own importance but I'm not fooled for one minute by her.'

'Why so?' Con asked

'There's a bit of hanky-panky going on between herself and Luke O'Gorman. I spotted the pair of them making eyes at each other. It's no wonder she makes muck of Ben Breen, but, from now on, Con, you'll hear me singing Postman Pat to annoy her.'

'Grow up, you amadhan,' Con was annoyed at his brother wasting his time talking about Norah. Surely the cute redhead Nigel met at the club the previous night was a much more interesting subject.

'Problem is, Nigel, she can't tell us apart,' Con joked, 'and, any night you're not up to it, you need look no further.'

'Dream on, boy,' Nigel replied, 'she's all mine and I intend to keep it that way.'

'You always were a miserable git. Even when I invited a lovely girl to my debs, you ran off with her.'

'I'm charming, irresistible, and right now I'm dismissible. Here comes Tom Hanley over the brow of the hill. Quick, jump on the mower, Con, and I'll start on the hedge.'

'Go on, grandma, please tell me what the surprise is, you know I'm dying to hear.'

'Get in the car, Jenny, and I'll tell you on the way to town. Honestly, you're like a bold child this morning.'

'That's exactly how I feel, grandma, giggly and mischievous, sort of like the O'Reilly twins. Norah didn't half let off steam at the pair of them earlier.'

'Sure it runs off them like water off a duck, all they want is the few bob and a good time, though I would like to see them saving towards college. By the way, I had a word with Norah, and in a round-about way, I told her to go easy on Ben Breen.'

'Well done, grandma! Let's get cracking.' Jenny offered to drive.

'It's okay dear I'll drive'. Parking at the Bank can be tricky, besides, I'm used to manoeuvring the car in the narrow street. Now, just sit back and enjoy the day.'

On this glorious June day, the locals waved or honked their horns in a friendly manner. Mary knew them all, she had lived in Sliabh na mBan all of her married life. 'Country life is so different from the hustle and bustle of the city,' she remarked to Jenny, 'kind of makes you lazy in one sense.'

'Never in your case, grandma, you look so smart and business like. Anyone would take you for a company director or some sort of professional dressed in that crisp navy suit.'

'Thanks Jenny'. I've some business with the bank manager today, that's why I've gone to a bit of extra trouble, it helps to boost one's confidence.'

'Is that the surprise?' Jenny was getting more and more impatient since they were now half way to town.

'It's part of it, Jenny, but firstly let me say how proud I am of you. It means so much to me to see your dreams being fulfilled. That means I'm happy and so is Mattie, and you saw how thrilled the farm staff were this morning. It spills over to our friends and neighbours. I know Clare Vaughan and her mother will be so excited to meet you again.'

'Clare Vaughan! Are you really serious, grandma? I haven't seen her since boarding school. Where are we meeting?'

'Kane's Hotel for lunch' she replied. I thought it would be nice to take you to The Milano Rooms. Since being newly refurbished the place looks wonderful and the food is excellent.'

Jenny welled up with emotion. Imagine seeing Clare again after all these years? What would they talk about? Pity they had lost touch in the first place.

She remembered the good old days at school when they had got up to plenty of devilment and had some great laughs together.

'I didn't know you had kept in touch with the Vaughan's. I don't recall ever hearing you speaking about them in the last few years.'

'Ever since I first met Alice Vaughan twelve years ago, we have been good friends.'

Jenny knew her grandma was referring to the morning her parents were killed. Alice Vaughan was the nurse in the casualty department that day and was so kind and sympathetic. 'We meet once or twice a year usually, and in between if she wants to discuss something important. Recently we met and she was talking about Clare. I just thought it would be nice if you two met up again.'

'It's made my day, grandma, I only wish I had more time to spare. Still we can catch up on the past five years.'

Mary smiled at her grandchild. Dressed in a green linen dress that complimented her peaches and cream complexion, she looked so beautiful.

'I hope you and Clare enjoy meeting again, Jenny. I understand from her mother that she is a fine person.'

Mary parked her car near the main entrance of the bank. They were ushered into the manager's office on the dot of midday. Harry Carmichael shook hands firmly, thanked her for coming on time and said he was pleased to meet Jenny.

'Please, sit down,' he said, keying data into the computer.

Jenny observed the manager as his slender fingers played on the keyboard almost like a concert-pianist. Sitting behind a great polished desk clad in a navy blue pinstriped suit with a red silk handkerchief peeping from his breast pocket, he reminded her of Gregory Peck. Even Harry's sleek black hair with a stray strand tumbling down his forehead and his wry smile were so characteristic of Peck.

'These things are a marvellous invention,' he remarked to Mary who agreed with him. She had taken some interest in computers since Mattie bought one for his office, and once she has mastered the jargon and had it translated into 'plain English' as she put it, she felt she understood the basics.

'How is Mattie and how are things on the farm?' he asked, looking up.

'He's fine, thank you, Harry, and doing well on the farm. Mind you, he grumbles all the time about the amount of office work he has to do to keep in step with Brussels and the Department of Agriculture.'

'Hmm! I can imagine they keep him on his toes right enough,' Harry replied. Having done business with the Andersons for a number of years, he had watched the farm turn over a tidy profit annually, and seen some of their investments pay good dividends. All in all, he considered they managed their affairs well.

'Well, I'm planning on handing the estate over to him shortly,' Mary announced. 'He's young, I'm getting old and it's time to make some changes. Simple as that!'

Harry nodded. 'When do you intend to hand over? If you need a good solicitor, I could recommend one. It's a big step and a huge responsibility.'

'I was thinking August would be a good time when Mattie reaches his twenty-third birthday. Of course, I haven't told him yet,' Mary remarked, glancing at Jenny. 'You won't breathe a word of this to your brother. I have some serious stuff to discuss with him beforehand'.

'Regarding a solicitor, Harry, I'll stick with the Gordon firm they have served us well, thanks just the same. Please hold on to the farm's deeds for the moment and I'll phone you at a later date.'

'Now, Jenny, what are your plans?' Harry asked, noticing how quiet she had remained throughout the conversation.

'I'm off to New York in about three weeks' time and really looking forward to it.'

'New York I've never been there.' Harry stretched his legs and did a few quick neck exercises. 'My problem is I'm scared of flying and I haven't the patience to sail. Anyway, what are you going to do there?'

'Social work' my cousin Mary has a job lined up for me so I'm fortunate.

'Best of luck Jenny'. I must say, you're a brave young lady and your grandma must be very proud of you.'

Mary nodded. Jenny has worked hard for her degree and I intend to reward her. I may be handing over the farm to Mattie but you, Jenny, must have your share too.'

Jenny wanted to point out to her grandma lots of reasons why she felt she had no claim on anything. In front of Harry Carmichael certainly wasn't the place to say how grateful she was for having been put through university, or indeed for the privileges she had enjoyed growing up. Surely that was enough and now it was high time to go and earn her living just like everyone else. But Mary was already giving her instructions to the bank manager.

Jenny gasped when she heard Mary telling Harry that she wanted to transfer a substantial sum of money from her own account to Jenny's. Totally flummoxed and not knowing what to say, she was relieved when Harry's assistant knocked on the door.

'Please excuse me for a moment,' Harry said, closing the door behind him.

Mary glanced at her watch. 'I hope he won't be long I'd hate to be late meeting the Vaughans. At any rate, we're nearly finished. A few signatures just to seal the deal and then our business will be complete. Happy?'

'Words fail me, grandma, except to say "Thank you" and even that seems totally inadequate. Of course I'm happy and happy for Mattie too, but what about you?'

'Let me explain Jenny.' 'I have done no more than hand over to you and Mattie what you are legally entitled to. It's your inheritance, and now seems to be just the perfect time to dispose of it. You're going to America, Mattie will take over the estate and I can retire. I have enough money to live comfortably on for the rest of my days and I intend to enjoy my freedom.'

'That's exactly what I want to hear, grandma, now what about a proper holiday?'

'When my cousin Tim Lucey, arrives, I'll make myself available and we'll hit the road to Kerry and Cork together. Tim always had a soft spot for Gouganebarra in West Cork, and I must confess I found Saint Finbarr's old habitat a heavenly place.'

Harry Carmichael charged back into the office apologising for the interruption. 'Well, that should keep you in shoe leather for a while,' he remarked to Jenny and all three laughed. 'You had better lend your signature to this agreement.' Harry handed her a pen and she signed the document.

'Thank you, Harry, it's been nice meeting you.'

'It's been a pleasure, Jenny, and perhaps some day you'll tell this old stick-in-the-mud all about New York.'

'It's a deal, but in the meantime, I'll send you a postcard. Okay?'

Harry got up and walked to the corner of his office. Carefully, he unlocked a small wall press with a brass door. From it he took a small presentation case and handed it to Jenny. 'I keep these for my special customers hope you like it.'

She opened it and was bowled over by the gold pen with the bank logo inscribed on it.

'Thank you so much, Harry, I'll always treasure it. Take a look, grandma.' Mary admired the gift, handed it back to Jenny and smiled appreciatively at Harry.

'It's a lovely gesture, Harry, and much appreciated, thank you so much.'

In the foyer of Kane's hotel, Alice Vaughan and Clare were waiting to greet them.

Big hugs and embraces were exchanged and it promised to be a wonderful reunion for Jenny and Clare.

Mary suggested a bottle of champagne to celebrate the occasion.

They seated themselves by a little fountain in the garden, and Toby Androtti, the headwaiter, brought the champagne on ice to the table. 'Special occasion?' he asked, popping the cork with great aplomb and enjoying the cheers of his guests. The suave handsome Italian had met everyone previously, except Jenny.

'Jenny and I are old school friends and it's our reunion today,' Clare told him.

'Where have you being hiding yourself?' Toby kissed her hand and said how pleased he was to meet such a beautiful woman.

'I'm delighted to meet you, Toby. I've been in college, I got my degree in Social Science today so grandma is spoiling me.'

Clare jumped up from the table and flung her arms round Jenny. 'This is wonderful news - congratulations!' Alice congratulated her too and Toby had a perfect excuse to hug Jenny.

'Brainy and beautiful,' he remarked, filling champagne into flutes. Toby didn't need much coaxing to join in the toast to Jenny and the party began.

'When you're ready to dine, just let me know. I have a table reserved for you and it would be my pleasure to look after you.'

'Thanks, Toby, but do you think we can split up for lunch?' Mary's suggestion brought a smile to Jenny's face. 'These young ladies will have lots of things to talk about and so have Alice and I.' Mary hadn't lost her sense of fun.

'Enjoy your lunch and remember you have all afternoon to yourselves,' Mary said, steering Alice to a quiet alcove.

Toby directed Jenny and Clare to a table overlooking the garden. He handed them the menu. 'Take as long as you wish and the wine waiter will be along presently.'

'He's gorgeous,' Jenny remarked to Clare, 'and so romantic too. I've never had a man kiss my hand before.'

'Don't be fooled by that class of stuff,' Clare replied. 'Sure he does that to every woman he meets - Continentals are all the same. Give me a Paddy any day!'

'All the same, you must admit it's nice, especially with Champagne. I'd say it's sort of the caviar equivalent of romantic technique,' Jenny said driving them both into convulsive laughter.

Toby was back. 'Have you decided or may I make some suggestions?'

'Please do,' Jenny replied. 'With so many gorgeous dishes to choose from, it's difficult.'

He leaned over Jenny's shoulder and she could smell his aftershave. 'I strongly recommend the glazed quail with spiced rice - its v-e-r-y different. Would you like to try it? By the way a Chablis wine goes well with it. What you think?

They nodded their agreement. He purposely lingered and flashed a perfect smile for Jenny's benefit. 'Do you like the choice of music? I could change it if you wish.

'It's fine Toby, honestly, we're perfectly happy,' Clare's tone of voice was slightly firm.

'Is he always this attentive to his customers?' Jenny asked after he left to collect their order.

'He is brilliant at his job and the Kane's think the world of him. I'm very fond of him too, Jenny, but in small doses.'

The restaurant was now almost full and Jenny noticed how popular Clare was. Almost everyone said 'Hi' as they passed by. It was the same at school, Jenny remembered. Effortlessly, she made friends and always seemed to be the leader of the pack. Clare had a natural, easy manner, lovely pleasant countenance with large brown eyes and a generous mouth. When Jenny remarked how well known she appeared to be, Clare laughed.

'It comes with working in the bank,' she replied. 'I know most of these people, of course that's the way in a country town, everyone knows everyone else and usually their business too.'

'All the same, it's nice to be part of the community, Clare, and obviously you enjoy your job. How long have you been in banking?'

'Five years, Jenny,' I went straight into training for the job after the Leaving Cert. Harry Carmichael, our manager, is a good old stick, and I enjoy being part of his staff. I'm on Foreign Exchange at present.'

'I met Harry Carmichael earlier. Grandma and I had a bit of business to sort out. I must say I liked the Gregory Peck look. All the same, Clare, I never associated you with banking somehow. At school, I remember you spent the holidays working at Purcell's stud farm, so I thought you might end up as a vet.'

Clare laughed heartily at the idea of it. 'Jenny, I mucked out the stables and shovelled horse manure just so I could get a peck on the cheek from his son, Tommy. I had absolutely no other interest in the job except for the few bob they paid me.'

'What about the love letters he sent you and the stories you told us at night in the dormitory? We all envied you back then, Clare, with your fabulous blonde hair, lovely legs and a rich boyfriend.'

'Ah, sure I was an awful idiot, Jenny, imagining for one moment that the Purcell's would allow their son to have anything to do with the local sergeant's daughter. Still, I enjoyed smuggling the letters to him and the convent gardener was so helpful. I used to hide them under Paddy Doran's prize geraniums and he would post them for me. In return, I stuck a few bulls' eyes in the pot and in that way we were all happy. Mind you, Jenny, I think Sister Ucharia began to get suspicious. .'

'They were good days, Clare, and you brought plenty of excitement into our lives.'

24

'There's plenty of excitement on the cards now, Jenny. You're about to experience the best lunchtime entertainment this side of the Atlantic and for free. Feast your eyes on the group just arriving and notice the dedication of Toby Androtti.'

Jenny observed the group, all women, impeccably groomed and in their early fifties, she supposed. Toby danced around them like a moth around a candle. He hadn't kissed their hands, she noticed, not yet at any rate, but then, they were matrons armed with stylish handbags.

He summoned extra staff to their table. The wine waiter stood to attention. He knew their individual likes by heart but he had to conform to the ritual of taking their orders. Owners Tita and Sam Kane arrived to greet them.

Clare finished her quail and dipped her fingers in the bowl of water provided. Jenny did likewise. Clare topped up the wine, remarking how kind it was of Mrs Anderson to have invited her and her mother.

'Grandma is great for keeping in touch, which is just as well, otherwise I'd have missed out on meeting you, Clare, not to mention the ladies at table seven. Who are they anyway and what's all the fuss about?' Jenny asked.

'They're known as the magnificent seven,' Clare replied. 'Magnificent in dress, bank balances, they throw lavish parties mainly to raise funds for charity and are married to successful men. However, when they come to Kane's for their monthly luncheon date, the god of Bacchus usually takes over, and confessions that would make Saint Augustine blush are heard. Yes, the fun will soon begin, Jenny.'

Mary Anderson and Alice Vaughan waved cheerily from the alcove.

'Would you just look at the pair of them in the cooers and peckers reserve? I'd love to a fly on the wall,' Jenny joked.

Clare took a long sip of wine and a glint came in her eye. 'Well, Jenny, what have you been up to in Dublin? Is it all wild parties and flamboyant lifestyles?'

'For some, yes, but I hasten to add that I'm not much of a party animal myself. Listening to music or a good book is my idea of relaxation. Besides, I have my sights set on New York and making a career there, so I kept the head down and studied. Sorry to disappoint you, Clare!'

Toby delivered scrumptious desserts. Clare chose pears and ice cream and Jenny opted for creme brulee with rhubarb.

'Are you actually planning on going to New York?' Clare hoped it was just an idea that crossed Jenny's mind at college.

'Definitely,' she replied. 'I have everything arranged and hope to be on my way shortly.'

'So it's hello and goodbye,' Clare tried to hide her disappointment at the thoughts of loosing her friend once again.

'Clare, New York is only seven hours from Shannon, and you can come out for a holiday. Besides, I'll phone often.'

'What about your boyfriend?'

'They'll be no-one with a red rose reciting poetry at the airport,' Jenny replied, reluctant to mention her friendship with Colin Maloney. After all, she hadn't heard from him since he went off to California to complete his studies in Astronomy. It had been almost a year since he left.

The magnificent seven were by now sufficiently inebriated to start their performance. The once beautifully coifed hairstyles were beginning to droop and Penny Granger was assisting her friend, Lil Barker, to the Ladies Room.

'Poor Lil has developed pins and needles in her left leg,' Toby announced when he delivered the coffee.

'Very unfortunate,' Clare replied, hoping he wouldn't detect the lack of sincerity in her voice. He poured the coffee and left.

'Lil is always the first one to make a show of herself. Pins and needles indeed,' Clare scoffed.

'I wouldn't be at all surprised if Toby hasn't some special remedy, Clare, so let's move on and talk about you. Something tells me that a popular girl like you hasn't escaped the clutches of some handsome guy.'

Without hesitation, Clare announced that Johnny Finnan was the love of her life. He owned his own building contracting firm and September would see them walk down the aisle of Saint Brendan's. 'You will come back for my wedding?' Clare hoped she wasn't putting Jenny in a spot but felt it was the appropriate time to ask.

'Yes, of course, I will, Clare, thanks for asking me. This is so exciting. I'm dying to meet him. He must be very special. Tell me, where did you two meet?'

Clare's eyes lit up. 'About two years ago, he came into the bank one afternoon, pebble-dashed from head to toe, hat on the Kildare side and he plonked a huge wad of notes on the counter. When I asked him if he wished to lodge all his money, he smiled and looked me straight in the eye. "Now why should I do a silly thing like that?" he asked.

'Because that's what banks are for,' I told him. 'Well, Ms Vaughan, I thought I'd take a beautiful woman out to dinner.'

'Oh, that's nice,' I replied, 'Have you some place special in mind?'

'I normally let the lady choose and you have until seven-thirty to decide, Ms Vaughan, and I won't take 'no' for an answer.' He shook hands. 'I'm Johnny Finnan.'

'That's how it all started, Jenny. There was no playing hard to get, just a straight forward meeting that has worked really well.'

'It's a lovely story, Clare What do your parents think of him?'

'Johnny smokes, enjoys a jar, and is fond of a flutter on the horses, all of which are taboos with my parents. I imagine they'll come round eventually but it makes no difference to us. We love each other and that's all that matters.'

'You're perfectly right, Clare, nothing should stand in the way of two people who really love each other.

Planning a home together, and marrying a man who will build you the perfect place is so romantic. I can just picture the scene.' Jenny took a sip of wine and dreamily stared ahead.

Clare wanted to talk about her new split-level bungalow that was almost ready, the lovely old trees that Johnny had so carefully retained, and the tiny stream that gurgled at the bottom of the garden. But she didn't. Today was Jenny's special day and that's how it would remain.

'Are you doing anything special Saturday evening?' Clare asked.

'No, except perhaps some packing and trying to organise my bedroom. That's about it. Why do you ask?

'I'd love you to come over to dinner and meet Johnny. Mind you, the old house where I stay is a bit rundown so you'll have to excuse the place, since the landlord is away most of the time. Still, I can manage to make it presentable when I have to.'

'That would be great. Don't fuss on my account.'

'Shall we say eight o'clock and please bring Mattie if he's free.'

Mary Anderson and Alice Vaughan were preparing to leave. Sam Kane was vigorously shaking their hands and obviously lapping up the compliments. Toby hotfooted over to Clare and Jenny. He kissed both their hands and thanked them for their custom.

'Hope to see you soon again,' he remarked, his gaze fixed on Jenny.

Clare smiled knowingly. She hadn't had time to tell Jenny about his relationship with Sam Kane's daughter. Mary Kane was a sort of lay missionary who travelled the world from India to South America. The kaftan-clad lady, with the enigmatic smile of Mona Lisa and long flowing dark tresses, usually came home in the summertime. Toby spent most of his spare time in her company, much to the relief of her family, who didn't understand her in the first place.

'Did you have a nice cosy chat?' Mary Anderson asked Jenny and Clare.

'It was wonderful, Mrs Anderson' Clare gently kissed her on the cheek.

'Thank you for the lovely meal and for Jenny'. I'm delighted to see her again before she leaves for New York and it's all down to you.'

Mary smiled gently. 'I've been hearing all about your plans too, Clare, I hope that you and Johnny will be very happy! Please bring him over to meet us soon.'

'I promise!' Clare replied, glancing at her mother. Had Mary given her some good advice? Clare was hoping for a change of attitude from her parents towards Johnny. Right now, Alice was busy taking to Jenny and wishing her well for the future.

'I'll be back for the wedding, Alice,' she said, cheerfully. 'Wild horses won't stop me.'

Alice hugged her. 'You're a great girl, Jenny, and we're all very proud of you.'

Back home, Norah Leahy had been busy answering the phone. She handed Jenny a list of the well- wishers that included Colin Maloney. 'By the way, that last gentleman said he'd call back later'.

'Thanks Norah, I hope you're not worn out between the phone and all your other chores.

'Sure it's a pleasure to speak to your nice educated friends instead of some of the ninnies I have to put up with.'

Jenny wasn't sure who she meant but the O'Reilly twins came to mind instantly. She slipped some notes into Norah's hand. 'Treat yourself to a movie and a meal, Norah, and thanks again.'

In her excitement, Norah mentioned that Luke would be delighted too. Then, realising she had let the cat out of the bag, she quickly tried to make an excuse, getting tongue-tied in the process. Jenny pretended she hadn't heard. Besides, her mind was preoccupied with the news that Colin Maloney had phoned.

'Like a cup of tea, grandma? Jenny asked.

'I'll join you in a moment, I just want a word with Norah first.'

Mary often had a quiet word with Norah before she went home. Running a big house and farm meant planning for the following day's meals with extra mouths to feed, depending on the workload.

The kitchen was peaceful except for the tick-tock of the large clock. A gentle breeze wafted through the geraniums and herbs on the windowsills. They sat opposite each other at the pine table and Jenny poured the tea. 'What an exciting day it has been for us, grandma, you must be exhausted.'

'Yes, I'm quite ready for a lie-down but I've enjoyed the day. It had been on my mind for some time to off-load the responsibilities of the farm and believe you me, Jenny, I feel lighter already.'

'And so you should after all the years of dedication and hard work,' Jenny clamped up quickly when she heard Mattie's footsteps.

He grabbed a mug from the dresser, filled it with buttermilk and downed it in one go. 'There's nothing like it to quench a thirst,' he said emphatically, 'and boy was I thirsty? How was lunch at Kane's? I bet you're still on a high, Jenny.'

'Grandma and I had a lovely time. Clare Vaughan and her mother joined us, and you are invited to dinner on Saturday night with me. How about that?'

'I guess I can make it, but I should really check my diary,' he grinned.

'Yea, you're right about the diary, a cow might be due to calve that night. That's about the height of your excitement these days. Find yourself a good woman and get a life,' Jenny advised him.

'Do you hear that, grandma? She wants me to ruin everything by letting a woman into my life and I a happy bachelor.'

'You could do a lot worse, Mattie, but right now I'm going to have a little siesta. Call me round six, Jenny.'

Colin Maloney phoned at the dot of six. 'Hi Jenny, it's me, Colin, I just got home from California, can we meet up, have lunch and plan for the summer?'

His sheer arrogance irritated her so much she almost slammed the phone down. Did he really think that she had been waiting on the shore for the past twelve months? There hadn't been one phone call, not a postcard, nothing, and yet he had plans.

'What plans?' she asked, her voice full of indignation.

'Sorry, Jenny, have I called at a bad time, you sound ......'

'Listen, Colin, this is one of the happiest days of my life, every moment has been a good one, that is, until you called, and yes, since you didn't bother to ask, 'I'm fine.'

'Jenny, can we start all over again? I'm sorry if I have upset you. Blame it on jetlag, bad manners or whatever, but please don't be mad at me. Honestly, I'm really sorry.'

Jenny had always known that Colin had his head in the clouds. 'This is planet earth,' Jenny reminded him. 'We have a good communications system, phones, post, etc., etc.

He laughed nervously at the other end. 'I've really blown it. I should have kept in touch, though that's not to say that I haven't thought about you often. Let me make it up to. Have lunch with me tomorrow. Please say yes!'

'Colin, I'm far too busy to travel to Dublin. I'm going to New York soon, and have loads of preparations to do. By the way, I got my degree and I've a job waiting for me in the Big Apple.'

'Congratulations!' Colin shouted in deafening decibels, even more intent on lunch. 'Let's celebrate in style. I'll drive down in the morning and whiz you off to a nice posh restaurant, just for old time's sake.'

Jenny could feel herself giving in. 'Okay, tomorrow at noon. I'll be waiting at Cill Chais church. 'She replaced the receiver and buried her head in her hands.

'Everything all right Jenny? Why are you upset?'

'Oh, there you are, grandma. I was just on my way to call you when the phone rang. An old friend from Dublin just phoned and wants me to have lunch tomorrow. It's kind of putting me under pressure with so much to do.'

'Always find time for your friends, Jenny. Norah and I will give you a dig out with the packing. I hope you said "yes".'

'I did,' Jenny replied. 'We're meeting at Cill Chais church at noon.'

'Good, and speaking of churches, I had better get off to the parish meeting. Father Rigney is planning a total refurbishment of the sanctuary in line with the other churches in the dioceses. I'm treasurer, so it should be interesting. Mary remarked.

'Any chance of fixing me up with a date?' Mattie asked, all fresh and eager after a shower.

'For your information, Mattie, my friend is a gentleman. Surely an eligible bachelor like yourself should have no problem finding a woman.'

'I must have, otherwise I wouldn't ask. Okay? You were the one who told me to get a life. I'm asking you to help me.'

'Keep your hair on, Mattie, with an attitude like that, I'm not at all surprised you're still looking. Besides, you'd need to take stock of yourself, tone up, get rid of that awful hairstyle and buy some trendy gear.'

'Damn it, woman, you make me sound like a total disaster. Have I any redeeming features?'

'Frankly, Mattie, you are a disaster. Take a day off, go shopping, find a new hairdresser and join a gym. Have you ever actually had a long-term girlfriend?'

'Yes. Chloe O'Donovan from the Beeches Pub. We went out together for about nine months.'

'What happened between you'?

'She got plastered one night and actually proposed to me. To tell you the truth, Jenny, she scared the daylights out of me. What's more, her old man seemed to be in on the act. With the pub in a dilapidated condition, he thought I might come to the rescue financially.'

'Does grandma know about this?'

'No, and please don't mention it to her. Mind you, I had an awful job shaking Chloe off. She even threatened to come over and tell grandma that we were unofficially engaged. I swear to you, Jenny, if I hadn't caught her with someone else I'd have been in big trouble. I was so relieved when I met them arm-in-arm coming out of the old briar lane. I could have clapped your man on the back for doing me a favour.'

'Listen, Mattie,' she whispered, 'I'll make a phone call later on and there is just a chance I can get you fixed up with a date. Don't hold me to it, mind, but I'll do my best.'

Jenny waited until he left the house to play pool in the local hall. She phoned Clare Vaughan, but she was out. She left a brief message on the answering machine.

'Urgent, please call me as soon as possible' Clare.

The big stone house was quiet at last. Jenny sat by the window in the sitting room and watched the sun setting through the maples, thinking about Mattie. He must be lonely enough, Jenny, thought. Their father died when he was eleven. Granddad Anderson had been wonderful when they were small but when Mattie got older, he needed his father. Suddenly she felt sorry for being so harsh earlier. First it had been Colin and then Mattie that she had lashed out at. The phone rang.

'Hi, Jenny,' Clare's voice was bright and cheerful. 'What's so urgent?'

'Mattie needs rescuing and fast. Please, Clare, you have to find him a date.'

Clare laughed heartily. 'You're joking,' she replied. 'The most eligible bachelor in Tipperary needs my help to find a woman.'

'It's true. He's just had the narrowest escape from Chloe O'Donovan. Ever heard of her?'

'Oh no, not Lilo Lil,' Clare sounded surprised. 'Sure everyone runs a mile from her and her old man. She is known for trying to get her claws into any man with a bit of land, let alone an estate like yours. Why didn't someone mark his card for him? Clare wondered. 'How did he manage to shake her off?'

'He saw her with someone else and broke it off.'

'Bully for Mattie, now, let's get down to business.' Clare said that Sylvia Kane of Kane's Hotel has just split with her boyfriend of two years. 'When I met her the other day, she was very down in the dumps. Perhaps I should invite her to dinner Saturday night. What do you think?'

Jenny shrieked with delight. Thanks Clare! Are you sure she'll be free?'

'She will be, trust me.' Clare replied confidently. 'By the way, Johnny is really looking forward to meeting you. We spent the past hour unwinding in a little roadside pub where Johnny usually calls to in the evening. He loves it there where he can enjoy a pint or two, and listen to me going on and on. Anyway, Jenny, you must be tired, thanks again for a really special day.'

Mattie's jeep screeched to a halt in the driveway. He caught his jacket in the door, reefing the entire left side into shreds. 'Curse a blazes on it anyway,' he thundered, striding into the living room.

Jenny jumped to her feet. 'What happened to you?' she asked, noticing the jacket in tatters and his fearsome expression.

'She'll kill me,' he replied, ripping the jacket off and rolling it into a tight bundle. 'That damn thing cost a fortune and now look at it fit for the bin. Grandma will do her nut when I tell her.'

Jenny examined the sorry mess and shook her head. 'You've made a right pig's ear of it. You may as well get rid of the evidence and quick. Maybe, just maybe, the shop might have another one,' she suggested hopefully.

Sighing heavily, he lay down on the couch. 'By any chance, did you make that phone call? I came home early hoping that you might have found me a nice blonde.'

'Blonde, eh? You'll take what's on offer and be grateful, besides, I'm a lot more vocal when I'm served a nice cup of tea.'

'Oh very well then.' He shuffled off into the kitchen, whistling the Gypsy Rover.

Judging by contents of the tray Mattie didn't put much emphasis on elegant service. He plonked a great mug of tea and a hefty chunk of Oxford lunch beside Jenny. 'I'm starving,' he remarked, making railways in the cake. Norah's a fine cook.'

'I take it you'll be on your best behaviour Saturday night,' Jenny said. 'No chomping on your food as if you never got a bite in your life, and remember to stand up when you're introduced.'

'You found someone? What's she like?

'I haven't the faintest notion' Jenny replied but she needs loving care and attention. Can I depend on you?'

'A blind date needing loving care and attention' How vague can you be? Mattie asked.

Mary hung her car keys on the key rack and slumped wearily into a chair.

'A cup of tea, grandma, or would you like something stronger?' Jenny asked.

'A glass of sherry would go down a treat, thank you.' 'I'm fed up listening to the committee debating and arguing the changes in the sanctuary. I'm off to bed after this.' 'Me too' said Jenny glancing in the direction of Mattie who had cheered up considerably.

Alone in her bedroom, Jenny fell exhausted unto the bed. Thank goodness Mattie had escaped the clutches of dipso Cloe O'Donovan. Imagine poor grandma handing over the farm to him if that wretch were in tow. She and that scheming father of hers would bleed them dry in no time.

She turned and twisted for hours before she dozed off. In the small hours, she heard the vet's car screech to a halt in the cobbled yard. She jumped out of bed and pulled the curtain. It was daybreak. Mattie ran from the house and jumped into the car with the vet. They sped in the direction of the byre.

Jenny could feel her heart beating as she waited for them to come back. An hour later there was still no sign of them. She desperately wanted to dress herself and follow them. Tears streamed down her cheeks when she thought of how hard Mattie worked. She tiptoed down the stairs just in time to meet him coming through the kitchen door.

'Is everything okay Mattie? What's the vet doing here at this hour?'

'Big Bertha had two lovely bull calves and all three are doing well,' he replied.

Sobbing uncontrollable, she hugged her brother. 'I'm really proud of you, Mattie. Do you want tea or coffee?

'No thanks, Jenny.' Go on back to bed.'

CHAPTER TWO

Colin Maloney packed a weekend case together with a bundle of poems he had written for Jenny. Although the previous evening's conversation on the telephone hadn't been that cordial, deep down he knew that he could peddle his way back in her favour. The same confident feeling didn't surge through his veins as he prepared to tell his mother of his plans. Last night, The Building Society's dinner had got in the way of breaking the news to her and she was never at her most approachable at breakfast time. Dressed in shorts, a t-shirt and wearing Moses sandals, he tripped lightly down the stairs to join his parents.

John Maloney left his newspaper to one side and greeted his son. 'This is a real treat, Colin, having you join us for breakfast. We've missed you this past year.'

'Me too,' Colin replied, quickly swallowing a glass of freshly squeezed orange juice.

'I'm glad you got over your jetlag,' his mother, Vera, remarked, 'in fact I was just about to bring you your breakfast.'

'Yeah, two days normally sees me rested and ready to rock-and- roll again, so no need to spoil me further mother.'

John studied his only child. He looked fit and tanned after his stint in California but he wished that he would get rid of that ponytail. When Colin was much younger and living at home, his father had been tempted to chop the ponytail off when he was asleep. When he mentioned this to Vera, she was not impressed.

'Finding it difficult to adjust to the time difference?' Vera asked, noticing Colin glancing at his watch regularly.

'Not really,' he replied, 'it's just I have a lunch date and I need to be heading off.'

'But it's only eight thirty. Lunchtime is hours away, now, relax and enjoy your breakfast,' Vera smiled at the idea of it.

'You don't understand, mother. I'm travelling to Tipperary to have lunch with a friend. I'm sorry I haven't had an opportunity to tell you.'

'Tipperary,' Vera's eyes almost popped out of her head. 'Are you listening, John? Our son has just got home and now he's off to have lunch with a friend one hundred and thirty miles away. This person must be very special.'

'I'd like to think so,' Colin replied. 'Do you remember Jenny Anderson from Sliabh na mBan?'

'You mean that lovely young woman who was studying Social Science, the one you brought to tea a few times.' Vera had never been good with names.

'Yes, she has just qualified and as a treat I'm taking her to lunch today.' Colin breathed a sigh of relief when a smile lit up Vera's face, and John was equally pleased that Jenny has passed the mama test.

'Oh, I'm so pleased she's done well. Now let me see,' Vera rummaged through the writing bureau and found a suitable card. She wrote a message congratulating Jenny and invited her husband to sign the card too. 'Bring some proper clothes with you and make sure you take Jenny to a nice restaurant. By the way, when will you be home?'

'I'll make a weekend of it at least but I'll phone you at some stage. Bye mother, bye dad.'

It was a calm June morning and Colin was looking forward to his trip to Tipperary. It was a chance to test his newly serviced gleaming red M.G. for speed and efficiency. Once he got on the motorway, he intended to enjoy the feel of the open top sports car and to let the wind blow through his hair.

'It's a long way to Tipperary, it's a long way to go,

'It's a long way to Tipperary to the sweetest girl I know'

The love ballad sung by the British Allies in World War One took on a whole new meaning for Colin. Jenny Anderson was the sweetest girl he knew and he couldn't wait to find her again. Problem was he had been stupid for not having kept in touch, and by the sound of things he hadn't much time left to let her know just how much she meant to him.

He glanced at his watch. He had made good ground and could afford to take a coffee break soon. The picturesque village of Stradbally in County Laois provided the perfect place. Amid the beautiful displays of window boxes, hanging baskets and pavement arrangements, he found a quaint little cafe. Entering through the brightly painted red half-door, he was greeted first by the friendly proprietor, and then by the magic aroma of freshly percolated coffee. Every conceivable homemade confection and preserves caught his eye.

He ordered coffee and a sultana scone. It was quiet and peaceful here as he seated himself by a window, its lace curtain drawn to one side, allowing the display of Cupid's bower and Tradescantia to trail attractively over the box. He hoped the Cupid's bower was a lucky omen. It was time to put his thinking cap on and prepare to explain why he hadn't kept in touch. Jenny had not taken too kindly to him when he phoned after a year's silence. He could still hear the anger in her voice when he mentioned that he had plans for them.

'What plans?' she asked indignantly and rightly so.

He lightly spread some butter on the scone and generously piled some delicious blackcurrant jelly on top. Tucking into the mouth-watering scone, he reflected on his first year in California. After receiving his college degree, he had gone to Los Angeles to study for a Ph.D. A bad move, he conceded, judging by the results of his exams. The partying had been endless, and the lifestyle of his American college friends left him gobsmacked. He remembered one occasion when Jane Berger brought him home to meet her father.

Ike Berger sat in a deck chair and swilled beer by the pool. 'Nice to meet you, Colin, now see if you can knock some sense into this dizzy daughter of mine.'

Colin shook hands. He didn't have to worry about a reply or further conversation since Ike suddenly dropped off to sleep.

'He's drunk,' Jane remarked. 'Let's go and join the party in the house.'

When Colin wondered about her father's safety sitting so close to the pool, Jane simply shrugged. 'His bodyguard will take care of him, now let's boogie.'

The rich and famous had remedies for everything, Colin mused, amazed at their strange attitude and liberal lifestyles. The last three months of his stay in LA had been the nearest thing to a life of debauchery, and he regretted it with all his heart.

How could he possibly make amends to Jenny? Poetry, however eloquently written or spoken, could do little to clear his conscious at this moment. The past had a knack of catching up, he thought, even in a beautiful village on a sunny

June morning. He paid for his coffee and smiled at the proprietor's daughter as she photographed his M.G. outside the cafe. Climbing aboard for the final leg of the journey, he planned to make a clean breast of things if Jenny asked him.

Jenny photographed the new arrivals and their mother. There had been a stream of staff calling to the byre to admire the latest additions. 'Have you decided on names yet, Mattie?' Jenny asked.

'I was thinking of Oisin and Fergus, what do you think?'

'Yeah, that's a good idea, calling them after the sons of Fionn Mac Chumaill is very appropriate, I'd say.'

'It should go down well with the judges when you enter them for the bonny calf competition,' Tom Hanley quipped. 'Anyway, let's all get back to work, Bertha and her babies need to rest awhile after their ordeal.' He patted Bertha gently on the head and closed the door.

'I'm off to town to do a bit of business,' Mattie's shopping spree was top of his agenda today and Jenny had a fairly busy schedule lined up too. It was already gone ten when she dashed back to the house to get ready. Colin would be well on his way by now,

Mary Anderson was looking forward to meeting Colin. She had checked the guest room earlier and everything was in apple pie order. Norah did a once-weekly check on the spare rooms, aired them and hung little fresheners in cupboards and closets. She was dependable, which was why Mary wondered why she was late today above all days.

'Has there been any message from Norah this morning?' she asked Jenny.

'Not a dickey bird,' She replied.

Just then, Norah arrived breathless and complaining that the surgery was packed when she took her mother to see the doctor. 'Sorry I'm late, Mrs Anderson'

'Never mind being late, Norah. More to the point, how is your mother?'

'It's the old ticker, the doctor said. He's put her on more pills and something for the swelling of her ankles. She has to rest more too. Anyway, I best get started on the lunch before the hungry hounds get in from the fields.'

'You know you only have to ask if you need any help, Norah. By the way, I've done most of the vegetables and the soup, so make a nice cup of tea for yourself.'

'Thanks, Mrs Anderson I could murder a brew this minute. Will you join me'? Norah asked.

'No thanks, Norah, I promised Jenny I'd walk as far as the road gate with her and pick up the mail.'

'Hi, Norah, you missed all the excitement this morning,' Jenny remarked, looking quite beautiful in a flowing floral dress and wearing comfortable sandals.

'What excitement?' Norah asked.

'Bertha had twins during the night, that's what. Gorgeous calves with beautiful markings, just like Bertha and Tan Bo. Tom Hanley suggested to Mattie to enter them in the bonny calf competition.'

'He would,' Norah remarked sarcastically, 'that old smart Alec will meet himself coming back one of these days.' Tom had recently started ribbing Norah about Luke and she was still furious with him. They hadn't exchanged the time of day in two weeks and Jenny regretted mentioning Tom just now.

'I'll only be a few minutes, Norah, and I'll give you a hand with the lunch.' Mary was aware that there were a few extra today on account of the milking parlour job.

'You've done your share already, Mrs Anderson, and thank you,' Norah suddenly looked more cheerful as she turned to Jenny.

'Meeting that nice young man who phoned yesterday, I take it, you look stunning Jenny.'

'Thanks Norah.' I'll bring him up and introduce him before we go to lunch.

Father Rigney was putting a folder in his car when Jenny arrived. 'Ah, nice to see you Jenny' he said extending both hands in welcome.

'You too Father Rigney. How are you?'

'I've just got the call from the clinic in Dublin and they have my bed ready for Sunday evening. Please come in for a few minutes Jenny.'

He hobbled into the house and lowered himself into a great leather armchair.

'Grandma told me you're for a hip replacement and I wish you the best of luck Father. I brought you some reading material to help you pass the time after the operation.' Jenny handed him the fat Biography and an Anthology of Poems.

'You're so sweet Jenny they're just what I love and thank you.' He clasped the books to his chest and smiled appreciatively.

'Congratulations on getting your degree we're all very proud of you but sorry to hear you're off to New York' ' Why are you leaving Ireland? I would have thought there was plenty of opportunity for Social Workers especially in the big cities.'

'Blame everything on my cousin Mary Rafferty. She has a job waiting for me and she sent me a first class airline ticket since it's my maiden voyage, so you can see it's an offer I can't refuse.'

'Ah well, perhaps some day you'll return home with loads of experience, meanwhile I wish you well.'

'Thanks Father.' 'I was hoping though, to air my Social Workers hat right here today, that is, if you have a few moments to spare. There is a little problem that needs to be dealt with, and I'm sure you can steer me in the right direction, if anyone can.'

Father Rigney glanced at his watch. 'I have exactly fifteen minutes before I do my last wedding for the time being, so the floor is yours.'

Jenny apologised for burdening him with the problem. 'You see, she began, I know of this young woman who has a drink problem, which in turn is leading to other problems, so I feel it's my duty to do something.'

'If I can help I certainly will' Father Rigney replied. 'It's very noble of you to take such an interest in this person Jenny. 'Do I happen to know the young woman?' he asked.

'Cloe O'Donovan from The Beeches' Jenny replied.

Father Rigney gingerly stood up and hobbled to the window. He stared out into the middle distance then he turned around and held Jenny by the hand.

'Is something wrong Father?' she asked nervously.

'Cloe O'Donovan is the young woman I'm about to marry ' he replied. She is teetotal for the past nine months and has attended the full pre marriage course.'

Jenny blushed scarlet. 'I'm so sorry Father I should have researched my subject properly please forgive me.'

Father Rigney patted her gently on the hand. 'There is nothing to forgive Jenny you were only doing what you felt you had to do, on the information you received. Think no more about it, and let's both be pleased that Jack Byrne is about to make an honest woman of her. God bless you Jenny and best of luck.

'God bless you Father' she replied ready to burst out crying. She rushed off wishing the ground would open. Her very first attempt at practicing her job had been so embarrassing, and with Father Rigney of all people. If only she had minded her own business she thought, instead of listening to Mattie. Still it was good to know that Cloe had found happiness, and she prayed it would last forever.

Outside the church the wedding party was assembling. She zigzagged her way through glamorous happy ladies and men in morning suits. A young man rushed past carrying a basket of buttonholes- carnations or roses she wasn't sure. Where had Colin got to she wondered. A limousine drew up just at the church gate.

The applause was deafening as the beautiful Cloe emerged, dressed in a lace white gown with a matching headdress. A portly middle- aged gentleman offered his arm and she linked him to the door.

Just then Jenny spotted Colin walking towards her. She felt a little awkward but managed to put on a brave face. 'Welcome to Sliabh na mBan, Colin.'

'It's lovely to see you, Jenny,' he replied, holding her in his arms. She responded like a child who was scared. If ever she had needed to be consoled and loved, it was right now. Colin was delighted. He was more than happy to lavish affection on her and strangely he could feel her need.

'I've missed you, Jenny, and being here with you means the world to me.'

'I'm glad you're here Colin really I am'.

Hand–in-hand, they walked towards his car. Together they surveyed the beautiful valley of Sliabh na mBan. In the distance, Cill Chais castle, built by the Butlers of Ormond, stood stately and steeped in history. Remembering the poem, 'A Lament For Cill Chais', Colin wondered if the woman mentioned in it was as beautiful as he imagined she was.

'That dwelling where lived the good lady
Most honoured and joyous of women
Earls made their way over wave there
And the sweet Mass once was said'.

He had blurted out the verse so accurately and she couldn't help thinking that he had practised it for her benefit.

'You have a good memory, Colin. I'm impressed.'

'It was one of the first poems I learned at school,' he replied. 'I guess it stuck in my mind. Let me ask you a question, Jenny,' he waited a moment and then a mischievous grin lit up his face.

'Ask away,' she replied.

'Is this Earl from Dublin permitted to tell you how beautiful you look today?' he squeezed her hand a little tighter as he spoke.

'Thank you, Earl Maloney,' she replied playfully, 'and the good lady would like to say how handsome you look yourself. Now let's go and meet the folks before we go to lunch.'

When he spotted the M.G. weaving up the driveway, Tom Hanley alerted Mary.

'Thanks, Tom.' She removed her apron and ordered him to lock Mr Tattoo in the fowl house. 'We can't take any more risks with that cantankerous old bird, not after what happened to Con O'Reilly,' she remarked.

'If you ask me,' Tom said, 'he provoked the gander in the first place. All those hissing noises he kept making earned him that colourful tattoo on his arm.'

'That's as may be,' Mary replied impatiently, 'but I certainly don't want our guest to be left with an indelible beak mark.'

Tom agreed. After coaxing the old bird into the hen house and securely bolting the door, he positioned himself behind the bushes to watch the arrival of Colin.

'Norah' Mrs Anderson's gentle voice summoned her to meet Colin.

'Coming, Mrs Anderson,' She quickly removed her apron, glanced in the hall mirror and joined the others in the sitting room.

Norah claimed she could always size a person up by the way they shook hands. Colin got a high rating straight away. There was nothing limp or half-hearted about him as he shook her hand firmly, and thanked her for having a room ready for him.

'I've persuaded him to stay for the weekend, Norah,' Mary Anderson announced.

Norah glanced through the big picture window wondering why Bran the sheep dog was barking so loudly.

'He's spotted your car, Colin,' Jenny remarked. 'Bran

always gets excited when a stranger comes around the place.'

'Wow! What a lovely car it is,' Norah was peering through the window full of admiration. 'It's like something you'd see in the movies, and come to think of it, Colin, you're a bit like a young Nigel Havers.'

Colin smiled. 'I haven't the faintest idea who you're talking about Norah.'

'He's a handsome British actor,' Jenny explained, 'and I'm inclined to agree with Norah except, of course, his hair is much shorter and his father is a Lord.'

'Two very big differences,' Colin remarked jocosely, grabbing Jenny by the hand and suggesting they go to lunch.

Lunch in a small family run motel called The Roost was very pleasant. Jenny was glad she remembered the place tucked away in the shadow of the Knockmealdown Mountains. The proprietor was an Australian and he and his wife, Mary, had settled there some years previous.

'The Roost is a favourite haunt of young ladies having a last fling before getting hitched,' Jenny told Colin. 'Mary Hawke once said that she had hosted more hen parties than anyone else in Australia and Ireland combined.'

'It's hard to imagine that a quiet place like this, would be so popular for hen parties. What's the attraction?' Colin wondered.

'Mary Hawke provides the best overnight accommodation and her morning-after remedies are legendary.' Jenny replied. 'More coffee?'

'Yes please,' he replied, visualising the wild young things lining up for the various concoctions. Heaven knows, in recent months, he had been in need of the hair-of-the dog on so many occasions.

'I've missed you, Jenny, and I want to make the most of the short time we have together. I'm so sorry that I haven't kept in touch,' Colin held her hand full of regrets for his behaviour in the past year.

'I expect you were very busy with projects, and studying for your exams. How did you fare out?' Jenny withdrew her hand and sipped her coffee.

He hesitated for a moment and fumbled with the envelope he brought with him. 'Let's say, Jenny, I don't want to lie, and neither do I wish to tell the truth, so you can draw your own conclusions. I've been foolish and reckless but I have learned one big lesson,' he said.

'Which is?'

'To hold on to the precious things in life,' he replied. 'I never realised how much you meant to me until .....' He stood up and took her hand. 'Let's find a quiet spot where we can talk and plan, but first I have to phone home.'

'How are your parents?'

'In great form and thrilled with your news' he replied. 'Look they sent you this card.' He handed her the card and the other larger envelope. 'Take a seat, Jenny, I won't be long.'

She sat on a wooden bench in the shade of a large chestnut tree. The MG was parked nearby. Colin had all the trappings of a spoilt only child, and she wondered if his good looks, and easy manner, had landed him in trouble in America. One thing for certain though, he wasn't too anxious to talk about the past year.

She opened the card from his parents. John and Vera sent

51

their congratulations and wished her good luck for the future. She was touched deeply by this gesture and touched even further when Colin returned beaming with excitement.

'Mother wants you to come and visit before you go to America. Please say, yes, Jenny, it would mean so much to all of us.'

'I'd love to see your parents again, but it's a question of time. Still, I promise I'll do my best.'

'I know you will,' Colin replied, kissing her on the cheek, 'now let's go and find that quiet spot where we can talk.'

A light breeze blew through the open-top car as they sped through the blue-tinged mountain on a June afternoon. Colin stopped at the entrance to Sugarloaf Hill. He parked the MG alongside some German and French registered cars. Arm-in-arm, they strolled along a nature trail filled with the smell of gorse, honeysuckle, cow parsley and wild herbs.

'This is real aromatherapy,' Colin remarked as they stopped to inhale the various aromas and revel in their soothing aromatic substances. A cascading mountain stream and the buzzing of the bees were the only sounds that broke the tranquil silence of the place.

'I haven't felt this relaxed for a long time,' Jenny remarked, lowering herself onto a large tree trunk. Colin sat beside her on a flat rock. For a few moments, they sat in silence, hypnotised by the magnificent view that the north side of the Sugar Loaf offered.

'This is our Shangri-La, Jenny, will you promise me you'll never leave me?' Colin was holding her close like a precious possession.

'If only things were that simple, Colin, but we both know

they're not' She could feel a quiver coming in her voice but she knew she had to remain strong.

A cuckoo bird sang in the distance. They both listened for a few moments.

'Its tune has changed,' Jenny remarked. 'Like me, it is preparing to leave for another continent.'

'Must you go, Jenny? I love you and I can't bear the thought of losing you again.'

'Yes, Colin, I have to go, everything is arranged and nothing is going to stop me. I've worked hard for my degree, and I'm really looking forward to meeting my cousin, and to working in New York.'

He was stuck for words now, nothing he could say would mean much, not after the way he had behaved this past year. He wished he could turn the clock back to when he first met her at the Trinity College ball. That was the year before he went to America.

'You've gone very quiet, Colin,' she said, jumping to her feet. 'Shall we climb the slope still further?'

He guided her gingerly up the slope remarking how like Tree Rock Mountain it was.

'Those were happy days,' Jenny replied, 'with you lugging the telescope, and me trailing behind with star chart equipment and film.'

'Remember the night we stayed very late to look at the summer constellations and a search party was sent out?'

'I'll never forget it,' Jenny replied, 'nor the fat man who was part of the search party. He really let me have it when I said how delighted I was to have seen Scorpio.'

'Scorpio indeed,' he yelled. 'So that's what deprived me of

my lovely juicy steak. I was just about to enjoy my anniversary dinner with my wife when the call came through. 'You stupid bloody stargazers', next time, inform your family if you intend to spend the night looking at that Orion fellow or, better still, bring a tent.'

'At least you were focused back then,' Jenny remarked jocosely.

'Pity I didn't remain focused,' Colin replied. 'I've really made a mess of things, Jenny, and I'm not even man enough to tell you or my parents.'

'I'm sure they'll understand, you're not the first person to fail an exam or to sow a few wild oats, for that matter.'

'That's true. But how do I explain that to my parents?'

'By giving me a full account of your yourself, so I can censor the report before you tell your parents.'

Colin blushed scarlet. 'You're right, Jenny and I'm not proud of what I did, so prepare yourself for some shocks.'

He paused for a moment and an anxious expression creased his forehead into a tramline of wrinkles. Jenny held his hand, knowing how painful it must be for someone to confess frankly, but she knew he wanted to tell her. He blurted everything out like a runaway train. There was no stopping now. She heard about the endless partying with the rich and famous college kids, the mansions they lived in, how he became part of their lives and loved it.

'It was like being in a movie,' he told Jenny. Swilling champagne by the pool, gorgeous leggy blondes by his side, and not returning to his apartment for days on end were the norm. 'I never in my wildest dreams thought I'd be part of such a lifestyle, but it happened.'

'Did their parents ever ask questions?' Jenny wondered.

'Sure, if they happened to be around or sober' he replied. 'For those who were interested, I seemed to be the perfect appendage for their daughters. An astronomer, who could speak five languages, studying or supposed to be, at a leading college, was a most welcome guest at any dinner party.'

'Somehow I just can't imagine you being part of such a wacky lifestyle, how did you manage to drag yourself away?'

'When a tragic accident happened late one night in the pool,' he replied.

'Two close friends drowned – they'd been drinking and taking drugs - and seeing them lying there, dead, scared the life out of me. At that moment I thought of you, Jenny, and I wanted to get home and be with you.'

He cradled her in his arms and stroked her hair.

Tears were streaming down her cheeks. 'I'm here for you, Colin. There's no need to feel embarrassed. We'll tell Vera and John together.'

'Promise?'

'Promise. I've already started censoring,' she replied. 'Do I get my reward now?'

He had waited all day for this moment. Tenderly, he kissed her. All his cares and worries suddenly vanished with that first real kiss. They were both carefree and relaxed strolling along the path towards the car. He noticed she was smiling.

'Happy?'

'Yes. It's been a good day for both of us.'

'Thanks for being so understanding, Jenny, because that confession has drained me.' He mopped his forehead and took a deep sigh. 'I'll never ever allow myself to go that road again, these last few days have been a nightmare.'

*

Mattie was in cheerful mood when Jenny came down for breakfast on Saturday morning. While filling the kettle, he whistled a catchy little tune and proceeded to set the table. 'You know, Jenny, I always love Saturdays.'

'Really?'

'Yeah, it's the only morning I afford myself an extra hour in bed, have a leisurely breakfast, a read of the paper, and feel a bit like the squire, if you get my drift.'

'Is it okay if I interrupt the pattern just this once? May I join the squire for breakfast?

'Certainly, madam, please be seated. Do you prefer tea or coffee'?

'Tea as usual,' she replied, 'and there's no need to go overboard.'

'I'm just practising my manners for tonight or have you forgotten?'

'No, I haven't but you've certainly forgotten something'

The smell of burnt toast permeated every corner of the kitchen and beyond and Jenny quickly flung the windows open. It was then she spotted her grandma and Colin in the rose garden.

'I'm surprised Colin is up so early. Have you met him?'

'He was having breakfast with grandma when I came downstairs and she introduced us.'

'Well?' Jenny waited while he put more toast on.

'He's a nice fellow, quiet and refined, I'd say, but then we only spoke briefly. I'll probably get to know him better over the weekend. He might even let me have a run in the M.G.'

The idea of her brother squeezing himself into Colin's car brought a smile to her face. 'You sound almost like a little boy wanting to play with his friend's toy, Mattie.'

He buttered his toast, piled on some marmalade, and topped up their teacups. 'I'm really looking forward to tonight it will be fun to dress up, and to meet this mysterious blonde. Is Colin coming too?

'I'm assuming he will and I've told Clare Vaughan that I'm bringing a friend.

Yes, it promises to be a fun evening.'

Colin drove past the kitchen window and parked his car at the farm entrance. Mattie's eyes lit up with excitement. 'This may be my opportunity to swap the tractor for the M.G.,' he remarked sprinting through the door. Jenny smiled as she cleared the breakfast table. She looked up when she heard Colin coming in, his arms full with a bouquet of red roses.

'They're beautiful, Colin. Thank you. I was just wondering where you had got to.'

'Poetry without roses is like a tree without leaves,' he whispered, kissing her on the cheek. 'See you later for lunch.' Jenny.

'Things are certainly changing around here,' Mary remarked to her grandchild. 'One minute it's just a humdrum farmhouse, and the next it's full of romance. Just look at those beautiful red roses. You're much happier since Colin arrived, I notice. How come you never mentioned him before?'

'It's kind of hard to explain, grandma,' Jenny replied honestly. 'We met at a Trinity Ball the year before last and became good friends. I met his parents, took an interest in astronomy and we hung out together till he went to California to do further studies and that's about it.'

57

'How long did he stay in California?'

'A year,' Jenny replied, hoping the inquisition was over.

'Ah well, absence makes the heart grow fonder,' her grandma sighed philosophically. 'Did he write?'

'Mostly poetry,' Jenny replied, trying to sound somewhat convincing. 'I must give them to you to read sometime, grandma.'

'I was never big into poetry. Your granddad and I always wrote letters to each other, in our young days. I still have them. It made my time in America much more exciting, when I received his letters from Sliabh na mBan. He would write pages of lovely interesting stuff, and invariably get around to tell me, how much he loved and missed me. I often read his letters in the quiet of the evening. Seeing you and Colin together brought it all back to me.'

'You were obviously very much in love with granddad, and I know you miss him loads, but you had a good life together,'

'More than words can tell' Mary replied pausing for prayer when the Angelus bell tolled.

Later that Saturday evening, it was a different Mattie Anderson who joined Jenny and Colin to go to dinner at Clare Vaughan's.

'Do I look okay, Jenny?' Mattie squared himself in front of the long hall mirror and adjusted his tie.

'You look great,' she told him, admiring the well-tailored dark grey suit, maroon shirt and tie. He flicked a none-existent flake from his shoulder in an effort to draw attention to his hairstyle. Jenny smiled and winked at Colin.

'How could anything escape from so much gel?' she asked.

'It's his first date with Sylvia,' she explained to Colin, 'so he's going all out.'

'She better be worth it,' Mattie replied rather gruffly. 'This suit has cost me an arm and a leg'.

'Perfect timing,' Jenny remarked as they arrived dead on eight o'clock at Clare's apartment. The place needed a lick of paint and certainly lived up to Clare's description. Even the side street where it was located not far from the bank looked shoddy.

Clare and Johnny greeted them warmly. The old-fashioned sitting room soon came alive with lively banter as everyone got to know each other.

'Sylvia will be along in a few minutes,' Clare announced, noticing the anxious expression on Mattie's face.

'Something smells absolutely mouth-watering,' Jenny remarked to Clare.

'I was just about to say that dinner will be a little later than planned,' Johnny Finnan's face was full of devilment as he spoke. 'My cement mixer broke down while mixing the vegetables.'

Clare gave him a poke in the ribs. 'Will you behave for once and look after the drinks.'

'He's a lovable rogue,' Jenny whispered to Clare while Mattie and Colin helped themselves to some tasty hors d'oeuvres.

'Mind the suits now, lads' Johnny cautioned. We don't want the Sunday best full of egg and salmon.' Now, for the gargle, who likes what?'

Jenny asked for a dry sherry. Colin wanted a beer and Mattie a coke. Clare and Johnny both opted for beer. Having looked after his guests, Johnny sat on the armrest of Clare's chair and placed his arm on her shoulder. 'Okay, sweetheart?' he whispered reassuringly.

Jenny almost envied them their easy relaxed charm. Clare wore a lovely sage green silk dress and gold sandals and her blonde hair fell loosely around her shoulders.

Johnny, dressed in casual beige slacks, cream shirt and brown loafers could be the man of the house. At twenty-eight, he had his own thriving building contracting business and soon he and Clare would wed. The doorbell rang.

'That will be Sylvia,' Johnny remarked, sprinting to the door. Clare followed.

Mattie could feel his heart racing as he stood up to meet her. All his birthdays had come together, he told himself when they were introduced. She looked beautiful. Her blonde hair fell seductively over her oval tanned face. Mattie almost forgot to let go of her hand as their eyes met. A gentle smile of satisfaction played on Clare's face as she introduced Sylvia to Jenny and Colin.

'Didn't I see you dining recently in the Milano Rooms?' Sylvia asked Jenny.

'Yes, Clare and I had lunch together during the week,' Jenny replied.

'I was working in the office that day,' Sylvia explained, 'and Toby Androtti came in swooning about the beautiful woman he met with Clare Vaughan. He hasn't stopped going on about you ever since.'

'A right Casanova by the sound of it,' Johnny Finnan remarked, winking at Colin. 'I'd watch that smarmy Italian if I were you.'

Colin shuffled his feet uneasily and held Jenny's hand. 'I'm flattered this Italian gentleman has such good taste,' he remarked with relish.

'Italian men are strange,' Sylvia sipped her sherry. 'I mean, Toby has been dating my sister Mary for a couple of years but they never seem to progress in the relationship. At this stage, you'd think they'd have an engagement ring or some sort of commitment to each other, but no.'

'Shall we start dinner?' Clare suggested, feeling that Toby was beginning to cause embarrassment all round.

'There are no special places allocated,' Johnny announced, 'so you may sit where you wish.' The large round mahogany table was laid with a beautiful damask tablecloth and a bowl of roses in the centre. Place settings were tastefully arranged with good silver ware, cut glass wine glasses and neatly folded damask serviettes.

'Gracious living ' Jenny remarked to Clare. 'I thought we had an understanding.'

'So we had, but Johnny insisted that since it's a very special occasion we would make the effort.'

'Consomme au Port' Johnny announced, carrying the soup tureen to the table.

'Bravo,' replied a chorus of voices while he ladled it into the bowls. Clare poured the wine and the chummy little group toasted each other's future.

Soon Clare and Johnny would wed, Jenny was off to New York, Mattie and Sylvia on their first date and Colin Maloney?

Clare had been watching Colin since he arrived. Who was he? What did he do for a living? And, how come Jenny never mentioned him the day they met for lunch. It was obvious they were no strangers to each other. She noticed how he held her hand at the mention of Toby Androtti. This was a serious relationship unless she was greatly mistaken.

'Let me help you, Clare,' Jenny placed the empty soup bowls on a tray and carried them to the kitchen. Clare followed her.

'Thanks, Jenny, but Johnny and I can manage. Now go and relax and enjoy your meal. By the way, your friend Colin is very dishy, you must fill me in later.'

'I'd love to,' Jenny replied, 'but prepare yourself for a few surprises.'

'Surprises, eh?' Johnny looked at them in amazement. 'Having an astronomer to dinner is a big enough surprise for me. Don't tell me there's more. 'Moon man and Earth woman,' he quipped, carving the lamb. 'Whoever would have thought?'

'There's an air of mystery about them and I wish Colin was a bit more chatty,' Clare said.

'Never fear, I've a remedy for that,' Johnny had a look of devilment in his eye as he spoke.

'Don't be foolish,' Clare retorted. 'You're not down in the local now surrounded by yobbos.'

Johnny carried the plates of lamb to the table and Jenny brought the vegetables.

Mattie was laughing heartily, trying to convince Sylvia that he didn't own the M.G. parked outside. 'It belongs to Colin, isn't that so, Jenny?'

Jenny nodded while Johnny assured Sylvia that she was the lucky lady who would ride home on a tractor. 'Didn't you notice it at the entrance to the street with a pair of Wellington boots sitting in the cab?' Johnny asked, keeping his face straight.

Sylvia shrugged. 'I've always wanted to ride on a tractor and can't wait to don the Wellingtons, so there.'

Johnny topped up the wine. 'Here's to the new Queen of the Land.'

'To Sylvia,' they all chorused.

Sylvia was obviously lapping up the attention and smiled seductively at Mattie, much to the delight of Clare and Jenny.

The phone rang. 'No peace from that thing,' Clare murmured, excusing herself to her guests. She breezed back full of apologies. 'That was mother with news that her sister Mary is coming from California for our wedding. She hasn't been back to Ireland for five years and already mother is in a tizzy.'

'I've just come back from California myself,' Colin told them, 'it's a really nice part of the world.'

'What were you doing there?' Clare asked.

'You really don't want to know, Clare, let's say I just ended up bumming around.'

'Ah look, everyone is entitled to let the hair down once in a while,' Clare was sympathetic, especially when she noticed Jenny was quite embarrassed.

'I hear it can be a wild spot,' Johnny remarked egging Colin on.

'Colin was lonely out there,' Jenny was eager to explain that he had gone out to do his Ph.D in Astronomy but became homesick and started living it up with his friends.

'That sums it up,' Colin said, 'besides I missed Jenny and I wanted to be with her. Can you blame me?' he asked, glancing admiringly in her direction.

'Let's drink to Jenny,' Johnny said, raising his glass.

Jenny smiled gratefully, hoping that would be the end of the subject.

'Black Forest Gateau and coffee for everyone,' Clare couldn't wait to give them a piece of her homemade gateau. She had mastered it to a fine art and proudly carried it ceremoniously to the table. Mattie declared it was his favourite.

There wasn't a word spoken until the entire gateau was eaten.

Johnny had one more chore to perform before dark. He was pleased when Bill, the taxi driver, arrived dead on the dot of nine thirty.

'Everyone ready for a mystery tour?' Johnny asked his surprised quests.

'Do we have a choice in the matter? Clare asked, puzzled by his behaviour.

'Frankly no, now if you would all pile into the cab we'll be on our way. Twenty minutes later, they arrived at the entrance to a house set in the trees. Clare laughed hysterically as the taxi wobbled its way up the rough laneway. Bill stopped his cab in front of the house and the passengers got out. Clare linked Johnny through a short path through the trees and the guests followed.

'Welcome to Knocknagow, the house where Clare and I will spend our future.'

On a bright June night with the birds still singing in the trees, they got their first glimpse of the splendid red-brick residence Johnny had built for his future bride.

One by one they admired the house. The lovely old copper beeches and oaks swayed in the light summer breeze, and the river Anner gurgled away like a contented baby.

'Come inside and take a look round,' Johnny said turning the key in the door.

'It's a palace, fit for a queen,' Jenny said, after they had looked over the whole house. 'Tell me, Johnny, why did you choose the name Knocknagow?'

'Well Jenny, on this very site in the nineteenth century, one of my ancestors, Ambrose Finnan, was born. The house then was modest enough, just two rooms. The story goes that he arrived home one day to find his few possessions in the yard. Apparently, he was in arrears with the rent and the landlord instructed the bailiff to evict him and his elderly mother. Charles Joseph Kickham wrote a book called Knocknagow and I'm quite sure Ambrose Finnan's house featured in it.'

Jenny nodded. She too had read the book and agreed that it was quite possible.

'Still, it's good to see things come full circle' Johnny said and 'I'm happy that the bad old days are gone for ever'.

'We'll drink to that' Mattie said.

CHAPTER THREE

In the days following Clare's party, Colin returned to Dublin and Mattie seemed besotted with Sylvia. They spoke frequently on the phone for long periods.

Jenny was thrilled. 'She's the best thing that ever happened to me," Mattie said.

'Wasn't their house at Knocknagow amazing' Jenny said. 'Maybe you could put some work Johnny's way, not that there's any shortage judging by the Finnan Construction placards on every new project.'

Mattie wasn't sure. 'What about Miley Contractors?' he asked. 'They've worked for us for years. I doubt grandma would want to change'

'What about them?' Jenny was angry. 'Mileys have always been a headache, shoddy half-finished work, demanding pay halfway through and arriving on the job at midday. Surely it won't be that difficult to persuade her to change? Besides, you need only look at the last job they did on the kitchen, to see that windows don't even fit properly.'

'You're right Jenny the windows are a botch job' Mattie replied. 'I'll talk grandma round. Hey up! We have a visitor,' he said, glancing through the window.

Clare breezed into the kitchen. Mattie greeted her with a great bear hug.

'Easy now, Mattie, shouldn't you be saving all the hugs for Sylvia?' She remarked cheerily.

'True, but there would be no Sylvia but for you, so forgive

me for losing the run of myself. Thanks for a great evening on Saturday. I owe you one.'

'Indeed, we did have a great evening,' Jenny agreed, giving Clare a peck on the cheek. 'How about a nice cup of tea?'

Mattie vamoosed allowing Jenny and Clare to get on with packing and ironing. There was only a week to go before her trip to New York

'Honestly. Clare, I feel embarrassed letting you near my bedroom. Do you know, I must have clothes in my wardrobe since I was at boarding school.'

'Well, now's the time to get rid of them Jenny and create more space.'

'You're beginning to sound like a Feng Shui expert Clare. Where do we start?'

'Let's have a look at the treasures hiding on the rails,' Clare suggested, 'and then we can divide them into categories.'

'Do you mean punk, hick, hippy, bohemian, peasant, gypsy and any fashion that suited the mood' Jenny asked, smiling.

'Well, not exactly,' Clare replied 'I was thinking more along the lines of Charity Shop, Recycling and, finally, what you might consider bringing with you. Jenny fetch two large bags, please, and label one Charity Shop and the other Recycle. We'll use the bed for what you intend to pack and bring with you. And, please, no crying into the garment you wore to your Aunt Frances' wedding anniversary, we have no time for being sentimental.'

'That won't be a problem. Who's Aunt Frances?' Jenny replied.

Clare worked speedily and methodically and it was up to

Jenny to make snap decisions. She would have dearly loved to try on that red blouse once again or slip into those flairs, but she was under starters' orders and the race was on. Two hours later, everything was sorted.

'Honestly, Clare, I'm really grateful for all your help. Will you stay for supper? I can make us a nice light chicken salad if you wish.'

Clare glanced at her watch. It was seven p.m. 'I'd love to, Jenny, but I'm meeting Johnny at eight. Tell you what, though, a cup of tea would go down a treat.'

'Shall we sit in the garden?' Jenny suggested, carrying the tea tray and leading the way. 'Thank God that's over. I'm off to Dublin in the morning to visit Colin's parents. They're anxious to see me before I leave.'

'Is this your first time meeting them?' Clare asked.

'No, I met them a few times before Colin went to California.'

'I don't mean to pry, Jenny, but I couldn't help noticing that Colin and you are more than just good friends, besides, you weren't very forthcoming that day in Kane's.'

'To tell you the truth, Clare, I didn't know where I stood with him. He hadn't been in touch for a full year until the day I had lunch with you. I got a surprise phone call from him that evening and he insisted on meeting and taking me to lunch. He told me that he went wild in California, flunked his exams, realised where his affections lay and now we are in love.'

'Colin's lovely. Johnny and I were very impressed. So what are his plans now?' Clare wondered.

'To join me in New York in the autumn and resume college there,' Jenny replied.

'That's wonderful, Jenny. Now I needn't worry about you. Oh, I'm so pleased.'

'Seeing Johnny and you so happy has strengthened our resolve to follow in your footsteps some day,' Jenny's eyes filled with tears as she told Clare how proud she was to be her friend. 'You've made an excellent choice in Johnny. He loves you to bits.'

Clare nodded and smiled gently. 'I better go to my love then, he likes punctuality especially when it comes to a good pint of beer.'

'Just one thing before you go, Clare, any ideas for a house warming present?'

'A rocking chair, please, that's what I'd really love.'

'Are you serious, Clare?' Jenny asked, sure she was joking.

'Yes,' she replied. 'I want to sit in the evenings in Knocknagow by the Anner River in the shadow of Sliabh na mBan and rock myself to sleep.'

'Two rocking chairs will be delivered this week, make sure you're at home Clare.'

*

The scene at Shannon Airport on the morning of the seventh of July was nothing short of hectic. Friends from all over the place had come to wish Jenny 'bon voyage' and 'good luck.'

Leading the group were her grandma and Mattie, Sylvia, Johnny and Clare and, of course, Colin. Since there was always something poignant about the departure area, her friends had planned an informal farewell party. Colin had helped her check her baggage through and there was an hour and a half to spare before boarding.

'Let's all have a drink,' Johnny suggested. 'No point in hiring a coach and taking the day off if we don't make the most of it.'

On a sweltering July day, they marched after him like parched soldiers in the Sahara desert. Bar tenders and waiters served the orders with the deftness of magicians.

'Cheers to Jenny,' Colin raised his glass.

'To Jenny,' they replied, clinking their glasses.

'You won't feel it till September,' Clare reminded her, 'I'll be here to greet you home for my wedding.'

'That's what's keeping me going right now,' Jenny replied, 'though I'm looking forward to meeting my cousin Mary in New York. Imagine she sent me a first class ticket so that I'd thoroughly enjoy my maiden voyage.'

'Imagine travelling first class with all the toffs,' Sylvia said. 'Honestly, Jenny, I'd love to be coming with you.'

'You'd leave me behind!' Mattie feigned a sad expression.

'Not really,' Sylvia replied with a cheeky grin on her face.

The voice on the public address system summoned Mr Mattie Anderson to 'please pick up the nearest telephone where an urgent message awaits him'. He rushed off leaving everyone worried that it might be bad news.

Fifteen minutes later, he came back, beaming. 'Jenny I am now the proud owner of a state-of-the-art tractor which I won in a competition,' That was Tom, he said they want me to arrange collection as soon as possible.'

Sylvia jumped to her feet and flung her arms around him while a chorus of 'congratulations' rang in his ear.

'Ms Kane, will you accompany me to the official handing over of my prize?'

Sylvia thought for a moment. 'I'm sure Kane's Hotel can spare me for a few hours.'

'You, my little treasure, will travel to Holland with me in the near future, where we will be wined and dined, all part and parcel of the prize. How about it?

'Would a cat drink milk?' she replied assuring him she'd love to.

Clare whispered to Johnny, 'Listen, sweetheart, I have to talk to Jenny for a moment my mother asked me to give her a little package'.

Jenny and Colin were spending the last few moments together when Clare caught up with them. She had her head on Colin's shoulder while he stroked her hair.

'September will be here in no time and we can be together again.' Clare hadn't meant to eavesdrop, or to intrude on the precious moments left to them. She walked in the opposite direction and approached them again. Jenny spotted her and smiled through her tears. The public address announcement to assemble at the departure gate saw her friends steeling themselves for the dreaded moment. Clare handed her the small package.

'Mother sent you this, Jenny. You're to open it when you arrive in New York,' she advised.

'Please thank her and tell her I'll call her soon.' Clare knew it contained the locket her mother had removed from Anne Anderson's neck the day she was killed. That day in the casualty department, Nurse Alice Vaughan pledged that one day she would give Jenny the gold locket containing the picture of her parents. Clare felt privileged to be asked to hand it over, and she was sure it would mean so much to Jenny.

Cruising at forty thousand feet above sea level and with over six hours before arriving at Kennedy International airport, Jenny settled down for the trip. Surrounded by all the creature comforts imaginable, she shared the compartment with about six others.

The Jumbo jet smoothly made its way towards New York and would land on schedule, Captain Eric Wilson said in his welcoming address.

Sipping champagne and munching on a tasty petit four, she reflected on the hectic week just past. The visit to Colin's parents had been very pleasant. Vera dismissed the news of Colin failing his exam off hand.

'You can't always be top of your class,' she remarked, adding, 'your father and I both know it wasn't for want of trying.' Jenny smiled to herself remembering the expression of relief on Colin's face. The dreaded moment had been cushioned by Jenny's presence and the fact that John had arranged a holiday in Madeira for Vera.

'It's where we spent our honeymoon,' she remarked to Jenny producing her wedding album. 'I've missed not having a daughter to share things with' Vera hugged her and a tear escaped from her eye. Jenny must have dosed off after the lovely meal and Champagne because now the giant aircraft was approaching Kennedy International.

Mary Rafferty waved madly when she spotted Jenny wheeling her luggage through the arrivals gate. Jenny quickened her pace behind the pile of suitcases that needed a beast of burden to haul them.

'I notice you've come for good,' Mary joked, throwing her arms around Jenny. They stood for a moment laughing, crying and hugging.

'Let's get you home, Jenny,' Mary said, dabbing her eyes. Already, Jenny felt bewildered in the crowded arrivals with its huge melting pot of nationalities. She felt awkward and unsure but obediently followed her cousin in the direction of home.

Speeding into Manhattan in Mary's black and red convertible Mercedes, she began to relax. With temperatures tipping eighty-six degrees Fahrenheit, the open top car was a God's send.

'Do all Americans have a built-in cooling system?' Jenny asked an amused Mary.

'Just look at you cool as a cucumber while I'm melting away here,' Jenny was envious of her ice queen cousin, dressed immaculately in white shorts and top with her massive thick black hair piled high on her head. There wasn't even a bead of perspiration on her forehead, while Jenny felt compelled to fan herself with a magazine and sip a soft drink.

'You'll get used to it eventually,' Mary assured her. 'The trick is to wear as little as possible and carry bathing togs. Yeah, we often head for the beach when we finish work.'

Mary swung into a beautiful tree- lined boulevard.

'Is this the scenic route' Jenny asked.

'This is Lincoln Boulevard where we live, number sixty-seven is our house.' She slowed down allowing Jenny to admire the mansions with their beautiful gardens and colour schemes. It runs for about two kilometres in one of the most fashionable neighbourhoods of Manhattan.

'It's very grand and not at all where I would expect social workers to hang out,' Jenny remarked, hoping she hadn't sounded rude.

'There's an interesting history attached to this house,' said Mary, parking her car in the car park with enough space for ten cars. Jenny admired the splendid residence with its red door, huge windows containing pots and window boxes of lovely flowers and greenery and a neatly manicured garden.

A man who had been clipping around the edges of the lawn turned and said 'hello'.

'Hello Jake,' Mary replied, 'come and meet my cousin from Ireland.' They shook hands warmly, chatted for a moment, and Jenny complimented the elderly gardener on such a colourful display of flowers.

Mary closed the door behind them and smiled at Jenny. 'Welcome to your new home, I hope you'll be happy here.' She led the way across the large entrance hall in the direction of a great sweeping staircase. Jenny stopped to admire a portrait of a woman with very stern features wearing a crimson and gold cloak.

'Countess Von Erlich, our dear departed benefactress' Mary told her.

'Was this her house?' Jenny asked, admiring some very fine paintings hanging in the hall.

'Yes' most of the paintings you see here were painted by her,' Mary replied 'She was a remarkable woman by all accounts as Jake will tell you.'

They walked slowly up the stairs. Jenny listened while Mary explained how she and four other social workers came to occupy this wonderful house. The Countess had come to New York from Austria after the Second World War. She had met and married Drew Melville, an architect from Boston. They had four children and everything was going well for them until Drew got mixed up in gambling and shady deals.

Soon he had plunged her and the family into severe financial problems. She turned her back on him vowing never to set eyes on him again. In her darkest hour, she relied on social workers to help her, while she attempted to get her career as an artist back on the rails again. With the help of some influential friends, her works sold like hot cakes and eventually she bought this house. Before she died, she instructed her grandson, a Dominican priest, to give this house to social workers and to use her paintings to help the poor.

'Where does the money come from for maintenance?' Jenny asked. 'It must cost a fortune to keep a house like this, not to mention the gardens.'

'The original group of social workers started a fund known as The Countess Von Erlich fund and we all contribute to it. Since we don't pay rent per se, this money goes to Father Ralph Melville who is in charge of the fund and he looks after everything.'

'Where is he based?'

'In New York City,' Mary replied. 'I meet him there on a regular basis. He owns a small apartment attached to a drug crisis centre but his main office is in the basement of this house where his grandmother's paintings are stored.' The phone rang.

'Hi mom, how are you? Yeah I'm fine, I'll put Jenny on while I make us some coffee.'

'Aunt Helen.' Jenny spent a while chatting and Mary managed to get the chicken casserole into the oven.

'I'm thrilled your mom invited me to Boston on Sunday. Gosh, I'm so looking forward to meeting Uncle Jack and herself, it's been a long time.'

'Yeah, dad was only saying last week that it was twelve years since he'd been home to Ireland, even though my mother would have loved him to go. Anyway, Sunday at the crack of dawn, we'll head up and stay for a few days. He hasn't been that well, you know.'

'Nothing serious, I hope,' Jenny was concerned.

'A major stroke, the doctor told us, but thankfully he's okay since he went on medication for his blood pressure. It left him a bit shaken and he has lost a lot of confidence. That's why he gave me his car.'

'How is Aunt Helen coping?'

'Her nursing qualifications have certainly come in useful, she keeps a strict eye on his diet, and he's only allowed two glasses of wine a week. Occasionally, he sneaks a small glass of Jack Daniels when his friends come for their card game. I caught him in the act one night and he begged me not to tell.'

They both giggled, especially when Jenny said she had brought a present of twelve-year old Jameson for him.

'Here, let me show you to your bedroom,' Mary said.

'It's the grandest bedroom I've ever seen,' Jenny remarked once inside. 'Just look at that four poster bed and the quilt with its Triple Irish Chain pattern sure I'm beginning to feel like a Countess myself.'

'The quilt is my welcoming gift to you,' Mary said, explaining that the quilt is traditionally given to a very dear friend.

Later, they dined on the little balcony overlooking the back garden, and Mary told Jenny that she was heading to Peru to do some missionary work in September.

'We're having a little welcoming party for you tomorrow evening,' Mary announced gleefully. 'Barbara Macy suggested a barbecue and Father Ralph said he'd love to come and bring some of his friends. Anyway, it will be a perfect opportunity for you to meet everyone.

'Is Barbara Macy a social worker too? Jenny asked.

'Yep, Barbara is a New Yorker and she shares her apartment above us with Mary Jo Shiner, a Kentuckian. 'You'll be trained in by Mary Jo and, I warn you, she is one tough cookie.'

'I better make the most of my weeks holidays so, before I'm whipped into line,' Jenny replied not realising the irony of her remark.

'Good,' Mary replied, jumping to her feet to answer the doorbell.

She returned accompanied by a petite frizzy-haired woman with piercing blue eyes carrying a bouquet of red roses. 'Jenny, meet Pip, our housekeeper.'

'I'm delighted to meet you, Pip' Jenny said, extending her hand.

'Welcome to New York, Mary has told me all about you. These roses came for you much earlier, Jenny, but I had to go on urgent business, sorry I'm so late!'

Jenny 'Are you going to tell me who sent them?' Mary asked, her voice full of curiosity. Mary coiled up on one of the French nineteenth-century silk-covered settees while Jenny sat, kitten-like, on a large Persian rug. The setting sun cast its golden shadows on the Venetian blown glass chandelier and mirrors, as Jenny told her cousin how she had fallen in love with Colin Maloney.

'He's joining me in the autumn to study right here in New York,' she said in a voice full of excitement.

'Gee, I can't wait to meet him,' Mary replied. .'How does he get on with your grandma and Mattie?'

'Grandma adores him for his old-fashioned manners and respect, and Mattie has fallen for his MG sports car.'

Mary smiled. She remembered Mattie as a shy awkward sort of chap and wondered if he had a young lady in his life.

'He has recently started dating Sylvia Kane,' Jenny said. 'She's lovely and works in her father's hotel. Between you and me, he hasn't had much luck so far, so I'm not pinning any hopes on this one being successful either. Mattie needs some fine-tuning if you get my drift. By the way, he sent you this.' Jenny handed Mary a neatly wrapped present from her brother.

Mary uncoiled herself and quickly unwrapped the gift. Clearly she was moved by his thoughtfulness as she surveyed the montage of animal photographs. Tan Bo looked impressive sporting a rosette he had won earlier at the Spring Show. His sons, Oisin and Fergal, suckled their mother Bertha, while Bran the sheep dog watched lazily. Finally, there was a recent picture of Jenny riding out on Flan, looking like something out of the Wild West.

'I'll murder him!' Jenny exclaimed, crimson with embarrassment.

'Steady on, Jenny, these pictures are beautiful, just the way I remember things in Sliabh na mBan. I think it's a lovely gesture on Mattie's part.'

Jenny struggled to her feet, clumsily catching her right foot in the strap of her handbag. 'I should have closed the damn thing properly in the first place, now look what I have done.'

They giggled helplessly at the contents strewn all over the Persian rug. 'Let me help you,' Mary said, picking up a neat little gift, wrapped in pink paper, and tied with a gold ribbon.

Jenny explained that her friend, Clare, had given it to her before leaving Shannon with instructions to open it on arrival in New York.

'Isn't it exciting?' Mary remarked as she watched her untie the bow and peel the wrapping off. Gingerly she opened the tiny green box that contained a locket. Deftly she clicked the locket open. For a moment, she studied the photographs it contained in silence.

'It's my mum and dad,' she revealed, her voice cracking with emotion, tears streaming down her cheeks.

Mary cradled her in her arms until she settled. 'I'm okay, thanks Mary, take a look.'

'Uncle John and Aunt Anne, they're just as I remember them.' Mary's mind flashed twelve years to a lonely graveside in Sliabh na mBan where she had bid a final farewell to them. It was the last time her father had set foot in Ireland, so profoundly had his sister's death affected him.

'There's a tiny note in the box' Mary observed.

'Please open and read it to me' Jenny said.

Mary did so. It read, 'Dearest Jenny. 'On your grandmother's instructions, I have kept this locket for the past twelve years. Today, I feel compelled to give it to you as you embark on a new life in America. Best wishes, all my love. Alice Vaughan.'

Jenny kissed the little photograph. 'I'm pleased Alice gave them to me,' she remarked, 'for in a strange way I think it was meant to be.'

CHAPTER FOUR

Jack and Helen Rafferty cried tears of sheer joy when Jenny arrived in Boston.

'You're more beautiful than your photographs,' Jack remarked his voice still a bit shaky after the stroke. He stood up, leaving his cane to one side while he hugged her.

She could feel the weight of his weak right side pulling heavily on her.

'It's so good to see you again, Uncle Jack, you too, Aunt Helen.' Helen embraced Jenny warmly before helping Jack back to his chair. To mark the occasion, she poured him a small Jack Daniels.

'I'm in good hands with your Aunt Helen here, Mary too. She comes home most weekends. I'll miss her when she goes to Peru.'

'Don't worry, Uncle Jack, I'll come often to see you both.' She stroked his hand and switched her conversation to Aunt Helen to allow him to overcome the emotion that suddenly gripped him.

'I think I'll go for a walk,' Jack said. The fresh air will do me good.'

Mary sprung to his side and arm-in-arm they walked to the garden. Helen explained that since he had his stroke, he was subject to mood swings. It was hard for him to adjust after years as a physical education instructor.'

'How are you coping, Aunt Helen'?

The former Massachusetts General Hospital nurse thought

for a few moments before she answered. 'I'm getting better with each day, Jenny, but I won't pretend that it's easy. I'm nearly sixty now and I had so many plans for our retirement years, even, would you believe, to attempt the Inca trail together.'

She looked fit enough for it, Jenny observed. She was slim and tanned and wore her years well. Dressed in white shorts and T-shirt, one could imagine her to have been one of Jack's star pupils.

Suddenly a smile lit up her pretty face and she adjusted the coloured bandana that held her greying hair in place. 'Let's join them in the garden for lunch. Jack appears to have settled again.'

The appearance of a tubby elderly man carrying a large tray of salads surprised Jenny. He hummed a little tune and seemed very happy while he placed the tray on a wooden table where Jack was sitting.

'Thanks Basil'. Come and meet my niece, Jenny, she has just come over from Ireland.'

He quickly rubbed his hands on his great white apron before shaking hands warmly with Jenny. Helen explained to Jenny that he had recently retired from his job as janitor at Massachusetts General Hospital, and had come to work for them.

'He's a godsend to both of us,' Jack said. 'He keeps me company when Helen has to slip out to her charity functions and other engagements.'

When lunch was over Jack got a second wind. 'I want to introduce Jenny to the Cradle of Liberty,' he announced.

'Are you sure you're up to going into Boston?' Helen asked, taken aback by this sudden surge of energy.

'You just do the driving, Helen, and I'll give the history lesson, okay?'

'You're the boss,' she replied, grabbing her car keys from the hall rack.

Despite a slight limp, Jack cut quite a dash in his beige twill shorts, polo jumper and Moses sandals. He supported his six-foot frame on a sturdy blackthorn walking stick, and steeled himself for the short distance to the car. He took a deep breath and squared his strong angular face against the gentle breeze coming from the harbour.

'Well, what do you think of Beacon Hill, Jenny?'

'Oh, it's very elegant,' she replied, 'and those cobblestones and quaint gaslights are timeless.'

'You should see this place at Christmas,' Mary closed her eyes for a moment and smiled sweetly as if remembering a wonderful fairytale.

Helen was already seated at the wheel and anxious to get going. 'Mind If I sit in the back with Maureen O'Hara?' Jack asked a bemused Helen.

'Not at all, John Wayne, so long as you're not planning to meet up with Dan Danaher, she said, referring to the well-known film, The Quiet Man.

'No ma'am,' he replied 'Right now I want you to drive us to the oldest house in Boston. I'm sure Jenny has heard of Paul Revere.'

She had learned Henry Longfellow's poem, Paul Revere's Ride, at school but never in her wildest dream thought she would visit his house. Eagerly Jenny entered the house, linking her uncle Jack. He pontificated at a great rate about the contents, so much so, that a group of visitors cocked their ears to hear what he was saying.

'They think he's the guide,' Mary whispered to her mother.

'Are you surprised?' Helen asked.

Mary shrugged her shoulders then tipped her father gently on the shoulder.

'Shall we move on?' she whispered in his ear. 'Jenny might like to visit the JFK Memorial Library. Besides we can come back here another time.'

He readily agreed. They made their way towards Boston harbour and the JFK library. Later, sitting by the harbour's edge, Jack told Jenny that tealeaves could still be seen floating in the harbour following the Boston Tea Party of 1773.

'Give over, Uncle Jack, I'm not that much of a green horn,' she replied jocosely.

'Of course not, my darling,' he replied, 'but I'm sure we could all do with a nice cup of tea right now.'

'A nod's as good as a wink' Helen replied. 'Where would you like to go for afternoon tea, Jack?

'Take me home please, Helen, I'm kind of tired'.

Later, Helen, Mary and Jenny sat in the conservatory, with a big pot of tea, as Helen adjusted the blinds, partially blocking the brilliant evening sunshine. Bluebirds and chickadees sang and flitted blithely through the luscious greenery surrounding the conservatory.

Mary poured a fresh cup for everyone. Jenny fumbled in her handbag and produced a photograph. She handed it to Helen. She studied it for a while and glanced first at Jenny then Mary.

'Well?'

'That's my boyfriend, Colin Maloney. He's an astronomer,' Jenny said, suddenly feeling almost boastful, and wishing she had led up to the subject more gently.

Helen placed her teacup to one side and sat up like an excited child about to listen to her favourite fairytale. 'How long have you known him and where did you two meet?'

'We met when I was a student at Trinity College in Dublin. We were just good friends for a while then he went to California to study. Since he didn't write or phone for a full year, I had almost forgotten about him till he phoned a few weeks ago. I can't wait for September to come till I see him again.'

'I take it you're madly in love with him, it reminds me of....' Helen stared out the window a faint smile on her face.

'Oh, go on, Aunt Helen, and tell me how you and Uncle Jack first met,' Jenny was only too delighted to rid herself of the spotlight.

'It all started in Massachusetts General Hospital when I was in my final year training as a nurse. I was asked to stand in on night duty for a friend. I hated night duty and having to work on the Orthopaedic Unit. That all changed when I spotted the handsome P.E. teacher with his arm in a sling. He had been admitted earlier in the day, having slipped and dislocated his shoulder, while helping a student who got into difficulty on an orienteering outing.'

'Later while checking his pulse I hoped he wouldn't notice how nervous I was. I knew straight away that Jack Rafferty was the man for me. I had only two nights to win his affections. I sat alone at breakfast the following morning, hungry and dreamy, but certainly not tired. Yep, a trip to the hairdresser was top of the agenda I told myself and although not allowed on duty, I intended to wear my most alluring perfume to net this fine fish.'

'Musk,' Mary teased and she and Jenny broke into laughter.

'Don't be ridiculous' Helen replied. 'It would have taken more than an extract from the gland of some old male musk deer to impress Jack Rafferty. No, I used my most exotic perfume reserved for special occasions and it worked.'

Just then the shuffle of feet could be heard along the corridor. Jack knocked gently at the door. Helen jumped to her feet. 'It's only eight o'clock, the poker players won't be here for another hour' she told him.

'I know,' he replied. 'I asked Basil to cancel the game tonight.' He walked straight over to Jenny and kissed her gently on the cheek. 'There's nothing more important than the colleen from Sliabh na mBan, forgive me for even mentioning poker.'

'You're forgiven, Uncle Jack, now come and sit down for a chat.'

It was late on Monday evening when Mary and Jenny arrived back in Manhattan. There were several messages for both of them, including one from Mary Jo Shinner for Jenny.

'Contact me as soon as you get back from Boston, there are a few points I'd like to clarify with you before you commence work'. It was signed MJ S.

'What do you suppose she wants to talk to me about?' Jenny asked Mary, her tummy full of butterflies.

'Relax, Jenny, she just wants to put you in the picture for

tomorrow's schedule. She generally leaves for work at eight a.m. like we all do, except I'll be staying here to help Father Ralph with some paper work for Peru.'

'You mean you're not coming with me on my first day,' Jenny said in a slightly raised voice.

'It's best you start with Mary Jo. After all, she is the senior social worker. Besides, she has instructions from Meg Greer to train you in. Meg is the head honcho and gives the orders so I'm afraid it's totally out of my hands. Sorry!'

The night was warm and humid. Jenny had spent a full hour talking to Colin. He was off to Madeira with his parents the following day. 'I'm so miserable without you, Jenny,' he told her. 'Honestly, this past week has been sheer hell.'

'I'm missing you too, Colin, and already I'm looking forward to Clare's wedding and to seeing you again.' The line started to crackle and a tear trickled down her cheek when she faintly heard her him say 'I love you'.

Jenny buried her face in the pillow and sobbed uncontrollable. All her emotions came to the surface like surf from a giant wave. There was Colin, whom she loved, on the other side of the Atlantic Ocean and Uncle Jack, who had never returned to Sliabh na mBan since her mother died. Why did life have to be so complicated, she wondered?

CHAPTER FIVE

Jenny was waiting in the main hall when Mary Jo appeared at the top of the great staircase. She smiled broadly and with a glint in her eye, she said, 'Top of the morning to you.'

Jenny glanced at her watch. It was precisely seven thirty and indeed it merited the same reply to Mary Jo.

'I like to get into the office early on a Monday,' she remarked to Jenny. 'It gives me a chance to check the email, read the post, and down loads of black coffee.'

Jenny smiled, imaging Mary Jo suffering from a major hangover.

'Hectic weekend?' she ventured.

'Bloody right,' Mary Jo replied. 'Know anything about horses?'

'I grew up on a farm and I own a pony, that's about it,' Jenny replied.

'Hold this a moment, please,' Mary Jo handed Jenny her briefcase and proceeded to fasten the buckle of her sandal by cocking her foot on the bonnet of the car. 'See what I mean about horses,' she remarked, pointing to a colossal bruise on her right leg.

'How on earth did that happen?' Jenny asked.

'I was in the forge chatting to the Blacksmith and while one of my horses was getting shod, I guess I got in the way. Good job it wasn't the stallion or I'd probably be on crutches with a broken leg,' she continued. 'Anyway we had best get going.'

On the way into Manhattan, Mary Jo talked about her love of horses. 'To tell you the truth, Jenny, I look forward so much to going home to Kentucky and galloping like mad around the ranch.'

Jenny was really getting to like this powerful horsewoman. Already she had managed to put her completely at ease with not a mention of work.

'Tell me, how did you end up becoming a social worker? I mean you sound as though you could have carved a great career in show jumping or as a trainer.'

'Yea, you're right Jenny. I have several trophies for horse jumping competitions but I wanted to do something really useful for people less fortunate. Sorry, I don't mean to come over all saintly but I do love my job,' Mary Jo said.

'And I'm looking forward to being trained in by you, and to getting started in what promises to be a very rewarding career.'

'In that case prepare yourself for the real world.' Mary Jo explained to Jenny how she had met the mottled, the bruised and the unfortunates every day in her line of work, and not all of it from a textbook.

'Sounds scary,' Jenny replied.

'Goes with the territory,' she replied, parking her car near the office.

The tall Kentuckian led the way to the office. Dressed in a cool blue linen shirt, navy linen skirt, and wearing Moses sandals that were designed for walking, she looked like she meant business. Inside the office, the fax was spitting out information and some of their colleagues were already at their desks, raising their heads briefly to nod a welcome to Jenny.

'Grab a notebook and pen from the desk in the corner,' Mary Jo told Jenny, 'then make us two mugs of coffee, please.'

Over coffee, they mulled over the day's schedule. 'We may not have time to cover everything on the list but we can but try. Incidentally, Meg Greer wants to meet you at four p.m. She likes to interview new recruits and spell out the rules, terms of employment, et cetera. I promised her I'd have you back on time.'

In temperatures reaching the high eighties, they made their way to the home of the Emmanuel family. The apartment was situated at the end of a street with graffiti and slogan-daubed walls. 'Best foot forward,' Mary Jo advised as they climbed to the fourth floor.

Through the intercom she announced their arrival. The bolts were pulled back on the heavy door revealing Angela Emmanuel, a low-sized Italian woman with beautiful brown expressive eyes dressed in black.

'Mary Jo, I'm so pleased to see you. Thank you, thank you,' she repeated. 'Victor has had a very poor night and I feel worn out too.'

Mary Jo introduced Jenny and they moved towards Victor. He was using his nebuliser to ease his asthma and appeared very distressed. He acknowledged them with a wave and closed his eyes.

'You like a cool drink?' Angela asked.

'Iced water would be fine please, Angela.'

Jenny noticed a photograph of a handsome young boy on the sideboard. She picked it up and admired it.

'Your son?' Angela nodded in the affirmative and handed her the glass of water.

'He's beautiful,' Jenny remarked.

'Not any more' Angela replied, tears streaming down her cheeks. She passed the glass of water to Mary Jo, who was seated on the end of Victor's couch.

'You have any news of my darling Sergio?' she asked Mary Jo.

'Our next visit is to Sergio and I promise to call you straight away,' Mary Jo replied.

'You think he has HIV / AIDS? Oh, my poor darling child, I hope they find the man who did this to him.' Angela was crying bitterly and Jenny tried to console her.

Mary Jo held her hand. 'Please be patient, Angela,' she advised. 'The doctor will have the results of the tests soon, meantime, try and be brave for Victor's sake.

We'll do all we can for you,' Mary Jo assured her, 'please take this voucher, it may help to buy some groceries.'

Angela thanked them profusely for everything and they left the apartment.

Mary Jo explained the background while they walked the ten-minutes to the Drug Treatment Centre. 'Angela and Victor came to New York from Naples some years ago and worked in the catering business. They had always managed to eke out an existence till Victor became too ill to work.

'Their sixteen-year-old son, Sergio, stepped into the breech and got a job as a courier. At first, everything went well, with Sergio bringing home enough money to pay the bills and provide food for them. When he started to stay out all night at parties and developed behavioural problems, Angela became suspicious. The police were contacted and investigations were soon underway.

'It transpired that Sergio was a courier for a notorious drug baron called Poppy. At these so-called parties, he was sucked into the drug culture and developed an addiction to heroin. A week ago, he was admitted to a Drug Treatment Centre.'

'What a dreadful mess,' Jenny remarked. 'It's bad enough for Angela having a sick husband and now her only child ruined by drugs.'

Mary Jo led the way across a courtyard that housed the Drug Rehabilitation Centre, a large cafe, a florist and a newsagent's shop.

'I'm dreading this,' Jenny said to Mary Jo, feeling almost overcome by the heat and the thoughts of facing the patients undergoing treatment.

'If you like, we can stop for an iced coke or something,' Mary Jo suggested.

'It's tempting,' Jenny replied, 'but I'd prefer to get this over with.'

The receptionist pointed to the day room where Sergio was sitting with a group of fellow patients. Mary Jo went straight over to him and shook hands. He eyed Jenny suspiciously when they were introduced but managed a faint smile.

'Have you seen the doctor?' Mary Jo asked.

'He will be here soon,' Sergio replied. 'I'm worried about the results of my tests. Did you visit my parents today?'

'I've just come from the apartment, and I promised to contact your mother after I've spoken to the doctor.'

'How are you feeling right now?' Mary Jo wasn't surprised when he replied that he was miserable. Jenny stared at the young seventeen-year old and saw no resemblance to his photograph. Instead, he had sunken eyes, a pale gaunt face, arms that were scarred from injections and trembling hands that scarcely could hold his paper cup of water.

'How is my father?' he asked.

'Poorly, I'm afraid,' Mary Jo replied. 'Don't worry, Sergio, we will do what we can to help.'

'How could I have done this to him?' he yelled, breaking into a cold sweat and collapsing in a heap on the floor. Mary Jo and Jenny tried to help him to his feet.

'Don't touch me,' he cried. 'I'm a junkie, a disgusting mean low-down rat, who doesn't deserve to see my father, or my mother, ever again.' He started frothing at the mouth and his body became rigid. A nurse and doctor were promptly at his side administering treatment.

'Let him rest awhile,' the doctor advised, adding 'I'd like to speak to his family as soon as possible.' Mary Jo and Jenny followed him to the observation room.

Doctor Cain was seated in front of the computer about to start work.

'Excuse me, Doctor Cain, may I have a word concerning Sergio Emmanuel?'

'Yes, of course, Mary Jo, please take a seat.'

'Thank you, doctor'. This is my colleague, Jenny Anderson who has just joined us.'

Doctor Cain shook hands and smiled at Jenny.

He listened politely while Mary Jo filled him in on the Emmanuel situation. For a few moments, he reflected on what she had said.

'Would his father not be better in hospital?' he asked. 'Sergio could do with a visit from his mother, he needs her support right now.'

'That's true,' Mary Jo replied, 'trouble is, Doctor, he won't go into hospital.'

'I've got to speak to his mother today if possible.' Doctor Cain told Mary Jo that while Sergio wasn't in any immediate danger, his parents needed to be kept informed.

'Have you any results to hand?' Mary Jo asked.

'Yes, his chest X-ray seems okay, liver function test shows Bilirubin slightly raised and I checked for hepatitis. There are other tests being carried out but the results are not back yet. Besides, I'd prefer to speak with his mother ...'

'I understand,' Mary Jo replied. 'I could bring you to the apartment if you wish.'

'Normally I prefer to interview relatives here,' he replied, 'but I guess the Emmanuel family are exceptions. Would two p.m. suit?'

She said 'yes' knowing they would have to work even harder to meet her schedule. Mary Jo suggested an early lunch, much to the Jenny's approval. 'I have one golden rule, Jenny, which is that we don't discuss work during breaks. But I regret that we can only spare thirty minutes for lunch today, with Doctor Cain's meeting thrown in.'

In the cafe in the courtyard, Jenny wearily joined Mary Jo for a salad sandwich. She wasn't even hungry, however the long drink of iced water was wonderful.

'How do you Americans always remain so cool?' she asked Mary Jo.

'Maybe it's because they stick us in the fridge at birth instead of the incubator,' she replied jocosely.

'I wish someone would lock me in a fridge for five minutes. I'm melting slowly away in this temperature,' Jenny remarked to a bemused Mary Jo.

They munched noisily on a sandwich of iceberg lettuce, cucumber, coleslaw, mayonnaise and tomato. Despite not being hungry, Jenny finished every morsel of the sandwich. 'I've actually enjoyed that,' she remarked. 'Have we time for a coffee?'

'Coffee it is,' Mary Jo summoned the waiter.

'Allow me,' the distinctive voice of Father Ralph Melville startled Mary Jo. 'Make that coffee for three please, waiter,' he called. 'May I join you?'

'Please do Ralph.' Mary Jo moved to the inside seat and made room for him. 'We understood you were busy preparing for Peru. How come you're here?'

'I've left all that business in Mary's capable hands after I got a call from Angela Emmanuel,' Ralph replied thoughtfully. 'I've just been to visit them and I'm on my way to see Sergio.'

Mary Jo wanted to explain about Sergio but time was running out. She apologised to Father Ralph that they had to rush. 'We have to make a call at the hospital and be back to meet Doctor Cain at two,' she told him.

'I'll run you to the hospital, I usually say Mass for the patients at one o'clock.'

In the courtyard they scrambled aboard his jeep. 'How's the new girl settling in?' Ralph asked Jenny as she seated herself in the rear seat.

'Please don't ask, Father Ralph,' she replied. 'The New York heat is getting to me.'

'In that case, why don't we all chill out in the garden after work'. I'll provide the drinks and food. Would seven o'clock be okay?'

'You're a star,' Jenny replied, provoking hilarious laughter from Mary Jo and Ralph.

Doctor Cain spoke to Angela and Victor Emmanuel, telling them the test results hadn't shown up anything more sinister than heroin addiction.' 'I'm not playing down the seriousness of his condition,' he continued, 'but I'm hopeful that with treatment, care and support, he will recover fully.'

'That is great news, Doctor Cain,' Angela said. 'Have you told Sergio'?

'No, he had a seizure this morning and I had to give him an injection,' Doctor Cain explained. 'He slept for some time afterwards but I will see him this afternoon.'

'You mentioned support, Doctor. Problem is that most of our family live in Italy. How am I going to give him any support with Victor so ill?'

'That's precisely why I've come to visit you,' he replied 'I'm afraid your husband must go to hospital. It would help you considerably, and facilitate Sergio too.'

'Will you explain to Victor?'

Victor was too weary to argue and simply nodded in agreement. 'I'll make arrangements and phone you later,' he told Angela. 'I'll also give you an update on Sergio.'

*

Jenny was exhausted after her first day as a social worker. She collected her mail from the pigeonhole and wearily ascended the great staircase. Glad to be home again, the thoughts of a long soak in the bath followed by a few cool drinks in the garden, was pure heaven.

She received three letters. Instantly she recognised Colin's handwriting, along with Clare's and her grandmother's.

Hurriedly she ripped open Colin's letter. A quick read revealed he was lonely and heartbroken in Madeira. She cast the letter angrily to one side. 'Imagine feeling sorry for yourself on such a beautiful island'

She lowered herself into a bath of relaxing balm and gently inhaled the fumes. Her mind drifted to Madeira with its lush growths of orchids, camellias, jacaranda and Mimosa trees. She remembered going there with her grandparents for her twenty-first birthday. When they had visited a remote village, she had travelled in a hammock carried on poles by two suntanned bearded men. She would willingly trade the intense heat of New York with the balmy temperature of Madeira right now.

'Have you disappeared down the plug hole?' Mary asked, knocking hard on the door.

'What time is it?' Jenny wondered.

'It's ten past seven, we're ready to eat,' Mary replied.

'Sorry, I'll be right down.' She dressed quickly selecting a lemon cotton crew neck sweater and casual floral pants. A quick flick of the brush through her hair, a dab of barrier cream on her face, a pair of open sandals and she was all set.

In the garden, the aroma of food from the barbecue vied with the scent of the flowers.

Father Ralph was busy mingling with the guests and dishing out food.

'Jenny, come and join the party,' Ralph said. 'Grab a plate and share the loaves and fishes. Now, what would you fancy?'

'Barbecued chicken and salad please,' she replied. Ralph helped her select from the huge range of salads available.

'Drink?'

'A glass of white wine would be lovely, please.' He poured

two glasses and placed them on a small table under an oak tree. 'Let's sit for a while and you can tell me all about your first day in work,' Ralph suggested.

'Are you going to have some food?' Jenny asked shyly.

'The truth is I have been sampling every dish as I went along, so I'm okay, thanks,' he replied.

Some of the guests had formed a little band in the corner of the garden and were playing lively music. A number of the young ladies spurred on by the music danced blithely round the duck pond.

'I guess that's the end of our chat,' Ralph laughed. 'Why don't we join them when you've finished eating.'

'I'd love to' she replied eagerly. Jenny noticed they were dancing barefoot and she relished the idea of the cool grass soothing her aching arches.

'Who are all these people anyway?' she asked. Aside from Mary, Mary Jo Shinner, Barbara Macy and the Wilton sisters who occupied the house with her, she didn't know anyone else, yet there were strangers all over the place.

'They're waifs and strays from the city,' Ralph replied 'Special people I meet everyday who normally wouldn't get a chance to frolic in a lovely garden on a summer's evening. Come and meet them!'

He held her hand and led her towards the dancers. They kept going, dancing and clapping while the musicians quickened the tempo. He clapped too, encouraging them, and keeping time with his foot. Jenny watched with excitement, enthralled by their performance. Suddenly they stopped, and one by one came to Ralph, and gave him a big hug. He seemed almost like a giant beside them. Casually dressed in chino pants, logo t-shirt, and wearing beige sneakers, nobody would have guessed, that the tall Dominican priest had trained this group of dancers, and musicians, to bring cheer to the underprivileged people he worked with.

He introduced them to Jenny calling each person by name. 'Let them dance in praise of Yahweh's name,' he said to Jenny quoting from Psalm 149.

'Where do you get all your energy from?' Jenny asked Ralph as the party was coming to an end.

'Hey, I'm only forty, you know, and believe it or not, I'm actually energised by all the wonderful people around me.'

'What will we all do when you go to Peru?' Although Jenny hardly knew him, she could already sense the vacuum of loneliness that his absence would create.

'Let's not waste time worrying about the future,' he replied. 'Instead, let's live and use each day to the fullest, for the betterment of our fellow man.'

Clutching bottles of coke and bags of goodies, the visitors climbed aboard the people carrier heading back to their various shelters and homes. They waved and blew kisses before disappearing down the tree-lined avenue.

'They'll sing the whole way back to town Jenny There's so much talent out there, all that's needed is someone to spot it and tap into it. I often wish I had more time to spare.' Ralph leaned against the bonnet of his jeep and folded his arms. 'Most of that group have no families anymore,' he told Jenny. 'I found them in shelters for the homeless, on the streets, and four of the young men are ex-prisoners who were jailed for petty offences.'

'How long did it take to get them to this stage'?

'Four years of hard practice,' he replied, 'but I didn't do it by myself. Some good friends have backed me on this one, like so many other projects. I'm a very fortunate man.'

*

'May I come in?' Mary asked, knocking gently on Jenny's bedroom door.

'Please do,' Jenny replied, glancing up from page twenty of her grandma's letter.

'I just wondered if you'd fancy a night cap, but I can see you're busy,' Mary remarked. 'Did the whole of Ireland write to you?' she asked, noticing the bed covered with writing paper.

'It's one of my grandma's epistles,' Jenny replied, 'and boy did she fill me in on the goings on at home.'

'So you'll have that night cap, I take it,' Mary was dying to hear the news.

'Yes, please. You don't mind if we sit on the balcony? I need to cool down.'

'Balcony it is,' Mary replied carrying the iced Tequilas.

'I'll ring his neck the very minute I see him,' Jenny exclaimed. 'I knew I couldn't trust him.' She flung the letter to one side and took a sip of her drink.

'Colin?' Mary ventured.

'No, Mattie's gone and messed things up between himself and Sylvia Kane'.

'What's gone wrong?' Mary asked.

'Apparently Mattie got the hots for some other fellows

girlfriend from the States. Sylvia flew into a rage and hasn't been seen since. I don't blame her.'

'He probably just got carried away,' said Mary.

'Maybe, but Mattie simply can't handle relationships. The previous one was a total disaster, and he's botched this one up after only a few weeks. I can't wait to go home for Clare Vaughan's wedding, I tell you, I'll give him what's for.'

'Speaking of weddings, when is Clare's big day?' Mary was anxious to change the subject.

'September fourth,' Jenny replied.

Jenny, Is there any word from Colin or have you forgotten all about him?' .

'Oh, he's miserable in Madeira,' Jenny replied. 'Honestly, Mary, there is no pleasing some men. Even in the Rock Garden of the Atlantic amid all the exotic blooms and greenery, he's missing me.'

'And here's his orchid, wilting in New York,' Mary teased.

*

One week on and Jenny was pleased with her progress. Lying in her bed on Saturday morning, she reflected on the week. Sergio Emmanuel had brightened up considerably now that his mother could visit him. He was also helping the police with their investigation into the drug baron – he had already given them the name of the mansion where he had delivered drugs as a courier. He also told the police that Poppy took deliveries of soft cushions and bedding stuffed with dope.

'That figures' the police replied 'It's time to put paid to his antics before he turns half Manhattan into Rip Van Winkles.

Jenny remembered how Mattie loved Saturdays. He had told her so on the very day he prepared for his first date with Sylvia. Now all that had changed. He was probably licking his wounds and feeling sorry for himself. She vowed to call him later in the day when she finished shopping with her cousin Mary.

'Any ideas for your wedding outfit?' Mary asked while they had breakfast.

Jenny browsed through a Vogue catalogue. 'What do you think?' she asked, pointing to a ravishing silk chiffon ensemble in black dot leaf with lace trimmings.

'Wow!' Mary exclaimed, 'it's drop-dead gorgeous. Go for it.'

'I kind of have my heart set on it, so let's hope I won't be disappointed,' Jenny replied.

'I know where to find the stockist, so let's get cracking,' Mary urged, 'and by the way they stock lovely accessories too.'

In a smart boutique near Fifth Avenue, Jenny found the ensemble. She tried it on and was more than happy with it, especially the long flowing skirt. In the hat department, she went from jaunty to cloche before deciding on a large-brimmed black one with a deep white band.

'I can't believe my luck,' Jenny remarked, when the first pair of Anne Klein sandals she tried fitted perfectly. 'They're so comfortable and stylish too, don't you agree, Mary?

Before Mary had time to blink, Jenny was clutching a Louis Vuitton bag and had made her mind up without further consultation.

'It will be years before I splash out again,' she whispered to Mary while the assistant carefully wrapped and bagged the purchases. 'I'm so looking forward to Clare's wedding - it's the first one I've ever been invited to.'

'So impressing Colin doesn't enter into this mad spending spree?' Mary teased.

'There's no fooling, Mary Rafferty,' Jenny replied. 'And, yes, I want him to see me at my very best. I do love him you know.'

They left the shop, soaking up the atmosphere of a bustling Fifth Avenue with its melting pot of nationalities, creeds and colours. Stylish and sophisticated shops fronted by lavish window dressing, Saint Patrick's Cathedral, the Empire State Building, Rockefeller Centre, that great landmark housing twenty-one buildings on twenty-three acres.

'It's good to be alive,' Jenny remarked to Mary.

'It is indeed,' Mary replied, leading the way into a bright and cheerful restaurant. The headwaiter showed them to a table for two, and handed them the lunch menu.

'If it's not the lovely Miss Anderson.' Jenny recognised the voice immediately and glanced up at her old friend, Dan Flynn. She quickly stood up and they hugged tenderly.

'Dan, fancy meeting you here' Jenny was surprised. 'Let me introduce you to my, cousin Mary.'

Jenny told Dan that Mary had taken her under her wing since she arrived ten days ago.

'You must have some hell of a wing span, Mary, to keep this one contained,' Dan joked 'Are you still mixed up with that star gazer, Jenny?'

'Yes, in fact, he's joining me here in September.'

'Very cosy, indeed, and speaking of cosy, I'm probably interrupting your lunch. I only popped in for a coffee,' Dan remarked.

'Please stay and have something to eat, it's my treat,' Jenny insisted.

'Thanks Jenny, I'll just have a coffee. I'm wrecked after a busy night on duty.'

Mary had been observing Dan since he joined them and reckoned that he must be a cop. He had the physique of a rugby player and stood six feet tall. His black hair was neatly cut, giving his long angular face a severe expression. Casually dressed in a black and yellow poplin shirt and a washed and worn looking twill pants, she figured he was aged about thirty-five or six.

'Dan's a surgeon,' Jenny remarked.

'I'd never have guessed,' Mary replied. 'When I heard you say you were tired after a busy night, I assumed you were a cop. May I ask how do you know one another?'

'We met in Dublin,' Jenny replied. 'A group of us hung out together, we met up once or twice a month for theatre and a meal, that sort of thing. Two years ago, Dan came to New York to specialise in neurological surgery.'

'You've chosen a tough one, Dan, how are you finding it?' Mary asked.

'Yea, it can be tedious as I found out last night, but having trained under Professor Manning at St. Mary's Hospital, I'm very fortunate,' Dan replied.

'Why, what happened last night?' Mary asked.

'The patient I performed surgery on had a clot on the brain. A man of fifty and his cohorts were involved in a shoot-out at his mansion. I've only sketchy details, as you can imagine, but it seems he was a drug baron called Poppy.'

'Poppy!' Mary and Jenny stared at each other incredulously. Did you save him?' Jenny asked nervously.

'I spent ten hours drilling and boring his skull till finally I released the clot,' Dan explained. 'He's on a life support machine, and I wouldn't give much hope for him, but you never know, he could rally.'

'Any news of the rest of his gang?' Mary wondered.

'Two or three were killed, one escaped, and more are in police custody but, like I say, I'm not sure.' Dan rubbed his weary eyes. 'I'm going home to get some sleep, ladies, so please forgive me.'

'Forgive you, we'll do more than that,' Jenny replied 'Why don't you come over for supper tonight, you can stay over if you wish?'

'I'd love to, Dan replied, 'but I'm sure you have other plans for the weekend. No, really I can't, some other time perhaps. Thanks for the invitation.'

'We've no plans for the weekend, Dan, and we'd both love to have you over for dinner tonight. Isn't that right, Mary?'

'How can I refuse two beautiful cousins such a heartfelt invitation? Would eight o'clock suit? Address and telephone number, please.'

*

The main story in the evening newspaper was the capture of Jeremiah Cobb, alias 'Poppy'. Mary and Jenny spent the afternoon reading several accounts of the drug baron and his gang. Described as 'New York's most notorious drug criminal', he had ruined the lives of a whole generation, the newspaper stated. Poppy supplied heroin, cocaine, cannabis, LSD and amphetamines.

'Should I call Angela Emmanuel?' Mary asked Jenny.

'If only to reassure her,' Jenny replied. 'Tell her we'll call to see her on Monday.'

Jenny folded the newspaper and put it to one side. The morbid reading had dampened an otherwise lovely day. But it wasn't going to get in the way of her plans for Dan Flynn and Mary.

'It's action stations now,' she called to Mary when she finished phoning Angela Emmanuel. 'We have precisely an hour-and-a-half before Dan arrives.'

'I'll prepare the meal and you can arrange the table,' Mary suggested. 'That way, we'll ensure that the poor doctor won't be poisoned.'

'Okay, point taken,' Jenny replied. 'I may not be much of a cook, but I sure as hell can detect romance a mile away.'

'Give over Jenny. Dan probably has loads of girls vying for his attention. Besides, who said I'd be interested?'

'Oh! It's like that, is it? Pardon me for intruding,' Jenny said, feigning mild offence.

She prepared the table, showered and changed for dinner. She had left Mary to do her own thing and the mouth-watering aromas coming from the kitchen were promising.

'How do I look?' Mary stood there, arms outstretched ready to do a twirl.

'Oh my goodness! What a transformation! You look lovely Mary and that black lace number is spot on.' The doorbell rang.

'You or I?' Mary asked.

'Please, Mary, you go and meet Dan. You can delay a little and tell him about the history of the house and the Countess.

It will give me time to uncork the wine and put on some music - Dan likes Vivaldi.'

Jenny checked the food. Everything was perfect and the sauces were on the Bain-Marie ready for serving. Mary was a wiz in the kitchen and she knew Dan would be impressed. She heard their footsteps approaching and went out to greet them. Dan was wearing a black suit, white shirt, and a paisley tie. He had a single red rose for each of them and a bottle of wine.

'For the ladies of the manor,' he said, handing them each a red rose accompanied by a hug.

'Cead mile failte,' Jenny said. 'It's lovely to see you again Dan.'

'Likewise Jenny' he replied. I'm really glad we had that chance meeting this morning. I think fate had something to do with it.'

Jenny insisted on serving the food. Dan poured wine for Mary and Jenny opting for a beer himself.

'Do you both do the cooking or who makes the decisions?' Dan asked, eyeing the juicy steak that Jenny served him.

Mary pointedly took a sip from her glass allowing Jenny to answer. 'I'm a disaster in the kitchen, Dan, as lethal as a crow with a shotgun, you might say. Mary, however, is as good as a trained chef as you are about to discover.'

'But you have improved, Jenny!'

'Only very slightly, Mary, I shudder to think what will become of me when you go to Peru.'

'Peru?' Dan looked puzzled. Jenny busied herself with the desserts, leaving Mary to explain. When she returned carrying the Pavlova Dan was deep in conversation with Mary. 'What's all this about Peru'? She heard him ask.

'I volunteered to go with Father Ralph Melville some time ago,' Mary replied. 'I'm really looking forward to it and we have most of the preparations done. From what Father Ralph has told me it promises to be very challenging.'

I've read some books and pamphlets too, so I have a fair idea of what to expect.'

'That's a brave move, Mary,' Dan said. 'It's just as well Colin is coming to New York to keep you company, Jenny.'

'That's true, Dan, I hope you'll keep in touch too. I can't guarantee cooking of Mary's standard but I have a good tin opener.'

'A bit like myself in the old bachelor pad over in Central Park West,' he replied in a good-natured tone. 'You must both come over some weekend to visit me. The apartment is modest by comparison to this palatial residence, but it's cosy and homely.'

'We'd love to come, Dan' they replied in unison. 'The weekend would probably suit us better,' Mary remarked. 'How about you, Dan?'

'Usually its fine,' he replied, 'though occasionally, I'm on call, like next weekend for instance. Oh damn! I forgot I'm going home to Dublin the following week for two weeks' holidays. Sounds like it will be the end of August before I'm free but ...

Just then, the phone rang. Mary glanced at her watch. It was precisely ten p.m. 'I'll get it,' she remarked to Jenny. 'It's probably my mother.'

'She's a remarkable lady, your cousin,' Dan remarked when Mary had gone.

'She's the sister I never had and I'm the sister she never

had,' Jenny replied, stopping when she saw Mary's white face flooded with tears.

'What is it, Mary?' she said, rushing over to cradle her in her arms.

'Dad's just died,' she said, shock etched in her face. 'I'll have to fly to Boston straight away. I can't leave Mom to cope alone.'

'Poor Uncle Jack,' Jenny cried, devastated. 'I'll pack our cases and we'll catch the midnight flight together.'

Dan offered his condolences and insisted he'd come, too. Mary protested through her tears. 'Dan, there's no need. Really, Jenny and I will cope.'

I insist' he said. 'Let me call a taxi and I'll travel with you. I'm so sorry, Mary, that our first meeting should end this way.' He held her in his arms and smoothed her glossy black hair.

Jenny packed and quickly made a few urgent phone calls to Sliabh na mBan. They too would have to make arrangements to come over for the funeral.

'Is there anything special we should bring?' her grandma asked, distraught.

'I'll call you later, grandma, when I've had a chance to talk to Aunt Helen.'

There was an eerie silence on the journey up to Boston. Dan held Mary's hand and tried to comfort her but to little avail. He could feel the sobs shaking every fibre of her body. Grief marked her face and she was obviously in shock too.

Jenny sat by herself on the flight, occasionally glancing across the aisle at them. The thought struck her that had she not gone on the shopping spree, Mary would probably have gone home to Boston. She glanced at her watch. It was just one a.m. and they were approaching O'Hare International Airport.

Basil had come to meet them. 'It was all very sudden,' he told them while offering his condolences. 'Your mother is showing remarkable courage,' he remarked to Mary.

'Is she, Basil? She's lucky you were here. I'd hate to think she had to go through it alone. Thanks Basil for coming to meet us at this late hour. 'This is Dan Flynn, a friend of ours, and you remember Jenny.'

'We met before briefly at Massachusetts Hospital,' Basil replied. 'Nice to see you again, Dr. Flynn.'

'And you, Basil, you have a good memory.'

'Your mother will be surprised, Mary,' Basil remarked.

'Why so?' Mary asked.

'She would have worked with Mr Flynn in the operating theatre, I expect.'

Mary looked at Dan. 'Theatre Sister Helen Rafferty. Does that ring a bell?'

'You mean you're Helen's daughter,' Dan was quite flabbergasted.

'I am indeed,' Mary replied 'I had no idea you worked in Massachusetts General.'

'I was only there for six weeks before I started in New York, but I did work with your mother. 'She taught me a lot,' Dan said.

Arriving at Beacon Hill, Basil led the way. He opened the hall door quietly and was met by Helen. Mary flung her arms around her mother. 'Poor mum' are you okay? You must be in shock. Thank God Basil was with you'. Jenny hugged her Aunt

Helen. Unable to speak Jenny moved away to allow Dan to offer his condolences. Helen thanked him and for coming. 'I didn't realise you were back at Massachusetts General Mr. Flynn' she remarked looking rather puzzled.

'I'm not Helen' he replied 'I'll let Mary explain later'.

Helen nodded. Please make some coffee Basil I'm sure they could all do with it after the journey.

'I've decided on a proper Irish wake for your father,' Helen told Mary. 'We'll keep him here for a few days to allow everyone to pay their respects. He'd want it that way.'

Mary and Jenny kissed his cold forehead. 'He looks very peaceful,' Mary remarked.

'Just as I remember Uncle Jack,' Jenny agreed. They sat silently and watched the candles flicker causing the silver cross on his rosary beads to shine brightly.

'You'll stay the night, Dan?' Mary asked as they sipped coffee in the kitchen.

'Thanks. I'll bunk down anywhere, but I must return to New York early. I have a list first thing Monday morning. I don't mean to sound insensitive, but I'd love to be more helpful,' he remarked sympathetically.'

Mary glanced round the kitchen. Familiar things like Jack's walking stick lay up against his favourite chair, his well-worn slippers placed beside a door leading to the garden, and his spectacles resting on the open newspaper, all reminded her of his daily routine.

'Would you like a few minutes to yourself?' Jenny asked. 'I'll give Aunt Helen a bit of support, she might even fancy a cup of tea.'

Mary nodded. Grief swelled up again leaving her unable to speak. Outside in the peacefulness of the garden, she heard the odd twitter of a bluebird. Her father had frequently left food and water for them in the winter. He loved nature, not surprising she thought, growing up in Sliabh na mBan.

She felt her mother's comforting hand on her shoulder. 'Sorry, mom, I should have been here,' she said, hugging her distraught mother. 'What time did he pass away?'

'At five past nine,' Helen replied. 'Basil was preparing him for bed and I was making his hot drink when I heard him call my name.' I rushed to his side and held him while Basil called the doctor and priest. He died peacefully, Mary, and we had had such a lovely day in the garden.'

CHAPTER SIX

Three weeks later, Dan Flynn returned from holiday. He phoned Jenny. 'I'd like to meet for a chat, just the two of us, it's kind of important.'

'Saturday, three p.m. at Jakes?'

'Jakes is perfect, Jenny. How have you been and how is Mary?'

'We're both okay thanks, trying to get back to normality. It's been difficult but we're getting there,' Jenny explained.

'You're two brave ladies. I am looking forward to Saturday, Jenny.'

Jenny had a fair idea what was important to Dan. Mary had received several phone calls from Dublin, a few postcards and a very sympathetic letter. He had left her in no doubt that she was special to him. Mary had made no comment other than 'Dan is so kind' and 'what a surprise that he knew Mom'.

With only one week to go before taking off for Peru her days were spent attending to every last detail. Together, they had gone shopping for what mainly amounted to sports gear. Jenny had helped with some of the packing following the list Mary had compiled and ticking off every item.

'I'm off home to visit mom tomorrow,' Mary announced late on Friday night. 'I'm hoping to persuade Mom to come down and spend the last few days with me here.'

'I'd come with you except I have things planned for the weekend,' Jenny said.

Dan was seated in the foyer of Jakes when Jenny arrived.

He stood up, kissed her on the cheek and thanked her for coming. They found a quiet table in a dimly lit corner. Jenny could sense Dan's unease.

'Shall we order afternoon tea?' she asked. 'I could murder a piece of gateau.'

'Why not? Dan replied. 'This place is renowned for its gorgeous Gateau and cinnamon doughnuts guaranteed to expand the waistline.'

'How was Dublin, did you enjoy you holiday?'

'Yea! It was fine. I swear to you, Jenny, my parents wait for me to come home to traipse from one art gallery to another, not to speak of museums. I have corns, bunions, and calluses for my troubles, all procured in the space of a week'

'Surely you exaggerate, Dan?' Jenny laughed.

'Only very slightly mind you, Jenny' and guess what my father has also started?'

'What?'

'The Flynn family tree' he replied. I also found myself in the Archives in Bishop Street handling musty old tomes tracing back the Flynn family. Apparently, we were known as O'Flynn till about seventy years ago.'

'What happened?'

'Some wise wag told them that the banshee followed the Macs and the O's so they decided they didn't want some wailing old witch, combing her hair and bawling her eyes out, when they passed away.'

'Okay, Dan, let's get to the real reason we're here. What's so important?

'Your cousin, Mary, I'm in love with her.'

'You don't beat about the bush, I'll say that for you.'

'Jenny, time is running out. I mean, if Mary has only a week left before going to Peru, then I have less time to ask her to change her mind and stay. Please, Jenny, you have to help me on this one.'

'Dan, you are asking the impossible,' Jenny replied. 'Why don't you talk to Mary and try to reach a compromise.'

'I feel embarrassed approaching her but I have to let her know how I feel, otherwise I might lose her. When do you suppose would be a good time to phone her?'

'She's in Boston but she'll be home tomorrow evening,' Jenny replied. 'You could try then. I know she plans to bring her mother down for a few days before going to Peru.'

'Gee, Jenny, I'm beginning to sound like desperate Dan at this stage. Look, I'll take a chance and phone her tomorrow evening.'

Jenny sat in the garden for most of Sunday afternoon. It was blissful, sitting beside the pool in the brilliant sunshine resting her bare feet on the cool flags. She glanced around at the quivering Aspens and the splendid colours of the flowers with their tantalising aromas. What a contrast to the places she had visited during her work.

She picked up her diary and leafed through it. Monday she had called on Angela Emmanuel and her son Sergio. The main topic of conversation had been the demise of Poppy. 'Thank God we no longer have to keep looking over our shoulders,' Angela remarked. 'Is it true that all his gang have been captured too?' Angela had read it in the paper but wanted Jenny to confirm it.

'Yes Angela, it is true - your worries are over,' Jenny assured her.

'Oh Sergio!' Angela hugged him with the relief of a mother who had nearly lost him. 'You're beginning to look your old self again,' she remarked to him. Jenny agreed with Angela, he was less drawn in appearance and the smile came more readily.

On Tuesday Jenny had met with Doctor Rob Cain. In her diary, she had noted how pleased he was with Victor Emmanuel. 'He's on new treatment for his asthma following a series of full pulmonary function tests,' Doctor Cain explained.

'When he is stabilised on his new regime, he should be capable of leading a reasonably decent lifestyle,' Doctor Cain pointed out.

Wednesday had been a day full of surprises and drama. Most of the day was spent in the Law Courts with Mary Jo and visiting prisoners. In the evening, Father Ralph took her to a beautiful lake about forty kilometres north of New York City. The shimmering clear waters of the lake stretched as far the eye could see. Within minutes of their arrival, Ralph noticed a distress signal coming from a small boat.

'Phone the emergency services, Jenny' he said before diving in and swimming with all his might to help. He rowed the boat back to the shoreline where paramedics helped to deliver the woman of a healthy baby boy. Her husband asked Father Ralph to christen the baby there and then and Jenny found herself being godparent along with one of the paramedics.

'Call him John Baptist,' the father said and his wife readily agreed. Turning to Father Ralph, he said, 'It's nothing short of a miracle you saved their lives and we are both grateful.'

Jenny closed her diary and smiled gently, recalling the happiness that the baby's arrival had brought.

'Hello, I'm back,' Mary announced from the garden gate.

'Hi Mary! Where's Aunt Helen?'

'She's not coming till Wednesday,' she replied. 'A charity group is collecting dad's clothes and she wants to give Basil a hand sorting things out.'

'Hope it won't be too painful for her,' Jenny replied. 'How is she bearing up?'

'So, so, the break here should help,' Mary replied. 'Her friends and neighbours have been fantastic you should see the floral displays, Jenny. Honeysuckle, amaryllis, magnolia, persimmon and roses.'

'Monet's garden,' Jenny replied, remembering the French painter's wonderful picture hanging in her grandma's sitting room. She could just imagine the sea of flowers, well chosen with every bloom carrying its own individual message. Honeysuckle= for generous and devoted attention. Helen and Jack had always been so devoted to each other. Magnolia= for love of nature. Jack had always loved nature. Amaryllis= for great beauty. Jack had always maintained that Helen was one of the great beauties of her time. And as for the Rose it symbolised their love for each other to the end.

'Poor Aunt Helen, I'll make sure to visit her when you go to Peru. 'You are still going?'

'Yes, I am,' Mary replied, surprised that she should ask. 'Father Ralph's going to say Mass here for a successful mission to Lima and, of course, for dad's soul.'

'He was wonderful at your dad's funeral service,' Jenny remarked.

'I love the prophet, Isaiah. It is such a beautiful reading and so full of hope and promise. "The Lord will wipe away the tears from every cheek",' she quoted.

*

Dan phoned just after supper. Mary must have spent an hour talking to him and Jenny wondered if he was making any progress. She busied herself clearing away the supper dishes and endeavouring to wrap the awkward going-away present she had chosen for Mary.

'That was Dan,' Mary announced. 'He wants to meet me on Tuesday at his apartment.'

'Are you going?'

'Of course,' Mary replied. 'I'd like to thank him personally for all his kindness when dad died. I might even treat him to a meal. You're welcome to come along if you wish.'

'Thanks, Mary, but Tuesday is out completely. I'll be lucky to get home by midnight if I'm to follow the heavy work schedule Mary Jo has lined up.'

'You exaggerate,' Mary quipped 'I know Mary Jo likes results, but she's no slave driver.'

'I know, and I'm getting great experience. But since it's so near Clare's wedding, I feel I owe it to her to keep my head down.'

'You must be so looking forward to seeing Colin and the rest of them.'

'I can't wait to see them and to hear all the news. I didn't really have much of a chance to speak to grandma and Mattie at the funeral.'

'Mattie was so honoured to carry the Irish soil to the altar at the offertory,' Mary remarked, her voice choking a little.

'Yes, it was very poignant,' Jenny agreed, before getting up to reach for Mary's present.

'This is to help make life a bit easier in Peru. Forgive the ungainly way it is wrapped, I'm not the most artistic'

'Thanks, Jenny,' said Mary, hugging her. Gingerly and ceremoniously, she unwrapped the gift.

'A laptop!' she exclaimed. 'Jenny! This is marvellous, only you would have thought of it, I'm over the moon.' How can I repay you?'

'By drinking your coffee before it's stone cold,' she replied.

'Seriously, Jenny, I never in my wildest dreams expected a laptop. Wait till I show Mom, she'll be thrilled too.'

On Tuesday, Dan greeted Mary with open arms when she arrived at his apartment. 'Mary, it's so good to see you, come in and make yourself comfortable.'

'Thanks Dan'. Sorry I'm a bit late, I got caught in the traffic.'

'Five minutes to be precise,' Dan replied. 'Anyway that's a lady's prerogative.'

'Are you hungry?'

'I am a bit peckish,' Mary replied, wondering what Dan was cooking.

'I've prepared the only dish I know - a good old-fashioned Irish Stew. My mother gave me the recipe so I wouldn't starve when I moved here!'

The table draped in a green gingham cloth with matching napkins, was laid out simply. Dan served the stew from a casserole onto plain white dinner plates. 'What would you like to drink? Dan asked.

'Buttermilk,' Mary replied with a smile.

'Damn! I haven't a drop of the stuff,' Dan replied. 'How about a glass of wine?'

'Perfect,' she replied.

They ate in silence. Dan wondered when she would give her verdict. She finished every morsel and requested some more.

'That's the tastiest meal I've had in a long time, Dan, you sure know how to cook. What did you say about a can opener?' Mary asked.

'That applies to the dessert,' he replied. 'A tin of fruit salad straight from the supermarket shelf topped off with fresh cream coming up.''Dan Flynn, you're a real treasure,' Mary said. His heart missed a beat and he hoped he had heard correctly.

'Dan, I wanted to thank you for all your kindness when dad died.'

'It was the least I could do,' he replied, taking her hand.. 'Sorry I couldn't stay longer, but the weekend was so busy and I had a theatre list to get through on Monday morning.'

'But you love your work,' Mary said.

'And I happen to love you, too, Mary. Is there any way I can persuade you not to go to Peru?' His remark was followed by a brief silence. Mary stood up and walked to the window.

'Sorry, Dan, this has been arranged for so long. I don't think it would be very fair for either of us to make any commitment just now. Do you understand where I'm coming from?'

'Yes, of course,' Dan didn't wish to appear too pushy. At the same time, he believed in the old adage 'that faint heart never won fair lady'.

'Shall we take a walk in the park?' Mary asked. 'It might help to clear my mind.'

Dan agreed. After walking in Central Park for fifteen minutes, they sat by the lakeside.

'I wish I could be more romantic,' Dan said, holding Mary's hand. 'I'm pushing you into a situation that perhaps you're not ready for.'

'Dan Flynn, you're the most wonderful man I've ever met,' Mary said, tears streaming down her cheeks. 'I'm afraid to allow myself to fall in love even though I have often wished my situation was different'

'Don't be afraid, Mary,' Dan reassured her 'If I had one wish, it would be to take care of you for the rest of your life.'

'Can we wait till Christmas?' Mary asked. 'I'll be home for a holiday. We can meet up and discuss how we feel after the three months.'

'You will keep in touch?' Dan asked, realising how much he would miss her.

They walked back to his apartment holding hands and enjoying the first shades of autumn that were turning the trees and shrubs into a kaleidoscope of splendid colours. Back in the apartment, the late evening sunshine gave his dull bachelor pad a lift. Dan insisted on afternoon tea. He liked camomile and Mary liked it too.

She told him about Peru and Father Ralph Melville.

'I'd have liked to meet the priest,' Dan said.

'Come over next Friday night if you're free, we're having a small get-together for family and friends before we go.'

'Thanks, I'd love to.'

From the mantelpiece he took a neatly wrapped box. 'I'd like you to have this, Mary, I brought it from Ireland for you.'

'You did?' Mary opened it with the excitement of a child.

'A Claddagh Brooch Dan', I've always wanted one. She flung her arms around him and kissed him firmly on the cheek. He held her and kissed her on the lips.

'I do love you, Mary. I wish we could spend more time together.'

'I know, Dan, but I have to go. See you Friday night?

Dan walked her to her car, kissed her goodbye and strolled back to his apartment. He felt like ringing a friend and going for a drink. Dick Evans had always been close.

He had come over from a large London hospital round the same time as Dan came from Dublin. Dick specialised in heart surgery. They often met to talk about things mainly their work. Dick had just come back from holidays in England a changed man. He told Dan about Emma, a gorgeous English rose whom he met at his cousin's home in Dorset. It was love at first sight in Dick and Emma's case and there was no obstacle. They would marry in England in December. So Dick said.

'Lucky devil,' Dan thought dialling Dick's number. He got the answering machine. 'He's probably still busy doing ward rounds or checking post op patients.' No harm done, he'd meet him tomorrow anyway for coffee and a chat.

Then he spotted a white envelope placed beside the Spider plant. He paused, knowing it hadn't been there earlier when he had flicked a duster round the room before Mary arrived.

He sat by the lounge window overlooking the park and opened the envelope.

It contained two pages neatly written.

My dear Dan,

It has taken some courage for me to write this letter. I suspect how you feel, but I've got to tell you something before this goes any further.

It seems I may have inherited a medical problem. Some time ago, while trawling through some old family records, I found out that one of my mother's grandparents' sisters had 'Huntington's Chorea.'

Forgive me for not discussing it with you today. I guess I couldn't bring myself to spoil our first date. Knowing that I may have this gene and realising there is no known cure, the prospects of having children frightens me.

I hate to spring this on you, but I feel it's only fair that I should tell you and that I will understand fully if your feelings towards me change. Incidentally, I have told no one else, not even my mother.

Best wishes, Mary.

Dan held his head in his hand and wished she were here with him now. The chances were that she was free of the gene and was punishing herself unnecessarily.

She was probably going to Peru to prolong the agony of finding out the truth.

Dan resolved to help her now. He mustn't let her go without at least bringing her to a good physician and having some tests done.

'Leave old skeletons in the cupboard where they belong,' Dan had said when his father started looking up his family tree. Perhaps Mary shouldn't have trawled through her family history either, but she had. He looked at the clock. It was just seven p.m. He phoned her.

'Hi Dan'. I've just got in.'

'And I've just found and read your letter,' Dan said. 'You poor dear' carrying this burden all by yourself. Please let me bring you to a doctor and have some tests done.'

'I'm not sure. When could I have them done?' she asked.

'Meet me tomorrow at the hospital,' Dan replied.

'But mother is coming for lunch. I promised to spend some time with her.'

'Listen, Mary, I can arrange for you to have the tests early. Just be at the hospital for nine, please.'

'You're not annoyed with me?'

'Of course not,' Dan replied. 'I love you, Mary, it's as simple as that.'

'Thanks, Dan.' I'll be at the hospital at nine a.m.

It was eight-thirty by the time Jenny trudged up the stairs. 'Thank God that day is over,' she said to Mary who was setting the table for supper.

'Anything strange?' Mary asked.

'Nothing really, the same depressing litany of problems as usual,' Jenny replied. 'Why don't we talk about your day instead? It's got to be far more exciting.'

'Hmm, it was most enjoyable,' Mary replied careful not to get Jenny's hopes too high. 'Dan had lunch ready when I arrived at his apartment. He makes a delicious Irish Stew you know.'

'Isn't that just so sweet,' Jenny was impressed. 'Keep talking while I eat, I'm ravenous.'

'I wish I could tell you that we were unofficially engaged, or, that we made passionate love but that's not the case.'

Jenny laughed. 'So, is there any spark at all between you or should I mind my own business?' She already knew Dan's feelings towards Mary.

'Dan has told me that he loves me and I'm very fond of

him,' Mary replied, 'but I think it might be prudent on my part to consider the situation carefully.'

'You won't meet someone like Dan Flynn too often,' Jenny reminded her cousin. 'Take my advice and make some commitment to him before you go to Peru.'

'Well, things are not as straightforward as you may think,' Mary replied.

'Look, let me show you something.' She took the gift from her handbag and handed it to Jenny.

'Dan gave you this?' Jenny asked, admiring the Claddagh brooch.

'He brought it back from holidays for me. Isn't it just beautiful?'

Jenny readily agreed, replacing it in its box. 'Hope it's an indication that a great and lasting relationship is budding between you,' Jenny said.

*

On the first of September, Mary and Father Ralph Melville left for Peru. They took an early morning flight leaving Kennedy International at seven a.m. Jenny wanted to accompany her cousin to the airport but Mary refused.

'It would be too painful saying goodbye,' Mary said. 'I'd prefer to go it alone with Ralph. Besides, you'd never be back in time for work.'

Tearfully hugging her cousin and Father Ralph goodbye at the door of the house, Jenny felt very lonely. The farewell party two days previously had been very enjoyable.

Dan and Mary seemed very happy. In her figure-hugging

red satin dress and black high-heeled sandals and his black suit, everyone said they made a lovely couple. Jenny agreed.

Dan wasn't pleased that Mary was going at all. The next few weeks would be crucial while he waited for the results of her test. He had promised to phone her the minute he got word.

When he had caught up with his friend, heart surgeon Dick Evans, he had every intention of confiding in him except that Dick had things on his mind.

'Dan, you wouldn't do me a huge favour?' Dick said.

'Spit it out,' Dan replied.

'I need a best man on December fourteenth. That's the day Emma and I will tie the knot.'

'I feel honoured to be asked,' Dan replied. 'I'll arrange some holidays for that time.'

Where does that leave me? Dan asked himself while driving back to his apartment that evening. A trip to England, Mary returning from Peru for Christmas and, no doubt, his family in Dublin asking when he'd be home for Christmas

December was always a tricky month. Trying to find time for job, family and shopping meant juggling his free time. He thought of his sister, Kit, in her cosy job with a firm of accountants. She had moved into a house near the sea and was in the process of buying it. Since leaving home, she had made a list of rules longer than the Ten Commandments.

'You must not visit me without first telephoning.

'You must not seek any favours like 'give me a hand with the Christmas shopping.

'You must not covet a minute of my spare time even if, in Dan's case, you are trying to divide yourself into four quarters.

It would have been cool to have an approachable sister whom you could ask to even wrap a few gifts when you arrived home breathless on Christmas Eve. Not so. Kit's gift for him had always been the first under the tree every year. Boring as a wet day, his six white handkerchiefs, two silk neckties, half dozen pairs of socks and aftershave had never altered. Still, it had meant he could save himself the bother of unwrapping it, not that Kit would have noticed anyway. She would be too busy calculating what she meant to everyone in terms of what she had received herself. Right now, Dan would be the first to admit that he was becoming a bit crotchety so he figured he needed the Nell treatment. He dialled her number.

'Nell any chance of joining me for a few beers?'

'I'm drying my blue rinse,' invariably meant that widow Nell Sheen was rearing to go.

'The taxi will be there in fifteen minutes,' Dan announced.

Nell had been theatre sister in Saint Mary's as long as the staff could remember. On duty, she was scalpel sharp and, while scrubbed up and waiting, she could deliver the smartest kick in the ankle to any surgeon who crossed her.

Dan had been on the receiving end once when his mask had opened during surgery.

'Tie the bloody thing correctly next time,' she shouted while Dan wrestled with his instrument and a stinging pain in his ankle.

'You won't ask for a second helping of that,' a colleague had whispered.

Dan didn't. He did, however, enjoy her wit and humour outside work. She was as good as any pick-me–up tonic once she had consumed a few drinks.

'Why are you depending on the company of a fifty-seven-year-old widow on a Saturday night?' Nell asked Dan in the cosiness of Sam's bar.

'Is a man not entitled to the best company in New York?' Dan replied tactfully.

'Pull the other one,' Nell said, her comic sallow features screwing her eyes into slits when she smiled. 'Seriously, Dan, have you a girlfriend?'

'Probably,' Dan replied, 'but she's away at present.'

'You're not very convincing, Dan, I wish I were twenty years younger'

'And I wish I were twenty years older,' Dan said, ordering another beer for them.

'Have you always worked in theatre, Nell?'

'Since I qualified,' Nell replied. 'If I had a dollar for every scalpel, retractor, probe, forceps, needle and suture I handed to all the surgeons I've worked for, I guess I'd be rich.'

'You're rich in experience, Nell, and that's why the surgeons feel so confident when you're around.'

'Thanks you Dan for keeping a lonely old widow company on a Saturday night'. I do miss George, you know.

'I know, Nell' Dan replied.

In the taxi home, they sang a Dean Martin number. Dan thought of Mary when he sang 'Hurry home, Hurry home' while Nell and the cab driver joined in.

Colin met Jenny at Shannon airport three days before Clare's wedding. It was worth everything to be in his arms again and to know they could look forward to ten blissful days together.

'I've missed you to the point of counting the minutes,' Colin told her after a long breath-taking kiss.

'Me too,' Jenny said. 'It's been a pretty rough time with one thing and another, I've lived for this day practically from the beginning.'

'Let's get you home. The reception committee were hanging out the bunting as I was leaving,' Colin said helping her with the luggage.

'The only bunting round our place at this time of year will be stray wisps of hay and corn hanging from the trees,' Jenny replied.

'You look beautiful and so relaxed, Jenny' Colin remarked as they sped through the Tipperary countryside. 'Was it tough in New York?' he asked.

'Very, very tough,' she replied. She gazed across the golden plains and the rolling hills graduating to mountains. Everything here was so beautiful and natural in contrast to the urban landscape she had left behind.

'Tell you what Colin I'll leave New York and my work behind me for now. It's been humbling working with drug addicts, alcoholics, visiting prisoners, et cetera but I'm glad to be free for ten days.'

Colin stopped the car. 'Let's take a break and get a coffee,' he suggested.

Hand-in-hand, they walked towards a little wayside cafe with its rambling roses trailing the whitewashed walls. Inside, the place was poky with an air of timelessness and a large old clock ticking the precise time. There was no rush, however, and the owner gave them a few minutes to soak up the ambience. The whitewashed walls were hung with old black and white photos. Oil lamps and storm lanterns spoke of the pre 1925 Ardnacrusha Power Station for rural electrification. A bank of peat and some hefty logs neatly arranged around the fireplace, in readiness for the cooler days ahead conjured a cosy picture.

Mrs Downer appeared all rosy cheeked and smiling, carrying a tray of willow pattern cups, saucers, cream jug, and sugar bowl. She placed them on the small pine table where Jenny and Colin were sitting.

'Lovely morning,' she remarked. 'Now, what would you like to order?'

Since there was no menu to browse through, they both looked at her for guidance.

'I have some lovely freshly baked buns or you might fancy a bit of carrot cake?'

'We'll try both please,' Colin replied.

'I think you'll enjoy them' she said 'What about some tea or coffee'? .'Tea for me please,' Jenny replied. 'And for me too please,' Colin said.

She returned with steaming hot buns, carrot cake and a large pot of tea covered with a multicoloured tea cosy. They tucked in while Jenny eyed the photos on the walls.

Wedding snaps, first communion, family gatherings they were all there. So too were some of the Tipperary footballers and hurdlers of bygone days. Jenny called Colin and pointed out her late Uncle Jack. He towered over most of the other players, but there was no mistaking him.

'Do you recognise anyone?' Mrs Downer asked.

'Jack Rafferty - he was my uncle' Jenny replied.

'Imagine that!' she exclaimed in sheer amazement.

'Did you know him?' Jenny asked.

'Listen child, I played the fiddle many a night while Jack and his friends danced inside on the kitchen floor. He was one of the most handsome men I ever laid eyes on. We were all saddened when his sister died and he never returned.

'There was a nice tribute to him in the Tipperary Star when he died' Mrs Downer remarked, sympathising with Jenny. 'It came as a bit of a shock to those of us who knew him well, God rest his soul. Did many of you go over for the funeral?'

'I work in New York but Grandma, Mattie and more relations came over to Boston. It was all very sudden in the end.'

'So you're the late John and Anne Anderson's daughter.'

'That's right, Mrs Downer, I'm Jenny, and this is Colin Maloney from Dublin.'

Norah and Mattie came out to meet them when they finally screeched to a halt, avoiding Bran at the front gate. 'She's lost the sight in her right eye,' Mattie told them, apologising for the near mishap.

'Poor Bran,' Jenny said, stroking the dog sympathetically. 'I hope you're not in any pain.'

'The vet has assured me she's not,' Mattie explained. 'It's old age apparently.'

'Where is grandma?' Jenny asked anxiously.

'She waited for you till quarter past two, then she had to drive Father Tim for an appointment with Father Rigney,' Norah told Jenny.

'We stopped for tea and delayed longer than we intended to,' Jenny explained 'I completely forgot that Father Tim would be here. When did he arrive?'

133

'About a week ago,' Norah replied. 'There's so much happening, Jenny, that I am losing all track of time.'

'Sounds like you're having a hectic time Norah'. Why don't I put the kettle on and let's have a good old chinwag while the place is quiet? Can you spare the time?

'Bloody sure I can,' Norah replied. 'But are you sure you're not too tired after your trip?'

'I'm fine, Norah, honestly, I wouldn't sleep now with the excitement. Besides, I'm dying to hear all the news,' Jenny replied.

'Mind if I nip into town?' Colin asked. 'Mattie and I have to pick something up for Johnny Finnan's stag party tonight.'

Norah poured the tea while Jenny quickly sorted the gifts she had brought for her from the suitcase. 'It's something very practical, Norah, I hope you like it.'

Norah stared at the bag advertising Bloomingdale's 3rd Avenue and 59th Street and she gasped with excitement.

'Imagine getting a gift from one of the most famous stores in the world,' she exclaimed 'Jenny I'm so thrilled, I can't wait to tell Luke.'

Jenny sipped her tea and watched while Norah ceremoniously removed the wrapping. 'Oh, they're so beautiful, so pretty and so American,' she said when she saw the white embroidered sheets, matching pillowcases and valance. 'I can just imagine Luke and I returning from our honeymoon, to the luxury of 'Beacon Hill' sheets sets by Wamsutta.'

'You've set a date then?' Jenny asked.

Norah casually stroked her chin with her left hand. 'Next

year, February twentieth,' she replied. 'It will be a very simple affair, mainly because we have to budget carefully.'

It was then that Jenny noticed Norah's engagement ring. 'When did it happen?' Jenny asked wishing her and Luke 'every happiness'. Norah extended her hand so that Jenny could get a better view of the neat solitaire ring.

'It's no wonder you're losing all track of time, Norah. Between the busy household here and planning your wedding, you must be run off your feet. Listen, why don't I treat you out to lunch someday next week?'

'Mrs Anderson has been most generous already allowing me some free time when I got engaged. Thanks for the lovely thought, Jenny, but there's no need.'

Oops! better not forget the Padre's birthday cake,' said Norah, checking the oven.

'Do you mean Father Tim?'

'I do indeed,' Norah replied. 'Mrs Anderson has booked the parish hall for Sunday night. It's his seventieth birthday with all proceeds going to the missions in Peru.'

'You can't have a birthday bash and in the same breath talk about a collection for the missions,' Jenny argued. 'It sounds ridiculous.'

'Not when you allow a much travelled missionary and a wily old parish priest to put their heads together,' Norah replied.

Beep, beep, beep 'I expect that's Father Tim and grandma. I had better go and say hello,' said Jenny.

'I'll slip out the back door,' said Norah. 'Welcome home! And thanks for the beautiful present and the chat.'

Jenny could feel all her emotions welling up as she walked

towards the car. Her grandma and Father Tim were smiling happily.

'It's great to see you home safe and well,' Mary said, hugging Jenny.

'Surely this can't be the pigtailed school girl that I once knew?' Father Tim asked teasingly, as he shook her hand. 'My, haven't you blossomed into a beautiful young lady?' he remarked.

'Thank you, Father Tim, fifteen years makes a big difference in all our lives. I still feel I cheated when I got five pounds' reward for writing the best essay with your help.

'You're wouldn't be the first ten-year-old to have received a little help from an adult,' Father Tim remarked, 'besides, I can remember lots of money coming from you for the missions.'

'How long are you staying in Ireland?' Jenny asked.

'Six weeks, then I'm off to the Dominican College in Rome to give a series of lectures. After that, it's back to Peru for Christmas.'

'I'd love to chat with you about Peru and the work you do in Lima.'

'And I'd love to chat with you about the work you do in New York,' Father Tim replied, 'so why don't we get together some evening later in the week.'

Jenny thought for a moment. 'I've a pretty packed schedule for the next ten days,' she replied, 'but I'm free Friday afternoon if you are.'

'Then we have a date,' Father Tim said, placing a folder on the kitchen table.

'You two are up early,' Jenny remarked to Colin and Mattie. 'Did you enjoy Johnny's stag party?'

'Yea, it was good fun,' Colin replied, 'except we didn't hang about for the tarring and feathering part, or whatever punishment his mates intended to inflict on him.'

'Cowards, the pair of you,' Jenny said, pouring the coffee. 'God help him if he was depending on you pair to rescue him. Gosh, Mattie, I hope you'll do a better job of being best man on Saturday.'

'Have no fears, dear sister, I have studied the wedding etiquette book and I know my duties thoroughly,' Mattie replied confidently. 'Johnny was more than pleased with me at the church rehearsal last Saturday,' he added.

'More like Clare was pleased,' Jenny replied. 'Sure Johnny wouldn't be dictated to by any book of rules. He'll probably do most of the talking on the day anyway.'

'All set for the hen party tonight?' Colin asked Jenny.

'I am indeed,' Jenny replied, 'and I'm really looking forward to one heck of a night with Clare and her friends.'

'Where is it being held?' Mattie asked.

'The Roost,' Jenny replied, observing the smirk on their faces.

'Aptly named,' Colin replied, winking at Mattie.

'Clare told me it's so popular, booked out for months in advance, and the Australian couple who run it are wonderful. Anyway Colin, you and I have loads to do today, so let's get a move on,' Jenny suggested.

CHAPTER SEVEN

Clare and Johnny's wedding day dawned somewhat misty but sunny intervals were promised for the afternoon. It was precisely seven fifty five a.m. when Jenny woke up to the weather announcement on the radio. The wedding was scheduled for two p.m. with two hundred guests booked for the reception in the Banqueting Hall at Kane's hotel.

'Hopefully the sun will shine,' Jenny remarked to Norah who had come to her room to see her gown.

'I should really have waited till you were all dressed up and ready to leave the house,' Norah remarked, 'but my curiosity got the better of me.'

Jenny removed the gown from the wardrobe, slipped into a pair of high- heeled shoes and held the gown against her body for Norah to see.

'It's truly magnificent, Jenny,' Norah remarked, standing in admiration. 'Colin and you will be the most handsome couple at the wedding.'

'Thanks, Norah.'

'Breakfast will be ready in half an hour,' Norah reminded Jenny. 'Mind you have a good hearty one, it might be late afternoon before the wedding reception gets started.'

In the quiet of her bedroom, Jenny placed her gown on the bed, thinking back to the day she had bought it near Fifth Avenue with Mary. The same day they met Dan Flynn. So much had happened since. She had been fairly optimistic that Dan and Mary might get together. But then Uncle Jack died and Mary had left for Peru.

She had only spoken to Mary once since she went to Peru. 'I'm fine,' Mary said, explaining that she and Father Ralph were settling in nicely.

'Where are Mattie and Colin?' she asked Norah as she sat down to breakfast.

'In the dining room' Norah replied, 'where they've been for the last half hour.'

'Oh!' Jenny was surprised. Normally, the two lads would be tucking into a good full Irish breakfast at this stage. 'Is there a crisis or something?' she asked.

'Mattie's taking this best man role very serious' Norah replied 'He and Colin have been practising solid and I wouldn't be surprised if you find the dining room re-arranged.

Jenny tapped lightly at the door. Colin answered. 'Breakfast is ready,' she announced, making sure she took a look round. Judging by the glass and spoon, Mattie was practising his speech.

'I now call on Mattie and Colin to have some breakfast,' Jenny said, banging on the glass with a spoon.

'It's okay for you to mock,' Mattie protested, 'but if I make a mess of this, I'll never forgive myself.'

'You'll be fine,' Colin said encouragingly. 'I'll keep an eye on you and, if necessary, whisper in your ear.'

'I feel better already,' Mattie replied, wiping a bead of sweat from his forehead.

Jenny glanced at her watch. She had fifteen minutes to make it in time for her hair appointment. Mattie and Colin had to dash into town to collect lounge suits and call to the florist. Johnny had given Mattie strict instructions to collect the bouquets for Clare's mother and his mother.

'These are two women I intend to keep sweet,' Johnny remarked to Mattie. 'God knows it's taken me long enough to convince Sergeant Vaughan and Nurse Alice that I'm even half worthy to be their son-in-law'

The day that had dawned misty had blossomed into glorious sunshine by the time a radiant Clare arrived at the church. Word was conveyed to a nervous Johnny that his bride-to-be had arrived. He and Mattie had taken their place just ten minutes earlier on the dot of two p.m. at Saint Brendan's church. Photographer John Edwards was poised and ready to get his first picture of Clare. A light breeze obediently calmed itself to allow Clare to pose with her father for her photograph. The sun picked up the hand-sewn beading on her elegant lace gown and train. A simple Lily–of–the-valley headdress held her shoulder-length veil in place, while her glossy crimped hair framed her pretty face.

Jenny gazed in admiration at her school friend. She remembered their reunion in Kane's Hotel back in June. Clare was starry eyed on that occasion when she told her that Johnny was the love of her life. Now she was ready to make a life commitment to him as she prepared to walk up the aisle. Her bridesmaid adjusted her train and checked her bouquet of wild orchids. Sergeant Vaughan proudly took his daughter on his right arm to the strains of 'Here Comes The Bride'.

'Twenty five is a perfect age to get married,' Alice Vaughan's sister remarked to her during the champagne reception afterwards.

'I've never heard of a perfect age as you put it,' Alice replied, knowing that Jenny was in hearing distance of them. Alice could gag her sister at times and now that she had downed three dry Sherries faster than the speed of sound, she was sure to have an opinion on every subject including marriage. The fact that she had remained a spinster, and was now sixty years old, didn't deter her one iota.

'Jenny, how good to see you,' Alice said, embracing her warmly. 'You look absolutely stunning.'

'Thank you, Alice,' Jenny replied. 'You look marvellous. Congratulations on such a wonderful turnout, you must be well pleased.'

'I'm grateful everything has gone so well,' Alice replied, careful not to stir any sad memories for Jenny. But she seemed in fine form and lit up when Clare and Johnny arrived.

'Mr and Mrs Finnan,' she said, greeting the happy couple.

'It rolls easily off the tongue,' Johnny replied, sipping his champagne. 'Where has Colin got to?'

'I'd like to meet him,' Alice said. 'Clare has told me so much about him.'

'Then let me find him, he can't be too far away,' Jenny remarked.

'Just as I expected,' Jenny remarked, finding Colin and Mattie hunched together, preparing for what Mattie referred to as the 'last hurdle.'

'So far, so good,' he said, feeling pleased with his performance so far. He had placed the air tickets, passports and travellers cheques in the hotel safe on arrival.

'Alice wants to meet you, Colin, so you had both better come'

'Alice?'

'Alice is Clare's mother,' Jenny explained.

'You two go ahead,' Mattie said, 'I want to have a word with Johnny. He asked me to help Clare and himself to make a quick getaway after the reception. Be ready to catch the bouquet, Jenny,' Mattie remarked jocosely.

Colin held her hand as they made their way to where Alice was chatting with Mary Anderson. Jenny introduced Colin to Alice.

'Lovely to meet you Colin I'm so pleased you came to the wedding.' 'I do hope you and Jenny enjoy yourselves.'

'It's lovely to meet you Alice' Congratulations! Clare and Johnny make a wonderful couple and are so full of fun and energy. 'Isn't that right Jenny?'

Jenny smiled and nodded in agreement. The guests were making their way to the banqueting hall. Colin and Jenny trailed behind stopping to have a word with Clare and Johnny.

'You're like a fairy princess' Jenny whispered to Clare and you Johnny are Prince Charming. 'Long life and happiness to you' she remarked sincerely.

The month of September had so far been kind and gentle weather-wise. Jenny and Colin enjoyed strolls in the many romantic lanes and boreens that are part of Sliabh na mBan, trying to plan their future in New York. Jenny knew she would miss Mary and Father Ralph when she returned but the prospects of Colin joining her in October cheered her up.

'Of course, we'll have to lay down some ground rules,' she told Colin.

'What on earth do you mean?' he asked.

'You'll have lots of studying and I have my job' she replied. 'We'll allow ourselves one date during the week, and have weekends together. How does that grab you?' she asked.

'I expected us to live together,' he replied. 'I was looking forward to finding an apartment, to making the first cup of tea or coffee for you in the morning - the way lots of couples in love behave, I imagine.'

'I'm a romantic, Colin, and old-fashioned too. Besides, I've promised to look after Mary's apartment in Lincoln Boulevard.'

'I'm sure she wouldn't object to me living there for a while. I could still make you that cup of coffee in the morning,' he smiled.

They rested a while in the shadow of the mountain. Sharing the trunk of a great old tree, hands entwined, they sat in silence. Jenny thought of Colin's time in California and the freedom he experienced there. But she wanted to take things slower. After all, they had only just got back together after a year apart, and she didn't want to ruin things by moving too quickly. And moving in together was moving too quickly, as far as she was concerned.

'I've been thinking, Colin.'

'Oh! Are you beginning to see the sense of my proposal?'

'You remember Dan Flynn, the guy we hung out with when he was a registrar in Vincent's hospital?'

'Yea, I remember him well,' Colin replied, anxious to know where this question was leading.

'He's a neurosurgeon in New York. He lives near Central Park now. I think he'd be delighted to share his house with you.'

'And what makes you think I want to share with him? And how come you know so much about Dan Flynn's whereabouts?'

'We met up one day when Mary and I were shopping. We had lunch together and later he came to dinner at Lincoln Boulevard. He was a good friend to Mary after her dad died.'

'Do you meet him often?' Colin asked resentfully.

'Now and then for a chat,' Jenny replied.

'I'm not happy with this news, Jenny. I don't want to sound jealous, but you seem to know too much about Dan Flynn for my liking.'

'It's not what you think …'

'What am I supposed to think?' he asked angrily. 'You're setting rules for us in New York, refusing to let me use your cousin's apartment and now it seems you've been meeting Dan Flynn. Well, I've got news for you, Jenny.'

'Hold on, Colin. Let me explain properly,' Jenny said, jumping to her feet.

'I've heard enough to convince me that you don't really love me, so I'm going home. I'll pack my bags and leave this evening.'

They walked silently back to the house. How could she prove to him that he had got the wrong handle to this story when he wasn't prepared to listen? He dashed upstairs to collect his things. Jenny picked up her post. Instantly, she recognised Mary's handwriting. She read the four-page letter quickly. Colin came to say a quick goodbye. Through her tears, she asked him to read the letter.

'Is it addressed to me?' he asked.

'No,' she replied.

'Then I'm not going to read it.'

'Please, Colin.'

'Fine, though I can't see why,' he replied.

He read the letter quickly then sank into the chair. He read it again this time slowly.

'Why didn't you tell me?' he asked.

'You didn't give me a chance,' she replied, 'and I didn't know that Mary left for Peru thinking she might be suffering from Huntington's Chorea. When I introduced Dan to her, I had no idea she would turn him down because she was afraid to have children. Anytime I've talked to Dan, it's always been about Mary.'

'Jenny, I'm so sorry,' Colin said. 'I suppose I was judging you based on my own experience in California, and that wasn't fair. Will you forgive me?'

'Yes,' she replied, wiping away the tears. He kissed her tenderly. They both reread the letter, and hugged when they got to the part where Mary said her tests had shown that she was free from Huntington's Chorea. And Dan was heading to Peru, with wedding bells in mind, according to Mary.

*

It was strange being back in New York after the whirlwind holiday in Ireland. Jenny flung open the big window overlooking the garden. The apartment was spotless, thanks to Pip. The house was eerily quiet – it was always quiet on Sunday, before her colleagues returned after the weekend around nine in the evening.

Mary's apartment door was open. Jenny took a peek round. It too was spotless. Strolling into the large drawing room, she saw her mail piled neatly on a small table near the window. There was a letter from Father Ralph, one from Aunt Helen and another whose handwriting she didn't recognise.

Tired after the flight from Ireland, she decided to rest for a while and headed back to her bedroom. She drifted off thinking lazily about Clare and Johnny's wedding.

Something woke her. Slowly opening her eyes, she saw a dark figure standing by her bed. Terrified, her eyes met his horrible stare.

'Who are you?' she shouted. 'What do you want?'

'Do as I tell you and I won't hurt you,' he threatened. Jenny stared at his large ugly face, noticing how his black jacket hung on his thin body like a scarecrow. His multicoloured curly hair could have been a wig but she wasn't sure.

'Get up and show me where you keep the paintings'

'What paintings?'

'Don't play games with me, or....' The doorbell rang.

He followed her down the stairs. Her legs turned to jelly when she saw the portrait of Countess Von Erlich in smithereens in the hall. 'Where is that music coming from?' he demanded.

'I don't know,' Jenny replied, aware that he must have activated the security system that in turn had set The Blue Danube disc off. The doorbell rang a second time. 'Persistent beggar,' he shouted 'Go and answer it and get rid of the caller. No hanky panky mind or ....'

With trembling hands, she opened the door. 'Jenny, it's good to see you,' Dan Flynn stood there smiling.

'I'm afraid you've got the wrong house,' Jenny replied, miming 'police' before closing the door. Dan twigged immediately.

'That wasn't too painful,' the intruder remarked. 'Now, where are the paintings?'

'I don't know anything about paintings. I only have an apartment here and I'm just back from Ireland,' she protested.

'Where is the owner?'

'Out, I presume, like I said, I've been away. Look, I can't help you, you'd better go.'

Quick as a flash, he smacked her across the face. 'Does that restore your memory?'

Jenny fell to the ground, blood gushing from her nose. Police sirens blazed outside.

'Traitor,' he screamed 'You'll pay for this.'

'Release the woman and give yourself up,' the voice on the loud speaker called.

'Now look what you have done.' He grabbed a rucksack he had hidden behind the sofa. He took out enough rope to tie Jenny up. Grabbing a pistol from his hip pocket, he headed for a window leading to the back garden. He realised he was cornered by the police and he panicked. Turning to run back through the room, he stumbled. Jenny heard a shot and screamed. She heard the intruder moaning and realised he must been shot. Struggling to free herself, she ran for the door.

'Are you okay?' Dan asked, cradling her in his arms.

'I think so,' she replied, on the verge of collapsing.

The police swarmed into the house. 'Where is he?' an officer asked. Jenny pointed to the back window.

'Is he dead?' Dan asked, noticing blood pumping from his head.

'Call an ambulance, he's unconscious,' the officer replied. 'Oh my God, I don't believe it,' he shouted as he recognised

Deadly Sammy, a vicious criminal who had escaped from prison two days earlier.

'She's a lucky lady,' the officer said to Dan, who was treating Jenny for shock and rendering first aid. Mary Jo Shinner and Barbara Macy arrived home earlier than usual to mayhem. The officer explained what happened.

'Is Jenny okay?' Mary Jo asked, while Barbara rushed to see if there was anything she could do.

'Make us all some strong coffee,' Dan said 'Jenny's had a huge shock.'

'How am I going to tell Father Ralph?' Jenny whispered 'This is a disaster.'

'Yes, but it could have been much worse,' said Mary Jo. 'Thank God you're safe, Jenny. We'll get the portrait restored, that's not a problem.'

The police were busy taking fingerprints. A detective was at the security alarm panel, wondering why the security system had failed. How had the intruder gained access and who else was involved in this crime? It was clear the paintings were no longer safe here nor were other valuables such as the piano and some antique furniture.

'Jenny, you need to take time to get over this,' advised Dan. 'I can give you the number of a counsellor if you need to talk to someone.'

'I suppose. I do feel pretty shaken up,' Jenny told Dan. But I should be okay in a few days. I'm a tough cookie, you know.

Dan smiled gently at the frail young woman in front of him, claiming to be tough despite the bruising all over her face.

'What about your family?' Dan asked 'Do you want me to ring anyone?'

'Grandma must never hear about this, she'd be horrified,' said Jenny quickly. 'Will you ring Colin Maloney please. Here's the number in Dublin.'

'What about your aunt Helen in Boston?'

'Gosh, yes, but break the news gently, she's still a bit fragile.'

Dan held her hand, suddenly remembering why he had come to see her in the first place.

'Did you get my letter?' he asked.

'I noticed strange handwriting on one of the letters in the drawing room but I haven't opened my mail yet,' she replied. 'Why, have you something to tell me?'

'Yea, I'm going to Peru for two weeks to visit Mary'

'That's wonderful. When are you going?'

'Next Friday and, what's more, I'm going to ask her to marry me.'

'I'm thrilled, Dan. I hope it works out. I'd love to celebrate but …'

Dan kissed her gently on the forehead. 'Why don't we wait until Mary comes home for Christmas?'

'It's a deal,' Jenny said, clasping his hand firmly.

The following morning the newspapers were full of the story, with headings like 'Deadly Sammy Strikes Again' and 'Escaped Prisoner Assaults Irish Social Worker.'

Bouquets of flowers arrived from well wishers along with scores of cards as the news filtered through. 'Thank God the papers haven't mentioned the paintings,' Jenny said to Mary Jo and the rest of her colleagues. 'How on earth did he know they were here?'

'Crooks sniff out these things,' Mary Jo explained. 'Anyway, Father Ralph will sort everything out when he gets home'

'You've spoken to him then?' Jenny seemed anxious.

'He phoned to know how you were immediately after Dan told him,' Mary Jo replied. 'To tell the truth, Jenny, he was only concerned about you and he said he'd fly home tomorrow.'

The following day Dan called on Jenny.

'How are you feeling Jenny? Dan asked, noticing that her right jaw was swollen.

'My jaw is sore when I try to eat, but I guess that's only to be expected after the blow he gave me.'

'I'm not happy with the look of it,' Dan said. 'I'm going to phone the hospital to arrange an X-ray.'

'You're to come straight away,' Dan told her when he finished speaking on the phone.

Dan was right. The X-ray revealed a hairline fracture, so she was booked in for a few days for monitoring.

Later in the afternoon, just as she was getting bored, Fr Ralph and Aunt Helen arrived together.

She greeted them with open arms and a stifled smile.

Helen and Ralph cradled her in their arms, noticing the haunted look on her face. Helen arranged the roses she had brought from the garden in Lincoln Boulevard and Ralph brought her some chocolates.

'How is Mary?' Jenny asked. 'Is she upset with the news?'

'She is,' said Father Ralph. 'She really wanted to come with me, but Dan has already made his arrangements to travel out. I promised to phone her the moment I visited you.'

'I'll speak to her in a day or two when my jaw is better,' Jenny said.

'What about the family and Colin?' Aunt Helen asked. 'Did anyone ring them?'

'Dan took care of everything,' Jenny replied. 'I asked him not to tell Grandma for the moment. I'll break the news to her gently when I'm fully back to myself.'

'You'll be glad to hear I've arranged to sell all the paintings, furniture and the piano tomorrow,' Ralph told Jenny. 'The basement apartment will then be free for Colin when he comes over, that is, if he wants it. You might all feel better having a man about the house.'

'Strangely enough, that was the last thing we argued about,' Jenny said. 'Still, if you're happy with that, I'm sure Colin will take you up on your offer.'

Dan returned to check on Jenny. Father Ralph shook his hand. 'If you hadn't called on her that Sunday evening, I shudder to think what might have happened,' he said.

Father Ralph and Helen returned to 67 Lincoln Boulevard to find the removal men ready to pack the paintings and furniture into a huge container for delivery to the auction rooms. 'I can't risk a repeat of what happened to Jenny,' Ralph told Helen.

'I can stay for a while to give a helping hand if you wish,' Helen suggested.

'I'd really appreciate that. I'll be having the painters and decorators in before Colin arrives and I'll have to get some new furniture. By the way, have you seen Pip?'

'I think she is getting ready to go home,' Helen replied noticing her basket in the hallway.

'Good, I'd like to have a few words before she goes,' Father Ralph replied.

Pip was putting her jacket on when Ralph caught up with her 'Pip, Helen is going to stay a little while, just until we get things sorted out. But, just so you know, Jenny doesn't want her grandmother in Ireland to know about the raid, so …

'Oh no. I've already talked to Mrs Anderson. She rang this morning and I told her Jenny was in hospital. I didn't say why, so she asked me if one of Jenny's colleagues could ring her later.'

'Helen, will you ring Jenny's grandmother?' Father Ralph asked. 'Pip told her Jenny was in hospital, so she's probably worried. Don't give her too many details, though.'

'Please God, let Mattie answer,' prayed Helen as she dialled the number. Mary's trembling voice left Helen in no doubt that the elderly woman was worried sick about her grandchild.

'Tell me the truth, Helen,' she pleaded, 'no frills or cover-ups, please.'

Helen explained as gently as possibly how an intruder had broken into Lincoln Boulevard looking for valuables. When Jenny didn't co-operate, he smacked her across the face and damaged her jawbone. The intruder was now in police custody and Jenny was doing really well.

'Oh, poor Jenny,' Mary cried.

Helen tried to comfort her from thousands of miles away. 'We've just come back from visiting her and, honestly, she's in good form,' she said.

'I have to talk to her,' Mary said, trying to be brave.

'Give me a few minutes to check the hospital number, Mary, and I'll phone you back,' Helen said. 'Try not to worry.'

Helen rang Jenny to tell her Mary knew she was in hospital.

'How is grandma?' Jenny asked anxiously. 'Is she very upset?'

'Well, she is, a little, but she'll feel better when she talks to you yourself,' Helen replied. 'Now, Jenny, I didn't tell her the intruder was armed, so you might want to leave that bit out. She'll only worry herself sick.

Helen replaced the receiver and found herself surrounded by what seemed a large family. All Jenny's colleagues had returned home from work. They gathered around the table and Helen made a large pot of coffee.

'Is this an all girls' club?' Father Ralph asked, dying for a mug of coffee.

'Grab a stool and join us, Father Ralph,' Helen said, placing a steaming mug of coffee in front of him.

'Thanks, Helen,' he said, taking a great mouthful of coffee with the gratitude of a parched Arabian. 'Marvellous stuff,' he declared.

'What's the news on Jenny?' Mary Jo asked.

Helen gave them an up-to-the-minute report. They were pleased to hear that she had already received counselling and that her assailant was due to return to prison.

Barbara suggested they make out a visiting roster. 'We could pop in for short intervals during the day and bring some books and magazines.'

The Wilton sisters Cora and Dawn agreed to look after the flowers for Jenny. 'I'm having a dental check in the morning,' Dawn said, 'I'll order a bouquet afterwards.'

'I promised to look in on Jenny tonight, so if anyone

wishes to send a message, speak now,' Ralph said.

The group hurriedly wrote their individual thoughts on a large 'Get Well' card supplied by Helen.

'See you all tomorrow,' Ralph said, clutching the card and his car keys.

Just then, the phone rang. 'Helen, is it okay if I call in for a few minutes seeing as my flight leaves early in the morning?'

'Sure Dan'. We can share the casserole I've prepared for supper.'

'I've brought you a small gift, Helen,' Dan said on his arrival.

'Whatever for?' Helen asked. 'Honestly, Dan, there is no need to spoil me like this.'

'Go on, open it, and see if you like it.'

'Dan, it's beautiful,' Helen fingered the delicate gold chain.

'Let me help you.' He fastened the chain on her neck and stood back. 'It's definitely you, Helen. Happy Birthday!'

'Who told you?' Helen asked.

'A certain person who unfortunately can't be with her mother next Wednesday, that's who,' He replied with a glint in his eye.

'Oh, you're so sweet, Dan, I'm lost for words.' She served the casserole, hoping she had remembered to season it properly.

Dan, who considered himself an expert on stews and casseroles, declared it was very palatable indeed. 'Have you made any plans for Christmas, Helen?'

'Quite frankly, Dan, I haven't given it any thought at all,' she replied. 'It won't be the same without Jack, but having

Mary home will mean everything. And you? Are you going home to Dublin?'

Dan thought for a few moments then he said, 'Probably, but I'm going to ask Mary to marry me first.'

Helen stared in total disbelief at him. 'That's wonderful,' she said slowly. 'But you hardly know her. Are you sure you're not rushing things?'

'Never more sure about anything,' Dan replied convincingly. 'From the moment I laid eyes on Mary, I made up my mind.'

'Have you talked things through with her?' Helen asked. 'Marriage is a very serious step.'

'Helen, Mary's come through a bad patch, and …' 'I don't follow you,' Helen replied, her expression grave.

'Remember when Mary looked into her family tree. Well, she got more than she bargained for. Seemingly, your late husband's side of the family had the gene of Huntington's Chorea and Mary was terrified she might have inherited that gene.

'When she told me, I persuaded her to undergo some tests. She had them done before going to Peru. Thankfully, there's no trace of this condition. We were so thrilled that we decided to get married early in the New Year.'

Helen stood up and hugged Dan. 'Congratulations! Poor Mary. I had no idea she was so worried.'

'Helen, I'd love you to spend Christmas in Dublin, and I'm almost sure I can persuade Mary.'

'Let me think about it. Now off home with you or you'll miss the flight,' Helen advised.

'Give Mary all my love and tell her I'm thrilled,' Helen said.

'Hi Jenny, I'm Claude Stanhope. Dan asked me to keep an eye on you while he's away.'

'Hi Claude' she replied. They shook hands and Jenny told him that she had no intention of spending two weeks in hospital.

'It's nice to know where I stand with my patient,' he teased, 'but the point is, the doctor knows best.'

He rubbed his hands vigorously, to generate some heat before examining her jaw. She winced slightly when he touched the tender spot. Beneath the make-up, he detected quite a bit of bruising still. 'How are you coping with food?'

'Everything is slipping down easily once it's minced,' she replied. 'I'm definitely on the mend and I'd love to go home for a while.'

He fixed his gaze intently and her pleading eyes met his. 'If you behave yourself, I'll consider allowing you out for a few hours in the afternoon.'

'Thank you so much, Doctor.'

'It's my day off tomorrow and I'd be delighted to drive you home 'Say two p.m.' By the way, I'd prefer if you called me Claude.'

'It's very kind of you to offer, Claude, but....'

'Dan asked me to care of you, so there are no ifs or buts. Okay?'

His bleep went off. 'I'm needed in surgery, Jenny, see you later.'

Claude headed off, leaving Jenny to think about his offer. He was certainly attractive. Of medium build, with dark hair and a tanned complexion, he looked younger than Dan. Jenny put him in his early to mid-thirties. Jenny cheered up immensely at the thought of getting out for a while and making lengthy phone calls to Colin and the family.

'You're in sparkling form,' her counsellor remarked when she came for her daily visit.

'If it weren't for my stiff jaw, I swear I'd break into song,' Jenny replied, much to the amusement of the other woman.

'So, what's put you in such good humour? 'Doctor Stanhope is allowing me home for a few hours tomorrow and, what's more, he's driving me there himself. Isn't that good news?'

'The French doctor certainly knows how to turn on the charm,' her counsellor remarked.

'He's a friend of Dan Flynn who has gone away for two weeks. Dan asked him to take care of me and that's it. Anyway, he didn't sound very French to me,' Jenny quipped.

'Take things slowly, Jenny,' she advised 'You've been through a very traumatic experience and you need kid-glove treatment for a while longer.'

Just then, a nurse dropped in a massive bouquet of flowers with messages from Mary Jo and the rest.

Her counsellor smiled and shook her head. 'I think these flowers will do more for your morale than I could possible do sitting here chatting.'

The following day, Helen served afternoon tea to Jenny and Doctor Stanhope. Jenny explained how Dan had put her in Doctor Stanhope's care.

Helen smiled. She detected a very good doctor patient relationship.

CHAPTER EIGHT

Father Ralph met Colin at Kennedy International Airport.

'Welcome to New York, Colin,' he said, shaking hands warmly.

'Lovely to meet you, Father Melville, thanks for meeting me,' Colin said 'I hope I haven't put you out too much. How's Jenny?'

'She's making a real good recovery I'm pleased to say. Another few weeks and she should be back in action. I'll take you to the hospital now.'

'I'm dying to see her but I must confess I am worried' Colin said.

'Colin everything is fine,' Ralph said, looking at Colin's drawn face. Colin felt he should have been by Jenny's side from the start, even though his parents had tried to reassure him that Jenny was doing okay.

They drove through the gates of Saint Mary's at five thirty p.m. precisely. Colin stopped to buy a bouquet of red roses from the florist beside the main entrance and, together, they walked to the second floor of the surgical unit.

'Room fifteen,' Ralph said, leading the way. He knocked gently at the door. 'I'll leave you to it, Colin, I have some calls to make'

Colin opened the door and rushed into Jenny's outstretched arms.

'I love you, Jenny,' Colin said, holding her in his arms. 'How is my darling precious angel?'

Jenny held him close. 'I'm so happy to see you, Colin. I love you too.'

Colin hadn't noticed Doctor Stanhope sitting behind the door writing notes on a file. Jenny introduced them. 'Nice to meet you, Doctor Stanhope,' Colin said, shaking his hand. Claude managed a weak smile and an even weaker handshake. He immediately disliked the tall handsome Irishman.

'Please give this letter to Father Melville and tell him if he wants any more information on your progress, I'll be happy to pass it on,' he remarked to Jenny before leaving. Colin was pleased to be alone with Jenny at last.

'Are you very tired?' Colin's question prompted her to glance in the mirror. She wished he had phoned to say he was coming today instead of tomorrow. That way she would have had a chance to have her hair done and dress in something special.

'I'm not in the least bit tired,' she replied. 'But I'm fed up sitting around here like I was sick or something.'

'How long more, do you know?' Colin asked 'I'm anxious to get you back to the apartment and look after you - bring you that cup of tea in the mornings. Remember?'

'Of course I do. Little did we think that things work out this way'. Still, it's great that you're here.

'I know,' Colin replied. 'I was worried sick so I decided to come prepared for college even if it is another two weeks before I start. At least I can be with you every day till then.'

'That's a great idea,' Jenny said excitedly.

'You think'?

'With you living in Lincoln Boulevard, sure there's no need for me to stay in hospital. I'll ask to go home tomorrow. I want to help you to settle in.'

*

Claude came into Jenny's room at eight the following morning.

'Are you sleep-walking?' Jenny asked, trying to bring a smile to his miserable face.

'I'm in theatre in twenty minutes,' he replied, 'but I thought you'd like to know that Deadly Sammy will be returning to prison later today. How are you feeling now Jenny?

'I'm feeling very well' thank you Claude in fact I was about to ask you if I can go home?

'That's not the deal I made with Dan,' Claude replied. 'I'm afraid you'll have to stay here till he returns from Peru. I promised to keep an eye on you and that's precisely what I intend to do. Now, if you'll forgive me, I have to go to theatre.'

Jenny noticed he wasn't as friendly as usual. Maybe it would be advisable to stay put till Dan got back.

'Oh damn!' Colin said when she phoned with the news. 'I really wanted you to put your stamp on the apartment but, never mind, it can't be helped, I suppose.'

'How do you like the place anyway?' she asked, her voice full of excitement.

'It's massive, imagine I have a study, sitting room and an en suite bedroom all newly refurbished. Father Ralph even helped me arrange my books and joked that I must have robbed the Carnegie Library.'

Will I see you later, Colin?'

'I'm driving into town with Father Ralph,' he replied. 'Ralph is going to the auction rooms and will drop me at the hospital.'

161

*

Nadine Stanhope answered the door to her son in the late afternoon.

'You look scruffy and dejected, Claude, what's come over you?' she asked gruffly.

'What happened to "Hello, Claude, good to see you,' he retorted.

'When you come home in a grumpy humour, it's usually one of two things. Either you've been working too hard at the hospital or woman trouble. Am I right?

'I suppose it's a combination of both,' he replied, requesting a glass of port.

Nadine opened the drinks cabinet and selected a bottle of finest port. She polished two gleaming cut glass wine glasses, to satisfy her obsession with cleanliness. Carefully she poured the wine. Claude watched the performance as he had many times before. 'This always brings me back to my Air France days,' she remarked with an expression of nostalgia.

'When you worked as a stewardess, looked like Catherine Deneuve and father selected you, from the other twelve cabin staff,' Claude said in a derisive tone.

'You may well scoff, Claude, but the point is that, thirty-six years later, your father and I are as happy as back then. Whilst you, at thirty-four are still coming home to mom with a sulky face just because you're not so lucky.'

Claude took a sip of port. 'I think I may have found someone,' he announced. 'The trouble is, I may need your help to win her over.'

'Please, please don't confront me with complications,'

Nadine replied 'If she's already married, leave her where she is. If she's in love with another man, then don't attempt to draw swords.'

'Everything isn't always straightforward, mother, but if a woman is worth fighting for, then you'll find me on the front line.'

'Dead,' his mother replied angrily.

'Oh, come on, mother, quit the dramatics, and hear me out. Here, take a look at this.' Claude handed his mother a photograph.

'Oh, she's a stunning young woman,' Nadine said, studying the photograph for a while. 'Not only is she beautiful, but stylish too.'

Claude finished his port and asked for another. He felt his mother softening a bit and hoped a second port would arouse her curiosity. He was right.

'Tell me, Claude, how long have you known this young woman?'

'Not very long, not very long at all, just a few days actually,' he replied, stroking his chin philosophically.

'Where did you meet her?'

'At the hospital,' he replied

'A medical colleague, I presume?'

'No, mother, she's a patient.'

'I beg your pardon, Claude. Are you telling me you're involved with one of your patients?'

'She's not a patient in the full sense, she's merely in for observation,' Claude explained.

'What's the matter with her?' Nadine asked.

'The Hippocratic oath binds me to secrecy in relation to

my patients'. That said mother I would like you to meet her.

'Claude, there are times when I find you exasperating and, dare I say, downright cheeky. You want me to meet this woman, on the strength of a photograph, with no information on her pedigree, and you expect me to comply.'

'Trust me, mother, you'll not be disappointed.'

'You always could twist me round your little finger, Claude,' Nadine said. 'Two glasses of port and my son has me won over - yet again.'

'Mother, you're wonderful,' Claude said, hugging his mother and preparing to go.

'Surely you'll stay for dinner, your father will be home soon?'

'No thanks I've got patients to look after. Remember?'

Nadine checked the casserole in the oven. It smelt delicious. She wished Claude had stayed to enjoy it with them. He must be very taken with this young woman when not even good cooking would tempt him to stay. She glanced at his picture on the kitchen wall. It was her favourite, taken when Claude was six years old at their home in Paris. They came to live in New York the following year, making annual trips to France ever since.

'I'm home,' Bill Stanhope called to his wife. 'I've brought you a surprise.'

'I'm off chocolates, thanks,' she replied cheerily. 'Be with you in a minute.'

Bill quickly unwrapped the painting and placed it strategically in the dinning room.

'Close your eyes, Nadine,' he said guiding her in.

'Say when, Bill, the suspense is killing me.'

'Now!' Bill replied, doing a quick step forward to catch her expression.

She opened her eyes and stood spellbound gazing at a landscape reminiscent of Vermont in the fall. She knelt down to take a closer look at the oil on canvass. Having studied art before she became an air stewardess, she appreciated the detail and perfect blending of colours beautifully executed by the artist.

'Do you like it?' Bill asked.

'It's a masterpiece, truly magnificent,' Nadine replied. 'I'd like to know more about the artist though. Maria Von Erlich doesn't mean anything to me.'

'I'll tell you over dinner,' Bill replied, delighted to be able to discuss a subject so dear to his wife's heart. They sat facing the painting and Bill talked her through the events of the day.

'I hadn't planned on going to the auction room,' Bill began, 'then the phone rang and my brother persuaded me to come along. And what's more, I met the artist's grandson. He was selling the entire collection and some antique furniture, including a grand piano.'

'I'd love to have gone with you,' Nadine remarked, 'Bill, why didn't you phone me?'

'Because my darling, I'm only Bill Stanhope, and not Rockefeller. If I let you loose in the auction room with a credit card, I shudder to think of the consequences.'

They both laughed. 'I am a bit reckless when it comes to paintings,' Nadine admitted, 'but I do consider them a good investment.'

'Yes but we have only so much to invest. Ten grand is

enough for one day and one painting, don't you agree?'

Nadine nodded anxious to hear more about the artist.

Bill explained that Maria Von Erlich was a Countess who came to America from Austria after the war. She had taken up painting again after her marriage failed. When she died, everything was left to her grandson, Ralph Melville.

Meanwhile, Claude had driven straight to Saint Mary's. Despite his mother telling him he looked scruffy, he went directly to Jenny's room.

'Hello, Claude,' Jenny said cheerfully.

'Hello, Jenny,' he replied. 'Why are you all dressed up?'

'Why not?' she replied. 'You said I couldn't go home, my boyfriend is here so I decided to make the most of things.'

Claude held both her hands. 'You look beautiful, Jenny, I wish we could dance.'

Jenny stared at him in amazement. 'Have you been drinking, Doctor Stanhope?'

'Two glasses of port with my mother,' he replied. 'I showed her your photograph and she said you were beautiful and stylish too.'

'Photograph, what photograph?' Jenny asked indignantly.

'Oops, sorry Jenny, I was so taken with the photograph you showed me of you at a recent wedding that I took the liberty of borrowing it.'

'You took it without my permission? May I please have it back?'

'Don't be cross with me, Jenny, I meant no harm. Can we still be friends?'

Jenny smiled and nodded.

'Actually, I've come to discharge you,' Claude announced, placing the photograph on her bedside locker.

'What's changed your mind, Claude?' she asked noticing his uneasiness.

'The truth is I have fallen in love with you, Jenny, and it's too painful trying to pretend any longer. It's best if I let you go.'

She was about to say something to him when Colin arrived.

'I'm coming with you, Colin. Will you help me pack my things? Doctor Stanhope said I can go home.'

Colin noticed the doctor left without saying a word.

'Why the sudden decision?' he asked holding her in his arms.

'Because you're here to look after me,' she whispered, 'and besides I've made a miraculous recovery.'

'Guess what?' Bill said to Nadine when he called from the office next day.

'You've managed to get me another painting,' she replied, crossing her fingers.

'Not quite,' he said, 'Ralph Melville has agreed to join us for dinner later.'

'Wonderful,' she replied, 'I must get on to Claude straight away.'

'I'd love to come home for a decent meal' Claude said when he got the invitation from his mother.

'Good, you're on time,' his mother remarked when Claude walked in the door, oblivious to the gruelling day he had put in. 'Go straight in and I'll pour you a port.'

'Just a small one,' he replied. 'I'm on call.'

He stopped to admire the painting that his father had hung in the dining room.

'When did you get this lovely landscape?' he asked Nadine who was carrying the drink on a tray to the drawing room.

'Come and meet the man who sold it to your father,' she replied.

'Doctor Stanhope, it's good to see you again,' Ralph said, shaking hands.

'You too Ralph,' he replied 'This is a surprise.'

Nadine looked from one to the other. 'Obviously you two need no introduction,' she remarked.

'How did the auction go?' Claude asked Ralph.

'Very well, thanks to the influence of your uncle and your father.'

Bill Stanhope smiled. 'I'm sorry to say I have little influence in the antique world. That preserve belongs to my brother.'

'Anyway, I sold everything,' Ralph continued, 'right down to the last stick of furniture and I made quite a bit of money.'

'That's wonderful news, Ralph, now you can return to Peru with a weight off your shoulders.

'Peru?' Nadine was more intrigued than ever.

'I've taken some time away from New York to work in Lima,' Ralph explained. 'I came back after my house was burgled to sort things out.'

'You were burgled, Ralph?' Nadine asked, horrified. 'Was there anyone in the house at the time?'

'Just one person, a young Irish social worker' She was lucky to have got away with her life,' Ralph replied. 'Claude has been looking after Jenny in Saint Mary's.'

Nadine knew instantly who she was. 'How is she, Claude?' his mother asked.

'Fine. I discharged her yesterday,' he replied

Nadine stood up. 'Claude, will you give me a hand to serve dinner?'

'Of course,' he replied.

She handed him the oven gloves. 'Lift the roast beef out, please, and let it stand for a while before I carve.' It smelt delicious, as did the vegetables that Nadine was transferring to dishes.

'Tell me, Claude, why is Ralph Melville working in Peru?'

'Because he is a priest, I presume,' Claude replied, shrugging.

Nadine carved the meat and arranged in on a platter. 'It's a pity you didn't bring Jenny to meet us and have dinner,' she remarked. 'Soon maybe?'

'Maybe,' he replied, wishing now that he had never told his mother about Jenny.

During dinner, Ralph told them how he intended to spend the fortune he had made at the auction. He already had a site to build a home for the homeless and he intended to dedicate it to Countess Von Erlich. He had other projects in mind too.

'Reformed alcoholics and drug abusers often find it difficult to slot back into the work force,' he said 'I intend to set up a centre where they can work to help others.'

He had in mind people like Sergio Emmanuel who had made a marvellous recovery.

Claude glanced at his watch. It was ten p.m. 'Duty calls, I must go,' he said regretfully.

'How did you get on with Professor Manning?' his father asked.

'So so,' Claude replied. 'He wants me to settle down and get married.'

'My sentiments entirely,' Nadine remarked. 'Now, will you consider bringing Jenny to meet us?'

Claude almost swallowed his tongue with embarrassment. Ralph smiled knowingly and shook hands with Claude.

'Thanks for the meal, mother,' Claude said, wondering how soon he would get an opportunity to confess to Ralph.

'I do worry about Claude,' Nadine remarked to Father Ralph after he had gone.

'He's a fine doctor, I'm told,' Ralph assured her.

'He seems to be very taken with Jenny. He showed me a photograph, she appears to be a lovely young woman.'

'You never mentioned this to me,' Bill said to his wife.

'I haven't had an opportunity, dear, with one thing and another it slipped my mind.'

'What do you think, Ralph?' Bill said.

'Oh, 'I believe that love is like a river. It must be allowed to run its course. Sometimes it can flow gently, other times an obstacle may appear.'

Nadine and Bill sensed the priest was trying to tell them something so they decided not to pursue the topic further.

'When do you return to Peru, Ralph?' Nadine asked.

'I fly back on Saturday,' Ralph replied, suddenly realising he had only three days left to finish his business.

CHAPTER NINE

Helen Rafferty was finishing packing her suitcase when Jenny and Colin arrived.

She stopped in her tracks, holding a pair of frilly pants in one hand and a folder in the other. Jenny and Colin both smiled at the surprised look on her face.

'Sorry, Aunt Helen, I didn't think to phone you when Doctor Stanhope discharged me.'

Helen flung her arms round Jenny. 'Welcome home. I'm so pleased you're back, and even more pleased, that Colin is here to keep an eye on you. Let me put the kettle on.'

'Sit down, Helen, and I'll make the coffee,' Colin said, dashing towards the kitchen.

'Any news from Mary and Dan?' Jenny asked, dying to catch up.

'They're unofficially engaged,' Helen announced. 'Mary phoned me earlier and I spoke to Dan too. He's going to buy the ring in Dublin at Christmas.'

'I'm thrilled for both of them and for you, Aunt Helen, you must be over the moon.

'Dan idolises her, Aunt Helen. I could see that, from the moment I introduced them. But I had no idea that Mary was worrying about....' Jenny stopped abruptly wondering if Helen knew about Huntington's.

'It's okay, Jenny, Dan told me all about the scare they had, which is why he wants to marry her as soon as possible.'

Colin arrived with the coffee and placed it on the table.

171

'I've got to phone home, why don't I leave you to chat,' he politely said.

'Don't feel you have to, Colin,' Helen said, thanking him for the coffee.

He smiled and closed the door behind him.

'Strange how things work out,' Jenny said to Helen. 'I bet you never in your wildest dreams, imagined Dan Flynn marrying your daughter, when you worked together in Massachusetts General.'

'Nor did you think he would marry your cousin, when you were friends in Dublin.'

'When have you to go back for a check up to Saint Mary's?' Helen asked

'Doctor Stanhope handed me my appointment when I was leaving,' Jenny said, rummaging in her handbag. 'I'm glad you reminded me.' She opened the envelope and stared incredulously at the piece of paper.

'Something the matter?' Helen asked.

'He wants me to contact him next week,' Jenny replied. 'He's given me his telephone number.'

'Phone him and put him straight, Jenny. You have to.' Helen spoke with caution. 'I noticed the way he danced attention on you when he drove you here last week.'

'I love Colin, and he loves me, and nobody, will come between us, Aunt Helen.'

Helen finished her coffee. 'You're a beautiful woman, Jenny. You can't blame Claude Stanhope for falling in love with you, but it's up to you to be truthful with him.'

Jenny scrunched the piece of paper and threw it in the bin. 'I'll write to him and explain that he is wasting his time, and I'll ask him not to contact me again.'

'Subject closed,' Helen said, handing her a pile of mail. 'I'll leave you in peace while I prepare some supper.'

Jenny left the mail to one side and went to the basement to visit Colin. She tapped gently on the door and waited. He was still on the phone. A gentle breeze rattled the garden door and for a moment she felt chilly. To stop the door rattling, she decided to bolt it. Suddenly she saw a tall shadow passing the window in the twilight. A knock on the door stiffened her with fright. Frantically, she banged on Colin's door.

'He's back again, Colin,' she shouted.

'Jenny what's wrong? Are you okay?

Speechless, she pointed to the door. Colin opened it and Father Ralph walked in.

'I can see you're taking the security seriously, Colin,' he said unaware that poor Jenny was reliving her nightmare.

'Sorry, Father Ralph,' she said 'I didn't know you were in the garden.'

'Did I frighten you? 'He asked noticing her pallor.

'A little' she replied It will take a while to get my confidence back, but now that Colin is here, I'll be fine,'

'Let's have a drink to christen the apartment,' Colin suggested.

'I'll nip up and get Aunt Helen, she might like to join us,' Jenny climbed the stairs slowly. Helen was basting the chicken, and welcomed the invitation since 'the bird' would take another forty minutes.

Colin and Ralph were chatting about the apartment when they arrived. 'It looks so much bigger,' Ralph said, 'now that the furniture and pictures are gone. I'm pleased that it suits you, Colin.'

The shelves were packed with books on astronomy, mathematics, geography and languages. The walls were hung with maps and charts replacing the works of Countess Von Erlich. In the space previously occupied by the grand piano was a large desk owned by Father Ralph. On it Colin had placed a beautiful photograph of Jenny and himself taken at Clare Vaughan's wedding.

Later that evening, Jenny and Colin prepared to settle into the love and contentment of being together.

'I'm so pleased you're here with me,' Jenny said as Colin stroked her hair.

'How's the jaw?' he asked.

'It's almost back to normal. You must have noticed how I'm able to eat nearly everything with the exception of an apple.'

'Okay, Eve, hurry up and get better so that Adam can give you a good old smackeroo.'

'You'll have to settle for a Victorian peck for a little while. Still, there is nothing to stop us from having a good night out soon. What do you say to that?'

'It's a splendid idea. Let's dress up in our finest attire and paint the Big Apple green white and gold. Let's dance the night away in Fitzpatrick's with the rest of the Paddies and afterwards go for a cruise on the river.'

Jenny laughed till the tears ran down her cheeks. 'You're as daft as a brush, Colin Maloney, and I love you.'

'I love you too Jenny and judging by this pile of fan mail, I'm not the only one who loves you. Now I'd like you to rest for a while, read your mail, and prevent yourself from getting lockjaw from all the laughter.'

'And what may I ask are you going to do?'

'I, my dear Jennifer, am going to register at the University, chat up some of the professors, and warn them, that I intend to be the first Irishman to challenge the theories of Galileo Galilei and Aristotle.

'You're even dafter than I first feared,' she replied.

'Look, this first letter is from Clare Vaughan Finnan.'

Jenny opened the envelope and made herself comfortable. Colin left her to it.

Clare had written the letter on a Sunday evening in her new home, Knocknagow. 'It was freezing outside,' she wrote and Johnny was sitting opposite her in front of a huge log fire, snoring his head off. Jenny smiled gently, visualising the scene. The honeymoon in the Caribbean had been wonderful but nothing could equal being with Johnny in the home he had built for them. For a while, Clare had considered going back to work part-time but then Johnny said 'he wanted her to control the financial side of his business'. She had a small office just off the kitchen and overlooking the river Anner. It was fitted with modern equipment, and their own website. The letter went on to say that Johnny was about to start working on a granny flat, and other improvements to Cloran House for Mattie.

What on earth was Mattie playing at, Jenny wondered? He couldn't possibly be making plans to settle down since, to her knowledge, there was no one to make plans with or for. Or was there?

She left Clare's letter to one side and quickly opened her grandma's. To her amazement, on the second page was a detailed account of Mattie's latest conquest.

Eleanor O'Driscoll was from Kinsale in Cork. Mattie had

met her while visiting a friend who had recently bought a boat and lived in Kinsale. His friend asked him to make up a foursome and, by all accounts, it was love at first sight. He had shown his grandma her photograph and she described her to Jenny as a fine looking woman.

'I've told him to bring her home for Halloween since she is a teacher and will have a break from school then,' she explained. 'All he talks about these days is the battle of Kinsale, The Lusitania , and that fellow Alexander Selkirk.' You'd think he was about to enter for Mastermind, he's so eager to learn more about Cork,' she continued.

Poor Mattie. Jenny remembered how he always had problems with history dates and the subject in general. History was supposed to be one long story, his teacher told the class, but Mattie invariably grew tired.

Jenny decided to phone Mattie and give him a bit of advice. If Eleanor truly loved him, it wouldn't matter a tinker's curse whether Selkirk called at Kinsale on his way to the Island of Juan Fernandez or not.

'1601,' she replied when Mattie answered the phone.

'So grandma has told you,' Mattie said by way of letting her know that The Battle of Kinsale date had finally sunk in.

'She did indeed,' Jenny replied. 'I'm thrilled for you. A word of advice, though, please don't allow a battle of wits to get in the way of the sweet nothings that you should be whispering in Eleanor's ear.'

'I'll bear that in mind. It's lovely to hear from you, Jenny, you seem in good form'

'I'm almost back to my old self thank God, and hoping to go back to work next week. By the way thank you for the cards and good wishes. I'll drop a note to you all in due course. Is there anything else exciting happening there?'

*

Jenny lay on her bed for a while wondering what she would cook for supper. She wanted to surprise Colin. A knock on her door made her jump. Nervously she asked, 'Who's there?'

'It's me,' Mary Jo replied. 'May I come in?'

'Please do,' Jenny said, delighted to see her colleague. 'Come through and I'll make some coffee. I'm dying to hear all the news on the work front.'

'That's not the reason I'm here, Jenny, no shoptalk please you're still at the convalescent stage remember.

'Not for much longer, I hasten to add. Anyway, how can I help?'

'We're having a girls' night out tonight and we want you to come,' Please Jenny say 'yes'. We miss you and we'd love to cheer you up.'

'I'd love to come. What time?'

'The cab will collect us at seven. Will that suit you?' Mary Jo asked.

'Perfectly. I'll leave a note for Colin.

'How is he?' she asked.

'Fine. It's registration day at the university so he went down earlier. He should really be back now except he's probably arguing with one of the eggheads about the shape of the moon or why the stars blow up.'

They both laughed heartily at the idea of it. Mary Jo finished her coffee. 'See you later, Jenny.'

At seven, the girls piled into the cab.

'Good evening ladies, where to?' the cabbie asked.

'Hastings Club, please,' Mary Jo replied, since everyone had left the choice of venue to her.

A group of musicians were preparing to liven the club up when the girls arrived. One of them approached Mary Jo.

'You look rather crestfallen, sweetie,' he remarked. 'Would you like me to sing for you?'

'That would be real nice,' she replied.

'Name your song,' he smiled.

'When Irish Eyes Are Smiling'. Will it be okay if we join in?'

'Sure.'

He positioned himself at the mike and a pianist and some guitarists started to play.

'This number, ladies and gentlemen, is for the Irish contingent on my right. If you happen to know the words, feel free to join in and please keep the requests coming.'

Mary Jo sang her heart out. The Wilton sisters, Kerry and Dawn, let it rip with The Irish Rover and Barbara Macy sang 'New York New York.'

'Can we have everyone on the floor, please, for a slow waltz?' the singer requested. 'Don't be shy.'

'May I have the pleasure of this dance, Jenny?' Dan Flynn steered her gracefully on to the dance floor.

'Dan! When did you get back from Peru?'

'Last night' he replied. 'I've been trying to get in contact with you all evening and I finally gave up.'

'Is this an old haunt of yours?' she asked.

'I come here sometimes with a colleague for a beer. Dick

Evans invited me for a chat tonight, and when I heard the Irish songs I was anxious to find out more. They don't normally concentrate on Irish numbers,' Dan remarked.

The music stopped. 'I had better go back to the bar. Dick he'll be wondering where I am.'

'Come and meet my colleagues, they'll be anxious to get to know Mary's beau a little better.'

Dan said a quick 'hello' to the group. 'Sorry I can't stay and chat,' he said apologetically, 'but I'm with someone else.'

'Mary's a lucky girl' Mary Jo said echoing the sentiments of the rest.

'And I'm a lucky man,' Dan replied, his face a picture of contentment. As he left, he almost bumped into a waiter with a tray full of drinks.

Jenny surveyed the drinks as the waiter placed them on the table, reaching for her wallet to pay. 'It's okay, Jenny, they're already paid for,' Mary Jo explained, smiling and waving to a gentleman in the far corner. 'He asked me to dance and, would you believe, for a date.'

'Did you tell him you're already engaged?' Jenny asked.

'Of course not,' Mary Jo replied. 'But if he asks me to dance again I'll put him straight.'

Jenny sipped her drink aware that her colleagues were amused at the whole situation.

'But he could be the wrong type' Jenny pointed out. 'I'd hate to think he was taking advantage because we're five girls on a night out. He is still staring in our direction. I think we should go.'

The band struck up a quick step. Despite having asked Mary Jo for a date, he invited Jenny for a dance. Reluctantly she agreed. 'I'll put him straight,' she vowed as she danced with military precision to the music.

'Cheer up, sweetie,' he whispered, as she felt his hand tightening round her waist.

She smiled politely feigning cramp. 'I'd like to sit down please.'

'Of course,' he replied walking her back to her table. 'By the way, the first lady you danced with is engaged. I thought I should point that out,' Jenny said solemnly.

'How right you are,' he replied, 'girls should always take care of each other, I say.'

'Thanks for the drinks, Bart' Mary Jo said 'It was quite a surprise meeting you here tonight.'

'You two know each other?' Jenny asked.

'Bart is my cousin,' Mary Jo explained amid laughter all round. Jenny felt a heel as she apologised to him. She could have thumped Mary Jo and was grateful she hadn't said too many derogatory things about Bart.

'Am I forgiven?' Mary Jo asked her when they got home.

'Sure,' Jenny replied 'Your cousin is a swell guy. I'd fancy him only.....'

'You go right to Colin's apartment and check him out,' said Mary Jo. 'Bart is no match for that groovy Irishman.'

Colin had left his door open. 'I'm home,' Jenny announced, tapping gently on the door.

'Did you have a good time?' he asked, switching off the television.

'It was fun, I suppose,' she replied, 'how was your day?'

'Disastrous,' he replied. 'Everything went pear-shaped. One of the professors called me a spoofer. He also said I was full of blarney.'

Jenny hugged him and apologised for being out when he got home. 'I fully intended cooking something for supper, except the girls wanted me to join them.'

'I'm glad you did,' he replied. 'God knows you need a break after all you've been through.'

She made some hot chocolate. 'Tell me what happened Colin.'

'It was kind of like going to confession,' he said. 'You always hope you'll get a nice compassionate confessor, except I seem to have got the deaf fellow who shouted, "Speak up, man".'

'He sounds cranky,' Jenny suggested.

'Too bloody right, especially when I mentioned I had done so badly in California. If only I had my time back again, I'd make better use of it.' Colin sat with his head in his hands. 'Then he gave me a long spiel about the excellent standards at the university, and its reputation for turning out top scientists.

'Why should we risk taking in somebody who has squandered his time and talents in the past?" He asked, glaring at me over his half moon spectacles

'I told him I realised I had made a mistake, and that from now on I intend to work hard'.

He looked through all my papers again, and again, and then scratched his head. 'There are some things in your favour however,' he remarked. "You seem to be an excellent mathematician and linguist, so on that basis, you must have worked hard at some stage, which is why I'm prepared to give you a trial run."

Jenny questioned the trial period.

'Till Christmas' Colin replied and then if I'm showing promising signs I'm in with a chance. 'I know I'll have to get extra tuition which will leave little time for socialising.'

'Can you afford the extra fees?'

'I sold my M.G. before I came over and got a very good deal. I'm solvent enough with the extras my parents gave me.'

'I'm sorry you had to part with your car. I'm going to miss it,' she said. 'Who bought it?'

'I sold it to a really nice guy called Mattie Anderson. Ever heard of him? He wanted to impress his new girlfriend Eleanor.'

Jenny stared at him in shock. 'Mattie bought your car and told you about his new girlfriend.' Is there anything else I should know about?

'Except that I love you,' he said, embracing her passionately.

'What happened to the Victorian peck?' she asked. 'But I know one thing for sure, my jaw seems a lot better.'

Listen, I'll give you all the help I can when it comes to your studies. I won't make any demands on your time, and I'll do the cooking. It will be like our days in Dublin when I helped with the charts. What do you say?'

'That would be great. I'll definitely chance your cooking at the risk of being poisoned.' He ducked smartly when she sent a cushion flying in his direction.

'By the way, I was going to offer to share Mary's Mercedes with you, but after that disparaging remark, I'm not so sure.'

'Surely you wouldn't let a Mercedes come between us,' he joked.

It was the late autumn when Jenny returned to work and Colin settled into college. During their lunch breaks, they often walked hand-in-hand in Central Park. It was so romantic seeing the leaves changing colour and making a carpet to walk on. Occasionally, they would enjoy a tasty snack and a coke as they sat on a bench. But it was up to Jenny to help keep his morale up, as he struggled with college. She had got a hero's welcome when she returned after her ordeal, while Colin was playing catch up and wrestling with grumpy professors.

'I'm so sorry, Jenny,' he said one day as they approached the steps of the college. 'I hate this place, and I'm not sure whether I can even stick it till Christmas. To think I had such high expectations when I came here, and now, I feel I've let you down badly.'

'Let me be the judge of that,' she said, squeezing his hand and encouraging him to put his best foot forward. 'You've got what it takes, Colin, all you have to do is prove yourself. Not to me mind, but to those who would have you think less of yourself.' He smiled and kissed her gently on the cheek in gratitude.

Jenny hurried back to meet a women's group that she had met previously with Mary Jo. If she was in any way shy meeting them today, they soon made her feel welcome.

'Thank God he didn't kill you,' the woman with the straw blonde hair and ruby- lips said. 'I lived with that dreadful fellow for twenty years,' she said, speaking of Deadly Sammy. 'He often beat me to a pulp in front of our three children and I have scars to prove it.' Jenny watched in horror as the woman unashamedly showed her scars to them. 'I can speak openly now, knowing that he is behind bars for good. He often threatened me and the children and we fled for our lives on a few occasions.'

Many of the other women told her similar stories. They said they had spent nights on the streets being tormented by other predators and pimps. Some of their children had been taken into care, they told her, tears streaming down their cheeks. 'Imagine seeing your own flesh and blood being taken from you, especially when we didn't set out to be bad mothers,' they said.

Jenny listened and wished she could do something to help them.

One lady made a large pot of coffee and carried it through. 'We usually stop for a break and a cigarette at this stage,' she said. 'Would you like a cup?' she asked politely.

'Please,' Jenny replied, seeing her take a china cup from the drawer while they used mugs. Jenny felt humbled by their kindness and honesty.

'We always used china when I was growing up, especially for visitors,' the coffee maker explained. 'I still remember all the lovely things my mother did to make people welcome. I hope you feel welcome among us.'

'I certainly do, thank you, and I'd like to come and chat soon again. One thing you all have in common is....'

Before Jenny had a chance to say 'a good heart', a woman dressed in black shouted 'V.D. And some of us are infected with H.I.V.' she added.

'I was going to say that you all have a good heart,' Jenny smiled.

'Well, it's that good heart that probably led us into our present situation,' the lady in black said. 'We were promised everything by our fellas, and, in our naivety, we believed them.

So much for 'street wise.'

'Have you all checked into a clinic?' Jenny asked in a gentle voice.

Most of them said they had and were on treatment. She hadn't planned on discussing Venereal Disease or Acquired Immune Deficiency Syndrome on this visit. But since it had been mentioned, she advised them to take responsibility for their ailments and attend for treatment and regular checkups.

'Jenny, are you ready for home?' Mary Jo asked as the last woman waved and left.

'Yea,' she answered with a sigh and Mary Jo understood.

Inside every cloud is a silver lining Jenny thought when she visited Sergio Emmanuel in the Drug Rehabilitation Centre the following day. He looked marvellous and smiled broadly when he met her. 'It's good to see you,' he said giving her a welcoming hug. 'How are you, Jenny?'

'Very well, Sergio,' she replied, 'and I'm delighted to see you have made a wonderful recovery. How are you parents?'

'My mother has found a job in a cafe and father is well enough to do light housework. All told, our fortunes have been reversed and we are now a happy family again,' Sergio announced proudly. 'I'm being paid to help here, so I too, contribute at home.'

Sergio rushed over to the office. 'Look what came for me today,' he said, handing Jenny a postcard. 'It's from Peru, please read it.'

'Dear Sergio, I arrived back safely a few days ago. It was good to see you and your parents, when I was in New York. You all look remarkably well, thank God. When I come home for Christmas, I'll bring a surprise for you. Meanwhile, take good care. God bless you. Ralph Melville O.P.'

'What does O.P. mean?' Sergio asked.

'It means Order of Preachers. Saint Dominic founded the Dominican Order back in 1216 and they are renowned preachers of God's word,' Jenny explained.

'I'd like to learn a little about them, so I can work with Father Ralph in the future,' Sergio said. 'He promised I could help him when he comes back to New York.'

'I'll help you with that,' Jenny said 'Together we can go to the library and read up on the subject, then you can make some notes.'

'Can you come and visit us on Sunday?' he asked. 'Just my parents and me, you could have lunch with us.'

'I'd love to Sergio, it's a date,' Jenny replied. 'See you then!'

In the late afternoon, she called to see a family whose two sons were playing truant from school. 'I can do nothing with them, love,' their father said, a can of beer in one hand and beef burger in the other. 'Find a home for them or lock them up is my advice to you,' he said, closing the door in her face.

CHAPTER TEN

Jenny sat drinking coffee in the kitchen. She had exactly one hour to spare before she and Colin would go into town and buy each other their Christmas present. A new wristwatch was what she wanted. Her old one had been losing a minute or two ever since Deadly Sammy attacked her. Colin said 'he'd like some classical music CDs and a shirt'. She glanced at the Advent calendar and opened the little door revealing December 16 and a chocolate sweet. With nine days till Christmas, her thoughts turned to Sliabh na mBan. Norah Leahy would be preparing to ice the cakes.

This would be her first Christmas away from home, ever, and little pangs of homesickness were already creeping in.

'Let's get cracking,' Colin said, as they both braved the wintry December morning. New York was bustling with excited shoppers and children, on a high going to visit Santa Claus.

'Is this for under the tree? The jeweller asked after Jenny had made her decision.

When Colin said 'yes', he wrapped it in gold wrapping paper and finished it with a neat bow. 'The card is free, sir,' he said. 'I hope you and the young lady have a lovely Christmas.' Colin thanked him and returned the compliment.

'There is something magical about Christmas,' Jenny remarked to Colin, even though they both felt the edge, of the biting sleety wind, that was now blowing. It was really romantic listening to the carol singers, and, being part of a

187

richly decorated city in full swing. Colin suggested they take cover for a while, in a cosy little cafe off Fifth Avenue. Piping hot coffee, and pancakes drizzled with maple syrup, brought a glow to their cheeks once again.

'It reminds me of the good old days in Dublin,' Colin said with a distinct air of nostalgia in his voice.

Jenny knew immediately he was not a happy camper. 'Can I suggest something?' she asked.

'I'm all ears,' he replied, cutting a chunk off the pancake and adding more syrup.

'You know how I have planned to spend Christmas working in the shelters, and wherever else I may be needed. Well, I've been thinking. It won't be much fun for you. So perhaps you might like to go home for the holiday and enjoy it with your parents. What do you say?'

'I'm staying right here with you, Jenny,' he smiled, 'and I'll even join you in helping out in the shelters or wherever.'

'That's very sweet of you, Colin, but please don't feel you have to.'

'I want to, it's as simple as that,' he replied. 'Now I think we should finish our shopping before we're snowed in completely.'

Jenny was sitting with her back to the window and couldn't see the huge blobs of snow that were landing on the windowpane. Outside, the snow mixed with icy rain had made conditions very uncomfortable. 'Be careful you don't slip,' Colin said, taking a firm grip of her hand. Clinging to each other, they made it to the music centre. Colin quickly found the discs he wanted. 'Imagine listening to these with a glass of mulled wine and some hot minced pies on Christmas Eve,' he whispered to Jenny.

They chuckled happily and agreed it was a cosy thought. At Daniel Cremieux's boutique, they found the most gorgeous Herringbone denim shirt in indigo blue.

Colin was very pleased and gave Jenny a big hug as he watched the salesman wrap it for under the tree.

'What would you like to do now?' Colin asked leaving the boutique.

'Don't laugh when I tell you I've got this wonderful recipe for duckling with apple sauce.' She didn't pretend to Colin that she had already done some of the preparations the previous day. 'I could have a meal on the table by six thirty,' she said enthusiastically.

'I have a nice bottle of Chateauneuf-du-pape' Colin said 'I'll chill it and bring it along.'

When they reached home, Colin's phone was ringing like mad. 'See you at six thirty,' Jenny said, leaving him to it.

She couldn't remember getting such pleasure out of preparing a meal. Everything was falling into place from the gratin potatoes to the two-tone courgettes, even the applesauce with a tablespoon of whiskey added tasted delicious. She set the table placing a single red rose in the centre. Quickly she browned the duck in hot oil and stuck it in the oven while she showered. Dressed in a black lace top with smart black pants and comfortable Anne Klein shoes, she was ready to serve.

On the dot of six thirty, Colin arrived clutching a bottle of wine and some luscious chocolate.

'If the food is half as tempting as the cook, I can tell I'm going to enjoy myself,' he remarked uncorking the wine. He complimented her on her outfit and said she looked stunning.

'You can't beat gracious living,' he remarked. 'I really enjoyed that meal and the duck was good too,' he added

She laughed heartily 'You didn't think I had it in me,' she remarked, carrying the coffee to the drawing room. Colin brought the remainder of the wine and they sat together watching the snow falling in front of the street lamp.

'Of course I knew you could cook,' he said, 'haven't you just proved it?' He leaned over and kissed her on the cheek.

'It was a real pleasure,' she said. By the way, what did you do this afternoon?' she asked pouring the coffee.

Colin stood up and walked across the room to the window. For a moment, he stood there gazing at the wintry sky. Inwardly, he was bracing himself to explain what happened in the afternoon. He turned and accepted the cup of coffee she had poured for him.

'My father telephoned,' he said.

'Everything okay?' Jenny asked taking a sip of her coffee.

'I have to go home tomorrow, there's a spot of family business I need to attend to.'

'But I don't understand, Colin. What on earth can be so pressing that you must go now, above all times?'

'My father didn't make himself very clear,' Colin replied 'All I know is he wants me home a.s.a.p. so that I can help him sort out the problem.'

'Surely he gave you some idea. I mean, it's most unlike your father to be vague, he usually spells things out clearly.'

'Not this time, I'm afraid,' Colin said. 'In fact, he didn't seem a bit like his old self'

'What arrangements have you made?' Jenny asked, her voice trembling.

'My airline ticket is still valid so I've booked myself on the flight to Dublin tomorrow evening,' he replied

'You would tell me if there is something seriously wrong?' she asked, trying hard to conceal her mixture of anger and doubt.

'Of course I would,' he replied. 'I'll probably be back in a few days and certainly for Christmas,' he added confidently. He held her close to him and told her she was the most precious person in the world to him. 'At this moment, I hate myself for having to put you through this after all you've been through already, and especially, after my commitment earlier.

'I know,' she replied, not totally convinced that he was telling the truth. She was about to ask him if he would like her to go with him, except, she had promised to help so many people around Christmas.

'I'll help you pack in the morning,' she said. 'Right now, I think we should have an early night.'

Colin turned and twisted all night long. He wished he could have told Jenny the true story that had his father screaming down the phone earlier. How could he possibly tell her, that a woman had flown in from California, arrived on his father's doorstep carrying a baby, and claiming that Colin was it's father.

'Get yourself home here at once,' his father said, 'and sort out the awful mess that you have landed yourself, and us in. We simply can't believe that you could do this to us.'

Jenny cried for a long time that night. Did anyone consider her for a moment? she wondered. It would be very uncharacteristic of Colin's parents to leave her in limbo, so the problem must be with Colin, she concluded. She drove to church early on Sunday morning. At Mass, she prayed for God to give her strength, and she offered Holy Communion for Colin and his family.

'I've made breakfast for both of us,' he told her, opening the door when he heard her arriving.

'Thanks. I could do with some strong coffee.'

He poured the coffee and removed the toast from the toaster. She buttered a slice but somehow found it difficult to eat it. A barrier had now come between them she felt.

'I'll phone you every day, Jenny,' he said. 'I love you with all my heart and I'm sorry I have to leave you like this.'

She swallowed her coffee and her pride at the same time. 'I'll help you with your packing and prepare some light lunch for us,' she said.

'I've done my packing. I'm travelling light, just taking the bare necessities and something to read.'

After she left Colin knew he had hurt her by not giving a proper reason for his sudden departure. He left the apartment and headed for the florist. He ordered twelve red roses to take to her now, and a further dozen to be delivered midweek. When he reached her apartment, she had the Christmas tree erected in the drawing room. It was still rather bare, but the few lights and decorations she had so far hung on it, were colourful, and added cheer to the room. He placed her present under it, and got a small bit of satisfaction that it was the first gift. At the same time, he left her card on the mantelpiece. It too, was the first one. He noticed a large pile of post not yet opened. If things had been different, he should be helping her open it, and reading the good wishes to them both.

Jenny came into the room and he gave her the roses and a kiss on the cheek.

'They're beautiful Colin, thank you. I'm sorry I'm not myself today,' she said, but I'm sure you can understand.

He held her in his arms. 'We're both upset, me, because I have to leave you and fly home to uncertainty, and you, because I haven't given you a proper explanation. Please bear with me, Jenny. I promise I'll make things right soon.'

Later, on his way to the airport he wondered if he should have made such a rash promise. Supposing, it turned out that he was in fact the father of Jean Judd's baby. What then? Ever since his father had said her name, he tried to place her but couldn't. He may have met her at one of the many parties he had gone to, but she, like the rest of the girls, was but a vague memory.

Once back in Dublin, the nearer he got to home, the more he hated himself. There would be no fatted calf for this son returning from a distant land, he told himself. How right he was! Not a word of welcome greeted him when his father opened the door. 'Season of goodwill' is right, he mumbled, leaving his bag in the hall.

'I suppose you expect us to greet you with open arms,' his father growled angrily.

'Did you ever hear that a man is innocent, till proven guilty?' Colin asked.

'Then what's that woman doing, coming all this way, bringing a tiny infant and claiming you're the father?' he replied. 'Surely she must be fairly certain of her claim.'

His mother had just finished cooking breakfast and invited him to sit in. 'Welcome home, son,' she whispered while her husband collected the post.

'Thanks mum,' he replied, aware that she too was under a lot of pressure.

He ate the mixed grill she had prepared and enjoyed it. 'I'll lie down for a while,' Colin said feeling his space was probably better than his company.

'You'll wait till I have made contact with that woman. We've got to talk to her and get this sorry business sorted out now,' his father said, dialling the hotel. Jean Judd answered promptly.

'John Maloney speaking,' he said. 'Colin has just got home from New York and we will be at the hotel at two p.m. Meet us in the foyer.' He barely gave her time to reply before he hung up. Everything was on his terms, it would seem, and even basic good manners were out the window.

'Be ready to leave the house at one-fifteen sharp,' he said to Colin as he proceeded to lay his head on the pillow. 'Make sure you wear your best suit,' he added.

At one fifteen p.m. John was dressed as if he were going to one of his executive meetings. Pinstriped dark suit, crisp white shirt, and maroon tie. Vera had a sober grey suit and carried a neat black bag. Colin was compelled to wear the only suit he possessed. He hated the dark blue waist-coated suit and felt like a jerk in it. His father led the way into the hotel with quick purposeful steps. A tall slim Grace Kelly look-alike came forward to meet them. She was elegantly dressed in a well-cut black trouser suit and appeared slightly nervous. She attempted a friendly smile, but soon changed her tune when John grimly asked her if she recognised Colin.'

'People look so different in shorts and shades, but I'm almost sure it's him,' she replied.

'One night fling, was it?' John asked harshly. 'Listen, Ms Judd, you either recognise my son or you don't, now please make your mind up.'

'I'd like a little co-operation from your son,' she replied. 'Surely he must remember me.'

'To my knowledge, I've never laid eyes on you before,' Colin said, 'and I'm certainly not the father of your child.'

'But you must remember that night at the pool when we drank champagne, and made love afterwards. Surely you're not going to deny your son's paternity?'

'I don't remember anything of this sort, but I would like to see the baby,' Colin said.

They followed her to her suite on the upper floor where the child's nanny was just finishing changing the baby.

'Please wait next door, nurse,' Jean said to her, 'while I talk with my visitors.'

John, Vera and Colin looked at the baby for a few moments. He was well cared for and healthy looking.

'What did you call him?' Vera asked.

'I haven't decided yet,' she replied, 'I wanted Colin to have a say.'

Colin straightened his tie. 'I told you I'm not the father of your child. He is beautiful, but his skin is darker than yours or mine. Let's solve this with a paternity test.'

'Absolutely not,' she said, bursting into tears.

'Listen, Ms Judd, and listen good,' Colin said. 'You have caused me and my family enough grief as it is, now, we either get a paternity test or you get on the next plane back to Los Angeles. Understood?'

'But my father is a millionaire and can give you anything you want,' she protested. 'Being the father of my child will benefit you enormously.'

'I don't believe what I'm hearing,' Colin said, his voice

raised in anger. 'You have my telephone number and if I don't hear from you in the next forty- eight hours regarding DNA, then don't call me ever again.'

He stormed out of the room followed by his parents. His father, who had behaved like a general up until now, suddenly became a cadet. Colin had amazed and impressed him in the manner he had dealt with the woman.

'You handled that very well, Colin, and I'm sorry I gave you such a rough time,' his father said on the way home

'How were you to know she was a fake?' Colin replied. 'She obviously got mixed up with someone dubious character who fathered her child, and her parents freaked and are prepared to pay a handsome sum for a surrogate father.'

'But why did they come after you?' his father asked.

'I probably impressed them at a dinner party,' Colin replied, 'and since millionaires can pick and choose, they saw me as a good catch.'

John smiled for the first time in a week. The very idea of a millionaire buying a father for his grandson amused him.

'Do you think she will have the paternity test?' Vera asked.

'The next forty-eight hours will tell,' Colin replied, 'though I'm sure she knows full well she's wasting her time.'

'What then?' Vera asked.

'Rich people always have plan B,' Colin replied.

'Which is?' his mother asked.

'If Paddy the Irishman doesn't respond, then she'll try elsewhere, I presume,' Colin said. 'The thing is, 'Jean Judd has been dispatched by her wealthy father to find a man suitable to be her child's father.'

'But that's preposterous,' Vera was shocked to think that

anyone would go to such lengths. 'It's ethically and morally wrong.'

Back home, Vera turned to Colin. 'I'm almost afraid to ask you about Jenny. How on earth did you explain the situation to her?'

'Not very well, I'm afraid. And I'm going to have an even bigger problem explaining myself, if that woman goes ahead with a paternity test. It takes at least ten days and, with Christmas included, probably two weeks.'

'What did you tell her?' Vera asked

'I told her a family problem had arisen but I don't think she bought my vagueness,' Colin replied. 'Besides I promised to be back in New York before Christmas.'

His mother sighed deeply. 'Would you like me to ring her?' she asked.

'And what good would that do?' he asked 'I don't intend to tell her about Jean Judd, and neither do I expect you to make excuses for me. Thanks for the offer, Mother, but this is one time in my life, when I'll have to act like a man.'

'Supposing Jenny phones when you're out, what am I to say?' Vera was anxious.

'Jenny is not likely to pry into our affairs,' Colin replied. 'I'll phone and explain that things are more complicated than I thought and I'll make arrangements to call her at a set time every day.'

'Fair enough,' his mother replied, 'but I don't want you to do anything that might hurt her.'

Later, he picked up courage and phoned her. Jenny answered the phone promptly. 'Colin, are you okay? I'm beside myself with worry, I was about to call you.'

'I'm fine, thanks Jenny' Sorry for the delay in contacting you but father decided to get cracking on the problem today.'

'And?'

'It's surmountable but may take a while. I'll phone you every day,' he replied.

'Does that mean you won't be back for Christmas?' she asked, her voice full of disappointment.

'The next forty-eight hours are crucial. If we get the answer we're hoping for, then I'll certainly be back.' Colin apologised again and again for the upset he was causing.

'I love you, Jenny, and I hope you're feeling well. Any news?'

'Something wonderful happened,' she replied. 'I'm so sorry you are not here to celebrate it with me, Colin.'

'Well, tell me,' he said.

'I've been elected Tipperary Person of the year and they're holding a ball in my honour in Fitzpatrick's on the 22nd. Isn't that marvellous?'

'Congratulations! darling. Tipperary and New York couldn't have bestowed the honour on a more deserving and beautiful person. I only wish I could be there with you.'

'So do I, Colin,' she replied, holding back the tears.

'Have you told your grandma and Mattie?'

'You're the very first person I've told. The gilt-edged invitation only came in this morning,' she said. 'I had better make the call to Sliabh na mBan. I love you and will be in touch real soon.'

'Love you too,' he replied

In New York, Jenny was having a ball. When Dan Flynn

heard Colin had gone back to Dublin, he promised Jenny he would find her an escort for her big night out. 'I'm so happy for you,' Dan said. 'I'd stand in for Colin myself, except I'm off to England to be best man for Dick Evans. Keep all newspaper accounts of the occasion for Mary and I.'

Mary Rafferty and Father Ralph Melville had arrived back in Boston from Peru. Mary had only two days to prepare for her trip to Dublin and was very excited. She immediately phoned Jenny. 'Dan has just told me the wonderful news. I'm thrilled for you, Jenny, and wish I could hug you to bits right now. Colin must be over the moon too.'

'He's very excited and so are all the family in Sliabh na mBan. They wanted to come over for the occasion, except, it might be too much for grandma so soon after Uncle Jack's death. They promised to come in the New Year instead.'

'Speaking of New Year,' Mary said, 'I can tell you and I will burn midnight oil for the whole month of January.'

'Yeah we'll have lots and lots of exciting news to talk about,' Jenny replied. 'I'm looking forward to seeing the sparkler.'

With no prince charming on the horizon, Jenny pressed ahead with preparations for the big occasion. Her colleagues booked a table at Fitzpatrick's and were squarely behind her, to ensure, it would be a night to remember. Normally at this time of year they would have gone to join their families for the holiday. But Mary Jo and the others had vowed to become honorary members of the Tipperary Association for one night.

Pip answered the door to the late evening caller. 'Is Ms Anderson at home? he asked.

'I'll check for you,' she replied. 'Who will I say?'

'Claude Stanhope,' he replied.

Pip spoke on the intercom. 'Claude Stanhope to see you, Jenny.'

'Thanks, Pip. Please tell him to come up.'

'Good evening Jenny'. Dan asked me to come. I believe congratulations are in order.' He shook hands warmly and she invited him to sit down.

'Thanks, Claude' 'I wondered what knight in shining armour Dan had lined up for me up this occasion,' Jenny remarked, 'but I wouldn't be surprised if you had come to say, that you are otherwise engaged on the twenty-second.'

'On the contrary, I'm quite free and would be delighted to be your escort for the great occasion,' he replied.

Colin answered the phone to Jean Judd. 'I've decided to go ahead with the paternity test,' Jean said 'Could you meet me and the baby at the clinic tomorrow?'

'What made you change your mind?' he asked.

'My parents flew in yesterday from L.A. and they persuaded me to go ahead. I told them what you said and they agreed.'

'What time?' Colin asked.

'The appointment is for eleven a.m. I hope that suits you.'

'I'll be there,' he replied. He replaced the receiver and put the kettle on.

'Put my name in the pot,' his mother said as she arrived armed with a basket of groceries. 'Are you still fond of Coconut Creams?' she asked, extracting the biscuits from underneath the bread.

'I'm not sure what I'm fond of anymore,' he replied in a dispirited tone.

She looked at his forlorn face. 'It's all getting to you, Colin. Isn't it?' Have you heard from Jenny?' she asked

'We talked for a while yesterday. She's been honoured with the Tipperary Person Of The Year award,' he told his delighted mother.

'That's wonderful. Surely you're going to join her in New York for the celebrations. When is the official announcement?' she asked.

'On Friday,' he replied. 'They're throwing a ball in Fitzpatrick's Hotel and she will be guest of honour.'

'You just have to fly over Colin'. you can't let her down. Who will escort her to the ball?' his mother asked frantically. 'Listen, Colin, you must phone that Judd woman, and tell her you've changed your mind about the paternity test. She wasn't on for it in the first place, so they'll be no harm done.'

'The harm is already done, mother,' he replied. 'She rang just before you came in. Jean has arranged a paternity test for tomorrow at eleven a.m. I promised to be there.'

'If she can change her mind, then so can you, Colin,' his mother said, undeterred. 'Cancel the appointment this instance and tell Jenny you're coming.'

'I wish it were that simple,' he replied. 'Don't you think I want to be with her more than anything else in the world but not with this dreadful problem hanging over me. I just want to get this Judd woman off my back for once and for all.'

'Then call the police. It's what your father and I should have done in the first place,' his mother retorted angrily.

'I don't want the police involved,' he replied. 'I wasn't exactly a saint in L.A. It was one non-stop round of parties dating one girl after another. Some of the time, I didn't know where I was when I woke up in the morning, so I've brought all this on myself.'

'Have you told Jenny all of this?' his mother asked, feeling that she was getting more information than a mother really needed to know.

'Sorry mother! I know it's the last thing you want to hear, but at least it will help you to understand. And yes, I have told Jenny about my debauched life in L.A.'

'So, to some extent, you're not all that surprised that a woman turns up with a baby? Honestly, Colin, I'm shocked at what you've told me.'

The phone ringing got him off the hook. His mother was surprised the call was from Jenny since Colin had promised to call her at a set time every day. She gathered from his conversation that a severe snowstorm had hit New York, and that Kennedy International Airport was closed. 'Even if I wanted to go I couldn't now,' Colin remarked to his mother. 'Kennedy is closed.'

'And to think that lovely woman is still involved with you, after the way you've treated her, makes me feel ashamed of you, Colin. She's better off without you.'

'Don't say that, mother. I love her with all my heart. At least what happened in L.A. made me realise the treasure I have in Jenny, and nothing is going to come between us.'

'I wish I could share your confidence,' his mother replied. 'You have a lot of growing up to do, Colin, believe me..' Vera lifted herself wearily out of the chair and went for a breath of fresh air in the garden. Usually she found solace in the quietness of her suburban garden. Not today. The chilly north wind blowing down from Tree Rock caused a shiver to run through her. She made her way back to the kitchen.

'I'm going to phone Jenny,' Vera announced. 'Have you the number handy, Colin?'

'Whatever for?' Colin asked, frightened of what his mother might say to her.

'I want to congratulate her on being conferred as Tipperary Person Of The Year,' Vera replied, 'and 'wish her Happy Christmas.'

'Jenny, how are you, it's Vera Maloney,' she said cheerfully when Jenny answered.

Jenny was thrilled to hear her voice. 'Colin is helping me with Christmas preparations but is broken-hearted because he can't be with you,' she said 'He loves you with all his heart Jenny. It's such a pity things happened the way they did. By the way, have you found a suitable escort for the ball?' Vera asked.

She listened intently as Jenny filled her in, taking note of the man's name. 'What's your gown like, Jenny?' Vera asked.

Vera gasped with admiration as Jenny described the green silk chiffon dress with gold beading. 'You'll be the toast of New York,' Vera said. 'Please send me some photographs. Have a wonderful time!' Vera said replacing the receiver. She was pleased she had made the call.

'Did she say who's escorting her to the ball?' Colin asked in a matter-of-fact tone.

'I'm hopeless with names,' Vera replied, 'but I think she said Stanhope. He's got a funny first name, sort of French, I think. Any ideas, Colin?'

'That'll be Doctor Claude Stanhope,' Colin replied.

'There you are then,' his mother said, 'she couldn't be in safer hands. You must be pleased, Colin, that she found someone at such short notice.'

Colin nodded though his heart had sunk to his boots. He pressed the zapper and cancelled 'Peace On Earth, Goodwill To Men.' He switched on the Christmas tree and sat back, admiring the lights flickering on and off.

Then he remembered how Jenny had started to decorate her tree before he left. It was a giant of a tree that filled the large picture window of the drawing room. Possibly Claude Stanhope would sip champagne with her before going to the ball, with just the lights of the tree shining on them. Why was he torturing himself, he wondered? Jenny had said that she loved him and he certainly loved her.

His father arrived home from work just as Vera was putting the finishing touches to the evening meal.

'Good day?' she asked her husband as they sat down to dine.

'Excellent,' he replied taking a large white envelope from his pocket. 'You can have the pleasure of opening it after dinner,' he said to Vera, 'and of spending it, I hope!' she added with a chuckle.

'Any news, Colin?' his father asked.

'Jean Judd wants to go ahead with the paternity test tomorrow,' he replied.

'It's just as well to get it done and over with,' his father said. 'When did she contact you and why did she change her mind?'

'She phoned this morning and told me her parents had arrived from L.A. and encouraged her to go ahead.'

'Best of luck, son, you have nothing to worry about.'

Vera Maloney opened the envelope. It contained a lovely

letter from the M.D. thanking John for his marvellous contribution to the company and rewarding him with a bonus of four thousand pounds sterling.

Vera hugged her husband. 'Congratulations, darling.'

'Would you like me to come with you in the morning?' John asked Colin as he prepared to go to bed. 'I'm free now till the New Year.'

'Thanks, dad, I'll be okay,' he replied, 'you enjoy a lie in now that you have the chance.'

Colin arrived ten minutes before the appointed time for the paternity test. Jean was already seated beside her parents nursing the baby.

'If it's not the great debater himself,' Glen Judd said to Colin, remembering him from one of his dinner parties. Colin shook hands. The debate was more of a head-to-head argument as Colin recalled. Glen was built like a sumo wrestler with a fearsome expression to go with a six-foot-four twenty stone physique. When he narrowed his eyes and smiled the smile of an ogre, one tended to agree with him.

His wife, by contrast, was tall, slim and dark haired. Her fine bone structure reminded Colin of Audrey Hepburn. What attracted them to each other, Colin failed to understand.

'I take it you'll be sticking around for a while,' Glen remarked to Colin after the D.N.A. test was finished.

'Yes sir,' Colin replied 'I'm staying in Ireland till the results come back, if that's what you mean.'

'I was thinking more along the lines of joining us for Christmas here at the hotel,' Glen said. 'It's what I'd expect of the child's father. Playing Santa, that sort of thing.'

Colin swallowed hard before answering. 'I'm sorry I can't

accept your invitation Mr Judd I've made other arrangements. Besides I have flown in from New York and left my girlfriend alone there for Christmas to accommodate your daughter.'

'What on earth are you talking about, man?' Glen asked. 'Jean said you're the father and that's enough for me. The D.N.A. will prove that conclusively.'

Colin could feel his blood boiling at the arrogance of Glen Judd. He stood up, preparing to leave.

'Thanks for your co-operation, Colin,' Mrs Judd said. 'We appreciate what you are doing and wish you, and your family a Merry Christmas.'

It was her politeness and gentleness that prompted Colin to take his next step. He hurried to the nearest toy store and bought the largest teddy bear he could find. Jostling with the Christmas traffic, he hurried to their hotel. It was his intention to leave it at reception but Jean was standing in the foyer when he arrived.

'This is for the baby,' he said, 'I doubt his natural father will even remember him.'

'It's very sweet of you, Colin,' she said, gazing at the giant teddy 'I've decided to call the baby after you.'

'Goodbye,' he said heading off.

He walked the three-and-a-half kilometres to his home. Darkness was descending over the Dublin Mountains as he reached Ticknock. Now and then on the way, he had stopped to take in the full panoramic view of the city with its millions of lights. The sky was clear and the star formation of The Great Bear, Orion, The Plough and The North Star brought him back to his aspiring astronomer days.

Back then, Jenny often helped him with telescopes and star

charts and life was infinitely easier. How he longed to hold her hand now, as he had then, while they scrambled down the mountain in carefree mood. He reached his house that stood at the foot of the mountain. Through the Lawson Cypress, he could see the well-lit Christmas tree beckoning. He turned the key and entered the hallway where the grandfather clock struck five p.m. A strange silence followed. He had become used to the hustle and bustle of New York and now found his home eerily quiet. Where were his parents, he wondered? A hastily scribbled note on the kitchen table informed him, that they had gone to a friend's house for Christmas drinks. He kicked off his shoes and socks and sat for a while to relieve his weary feet. For a few precious moments, he allowed his body the pleasure of being intoxicated with Christmas spices. Cinnamon, nutmeg, and cloves seemed to permeate every part of the kitchen.

A freshly iced and decorated cake with colourful frill stood centre stage on the table. Jars of mincemeat with great tartan bows vied for attention on the dresser while a plum pudding perched beside a bottle of Remy Martin had a shelf to itself.

He uncapped a beer trying desperately to enter into the magical world his mother had created in her kitchen. He took a long swig remembering that not alone had he entered the Winter Solstice, but that tonight, December twenty second, Jenny would be named Tipperary Person Of The Year.

The longest night in the calendar year would be a sad, lonely, and long one for him.

Choking with emotion, he dialled her number. Pip told him that Jenny had gone to the hairdressing salon. He drank several more beers and waited for what seemed like an eternity.

The phone rang at almost midnight. He jumped with excitement and promptly answered it. 'I thought you'd never call,' he said. But to his great disappointment, it was the voice of Jean Judd at the other end of the line expressing her gratitude for the teddy bear.

'Thank you for the call,' he said politely. 'I'm expecting an overseas call and must hang up.' He waited another half–hour, hoping to hear from Jenny but no call came. He then decided to call her and finally left a message on the answering machine. In his half drunken state it was a message punctuated by sloppy drivel and excuses.

*

The glittering event in Fitzpatrick's Hotel was attended by the who's who of New York society and the Tipperary diaspora. Social diarists photographed and interviewed Jenny, as she arrived on the arm of the dashing Doctor Claude Stanhope. The president of the Tipperary Organisation said 'It was a real change to honour a beautiful young woman from Sliabh na mBan for a number of reasons'. 'In the past, we have honoured footballers, hurlers, business people, and musicians but, tonight, the honour goes to Jenny Anderson.'

The president spoke about her recent heroism and the brave way she had returned to her job as a social worker. Many more lovely tributes followed much to the delight of the distinguished assembly. Finally she received a standing ovation when she accepted a beautiful piece of Tipperary Crystal, specially commissioned, and flown in for the occasion. The dancing and celebrations went on into the small hours, ending with Claude and Jenny leading the waltzing to the strains of Sliabh na mBan.

'Thank you for a wonderful evening,' Claude said as they returned to their table. 'It's a great occasion and I know I'm the envy of all the bachelors here tonight. You look stunning, Jenny.'

She smiled broadly and their eyes met. 'I couldn't have done this without you, Claude,' she whispered. 'I want you to know that you are very special and 'thank you'.

He knew he had to continue to woo her. 'Will you come out to dinner with me some evening?'

'I'd love to,' she replied. 'How about Saint Stephen's night?'

'Perfect,' he replied, kissing her goodnight.

Nadine and Bill Stanhope spent the following morning reading about Jenny and Claude. Their photos graced the social columns of every newspaper.

'I'm going to phone Claude and invite Jenny and himself to dinner,' Nadine announced excitedly.

'Don't forget Father Ralph Melville,' Bill said. 'Remember he did promise he'd call at Christmas time.'

Nadine Stanhope lost no time in contacting Claude. 'You're as bad as Professor Manning,' Claude said after his mother had hinted at a short romance, a quick engagement and marriage.

'Steady on, mother, I'm out of breath listening to you,' Claude replied. 'Now, why have you called me in the first place?'

'To invite you and Jenny to dinner real soon,' she replied.

'I'll get back to you when I have spoken to Jenny, on one condition.'

'That you will not engage in conversation likely to turn Jenny away from us for good. And please don't give her your five tips for a successful relationship.'

Nadine smiled at the other end of the phone. 'I'll play it your way, Claude.'

*

After several vain attempts to contact Jenny, Colin finally reached her on Christmas Eve. During the hour-long conversation, Jenny purposely didn't mention or question Colin's so-called family problem, preferring to eagerly tell him all about the ball. He was more than happy to listen since it deflected from his miserable frame of mind and melancholy. Not once had she mentioned Claude Stanhope. For that he was grateful but, deep in his psyche, he felt cheated and ashamed. Why did Jean Judd deprive him of what had promised to be one of the happiest Christmases of his entire life? He could never live without Jenny but did she feel the same about him now?

'I love you, Jenny,' he said in a voice so choked with emotion that he had to hang up. He lay on his bed, his heart pounding as if it were going to burst. He heard his mother speaking to Jenny when she called back to see if he was okay.

'Holy smoke,' he uttered, jumping out of bed. God knows what she would say to Jenny if she sounded worried, especially after she had drunk a few glasses of wine with Christmas Eve friends.

'I'll talk to Jenny,' he called from the landing, 'just replace the receiver mother.'

'Sorry about earlier,' Colin begun, 'it's just I'm missing you so much it's kind of getting to me.'

'At least you're with your family, Colin, and that must surely count for something,' Jenny said. 'We both have to make the most of the situation we find ourselves in and try to enjoy Christmas.'

It was a long time since Colin had placed any significance on The Nativity. Maybe it was time to stop feeling sorry for himself he thought.

'You're right. I'll visit the crib tonight at midnight Mass and say a special prayer for you, Jenny.'

'Me too,' Jenny replied. 'I'll go to Saint Patrick's Cathedral and light a candle for you.'

'And tomorrow?'

'I'll be at the shelters serving Christmas dinner to the homeless with all the other volunteers,' she replied. 'I'm quite looking forward to being part of the huge melting pot of people' who will be a family for one day. It would have been nice to have you here too but, since that's not possible, I hope you and your family will enjoy the day. Merry Christmas, Colin.'

'Merry Christmas to you, my darling! Call you soon.' He replaced the receiver wishing she had said 'I love you' She seemed so distant in every sense of the word, almost as if she were a stranger. He could feel the hurt in her voice when she said 'it would be nice to have you here.'

A volley of raindrops hit hard at the windowpane as he donned his raincoat. It was only a kilometre to the church and he had exactly fifteen minutes before the service would start. He slipped quietly from the house and braved the chilly

December night. Once inside the church, he felt great. Scores of candles in ornate candelabras lit the high altar and others were placed strategically around the church. The service was lengthy and included the placing of the child Jesus in the crib. He had almost forgotten how touching the story of the Nativity was.

Later, as he lit a candle for Jenny, it occurred to him that had she not mentioned The Nativity, he would never have gone to church at all. The rain had eased off when he started for home. Several people wished him 'Merry Christmas' and he did likewise.

As he reached home, he studied the Christmas candle flickering in the bay window. Gently, he turned the key and his mother's voice startled him.

'Where on earth have you been?' she asked, her face smothered in night cream.

'Visiting the crib,' he replied, 'and lighting a candle. Why do you ask?'

'You didn't say you were going out and since it's now one in the morning, I was worried.'

'Sorry, I should have said,' he replied, giving her a hug. 'Happy Christmas, mother.'

*

The feast of the Epiphany came and went and there was still no sign of Colin coming back to New York. Dan and Mary had returned from Dublin in high spirits. Mary was proudly wearing a fabulous antique engagement ring and she and Dan planned an Easter wedding. Together with Helen, they had called to visit Mary Anderson and Mattie in Sliabh na mBan.

'Will you be my bridesmaid, Jenny? Mary asked timidly.

'Of course I will,' Jenny replied. 'It will be my first time being bridesmaid. I'm really looking forward to it. Thank you so much for asking me.'

'Have you fixed a date?' Jenny asked.

'Easter Monday, the nineteenth of April, is D-Day,' Mary replied excitedly.

'Let's have a celebratory drink,' Jenny suggested. She poured two vodkas and tonic and they settled comfortably in the glow of the final night of the Christmas tree.

'Here's to the future,' Jenny said. 'I hope you and Dan will have every happiness together.'

'Cheers Jenny! Thanks for bringing us together,' Mary replied.

'What are your plans now?' Jenny asked.

'In two weeks, I return to Peru with Father Ralph. Then I hope to come home mid-March for good to start planning the wedding.'

'You're not giving yourself much time,' Jenny remarked.

'We are only having our families since it's too soon after dad's death for anything elaborate,' Mary explained.

'Will you be wearing a traditional white gown?'

'Most definitely,' Mary replied. 'I'm having a figure hugging graceful lace dress with matching veil and a lace train. I just love old-world styles and a bit of romance,' Mary continued.

'Sounds divine,' Jenny remarked. 'Aunt Helen must be over the moon with excitement.'

'She's pretty chuffed,' Mary replied, 'and thrilled to have loads to do in the next few months. I can see her playing the mother of the bride to the fullest. Since she will only get one shot at it, I know she'll enjoy every minute of it.'

Jenny poured another drink. 'What colour bridesmaid dress do you have in mind, Mary?'

'I'm going to let you decide, Jenny. You can choose a colour you really like and have the gown designed in whatever style you wish. How's that?'

'It's very generous of you, Mary, and thank you for the vote of confidence. Has Dan decided on his best man?'

'Not yet, though I'm sure he has someone in mind,' Mary replied.

There was a pause. Mary took a sip of vodka, re-arranged the cushion behind her back and asked Jenny what her plans for the New Year were.

'I'm moving out of the apartment in ten days' time,' she told Mary. 'I want a place all on my own. Doctor Cain has a comfy modest little place behind his office. He told me I could have it.'

'Does Father Ralph know?'

'I told him last week and he was very understanding,' Jenny replied. 'I explained to him that I'd miss you when you go. Besides, I'm not sure about Colin's plans.'

'Have you heard from him?'

'Oh yeah, he's been in touch all right,' Jenny replied, 'but I don't ask questions any more. That family problem seems to have dragged on far too long.'

'Do I detect an air of disappointment in your voice?' Mary asked gently.

'You do. I thought we were close enough not to have secrets but Colin seems to have shut me out completely.'

'Have you found any comfort from Claude Stanhope?' Mary had her eyes riveted on a copy of the newspaper, carrying a large photograph of the pair of them at the ball.

'Claude has been wonderful,' she replied, 'and, yes, he has comforted me.'

'So has Colin a serious rival? I mean, if you had to choose, could you?'

'Things haven't reached that stage yet,' Jenny replied. 'I've gone out to dinner with Claude and met his parents, that's about it really.'

'Well, how did you get on with his parents?'

'Very well,' she replied. 'Nadine is very young at heart and Bill is sound. Don't read too much into the situation,' Jenny warned Mary. 'After all, American families tend to make one welcome at all times and especially at Christmas.'

Mary wasn't so sure. Colin might have to fight hard for Jenny yet.

Colin got the news he was waiting for mid-January. The paternity test proved that he was not the father of Jean Judd's child. Glen Judd scrutinised the result with disbelief written all over his face.

'How accurate are these tests anyway?' he asked gruffly.

'Ninety nine point nine per cent,' Colin replied. 'Now, if you'll excuse me, I have my life to get on with.' As he left, he could hear Glen Judd yelling something like, 'You haven't heard the last of this, Maloney.' But Colin knew the old buzzard was bluffing. 'Go and prey on someone else'. Colin replied angrily.

There was a flight to catch to New York and time was ticking away fast. He hurried home, gave his parents the news and headed for the airport. Vera and John saw him off with a tinge of sadness. It hadn't been the easiest few weeks for them but they were pleased that things had worked out for him.

'Give Jenny our love,' Vera called as he went through the departure gate.

It was still bleak and icy cold when he arrived in New York. He grabbed a limo and headed for 67 Lincoln Boulevard. Pip had just finished dusting and polishing his apartment. 'Happy New Year, Pip,' he said, giving her a peck on the cheek.

'Happy New Year to you, Colin, I'm glad you're back. Did you have a good time?'

'I did, thank you' he replied. 'How was your Christmas Pip?'

'Lonely and sad,' she replied. 'I missed you all, but Jenny was very kind to me.'

'Is she in her apartment?' Colin asked.

'Have you two had a falling out or something? You know Jenny doesn't live here anymore. She left about five days ago.'

'I didn't know,' he replied

'Is Mary in?' Colin asked, trying to hide his frustration.

'She's gone home to Boston and won't be coming back either.'

'Did Jenny leave a forwarding address or a telephone number?'

'I'm sorry, Colin. She promised to call me in a little while when she gets settled in to her new apartment.'

'Thanks, Pip.' Colin closed the apartment door and felt as if he had walked into a ghost house. He made himself some coffee and phoned his parents. He left a message on the answering machine saying he got back safely. He had to locate Jenny he simply must speak with her. Would Dan know where she was, he wondered?

He dialled the number. Dan answered immediately. He was on call at the hospital, he told Colin, and couldn't speak for long.

'I'm back in New York and anxious to locate Jenny,' Colin said.

'I think you and I had better have a little chat first,' Dan said. 'Would tomorrow lunchtime suit?'

'Is something wrong?' Colin asked nervously. 'Is it Stanhope?'

'Leave Claude out of it,' Dan answered curtly. 'Meet me at The Gem at one p.m.'

'I'll be there, Dan,' Colin replied, replacing the receiver.

The following day, Dan was already in The Gem when Colin arrived. They sat in a quiet corner and Colin ordered coffee for both of them. It was a bit early for something stronger, he supposed.

The pub was small and intimate and most of the clientele were huddled in small groups sipping and chatting.

'Had you a good Christmas?' Dan asked.

'Not really,' Colin replied. 'I had some personal problems to attend to that sort of got in the way of any real enjoyment. How about you, Dan?'

'Yes, Mary and Helen made Christmas very good for me and my family'. We all got on very well indeed. By the way, Colin, I saw you in Dublin on two occasions.'

Colin could feel the blood rushing to his face. 'I take it

you saw me in a certain hotel,' Colin said, truly embarrassed.

'My cousin runs it and I took Mary and Helen to dinner there on a few occasions,' Dan remarked.

'I can explain everything Dan. Honestly it's not what you think. There is no other woman. I love Jenny. Please don't jump to conclusions. I was a bit wild in L.A. and that woman tried to foist paternity on me for her son. I only went home to prove my innocence. I had to, Dan. I couldn't tell Jenny at the time but I intend to make a full confession when I see her.'

'You've hurt Jenny deeply' Dan said, and I for one, am not prepared to stand by and let that happen.' Can you prove categorically that there aren't more skeletons in the cupboard? 'I saw you delivering a giant Teddy Bear to a very beautiful woman, presumably for the baby. Does that suggest that you are not the father?' Dan's tone was caustic.

'I only did that on account of the child's grandmother who appreciated the trouble I had taken to prove I was not the father.'

Colin rummaged in his wallet and produced the evidence of the recent paternity test.

Dan Flynn examined the document. 'So you've proved you're not the father of this child,' he remarked, 'but who's to know what may happen in the future? When you say you were wild in L.A., what exactly did you get up to? On second thoughts, tell me to mind my own business and suffer the loss of Jenny.'

'I've told Jenny all about the wild life I led in California,' Colin replied. 'She knows everything about me except the recent allegation.'

'If you fooled around that much, are you sure you're okay

on the health front?' Dan asked.

'I'm okay Dan'. I did take precautions.

'So you won't object to me arranging some tests, just to be sure,' Dan suggested.

'Just say when' Colin replied, 'and I'll be there'. Now may I please have Jenny's address and telephone number?'

Dan gave them to him. 'I suggest you phone her before visiting,' he said 'She has taken on some new projects recently and may not be available.'

Colin went straight home after his meeting with Dan. He hadn't cancelled his newspaper before going to Ireland, and hoped Pip had put them in a press near the garden door. They had come to that arrangement when he first arrived. Sure enough, they were there. Every copy placed in chronological order on a shelf. Now he could read about the ball. On finding the copy dated December twenty-third, he leafed through it and found the photograph and write up. He studied the photo for a few moments. Jenny looked stunning in a green and gold gown that complimented her hair and perfect figure. Standing slightly behind her, was the man described by the diarist as the dashing Neurosurgeon Claude Stanhope.

Colin folded the photograph neatly down the centre, and with a pair of scissors cut Claude Stanhope out of the picture. He scrunched him into a little ball and threw him in the bin. 'Leave Claude Stanhope out of it,' Dan had said. 'With pleasure,' Colin added. He knew he was behaving badly but somehow he couldn't help himself.

He felt hungry but had forgotten to shop for groceries. 'Great,' he shouted, remembering his mother had packed

Christmas cake, plum pudding and lots of home made cookies. Painstakingly, he arranged the goodies on little dishes and brewed a mug of steaming hot coffee. He was about to tuck in when his bell rang. Grudgingly, he answered on the intercom.

'It's Ralph, may I come in for a few minutes, please?' He opened the door and extended his hand in a warm greeting.

'Pip told me you were back, Colin. I hope I'm not intruding.'

'On the contrary, you're most welcome, Father Ralph, have a seat. As you can see, I'm about to enjoy some of my mother's Christmas cooking. You're welcome to join me if you wish.'

'Gladly,' Father Ralph replied. 'I simply can't refuse such a tempting display.' He patted his stomach and vowed to lose the stone he had gained during the festival.

Colin brewed a mug of coffee for him and they ate in silence till the dishes were empty.

'Your mother sure is a lovely cook, God bless her. You must be missing Mary and Jenny now,' Father Ralph remarked.

'I am indeed Father Ralph. To tell the truth I'm in big trouble with Jenny'.

'I'm sure you kids can patch things up and start afresh for the New Year'

'It mightn't be so easy because I've messed things up big time,' Colin confessed, 'in fact if I were to tell you everything, Father, the hair would stand on your head.'

'I'm a priest, Colin. I'm used to hearing hair-raising stuff, so don't be too hard on yourself'. The just man fall seven times etc, etc. Have you spoken to Jenny recently?'

'It's been a little while, but I detected a coolness in her voice, not that I blame her. The so-called family problem that sent me scurrying back to Dublin before Christmas was in fact a paternity claim against me. Jenny doesn't know yet.'

'And are you the father?' Ralph asked.

'Thankfully I'm not, though I did lead a pretty loose life in L.A. but with precaution. Does this change whatever perception you had of me, Ralph?'

'I'm not sitting in judgement, Colin,' Ralph replied reassuringly. 'I take it you'd like to see Jenny and talk things through. I think it might be for the best.'

'You're so right Father' Colin replied glancing at his watch. 'Dan said she was busy but maybe I should phone her.'

'I'm going into town and I know where she is living. If you like, you can mention that I'm coming too.'

It was on account of Father Ralph coming that Jenny agreed to see him, Colin felt.

Jenny was cheerful and friendly when she greeted them in her new apartment.

'This is a surprise,' she said, leading the way to a cosy sitting room. Sage green and magnolia was the dominant colour of the doors and walls. It blended nicely with the furnishings, Colin observed. Jenny seemed content in her new abode.

'I can have an extra half hour in the mornings,' she joked when Ralph remarked on its proximity to work. 'On the other hand, there is no excuse for arriving late since I'm within walking distance of the office.'

'I'd love to stay and chat,' Ralph said, making an excuse that he had to meet someone back in his own apartment.

'Surely you have time for a coffee,' Jenny suggested.

'Save it till Thursday when I'll drop by to see you before

going to Peru,' he replied. 'Enjoy your evening!'

When Ralph left the atmosphere changed dramatically. Even the cosiness of the apartment suddenly dropped a few degrees in heat. Ice had started to build on the windowpanes closing out the grim view of the multi-storey grey apartment blocks.

'There's enough food in the casserole for both of us,' Jenny said politely. 'Are you hungry?'

'Not really,' he replied, 'but I'll have a little just to keep you company.' He watched her serve the steaming hot chicken dish and wished it were like old times again. But he knew it wasn't, and he was here to make a clean breast of things.

She placed an extra setting of cutlery on the small table and invited him to sit in.

Despite being dressed in his best gear and the shirt she bought him at Christmas, she made no comment whatsoever. In fact, there had been no eye contact since he arrived. She seemed to be deliberately concentrating on her meal just as if they were strangers.

'I've missed you,' he ventured, topping up the mineral water. 'Not a moment passed in the past few weeks that I didn't think about you, Jenny. How about you?'

'I gathered that from the number of phone calls,' Jenny replied. 'But what I have failed to understand is your reluctance to explain, either by letter or phone, your sudden departure to Dublin. Is that why you're here now?'

'Yes,' he replied. 'But before I tell you, I want you to know that I love you with all my heart. These past few weeks have been a pure nightmare.'

'That bad?' Jenny asked, looking at him curiously. For the

first time, she noticed the pained look on his face, and saw the strain of the problem on his furrowed brow. She felt sorry for him, realising that he had suffered greatly under the strain of it all. He was trying to make amends, even wearing her Christmas present in an effort to win her admiration.

'I can't go through with it, Jenny,' he said. 'It's too embarrassing; you'll have to talk to Dan. I'm sorry, really, really sorry.'

'I'd prefer to hear it from you, Colin. Would a glass of wine help you to relax?'

He walked over to the sofa and sat down, his head slumped to one side. Jenny poured two glasses of wine. She handed him one. He took a sip and remarked how good it tasted. She smiled gently and patted him on the shoulder.

'You're right, Jenny, it's up to me to tell you,' he said. 'Why should I act like a coward and hide behind Dan?'

'Indeed! Why should you?' Jenny held his hand encouragingly.

He then related the story from the moment his father made the phone call to him in Lincoln Boulevard to when he got the D.N.A. results. 'My parents were so upset that I suggested a paternity test, even though the baby was clearly not mine. And I was so sorry for that poor baby that I gave him a present of a Teddy Bear, mainly due to the ladylike way the baby's grandmother treated me.

Jenny was silent for a few moments, trying to come to terms with what she had just heard.

'Where are the Judds now?' she asked.

'Roaming the world, waving wads of dollars, and trying to inveigle a suitable male to be the father of the baby, while denying the child his natural father, I suspect,' Colin replied.

'It's horrible, really horrible, Colin. How could any human being do that to an innocent little baby, no matter what the colour of its father? You must be very traumatised.'

'Yes I am,' he replied. 'It was horrible being drawn into this, knowing I had nothing to do with it, and trying to convince everyone that I was telling the truth.'

'Are Vera and John okay?'

'Yeah, they're fine now, but it was a very different story when I arrived home before Christmas. My father gave me a rough time, but I suppose you can't blame him. He felt I had let him down badly.'

'Have you made any plans to get help after what's happened?'

'Like what?'

'Counselling, I suppose,' Jenny replied. 'After all, this whole business is bound to have affected your ego and might even impact on your studies.'

'I'm really shattered after the whole sad debacle, and I'm not sure how I can get my life back on track'. Colin sipped his wine and thought for a while. Maybe I should talk to an expert to help me get my self-esteem back again. I want to do well in college. I also want us to get back to where we were.'

'That may take some time, Colin. I moved out of Lincoln Boulevard to allow us both much-needed space.'

'But I keep telling you, Jenny, that I love you and I always will. I need you now. You are the one person who kept me going through all of this and it broke my heart to be so secretive. Please understand.'

'I do understand, Colin. But you must realise that I've been very hurt by all this. It can't be about you all the time, you know, you have to consider my feelings too.'

He looked at her with the surprised expression, of someone who had suddenly been brought to his senses. 'Am I that selfish in your eyes?' he asked.

'At the moment yes' she replied. I'm trying to tell you that I need my space right now Colin. It's the only way that I can deal with what's happened these past weeks. I need some time alone.

'How much time?'

'It's hard to say,' Jenny replied thoughtfully. 'Let's take it slowly for a while.'

CHAPTER ELEVEN

It turned out to be one of the coldest winters in decades in New York. Snowploughs and gritters worked round the clock to keep the streets and highways passable. Snow fell almost continuously and an icy wind added to the misery of commuting. Colin managed to travel into college most mornings with Mary Jo Shinner or Barbara Macy. Lectures were often mid-morning or early afternoon, which meant he spent lots of time in the library or the lab. He began to marvel at how well he had adjusted to college after only two sessions with a counsellor.

'Jenny was right,' he told Dan one Friday evening. 'If it weren't for her, I'd never have sought the advice of a counsellor and I'm glad I did.'

'How are things between you and Jenny?' Dan asked. 'I haven't seen her for a while.'

'Let's put it this way,' Colin replied 'I'm on probation for an indefinite period. Everything hinges on my performance at college and my progress with the counsellor.'

'Sounds like you're being whipped into line, Colin,' Dan quipped, ordering two pints of beer for them.

'It's just the place to dodge the elements,' Colin remarked in the cosiness of Sam's bar. 'Thanks for inviting me, Dan.'

'Our last meeting wasn't very cordial, as I remember,' Dan remarked. 'I didn't even offer you a bite of lunch, which is why I intend to make amends this time.'

'I deserved everything I got,' Colin replied 'I need straight-talking people around me since I've been a right maverick in the past.'

'How's college going?'

'Marvellous,' Colin replied. 'I'm pleased to say I'm no longer playing catch-up. The last semester proved very rewarding, even if I say so myself. How's Mary and how are the wedding plans coming along?'

'Great thanks'. As for the wedding plans, I can't do much till she comes home in March. But there is one thing you can do, Colin.'

'Buy you another pint of beer. It's my round.'

Dan wasn't a great pint drinker. 'If it's all the same with you, Colin, I'd prefer a Jameson with ice and a dash of soda. Listen, Colin, I'm getting married on the nineteenth of April and I'd like you to be my best man.'

'Whoopee!' Colin exclaimed. 'Nothing would give me greater pleasure. I'm deeply honoured. Thanks, Dan!'

'Have you ever performed the duty before?' Dan asked in a slightly slurred voice.

'No, I never had the opportunity and I promise to do a good job,' Colin replied, wondering if Dan would remember he asked him tomorrow.

'I'll tell you what I'll explain to you how to be best man for me. It's simple really. Don't forget the rings and get me to the church on time.'

'Couldn't be easier,' Colin replied. 'Now I think I had better get you home while we still can walk.'

'Is a fellow not permitted to go over the limit on his stag night?' Dan asked.

'Don't be ridiculous, Dan. Surely we can organise a proper

stag night in the coming weeks?'

'Everything in proportion,' Dan replied. 'So far as I'm concerned, tonight will do fine. Small wedding, small stag night, and that's the end of the matter. Now, order a cab and we'll both go back to my place.'

Colin didn't remember much after struggling to get Dan into bed. Even the black coffee Dan ordered was sitting on his locker the following morning.

'I'm glad Professor Manning gave me a free day,' Dan remarked while mixing a hair of the dog at the kitchen counter. 'How are you, Colin?'

'Absolutely fine, thank you,' Colin replied. 'Am I still your best man?'

'Yes sir,' Dan replied. 'Now smarten yourself up and I'll buy us some lunch.'

*

The winter months in the career of a social worker were very difficult. Hardship cases presented on a daily basis and the inclement weather didn't help. Requests for blankets, fuel and food greeted Jenny round every corner. The shelters were full to the door, as homeless people sought refuge from the blizzard that reigned relentlessly, day after day. Jenny and her colleagues were missing Father Ralph.

'No matter how dire the situation was, he invariably came up with some solution,' Doctor Cain told Jenny. 'In similar conditions, I've known him to open a church, fill it with waifs and strays and carry soup and bread to them.'

On that Monday evening in February, Jenny arrived home

tired, hungry and feeling totally inadequate. On her way, she had passed scantly clad beggars pleading with passers-by for a few cents. She had emptied her pockets to a woman with small children, only to discover, that all it amounted to was three dollars in total. She figured it wouldn't buy them fish and chips. Then where were they going to spend the night?

She decided to go back and offer them shelter. On her way out, she bumped into Doctor Cain. She explained her position to him.

'You can use the old recreation hall across the way,' he replied. 'I have a key.'

'What about heating and some blankets?' she asked.

'There is enough fuel in the tank for a week,' he replied 'I'll see what blankets I can rustle up from the emergency supplies at the hospital.'

In an hour, they filled the old hall and the mobile soup kitchen provided hot soup for everyone. Doctor Cain nominated a few of the more reliable ones to keep law and order, and in the event of a fracas, he was to be contacted immediately.

'That's the best we can do for now,' Doctor Cain remarked to Jenny as they prepared to call it a day.

'I'm relieved that they have a roof over their heads, in these conditions,' she replied. 'Thanks for your help, Doctor.'

Wearily, she made her way back to the apartment. She checked for messages. Nadine Stanhope topped the list, insisting it was urgent. They had become close in recent weeks. Jenny dialled the number.

'Are you okay?' Nadine asked. 'It's just that I've called several times and when I got no answer, I became concerned.'

'Doctor Cain and I have been looking after the homeless,' Jenny explained. 'They'd die from exposure if we didn't get them indoors.'

'I'll gather an army of my friends tomorrow and we'll give you a dig out,' Nadine said. 'I'm sure we all have clothes, blankets and food to spare. What time would suit to link up with you?'

'As early as possible, Nadine, say midday,' Jenny replied. True to her word, at midday the following day, Nadine and her band of loyal supporters drove their convoy of welcome supplies to the old recreation centre.

Jenny and her colleagues rowed in behind them, carrying the supplies into the centre.

The relieved expression on the faces of the hungry was evident, as soup and sandwiches were handed out. Nadine and her crew formed a little crèche, giving much-needed respite to worn-out mothers. The experience of changing pampers, and cradling little mites, who were too tiny and innocent to appreciate the harsh life facing them, was very rewarding. Late in the afternoon, the cavalcade pulled out to a rapturous round of applause by the homeless.

'We'll be back with more food tomorrow,' Nadine told a grateful Jenny and her colleagues.

'I'm very impressed,' Mary Jo remarked to Jenny after they left. 'Where did you meet Nadine?'

'She's Doctor Claude Stanhope's mother,' Jenny replied. 'I met her a few times during the festive season.'

'And what about Claude?' Mary Jo asked, wondering if he and Jenny were romantically involved.

'We're good friends,' Jenny replied. 'Matter of fact, he is

coming over to the women's group to give a lecture on their various health problems. He volunteered, when I explained, that I was concerned that some of them weren't keeping their appointments.

'There's nothing like a handsome doctor to spur their curiosity and I expect a full house,' Jenny said.

'And plenty of cleavage, I wouldn't be surprised,' Mary Jo added jocosely.

Later that evening, Jenny phoned Nadine to thank her for coming to the rescue.

'I'm delighted to be involved, Jenny, and so are all my friends,' Nadine replied cheerfully. 'I didn't realise what a tough job you social workers have until today. It will make some of us come down from our ivory towers, and get involved in relieving the everyday hardships that others have to endure.'

'We appreciate your help while the cold snap lasts,' Jenny replied. 'Indeed, any help to add a bit of cheer to the lives of the poor is always welcome.'

'Then what would you say if I were to start something recreational with them?' Nadine asked. 'I had intended to go back to art classes, but would love to teach a group some basic sketching and drawing, if you think it would help.'

'Most definitely,' Jenny replied. 'I'll look into it and get back to you, Nadine. We could even organise an exhibition later on. I'm sure that would be a great incentive.'

'It's rather ambitious, Jenny, but thanks for your vote of confidence,' Nadine said. 'But let's see how things work out.'

Bill wasn't so enthusiastic when Nadine told him of her plans. He pointed out that from the little he knew about such projects, while they started off well, they usually ended up a damp squib.

'You're putting a hex on me before I even start,' Nadine protested. 'I thought you'd be proud of me and encourage my efforts to do something constructive with my spare time.'

'Very well, give yourself a three-month trial period,' Bill said. 'I'll be waiting with bated breath to see how things work out.'

'That's fair enough,' Nadine replied, already fired with zeal and anxious to make a success of the venture. She was anxious too, for Jenny to spend more time with Claude.

On that score, she decided to throw a bash for his birthday. In the quiet of her Study, she drew up a list of guests including a number of young ladies whom she believed had a crush on Claude. 'This should set the cat among the pigeons,' she chuckled, hoping that Jenny would be the clear favourite. 'I need confirmation,' she told herself. 'How else am I ever going to find out what's happening?'

Claude's thirty-fourth birthday party was a great success. So far as Nadine was concerned it proved that Claude had eyes for Jenny only. He didn't seem to notice the beautiful competition, dressed in designer outfits, with expertly applied make-up vying for his affections. As one disappointed admirer of his remarked to her friend, 'I might just as well have arrived in my pyjamas and curlers, at least that way I might have got a sympathetic glance.'

But sympathy had no place in Nadine's formula. She pressed ahead with her art classes, when Jenny gave her the go-ahead. Bill looked askance at the easels, palates, brushes, rolls of paper and sketching pads ready for loading into the boot of her car.

'I presume you want a hand with this lot,' he remarked cynically.

'This lot, as you refer to it, will transform the lives of many,' Nadine retorted. 'And, yes, I would like a hand please. Oh! In case you need to contact me for one reason or another this morning, I'm using the pseudonym Henri.'

'What ever for?' Bill asked, trying to hide his amusement.

'Two reasons,' she replied. 'If the project ends up a damp squib as you seem to think it will, then I won't cause you any embarrassment. On the other hand, if I'm a success, they may liken my work to Henri Matisse.'

'Come here, my precious one,' Bill said, holding her in his arms. 'You know I love you and I wish you all the best. When you reach exhibition stage, Henri, be sure and let me have a sneak preview.'

Jenny was waiting to introduce her to the group when she arrived at the centre. 'I'd prefer if you call me Henri,' she remarked to Jenny. 'What with Claude giving them some lectures on health, I think it might be better if they don't identify me as his mother.'

'I totally agree,' Jenny replied, 'but don't be surprised if your son's name comes into the conversation. They have taken a shine to him after his first talk.' Jenny wished her luck advising her not to be too sensitive.

'I'm French and pretty broad minded,' Nadine replied with a smile.

Just as Jenny was about to continue on her duties, Claude drove up at the door of the centre. 'Give me two minutes,' he said. 'I have misplaced my Filofax and am hoping I left it here.'

'But you can't go in there, Claude, I'll check instead. Wait here.' Claude suddenly copped his mother's car and wondered what on earth was going on.

'Here you are,' Jenny said, handing him the Filofax.

'What's my mother doing in there?' he asked.

Jenny smiled. 'Obviously she hasn't told you about the art classes.'

'Art classes?' Claude repeated. 'Has she gone mad?'

'Nadine, aka Henri; is fine and has the undivided attention of her pupils. They didn't even bat an eyelid when I collected your Filofax.'

'Is this the same group that I lectured to?'

'Yes it is,' Jenny replied, 'hence the pseudonym Henri. Your mother thought it would be wiser to keep your relationship a secret.'

'That's about the only sensible thing I've heard so far,' Claude was not impressed by his mother's efforts. 'Nadine is acting strangely, Jenny, and I'm concerned.'

'Listen, Claude, you've got it all wrong. Your mother has found an outlet for her creativity. Those women will benefit from her talent, and she so wants to share it with them. Now what is wrong with that?'

'Meet me for dinner tonight and I'll tell you,' he replied.

'Gladly,' Jenny replied. 'I look forward to putting you right on a few matters. Shall we say eight o'clock?'

'Thanks, Jenny! You've made my day.'

*

Norah Leahy had a habit of phoning late at night. She told Jenny that she could never get her head around the time differences. 'It's ten thirty p.m. here,' she said. 'But it's the only time I get a chance to speak without my mother butting in on the conversation.'

'I take it she's tucked up in bed, Norah, and how is she anyway?'

'She's better than ever she was, I'm pleased to say,' Norah replied. 'All she talks about these days is my wedding.'

'And how is Luke?'

'A bit nervous, now that it's near our wedding day,' Norah replied. He pretends to be calm and collected but underneath that facade he's terrified I'll leave him standing at the altar.'

'You're an awful woman, Norah Leahy, and I'm glad I'm not near you right now.'

'Sure I'm only joking,' Norah replied. 'I love the guy to bits and can't wait to say 'I do.''

'Are you all set for the big day?'

That was the question that got Norah going. She talked non-stop for the next fifteen minutes about the wedding dress, her shoes, and going-away outfit. How she and Jenny's grandma had iced and decorated the wedding cake and photographed it. 'I'll send you a good chunk with the photographs,' Norah said.

'Is everyone else well?' Jenny asked when Norah finally stopped to catch her breath.

'They're all in top form, and looking forward to celebrating with me. Guess what, Jenny, I've invited Eleanor too, and she's coming.'

Claude phoned at seven thirty p.m. 'I may be a few minutes late, Jenny,' he said apologetically. 'One of my patients has reacted badly to his anaesthetic and I'm waiting for the anaesthetist to check him out.'

'Of course Claude I understand'. Take your time your patient is far more important.

Since they hadn't even discussed where they were dining, Jenny assumed Claude would let her decide. There was a cosy little place called Joel's where she always enjoyed herself. The food was good, the atmosphere brilliant and not too formal.

After some deliberation, she decided to wear her cream silk blouse and full-length cream skirt. This would be her third dinner date with Claude and time for serious talking. At eight fifteen, he arrived full of apologies.

'How's the patient?' Jenny asked.

'Much better" Claude replied, 'though I may have to check him out later tonight. The nurses know my cell phone number and will contact me if necessary.'

'We could cancel if you like,' Jenny was concerned.

Claude held her and kissed her cheek. 'I'm looking forward to dinner and to spending the evening with the most beautiful girl in the whole world. Now let's go.'

'Joel's please,' he told the cab driver, smiling knowingly at her.

'You're a mind reader,' she whispered. 'I'm so pleased.'

'And so am I,' Claude said gently squeezing her hand.

Joel's was buzzing with patrons enjoying candle lit supper. The waiter led them to their table and left them to browse the menu.

'Marvellous!' Jenny exclaimed, spotting coconut chicken on the menu while Claude was equally pleased to see dry spiced roast lamb. Claude recommended tangy lime sherbet to drink and Jenny was willing to sample it. 'Indian food is ideal in this very cold weather,' Claude remarked, tucking in. He particularly liked the combination of cloves, chillies, and almonds in the cooking of it and remarked to Jenny that the proportions were just right.

'I'll take you at your word. I'm no expert on Indian food,' Jenny confessed.

'Nadine loves doing Indian cooking and lamb is one of her specialties. I've watched her prepare and cook it, on a number of occasions, and I have developed a palate for it. However, tonight I'd much prefer to talk about Jenny Anderson.'

'I feared that sooner or later, we might get on to the subject of boring old me,' she remarked with a smile.

Claude shook his head in disbelief. 'How could a beautiful woman, whose photograph had graced all the newspapers a few weeks ago, consider herself boring? I want to know all about you, Jenny.'

'Very well,' she replied. 'You've asked for it, now, don't blame me if you find yourself nodding off.'

He listened with rapt attention, to the story of the girl from a rural background who grew up, on a large farm in Sliabh na mBan, County Tipperary. He heard how she and her brother Mattie were orphaned at a young age, when their parents were killed in a car crash. She told him about her grandmother, who had reared and educated them, and who recently retired and gave the reins to Mattie. Then there was the wonderful Mary Rafferty, her cousin, who got her the job as social worker and was now engaged to Dan Flynn.

'Let's move on to Colin Maloney. What's become of the astronomer?' he asked.

'We've decided to take a break for a while,' she replied. 'We've hit a rocky patch recently and both of us need some space to think things through'.

'Do you suppose he'd be upset if he were to find out about us?'

'I think it's healthy to have a social life,' she replied. 'Neither of us would begrudge a dinner date with a friend or colleague'.

'All very civilised I'm sure' Claude remarked except I'd prefer to take our relationship to a more serious level. What do you think Jenny?

'I'm enjoying things as they are Claude. I'm also very grateful for all the help you are giving to the women's group. Please bear along with me for now.

'Okay, if that's the way you want it, but remember I do love you Jenny.'

She smiled and nodded. 'Claude, I'm fragile and confused at the moment and it's not the time to make decisions. Please understand.

The conversation switched to his mother and her Art classes. 'She's out of her depth altogether with that group,' he told Jenny.

'Since I haven't spoken with her, I really don't know,' Jenny replied. 'But her support will be very beneficial to persons suffering with HIV/AIDS and other STD's. How did you find the group?'

'Like you said, Jenny, in regard to their appointments and their treatments, I'm afraid I'll have to spend an entire day with them.'

'But you don't have the time,' Jenny protested.

'I'm going to make time to impress on each one how important treatment and counselling is. I'll go through the Antiretrovirol Therapy with the AIDS sufferers.'

'I can give you a helping hand to get charts and things sorted. Since I know them a little better than you, I can point out the ones who need special guidance.

'Enough of shop talk for one evening,' Claude said. 'I've got a little gift for you.'

He fumbled in his pocket and produced a tiny box. 'Hope you like it.'

She undid the wrapping. 'It's beautiful,' she said, admiring the gold chain.

'Thank you so much, Claude. I'll wear it with pride.'

'It's my pleasure,' he replied as he was called back on duty.

CHAPTER TWELVE

It was now mid-February and the worst of the recent cold weather seemed to have passed. Already the harbingers of spring had shot up, with clumps of snowdrops and crocuses appearing in the parks and gardens. The birds too were in fine voice most mornings and there was a general air of expectancy about. Jenny rejoiced with her friend Clare on receiving her letter with news that she was pregnant. The baby was due in September, Clare said.

'I'd love you to be godmother, if at all possible,' she told Jenny.

'And I certainly will,' Jenny replied aloud, reaching for diary and writing paper at the same time. 'I'll even help you push,' she promised Clare jocosely in a letter promptly dispatched.

Her mind and thoughts turned to Knocknagow. She visualised the happiness the baby would bring to Clare and Johnny. Although it was early days, they were probably having fun decorating the nursery, and choosing names. She wondered if her grandma and Mattie were privy to this wonderful news. There was only one way to find out, she thought, dialling her home number. Norah Leahy answered the phone.

'You're lucky to have got me,' Norah said in a rather breathless voice. Jenny hadn't planned on speaking with Norah at all, since her wedding to Luke was in four days time, but she played along with Norah anyway.

'Lucky indeed, Norah, sure you must be run off your feet

with last minute arrangements,' Jenny replied. 'I hope you and Luke have a wonderful day on Saturday. I'll be thinking of you.'

'Thanks Jenny, sorry you can't be with us,' Norah replied. 'I'll send on some cake and photos.'

Before Jenny had time to reply, Norah handed the phone to Mattie. 'I'm off,' she said almost taking the door and its hinges with her.

'She has a very bad dose of pre-wedding nerves' Mattie told Jenny.

'I don't believe you. Sure Norah never gets flustered.'

'She's been racing between the cooker and the phone all week, and nearly set the house on fire in the process,' Mattie explained. 'I had to resort to the fire blanket on one occasion.'

'You're joking?

'Well, maybe a little,' he replied, 'but the food is definitely crunchier than before.'

'Trouble with you, Mattie Anderson, is that Norah Leahy has spoiled you all these years, and she is going to be a hard act to follow. Luke is one lucky fellow.'

Mattie hadn't heard that Johnny and Clare were expecting their first child, and promised not to tell anyone except his grandmother.

'How is grandma?' Jenny asked.

'She's down in the travel agents making arrangements to go to Rome,' Mattie replied. 'Immediately after Norah's wedding, she's off to visit Father Tim Lucey. He wants to show her the eternal city before he goes back to Peru.'

'I'm thrilled for her, in fact I'd love to be going with her,' Jenny said. 'Any other news?'

'Matter of fact there is,' he replied. 'Mary Rafferty has invited us to her wedding. The invites came in yesterday, and we're so looking forward to travelling to Boston in April.'

'This is good news, Mattie, since I'm just beginning to feel a small bit homesick.'

'Oh?'

'Well, with not being home for Christmas, I guess I missed everyone. You know, the first time being away from home ever at Christmas time was lonely. I can't wait to see you all again.'

'Hey, I'm coming over all weepy now,' Mattie replied. 'We missed you too, Jenny, really we did. But I suppose we thought that Colin and you would work something out together in New York. Did you?'

'Not really'. I'll tell you all about it in a letter. But promise me you won't tell a soul.'

'Hand on heart,' he replied. 'Are you okay?'

'Yes, I'm fine,' she replied.

Mattie strolled down the headland after the phone call. He would do so every day for the next week, waiting for that letter. He worried day and night about Jenny. She had always been so self-assured, giving him advice in so many different areas. Now it might be his turn to give advice and support. If so, he was more than ready and willing to help, even if it meant going to New York at the drop of a hat.

Strange, he thought, how we become complacent when things are going well. Having met Eleanor, taking over the running of the farm and being generally preoccupied with day-to-day living, he had forgotten that Jenny might have needs too. In the snug and secure life that Sliabh na mBan offered, it was not surprising that he had become selfish. She had chosen a different life, living amongst strangers and working in difficult circumstances.

He walked back quickly to the house when he heard his grandma drive in. She was juggling with an arm full of brochures and her car keys when he caught up.

'Jenny called while you were out,' Mattie announced casually.

'Sorry to have missed her,' she replied. 'How is she?'

'Fine, she just wanted to tell us that Clare and Johnny are expecting a baby.'

'Ah, that's wonderful,' she replied. 'Jenny must have been the first to be told.'

'It appears so,' Mattie said. 'We're to keep it a secret for the time being.'

Grandma nodded. 'No doubt I'll have a phone call from Alice Vaughan soon. She'll be eager to share the news of her first grandchild with me. Meantime, mum's the word.'

A week later, Jenny's letter arrived. Mattie hurried to his office and quickly read through the seven pages. He was furious when she told him that she had spent Christmas without Colin. What way was that bloody man treating his sister, he wondered. He phoned her straight away.

'I'm coming to New York just as soon as I can make arrangements,' he said in a voice that meant business.

'You don't have to do that, Mattie,' she replied. 'Listen, I didn't mean to upset you it was more a case of getting things off my chest. At the moment, I'm busy with different projects and with grandma gone to Rome you're needed at home. Thanks Mattie, now don't worry.'

Jenny never thought for a moment that her letter would spark this reaction.

'If you say so,' he replied, less than convinced.

She quickly changed the subject and enquired about Eleanor and how much she looked forward to meeting her.

'I'm bringing her to Boston for the wedding,' he told Jenny excitedly. 'She has never been to America and she's dying to see Boston given her interest in history. I know it will be a great treat for her.'

Jenny agreed. 'By the way, how is the new housekeeper getting on?' she asked.

'Sheila is doing fine and settling in well,' he replied. 'Norah made sure to train her to carry out her duties, in the same manner in which she had done them. Anyway, she loves it here and is getting along great with grandma. Listen Jenny, I hate to cut you short, but I have to go. Andy Sheehan has arrived to check the cattle. I'll write soon and I'm looking forward to April.'

'Me too,' Jenny replied. 'Thanks, Mattie, for your support and for offering to come over and please don't worry. I'm fine.'

Jenny realised how stupid she had been to write that letter to her brother in the first place. Mattie had absolutely no experience in teasing out problems of the heart. His own record in that department wasn't very impressive, and certainly didn't earn him agony aunt status.

What on earth possessed her to do such a thing she wondered? Self pity perhaps? Anyway, she vowed never ever again, to tell her problems to Mattie or any unqualified person for that matter.

The arrival of Sergio Emmanuel for his weekly chat about the Dominican way of life, cheered Jenny up no end. He looked so well these days, she thought, inviting him to share supper with her. He left his portfolio to one side and joined her at the table.

'Take a look,' he said, handing her a large white envelope.

Jenny smiled. She opened the invitation to Mary and Dan's wedding.

'Isn't that real sweet, Sergio? You must be delighted.'

'I am, Jenny. Look it, says "Sergio and friend".'

'Who are you going to bring along?'

Without the slightest hesitation, Sergio said he was bringing his mother.

'I can arrange for your father to come too,' Jenny told a delighted Sergio. 'I'll arrange accommodation for you in Boston, it will be a nice break for the three of you.'

'It's been so long since we had a holiday together, Jenny. I know my parents will be delighted,' Sergio remarked giving Jenny a big hug.

'How are you getting on with your research into Saint Dominic?' She asked.

'Some of it is very difficult, because the books I got in the library have very big words, and I don't understand some of them,' he replied.

'Look, I've set out some questions for you and I'd like you to try and answer them. After I've washed the supper dishes and tidied up, we can sit down and have a little discussion. I may be able to simplify things for you. Okay?'

He shook his head obediently and got down to business. While piling the dishes on a tray, she observed the diligent young man who had come through drug addiction, and was once again making a new start. He deserved every bit of help she could give him, and that's how it would be.

More than anything else, he wanted to prepare himself for a life with the Dominicans. Father Ralph Melville was his role model and he hoped one day to work with him. He spoke of little else every time he met Jenny. Later, when she examined his work it was clear that he needed to spend more time learning English. His handwriting was spidery, and certainly he needed to practice letter formation and pay attention to spelling.

'Would you like to go back to school, Sergio?' she asked. 'It will be just for a while, till you get the feel of the classroom and having a proper teacher. I can arrange everything for you.'

He stared at his work for a few moments, and a wry smile indicated he knew she was right. 'I'm not doing very well, it seems,' he replied, 'but one thing bothers me.'

'Which is?'

'How is my mother going to make out financially? She relies on the bit I earn from working at the rehabilitation centre, you know.'

'I'll have a chat with your parents tomorrow, to see if we can come to some sort of arrangement,' she replied. Jenny felt sure, there would be no difficulty with Victor and Angela Emmanuel agreeing with her suggestion. They had spoken often enough of the sacrifice their son made when times were hard.

Nadine Stanhope was showing visible signs of difficulties with her art classes. She confided in Jenny when they met for lunch on Monday 'They were not in the mood for art after the weekend cavorting in Hastings bar'. 'They speak about Claude as if he was some sort of Lothario instead of a very dedicated doctor. I feel so hurt at times,' Nadine explained, wishing she could defend her son.

'Maybe you should take a break,' Jenny suggested sympathetically. 'I know how difficult it can be trying to keep the momentum going, believe me, I do.'

'I don't want to give in yet,' Nadine replied. 'They were so enthusiastic at the beginning, and some of them actually showed real promise. I wonder if it's me?' Nadine asked stroking her chin.

'Of course, it's nothing to do with you, Nadine, it's just how they are,' Jenny explained hoping to cheer her up a little. 'Friday will probably be altogether different, and it might be a good idea to throw in a little perk,' Jenny suggested.

'Like what?' Nadine wondered.

'A visit to an art gallery and a light lunch afterwards,' Jenny knew she was probably being a little too ambitious, but it was all she could come up with.

'I'm not so sure,' Nadine replied. 'I agree I'll have to find some way of making the course more exciting, maybe a little retail therapy might be the solution.'

'And costly,' Jenny reminded her.

Then Nadine remembered that a close friend of hers was having a closing- down sale. 'I'll phone Jackie tonight to see if I can arrange an after-hours shopping spree for them. I'm sure she'll agree,' Nadine said confidently.

'Best of luck,' Jenny said, wondering why Nadine was going to such lengths, to make the project work.

Nadine knew she had her work cut out, when it came to presenting this wild bunch of women as mature students. She hoped her friend Jackie wouldn't ask any awkward questions.

'Everything going well with the art classes?' Bill Stanhope asked his wife when he noticed she was less bubbly than usual.

'Fine,' she replied philosophically. 'Matter of fact, I'm finding it both exciting and challenging, and I'm glad I started the project.' She dare not let Bill know just how difficult things were, and the measures she was taking to keep going. The last thing she needed to hear was 'I warned you'.

'Let me know when you are ready to exhibit and I'll arrange a venue,' Bill said, adding, 'I'll make sure it is well advertised.'

'Thanks, sweetheart, what would I do without you?' she asked, receiving a peck on the cheek. Suddenly she felt more confident.

On the Friday the group were in great form. They had everything set out when she arrived. She hadn't noticed Claude sitting in the small office drinking tea.

'Doctor Claude wants a word with you, Henri,' said one of the women pointing in his direction.

'Cup of tea?' The tea maker poured the tea and popped two cookies on a plate. 'Don't spend too much time with him or we might get jealous,' she quipped.

Nadine made sure not to let her guard drop. 'Good morning, Doctor Stanhope.'

Claude stood up and shook hands. 'Good morning, Henri, I have a favour to ask.'

Aware that the group had their antennae cocked, she gently closed the door behind her. 'Fire ahead, Claude,' she said.

'I am wondering if you could let me have the entire morning with the group, to sort out their charts and appointments? It would facilitate me greatly.

'I appreciate their health is more important than an art class' Nadine said. However, I would like just ten minutes to speak with them if that's okay?'

'That's fair enough,' he replied. 'I can make some notes till you're ready.'

She thanked him and invited him home for dinner and a chat. He gladly accepted and promised to come for seven thirty.

'Doctor Stanhope is spending the entire morning with you, which means we have to forego our art class,' Nadine announced, observing the gleeful expression on their faces. 'However, I had intended to have a little chat with you concerning a treat I have planned for you, so if you'll bear with me, I'll explain what it is. How does a little shopping spree grab you?' she asked.

Suddenly, there was an outburst of fancy dancing and displays of gratitude she had never encountered before.

'Calm down, ladies, or Doctor Stanhope will be wondering if we have taken leave of our senses. Let me explain the plan of action. On Monday night we will go to the shop. The owner has very kindly agreed to allow us in after regular shopping hours. I'm also planning an exhibition of our work at a later date.

'Henri, you're wonderful, we had no idea you had such faith in us,' Martha said, adopting the role of spokeswoman. The rest agreed wholeheartedly.

'Not a word to anyone please' Nadine said indicating to Claude that she had finished. She headed straight for Jackie's shop.

'This is a lovely surprise, Nadine, why don't we do lunch someplace nice?' Jackie was genuinely pleased to see her.

'I'm not exactly dressed for a posh restaurant,' Nadine replied. 'I was meant to be working with my art group this morning, but the doctor wanted to sort medical matters out with them.'

Jackie gave Nadine a strange look. 'I don't understand, have they all suddenly developed some virus or other?'

Nadine laughed nervously. 'Of course not,' she replied 'Look Jackie I'd like to talk to you about the group. Is it okay if I order a takeaway and maybe we could just eat here today?'

'It's fine by me,' Jackie replied, sensing Nadine's uneasiness. 'I'll make us some coffee. But remember that luncheon date still stands.'

Nadine sat on a straight back chair while Jackie opted for a stool. The small room was anything but conducive to a cosy chat. It was packed with piles of sweaters and jeans, empty cartons, and God knows what else. Jackie quickly cleared the table to make space for the takeaway and the coffee. 'I'll be glad to be out of this place,' she remarked, apologising for the state of the room. 'This closing down sale is doing my head in, but there is no way I could keep things going, now that Josh has passed on. Although he left me very comfortable, bless him, I'll soon be sixty and more than ready to put my feet up.'

'Good for you,' Nadine replied. 'If it weren't for my art classes, I'd be stuck in the kitchen concocting new dishes for Bill and his friends, who seem to have insatiable appetites.'

'So are you enjoying the easel and brush again?' Jackie asked, unwrapping the food.

Nadine hesitated before answering. 'That looks good,' she said, referring to the French bread with cottage cheese and a side salad. She took a bite of bread, playing for time and trying to fathom out the best angle to approach the story of her art pupils. Finally she plucked up the courage to begin. 'The truth is, Jackie, I'm helping a social worker friend to help in the rehabilitation of a group of women, who have been very traumatised by their experiences in life.'

'You mean you're working with prostitutes?' Jackie was direct.

'Prostitutes, AIDS sufferers, reformed drug addicts. Some of them have horrifying stories of being abused and battered, the list is endless,' Nadine replied

'But you have no special skills, Nadine, how do you cope?'

'We have good days and not so good ones,' she replied. 'They find it hard to concentrate all the time, which is why I have to offer the odd carrot.'

'Like a shopping spree,' Jackie said with a chuckle.

Nadine nodded. 'They're ever so excited Jackie, and I do hope you won't find them too boisterous. Most of them never had a treat like this.'

'Then I only hope they'll strip the rails naked on Monday night,' Jackie said compassionately. 'I intended giving everything left over to charity, so you're doing me a huge favour.'

'I'm really grateful to you Jackie for making everything so easy. They are a wonderful bunch and deserve a few breaks in life.

'I'm proud of you Nadine and remember that lunch date still stands'.

'Till Monday then and thanks for everything,' Nadine said.

Later that evening, as Nadine prepared supper for Bill and Claude, her thoughts strayed to Jackie and the closing down sale. 'I only hope they will strip the rails naked,' she said and Nadine smiled as she visualised the women, scrambling like bees around a honey pot to find the most risqué garments on offer.

'Something smells delicious,' Bill said, arriving home after a long day negotiating one business deal after another. 'Who's the third place setting for?'

'Claude,' she replied hopefully. Her son wasn't the most reliable guest, and often phoned at the last minute, when he was needed at the hospital. Just then, she heard him turning the key in the door and was grateful he made it on time.

'Let me guess' Claude said sniffing the gorgeous aromas. 'It's salmon parcels, new potatoes and cauliflower with cheese sauce.'

'You're almost right,' Nadine replied, urging him to be seated, since she would be serving pronto. She liked to get this dish to the table at the precise time, to ensure, that the flavour and texture of the salmon was just perfect. They ate in silence since the food was so good and appetites sharp. Conversation could hold till every morsel including dessert was consumed.

Later, sipping coffee in front of a great log fire, Nadine broached the subject of Claude's love life. He was enjoying the atmosphere of the glowing timber reflecting on the ceiling, when his mother started the inquisition. Bill, sensing what was coming, poured himself a stiff drink in the hope that it would induce deep narcosis.

'How are things progressing between you and Jenny?' Nadine asked, placing a great log on the fire and curling up in the chair in anticipation.

'We're still good friends,' Claude replied, finishing his coffee. 'To be honest, mother, that is as far as the relationship between Jenny and I will go.'

'You can't mean that, Claude. I have never known a couple more suited. It's obvious you're not showing Jenny that you mean business.

'Isn't that right, Bill?'

Bill glanced at his wife. Why did she insist on running her son's love life, he wondered? He took a sip of his brandy and prepared to nail this conversation for once and for all. 'Look, Nadine, as I understand from what Claude has just said, there is no real romance between himself and Jenny. Am I right Claude?'

'Sadly, that is the case, father,' he replied. 'I love her with all my heart but I know she doesn't feel the same about me.'

'That's just it, you can't make someone love you,' his father said. 'Besides if the chemistry is not right between you, it just won't work.'

'So the relationship has been a complete waste of time,' Nadine sounded sour and resentful, and simply didn't relish the truth.

'Mother, I know you have put a great deal of work into trying to bring us together. Sorry it hasn't worked out the way you would have wished it to, but for me, it has been anything but a waste of time,' Claude said emphatically.

'If it weren't for Jenny, our lives would be much different. Think of the pleasure your art classes are giving those women, as for me, it has opened my eyes to a world I preferred to ignore. In fact, I'm seriously thinking of turning my attention to the treatment of AIDS sufferers. When I have finished my stint with Professor Manning, I intend doing more research into this area.' He said.

'But I thought you were going to specialise in brain surgery,' Bill said failing to understand why his son would give up a promising future as a neurosurgeon, to look after people suffering from AIDS.

'Does Professor Manning know about your plans?'

'Frankly no,' Claude replied. 'I haven't told him yet, because I have only just made my mind up. But I'm sure he will give me his blessing.'

Bill finished his drink and stared into the glowing embers. Suddenly, his only child was like a stranger. He knew very little about what made him tick. When he thought about it, he had never got to know him in a father and son way. They hadn't done things together, or shared any precious moments. His visits home were few enough and never seemed to be fun occasions. It was time to make a few changes, Bill thought.

'What are you doing tomorrow, Claude?'

'It's my day off,' he replied, 'and I haven't made any plans. Why do you ask, father?'

'I would like us to spend the day together, doing something that would please you, that's of course, if your mother has made no plans.'

Saturday for Nadine usually meant going to the hairdresser, doing a spot of shopping and having lunch with a friend.

'I'll spend the day as I usually do,' she told them. You two go on a mystery tour and come home to a nice supper and tell me all about it.'

*

Dan phoned Jenny at midday on Saturday and invited her to his house for lunch.

'I'd be delighted. In fact, I was only thinking about you yesterday, and wondering how the wedding plans are coming along,' Jenny said.

'That's exactly what I want to discuss with you. It's only two weeks till Mary gets home,' he reminded her. 'Would one thirty p.m. suit?'

'Perfect,' she replied, 'see you then.'

How time was flying, Jenny thought, as she scrambled around the apartment doing a bit of tidying up on Saturday morning. She had successfully managed to get Sergio Emmanuel back to school, and Social Services were providing some extra money for Angela and Victor. Her Aunt Helen was thrilled to hear that Mary had invited them to the wedding. She told Jenny that she would book them into a family run hotel near the centre of town. Everything was falling into place nicely Jenny thought.

There were many changes ahead with the news that Father Ralph was considering selling 67 Lincoln Boulevard. The present group of social workers were moving on either to get married or live nearer to their work.

The other bit of exciting news from Mary was that Ralph would be made a bishop in a year's time. He's so young, Jenny thought, remembering the few bishops she knew in Ireland who were always older men. She looked forward to seeing him soon at the wedding and hoped to have a long chat.

Dan greeted her with a big hug and ushered her into his cosy sitting room. 'Make yourself comfortable, Jenny, and let me get you something to warm you up. That wind would shave a monkey,' he continued.

'It's great to see you, Dan,' she said and she meant it. He handed her a medium dry sherry and poured one for himself. 'Lunch will be ready in about fifteen minutes, hope you're not too hungry.'

'I'll survive for fifteen minutes, just about,' she replied humorously. 'How are the wedding plans coming along?'

'Everything is progressing nicely,' Dan replied. 'All forty guests who have been invited are coming, and Helen has arranged the church, the flowers, and a singer with the most amazing soprano voice imaginable. Mary and I decided on the hymns when I visited her in Peru.'

'Oh Dan! I'm delighted for both of you, and your family. Have you seen Aunt Helen recently?'

'I was in Boston two weeks ago and we speak regularly on the phone,' he replied. 'She wants us all to go up next weekend. That's why I've invited you and Colin for lunch today.'

'Colin is coming here today?' Jenny suddenly felt uneasy since she hadn't seen Colin for a month.

'Yeah, I thought it was high time to have an informal chat with my best man and bridesmaid. Everything okay between you?'

'Of course it is,' she replied, not wanting to spoil Dan's plans. 'I'm beginning to miss Colin, and today is the perfect time to catch up, and see what he's been up to.'

'That'll be him now,' Dan said, responding to the very loud ding-dong that was part of this old house.

Jenny quickly quaffed the remainder of her sherry, and glanced in the large mirror over the fireplace. The sherry had given her cheeks a pink glow almost like a blush. Unceremoniously, she found herself in Colin's arms while Dan made himself scarce in the kitchen.

'It's great to see you again, Jenny,' Colin whispered, still holding her close.

She didn't reply for a few moments, trying desperately to muffle sobs of emotion.

'Are you okay, Colin?' she asked, tears trickling down her cheeks.

'Never better,' he replied, dabbing away her tears with his handkerchief. 'This is the moment I've longed for since I last saw you. Am I forgiven?'

She kissed him tenderly trying to make everything right between them again. They sat down quietly on Dan's sofa gently holding hands. Standing in the doorway, Dan shook his head wistfully and announced that lunch was ready, glad to see them happy again.

*

Bill Stanhope was very quiet in himself all day Sunday. Nadine wondered if he was coming down with flu, and suggested he go to bed early. She had looked forward to snuggling up in front of the fire with a book, but the sight of her husband looking pale and worried meant she couldn't concentrate.

'I'm just having a down day,' he insisted when she repeatedly asked him if he was okay.

'Is it something Claude said or did that is bothering you?' Nadine asked, fed up with the silent treatment.

Bill finally broke his silence. 'Nadine, you're not going to like what I have to tell you. In fact, I've been putting this moment off all day.'

'Maybe when you share it with me, it won't appear so bad,' she replied, feeling her tummy fill with butterflies.

'Claude is going abroad indefinitely. He plans on going to Africa, Asia and Europe to research HIV/AIDS and he's going quite soon.' Bill sighed heavily when he finished speaking. 'I tried to persuade him not to go but he was having none of it. He's all fired up about trying to make his mark for the greater good.'

Nadine stood up and walked across to her husband. 'Honestly, Bill, we should be proud of him for taking such a stand,' she said. 'Let's do all we can to support him. After all, he's the one that is about to make sacrifices. Does Jenny know?'

'It wouldn't make a scrap of difference,' Bill replied. 'Claude knows his relationship with Jenny will never amount to anything, neither would his going away make any difference, though he did say she would always be close to his heart where ever he goes.'

'Still, I think she should know,' Nadine said.

Jackie threw her shop open to Nadine and her art group on Monday night. Within the space of an hour, they had gutted the place. Not a single item of clothing remained, and every shopping bag bearing the name 'Jackie's' was jam-packed with clothes. Martha, the spokes-woman for the group, presented Jackie with a huge bunch of flowers and some handmade chocolates.

'We are all grateful for your kindness, Jackie,' she said. 'As you can see, we are a pretty motley crew, who won't even recognise ourselves, once we get dressed up in this lovely gear.'

'You'll knock them dead when you go clubbing in those outfits,' Jackie assured them.

Nadine helped the girls load their treasures onto the bus. They waved happily and sped off into the night.

Jackie sat on a stool and looked around her bare shop. 'You've done me a big favour Nadine,' she remarked. 'I had no idea that closing down would be so simple in the end.'

'What do you intend doing with the shop - sell or rent?'

'Sell, I suppose, if I get a good offer,' Jackie replied.

Nadine surveyed the empty premises and noted it was much more spacious than she imagined. 'I'd like to buy this place and use it as an art shop,' she remarked to a very surprised Jackie.

'Just like that,' Jackie replied, hardly able to believe her luck. 'First you help me to get rid of the stock and now you want to buy the place. This calls for a good luck drink.'

She produced a bottle of sherry with just about enough left in it for two drinks.

'I always kept a drop handy for brides who came in to buy their going-away outfits,' Jackie explained.

'Nice idea,' Nadine said as they clinked their glasses and wished each other good luck in the future.

They agreed a price, and Nadine promised to get back to her as soon as she had spoken to Bill, and got his blessing. She was sure there wouldn't be a problem. After all, he had promised to get her a place to exhibit her work when she was ready. Jackie was over the moon that her close friend was about to take over the shop.

'I can pop in from time to time for a chat. Who knows if business is thriving, you might even need a sales assistant in the future,' Jackie remarked jocosely.

Nadine phoned Jenny when she got home. 'I'd like to meet for coffee tomorrow if possible, there's a few things I think you should know.'

'I have a very tight schedule as it happens,' Jenny replied, 'but I could squeeze in a brief meeting at lunchtime.' Nadine had been so kind that she didn't like to disappoint her.

Tuesday was one of the most hectic days of the week. Jenny scurried back from the courts to find Nadine sitting in the little cafe near the rehabilitation centre.

'Sorry I'm late,' Jenny said, slipping her coat off, aware that she looked a right mess in comparison to the elegant Nadine. How did she always manage to look as if she had stepped out of a beauty parlour? Sleek short cropped hair, perfect complexion and dressed in a neat full-length black coat that made her look taller, than her five feet four inches.

'Hope I'm not running you into the ground, Jenny, but I was dying to see you.'

'Me too,' Jenny replied, wishing she had more time. Ricky

the waiter brought the coffees and salad sandwiches that Nadine had ordered.

'Hope these are okay, Jenny, I know you're pushed for time.'

'They're perfect, thanks,' Jenny said, tucking in. 'What news have you for me, Nadine?'

'Claude is going abroad indefinitely to research HIV/AIDS. I'm not sure how soon but he plans to visit Africa and Europe and gather all the data he can.'

'When did he decide to do this?' Jenny asked. 'I mean, he never mentioned it, not even this morning when I spoke to him.'

'He seems to have made his mind up over the weekend, but I dare say he has been thinking about moving for a little while,' Nadine replied. 'By the way, what is the relationship between you and Claude?'

'We've become close friends these past few months, ever since I won the Tipperary Person Of The Year. He is the most charming and caring man and this proves it.. As you know, Nadine, the group of women that he is helping at the moment think the world of him. They will be devastated when he tells them.'

'What about you, Jenny? I mean, you're the only person who could make him change his mind.'

'Even if I wanted to, Nadine, I wouldn't do that,' Jenny replied. 'Claude knows how I feel, and he has always shown great sensitivity. I know he cares deeply for me, he told me so, but my affections are elsewhere. Sorry, Nadine.'

'I'm sorry too, Jenny, because the one thing in the world I would have wished for, was for you and Claude to have fallen in love and married.' Tears flowed from her beautiful brown eyes, as she made Jenny promise, never to mention what had passed between them to a soul.

Drying her eyes, she said, 'Before you go, I'd like to say that I certainly will continue art classes, and I have just bought a new place that I intend turning into an art shop. You must come and visit it soon Jenny'.

'Congratulations, Nadine, this is wonderful news. I wish you all the luck in the world.'

Jenny got through her afternoon's workload with a heavier heart than usual. Twice, Mary Jo urged her to cheer up. 'I've never seen you so downcast, Jenny,' she remarked. 'What's the matter?'

'Claude Stanhope is leaving for Africa shortly, his mother told me today. This is a sad day for me, and the group of women he has been helping. You have no idea how much we will miss him.'

'I think I do,' Mary Jo replied. 'Word has got around that he has changed their outlook and given them hope when things seemed hopeless. '

Nadine knew Claude was serious about going away, when she found him clearing out his room and doing stocktaking. He hadn't used the room much in the past few years, since he lived in the doctor's quarters at Saint Mary's. Sitting on the edge of the bed, he browsed through old photos of his college days and family holidays in Paris. He studied the family holiday photos for some time, occasionally smiling to himself, when he remembered something special about the occasion.

'Those were happy times, mother,' he remarked. 'I'll always treasure my childhood days with my grandparents in Paris.' He wrapped the photos carefully and placed them in a suitcase with gifts given him by his grandparents. A toy aeroplane, a replica of the Eiffel Tower and some pictures painted by an African street artist in the Latin Quarter meant a lot to him.

'I've made up my mind to visit my grandparents before I go to Africa,' Claude told his mother. 'I fancy spending a short time in Paris just to say goodbye.'

'I'll come with you Claude it's time I visited them myself. We might persuade your father to come along too.'

It didn't take much persuading for Bill to agree to visit Paris. He had always loved the place, and jumped at the idea. However, when Nadine told him she had bought a shop, it was a different story.

'You're putting the cart before the horse, Nadine,' he said in tones that were anything but dulcet. 'What are you going to stock this place with? I know I said I'd find you a place to exhibit your work, but I never intended to buy a shop for you.'

'But this place is a real bargain, you'll agree when you see it,' she said, undeterred by Bill's anger. 'Will you and Claude come and look at the place tonight?'

'There is no harm in looking, Nadine, but I can't promise anything,' he replied. 'I suppose I should be grateful it's not the Empire State Building that you are bidding for.'

Bill hummed and hawed and scratched his head as he surveyed the shop. He saw many faults with the property. It would need to be rewired and plastered and what about those window frames? 'In my opinion, this whole building needs to be revamped. It's no wonder the previous owner wants out,' he continued.

When Nadine told him the asking price, it was clear that

the owner was in a hurry to sell. 'How did you come by this property?' Bill asked.

'Jackie is an old friend who ran a clothes shop here. Her husband died a while ago and she was finding things tough and decided to call it a day.'

How many old friends did Nadine have, Bill wondered. 'I'd like to meet Jackie,' he said. 'Although the price is reasonable enough, I may be able to negotiate an even better deal. What with so many things needing replacing and repairs, it might be worth haggling for three thousand dollars less. What do you say, Claude?'

'You're the businessman, dad,' he replied. 'I have no experience in this area, though I have to say it looks ideal for what mother has in mind.'

Claude threw in a few suggestions and advised his mother to buy some paintings from artists on The Left Bank in Paris. 'I'll go with you when we get there,' he said.

'For God's sake, stop filling her head with more ideas,' Bill said. 'Between the two of you I'll end up with no trousers.'

'Now there's something to ponder on,' Claude said. 'Surely we can drape you in mother's art work and leave you to do the advertising on the pavement outside?'

'Very funny,' Bill replied. 'I knew all along that I'd probably come in handy somewhere in the equation.'

Bill met Jackie two days later. When he heard how kind she had been to Nadine's group, he threw his bargaining hat away and agreed on the original asking price. They shook hands on the deal when everything became legal and Nadine was happy to be the new owner. It was the easiest transaction Bill had executed in a long time.

'While we are in Paris, I'll have the workmen in to do the renovations,' he told a delighted Nadine.

'I'll make you the proudest husband and business in the whole of Manhattan yet,' she said, sealing the promise with a kiss.

'I'm that as it is, Nadine,' he replied.

CHAPTER THIRTEEN

Helen Rafferty was in tiptop form when Dan, Colin and Jenny arrived in Boston to discuss the wedding plans. 'It's great to see you guys,' she said warmly, embracing them 'Now I really feel everything is falling into place for the wedding.'

'You must be run off your feet, Aunt Helen,' Jenny remarked.

'It's been hectic,' Helen remarked, 'but most enjoyable, I have to say, and everyone is just as excited as I am. That's the beauty of living in a place all your life, everyone rejoices with you and it puts an extra spring in your step. Any luck with the house hunting, Dan?'

'Helen, you won't believe my good fortune,' he replied, anxious to tell her all about his Dublin uncle, Peter O'Brien, who had lived in New York for years.

'He's on my mother's side,' Dan explained, 'and prefers to keep to himself. By all accounts, uncle Peter's an odd bod who writes thrillers and poetry, and likes to travel. Anyway, to make a long story short, he wants Mary and I to have his house, or so my mother told me on the phone last night.'

'That's wonderful news, Dan. When are you meeting him?'

'He'll be back in New York next week and I hope to meet him then. Keep your fingers crossed, Helen. Uncle Peter is a bachelor and I imagine the house will need the once-over big time. Still, it will be up to Mary ultimately as to whether she would like to live in it or not.'

'I'm so happy for you both,' Helen said. 'It's a very

generous gift and a great start to your marriage. I just know everything will work out.'

Colin and Jenny, who had given Basil a hand in the kitchen, announced that dinner was ready. On a chilly March night, what could be nicer than Irish stew and apple pie and custard for dessert? Helen had a great knack of making everyone feel at home.

Normally, after dinner when the kitchen table was cleared, a game of poker was played when Jack was alive. Not tonight. Instead, Colin and Dan were left to discuss groom and best man stuff over a pint of Guinness while Helen and Jenny retired to the sitting room, to catch up on all the latest gossip and fill Jenny in on her progress with her daughter's wedding.

'I'll bring you to the little private chapel tomorrow,' Helen said. 'It's attached to the convent where Mary went to school. I thought it would be ideal since it's a small wedding group and Sister Bernadine, who is an expert at flower arranging, offered to do them for me. Given that it will be Easter, Mary plans to adorn the chapel with lilies.'

'That sounds lovely, Aunt Helen,' Jenny closed her eyes, visualising the little chapel and Mary entering to the strains of 'Here Comes The Bride.'

Then a thought suddenly struck her. Who would give Mary away? Helen seemed to read her mind.

'Things would have been so different if Jack had lived,' she remarked wistfully. 'We would have invited hundreds of guests and the service would have taken place in our parish church. Jack always said that Mary's wedding day would be a reunion of Boston and Tipperary relations and he wouldn't care if it lasted for a week,' Helen's voice cracked with emotion and tears trickled down her cheeks. Jenny placed a consoling arm around her aunt.

'Don't upset yourself, Helen. It's understandable that Jack's memory will dominate the occasion, but you must be brave for Mary.'

'And I shall, Jenny,' Helen replied 'It's just that it's difficult at times when I think of how proud he would have been to see his only child marry a man like Dan. My brother Anthony is giving her away you know,' Helen announced.

'That's marvellous news. I wondered who was doing the honours,' Jenny replied.

Helen leafed through the bridal catalogue. 'There it is,' she said, pointing to a very elegant lace gown. 'The bridal boutique downtown is storing it for her.'

Jenny gazed at the stunning gown that would look a million dollars on her cousin.

'What do you think, Jenny?'

'I'm totally bowled over,' Jenny replied. 'It's magic. She'll be like someone straight from the pages of a fairytale. Oh! It's all so exciting. I feel great at the prospects of being her bridesmaid.'

Jenny took a sample of the material from her bag and showed it to Helen. She was very impressed with her choice of sage green silk. 'Mary left the choice and design to me and I hope she'll like it,' Jenny said.

'A wedding should have a little surprise element to it,' Helen said. 'I'm prepared to wait till the actual day to see your gown and I have no doubt it will be lovely.'

She handed Jenny a pile of old photographs. 'I'd like you to look through those for me I'm in the process of compiling a sort of montage of memories for Mary. Meantime, I had better check on the men folk.'

Colin and Dan had gone through their list and decided to call it a day. 'We'll let you run your eye over it tomorrow, Helen,' Dan said as he and Colin prepared to go to Massachusetts General Hospital to say 'hello' to some of Dan's colleagues. 'We won't be too long,' he said, 'just a few beers and a chat for old time sake.'

'No reason why you and I shouldn't have a glass of port,' Helen said to Jenny when they left. 'We probably won't get many moments to ourselves over the weekend,' she continued. Helen was anxious to hear how Colin and Jenny were getting along, and if they had any long term plans to follow in Mary and Dan's footsteps.

'Things have been difficult since Christmas,' Jenny told a surprised Helen. Jenny dwelt for a few moments on a photograph of Mary riding Flan on holidays in Sliabh na mBan.

'That is definitely one for your collection, Aunt Helen,' she remarked in the hope that her Aunt would get sidetracked. Helen agreed and smiled lovingly at her then fifteen-year-old daughter who looked so happy.

'Had Claude Stanhope anything to do with it?' Helen asked, her mind very much on the topic of conversation.

'Certainly not,' Jenny replied. 'If anything, he was the one person who helped me through this crisis and I owe him a debt of gratitude, I may say.'

'Crisis, what crisis?' Helen asked. 'I seem to be totally out of touch with things. Why didn't you call me, Jenny?'

'Because I didn't want to upset you, Aunt Helen' she

replied. Besides it was a rather delicate problem which thankfully has been resolved.'

'Do you wish to tell me more?' Helen asked gently.

'Colin was pursued by a young woman from California who claimed he was the father of her child, but a DNA test proved he was not. It put a great strain on our relationship, as you can imagine.'

'You must really love him,' Helen remarked. 'There are few who would have been so forgiving under those circumstances, but I'm pleased everything is going well now. I'm also delighted that you are both playing such an important role in Dan and Mary's wedding. I'm really very excited, Jenny, and I'm so looking forward to Mary's homecoming.'

'And so am I,' Jenny said. 'She has been like a sister to me and I miss her so much. It will be nice to have her back in New York.'

'By the way, how is Claude Stanhope?'

'He's gone to Africa,' Jenny replied. 'Yeah, he left a few days ago to work with and research AIDS victims.'

'That's surprising news, I had no idea,' Helen remarked.

'It was a snap decision, really, he took everyone by surprise, including his parents,' Jenny said. 'His mother even asked me to try and dissuade him from going, saying that I was the only person whom he might respond to.'

'And?'

'I choose not to, Aunt Helen, because he had done voluntary work with a group of women that I too work with, with phenomenal success. He seemed cut out to work in that field.'

'It's a tough call,' Helen replied. Still she couldn't help

feeling that Claude Stanhope left for Africa nursing a broken heart. She knew how taken he was with Jenny and wondered if Colin really appreciated how lucky he was.

On Saturday afternoon, Helen, Jenny, Dan and Colin visited the little convent chapel. Dan had his first glimpse of where he and Mary would wed. He surveyed with great interest the chapel that was part of Mary's old Alma Mater. From the ornate ceiling with the Ascension of Christ as its centrepiece, to the simple altar adorned with flowers and shining brass candlesticks, it pleased him totally. A ray of sunshine through the stained glass windows formed a rainbow of colour on the cream walls. The clinical smell of beeswax and incense, so typical of convent chapels.

Presently, Sister Bernadine, accompanied by Sister Angela, made their appearance from behind the altar. Recognising Helen, they hotfooted it down the isle to greet her.

'Which of you gentlemen is Dan?' Sister Bernadine asked before Helen got a chance to properly introduce them. He extended his hand, telling her how pleased he was to meet Mary's former teacher.

'I've heard so much about you, Dan. It's only recently I was told that you had worked at Massachusetts General. It's a fine hospital, as well we know,' she said.

The sisters were delighted to meet Jenny and Colin too and insisted that Helen bring them into the parlour for afternoon tea.

'We only called to see the chapel,' Helen replied politely. 'We couldn't possibly intrude like this on a Saturday afternoon.'

'Nonsense,' Sister Bernadine said. 'Please come, it will liven the afternoon up considerably.'

In the parlour, the Sisters fussed about them and chatted mainly about Mary. 'She was terrific at sports, especially net ball,' Sister Angela said. 'A good all rounder' was how Sister Bernadine described Mary, tapping on the service hatch. As if by a miracle, a batch of freshly baked scones arrived neatly arranged on a doyley. Angela poured the tea and Bernadine told Dan how much she was looking forward to the wedding.

'We'll wear our habits to the ceremony then it's into mufti for the hotel. We both love to dance,' she declared, with a glint in her eye.

'You'll save one for me, Sister Bernadine,' Dan teased noticing a slight blush on poor Sister Angela's face.

On hearing that Colin was an astronomer and Jenny a social worker, Bernadine nodded in the direction of Sister Angela. 'To think we were honoured when the bishop called last week for lunch. Wait till I tell him that, in one swoop, we had a surgeon, an astronomer and a social worker, he'll be knocked into a cocked mitre.'

Everyone laughed heartily at her remark. Sister Bernadine was a riot, Dan thought, and he quite looked forward to meeting her at the wedding. Helen and Jenny offered a helping hand with clearing the table but were soon told that 'aside from evening prayer, we have nothing else to do. Sure, Sister Angela and I have had a very entertaining afternoon,' Bernadine said.

'Judging by those beautiful scones, I think I should have engaged the convent kitchen staff to look after the catering for the wedding,' Helen remarked, to the very chuffed Sisters Bernadine and Angela.

Sunday passed quickly. After attending Mass, the party paid a visit to Jack's grave and prayed silently for a few moments. Helen placed a fresh wreath of flowers, remembering how much he loved the springtime of the year.

Dan quietly read the inscription on the newly erected tombstone taken from psalm 22.

'Surely goodness and kindness shall follow me
all the days of my life.
In the Lord's own house shall I dwell
for ever and ever.

Back in New York, Colin was relieved that Claude Stanhope had gone to Africa. As far as he was concerned, it wasn't half far enough and he hoped he would take his time in returning. He reckoned Claude had been a threat to his relationship with Jenny, ever since he had first clapped eyes on him at her bedside in Saint Mary's. Now that the coast was clear, he resolved to let nothing get in the way of making amends to Jenny and catching up on lost time.

Since the Easter holidays from college was fast approaching and studies and exams were well in hand, he decided to take Jenny out on the town every chance he got. She welcomed her new lifestyle with Colin, and hoped they could put the past behind for good.

'Look what came in the post this morning,' he said to Jenny, handing her the envelope. They were relaxing in her apartment after seeing a movie. Jenny opened the envelope and was thrilled with the invitation from Johnny and Clare Vaughan for Colin to be godfather to their child.

'We're very much in demand these days,' she said with a

chuckle. 'I'm delighted, Colin.'

'It's perfect timing,' he remarked. 'We can book our holidays for September since I don't start my final year till October. If you wish, we can spend the whole time in Sliabh na mBan and plan for our future. What do you think?

It was precisely what she wanted to hear but she remained cool and calm.

'Let's take each day as it comes and, well and good, in September, if things pan out in our favour, then we can do as you say,' she replied.

'I love you more than anything else in this world, Jenny, so forgive me if I sound anxious to forge ahead.'

'And I love you too, Colin, but let's enjoy ourselves for now and worry about other things later.'

His tender kiss assured her of his love. As she saw him out and closed the door, it was her brother Mattie that she would have to convince.

Dan searched his pockets for Peter O'Brien's address. It turned out that he lived a stone's throw from Dan's leased house in Central Park. It was seven p.m. on a cold dank March evening when he went to see his uncle and survey the house he had promised him as a wedding present. On the exterior, the house looked as well maintained as the others except for the small higgledy-piggledy railed garden.

Peter obviously hadn't green fingers, he thought, as he pressed the doorbell.

'Uncle Peter!' Dan shook hands warmly with his bearded uncle who greeted him with a broad smile.

'Any trouble finding me?' Peter asked, leading the way

through a fairly spacious hall to the sitting room.

'Not a bit,' Dan replied, 'sure we're neighbours. I only live round the corner.'

'That's good,' Peter said. 'Hope the place suits you and your bride-to-be.'

'It's more than generous of you, Uncle Peter I know Mary will love the place. We're both very grateful for such a handsome wedding present.'

'Think nothing of it, Dan,' said Peter. 'After twenty-five years living here, I plan to move on. Not that I have used it much mind, I always seem to be on the move around the world.'

'What do you plan to do, Uncle Peter?'

He stroked his beard thoughtfully and his eyes lit up with excitement. 'I'm off to Kenya in a few days time on Safari with some friends. It's always been an ambition of mine to explore the Serengeti Plain, shake the hand of a Masai Chief and collect a few spices in Zanzibar on the way home. By the way, I'm sorry I can't be here for your wedding but thanks for the invitation anyway.'

'We're sorry too, Uncle Peter, but maybe you'll come back to New York and spend some time with us.'

'That's very kind of you Dan I may take up the offer sometime but eventually I hope to retire in Dublin.' Peter produced a bottle of Cognac with the seal still in tact. 'I was waiting for an occasion to crack this open' he said inviting Dan to take two glasses from the cabinet. He examined them carefully then strolled into the kitchen and returned with a linen cloth. 'Can't be too careful' he joked in the presence of a doctor. He polished the glasses vigorously and poured a double each.

'To you and Mary wishing you both every happiness together' he said clinking his glass with Dan's.

'Thanks Uncle Peter' and may I on behalf of Mary, wish you safe travels and good health' Slainte!

'Marriage is a wonderful institution' Peter said and family life in the true sense I fully endorse, though sadly I never entered into that holy state myself. I may have proposed to the odd lady on my travels' he continued, usually at the end of a poetry reading or on some such occasion. Obviously I didn't impress them enough to be taken serious. Then it didn't surprise the family either that I remained a bachelor. Your mother always referred to me as 'a boil on the arse of society.' She hadn't much time for an untidy poet and writer.

Dan could easily appreciate his mother's attitude towards her brother. Presently his bread- crumbed beard and sloppy pullover didn't conjure a picture of a man who dressed to impress. By contrast she and his father had always dressed smartly and Peter on the odd occasion he visited them was obviously a let down.

'How is the writing and poetry going these days?'

'I'm still making a good living from it' he replied though I am spending less time at my laptop, and more time enjoying my travels. Why don't I show you the rest of the house before I pour another shot of brandy?

'Why not?' Dan replied thoroughly enjoying his uncles company. He followed the tall gangly man, with his corduroy pants bagging round his backside to the stairs. Peter stopped to yank up his breeches before ascending. He scaled the stairs with the agility of a mountain climber.

'The furniture and furnishings go with the house' he

remarked entering the first bedroom. It's all good solid stuff, old- fashioned maybe, but then good workmanship endures.

'It's beautiful Uncle Peter and I have an eye for this type of thing' Dan said.

Two spacious bright bedrooms were fully kitted out and two unfurnished. Peter had converted one into a study. It contained a large mahogany desk filled with books neatly stashed -among them works of some Irish writers.

'They'll be packed tomorrow by a professional packer ready for collection by a shipping and forwarding agent he told Dan. I'm sending them to a warehouse in Dublin for storage along with some other personal items.

For all his untidy appearance Peter seemed to have his head well screwed on Dan observed. 'How did you manage to keep this place so well maintained?' Dan asked. 'I mean you seem to have been away for long periods on your travels'

'Well Danny boy it's like this. When you have met as many people as I have, you'll always find someone who wants to visit New York. It suited me to give them a key to the house, for a whole year, in some cases. They were people I knew I could trust, mainly scribblers like myself. The house was minded and I had peace of mind.

Dan nodded and followed him to the landing. He stood with arms outstretched pointing to two doors at either end.

'A his and hers' he said meaning the two bathrooms. Take a look Dan.

Dan did. They were on a grand scale with fittings and fixtures of the very best quality and a great circular tub. 'I'm very impressed' Uncle Peter.

'No need to hold knees together or dance up and down in

this house' Peter joked. The architect who designed the place saw to that. A sizeable hot press and water tank completed the viewing.

'I'm the luckiest man in New York' Uncle Peter 'I almost feel guilty accepting all this. After all it's worth a fortune, and way beyond anything I had ever expected.'

'That's what makes it all the more pleasurably for me' Peter replied. 'Like I said, I have now decided to leave New York and it's good to know that a fine doctor and his wife will take over.'

'When did you say you leave for Kenya Uncle Peter?'

'On Friday' Peter replied.

'Then you'll have dinner with me tomorrow night' Dan suggested 'I know just the place.'

'Only if you're sure Dan'. I know how busy you surgeons can be'

'It will be my pleasure' Dan replied.

'So you won't object to a bit of supper here tonight' Peter said 'I make a grand ploughman sandwich with all the trimmings. You can view the rest of the place while I prepare.

Dan couldn't wait to tell Mary about the house. He knew she would love it even as it stood. They had the rest of their lives to make changes and decorate to their own taste.

The ploughman's tasted every bit as good as Peter had said. Washed down with two steaming mugs of well- brewed coffee it went down a treat.

'I believe you're marrying a lovely girl from Boston' your mother told me. She also mentioned her mother as a fine woman who has lost her husband recently.

'Mary is an exceptional woman Uncle Peter' I'm very

fortunate to have met her. And I worked with her mother in Massachusetts General where she was a nurse.

'I feel the need for some loving care and attention' Uncle Peter said eyeing Dan curiously.

'I could always arrange a meeting with Helen' Dan said.

'Tell me honestly Dan how do you think I'd measure up?'

Dan drained his coffee mug and gazed into the face of the George Bernard Shaw look alike. 'You come from opposite ends of the spectrum Peter' Helen is a home bird who has worked and lived in Boston all her life while you like to explore the world.

'A nurse conjures the imagine of one who would lead me to a barbers shop and then fumigate me' Peter joked 'I think I'll forget about it and remain a bachelor'

'Let's finish the bottle Dan and we can turn in for the night' you have to test those bedsprings you know

'That's very important' Dan replied amused at his uncles warped sense of humour.

Mary Anderson enjoyed her holiday in Rome. She had an endless amount of photographs and memorabilia to show to all her friends. Father Rigney was in his element and quite capable of giving a running commentary on the Eternal City. He had studied there for a time, preparing for the priesthood and claimed to have seen almost everything. 'Maybe you'd put a montage together for me, Father,' Mary suggested not quite knowing where to begin.

'When you return from America, Mary, I'll have it completed and I know you'll be pleased with the result. I'll start with Vatican City and work from there,' he said, delighted with the task ahead. Having left him various albums and materials for the job, she headed to visit Alice Vaughan.

Alice was busy with knitting needles and lemon wool together with a pattern for a baby's matinee coat.

'What news are you hiding from me, Alice?' she asked feigning surprise.

'Clare is three months pregnant,' she replied excitedly, 'and I'm looking forward to being a grandmother.'

'This is wonderful news, Alice. Congratulations! How is Clare?'

'Absolutely blooming'. She and Johnny are busy decorating the nursery. I believe Jenny and Colin are going to be the godparents,' Alice said.

'The news gets better by the minute,' Mary replied. 'I'd like to do something special too, Alice, if you wouldn't mind.'

'I'd be delighted. What have you in mind, Mary?'

'I'd like to buy the christening robe when I go to America, that is if Clare and Johnny have no objections.' What do you think, Alice?

'It's a beautiful idea. They'll be thrilled ' Alice replied dying to tell Clare. 'Are you looking forward to going to America?' Alice asked while making a pot of tea for them.

'I am of course,' Mary replied, 'though I would have preferred more time after Rome.'

'How is Mattie these days? I never see him at Kane's or about town.'

'He saves all his energy for Eleanor when she comes up from Cork, which is not that often. Of course, he goes to Kinsale occasionally and they are excited about their trip to Boston.'

'Is it the real thing this time?' Alice asked.

'I would hope so but, with Mattie, you can never be sure,' she replied. 'He has a habit of putting his size tens in it. Still, Clare and Johnny have set the ball rolling and I hope that both he and Jenny will follow in their footsteps soon.'

*

Nadine Stanhope returned from Paris full of the joys of spring. She couldn't believe the transformation to her shop. Bill shared her joy and enthusiasm as he carried the newly framed prints she had bought in Paris. They spent a few days hanging pictures and arranging plants in strategic positions before opening the premises to the public.

Claude had bought her a replica of Claude Monet's 'Water Lilies' that would be the main feature in the shop. She was pleasantly surprised when a number of local artists called and asked to have their paintings exhibited.

'I had no idea that things would work out so well,' Bill remarked, shedding any former doubts he had about Nadine's project. He also agreed that the newly decorated and bright Art Shop would enhance the rather dowdy street where it was located. 'It might spur the other traders to smarten up their shops,' he remarked to her. Secretly, Nadine was gloating as she drove to see how her group had done in her absence. Jackie, the former owner of the shop, had very kindly offered to stand in while she was away. It came as no surprise to her that they had been models of good behaviour and had taken well to Jackie.

In the short space of a week, Nadine was glad to see they

had finished some lovely paintings ready for framing.

'I'm opening the Art Shop on Saturday' she told them. 'I'd like to invite you all to the opening. We can display your work, and each of you can talk prospective buyers through your own painting. Jackie will brief you about sales technique. How does that sound?'

'We can't wait, Henri,' they replied in unison.

Later in the day, Jenny met Nadine. 'Any news from Claude?' she asked.

'Just a phone call to say he'd arrived safely in Kigali and he's feeling okay.'

'The women's group were just saying how much they missed him,' Jenny told Nadine, who agreed that if it weren't for the Art Shop she too would be devastated.

'I'm still not convinced he's done the right thing. Call it a mother's intuition,' Nadine said with a deep sigh. 'Will you be free on Saturday, Jenny?'

'Yes, Nadine,' she replied. 'I wouldn't miss the grand opening for anything.'

Jenny hugged Nadine and wished her luck. 'See you on Saturday' she said before rushing off to meet Dan.

Dan met her as arranged at a cafe near Central Park. He was anxious for her to take a look at his new house, especially the garden. 'I didn't get a proper look the other night since it was late and Uncle Peter and I had demolished a bottle of Cognac between us,' he remarked to an amused Jenny.

'He sounds like a great character,' said Jenny.

'You don't know the half of it, Jenny. He's like a two-year-old and gone to Kenya on safari, would you believe. Not bad for a fellow pushing seventy' Dan remarked, arriving at the house. Inside, Jenny was amazed at the spaciousness of every room. The workmanship was quite staggering with ceilings and woodwork finished to perfection.

'Do you think Mary will like it?' he asked Jenny who was busy examining the period- furniture.

'I have no doubt, Dan, and if I know my cousin, it's just the perfect place for her.'

'Let's explore the garden,' Dan suggested, going through the small conservatory. Jenny followed. A short crazy paved path led to a wooden gate. Dan had some difficulty opening it. He giggled helplessly at the mass of tangled shrubbery and over-grown grass that confronted him.

'Just as I expected,' he remarked to an equally amused Jenny. The long winter months had taken their toll resulting in moss and fungus everywhere.

'I need a gardener and quick,' he said. 'Do you happen to know a good one, Jenny?'

'Matter of fact I do,' she replied. 'Jake who kept the gardens in Lincoln Boulevard, he's regarded as top notch. He'll cost you though.'

With only a week to go till Mary would arrive home, Dan wasn't particularly worried regarding the cost.

'When can you get hold of Jake?'

'I could have him here for Saturday and, knowing Jake, he'll have this place transformed in no time. Look, Dan, there are some lovely blooms behind the cupola,' Jenny announced joyfully on making the observation.

Dan made his way through the briars and there, in full bloom, was a lovely Magnolia and Camellia. 'Maybe it's not so bad after all,' he remarked while a bluebird singing in a

Forsythia shrub seemed to agree with him.

Jenny was one of the first to arrive for the opening of Nadine's shop. Bill and Nadine were putting the finishing touches to some lovely fresh blooms just delivered while Jackie took care of the sherry and champagne reception area.

She gazed in utter amazement at the magnificent art display so gracefully displayed. Nadine and Bill welcomed her with open arms and hugs. Jackie did likewise.

'Mind if I have a leisurely look round before the throngs arrive?' Jenny asked.

'Please do,' Nadine replied.

It was the first time Bill met his wife's art students. He stood open mouthed as the lavishly clad group of women descended on the shop. While Nadine and Jackie briefed them on their duties, Bill made a few observations. Despite the fine clothes, it was obvious these women had a colourful past, he thought. What was his wife thinking about bringing them about the place on opening day? He decided that he wasn't going to stick around to find out. Damn silly woman, he muttered, putting on his jacket.

'And where are you off to?' Nadine asked, about to introduce him to the group.

'I'm going home,' he replied, 'where I should have stayed in the first place.'

'What's got into you, Bill?

'We'll discuss this later,' he said, storming off.

Nadine returned as if nothing happened. Nobody had noticed Bill's tantrum or the fact that he had left altogether. She resolved not to let whatever it was that was bugging him get in the way of business. It didn't. Crowds poured in throughout the day. The women played a stormer under Jackie's watchful eye. Patrons sipped champagne, purchased several paintings and first-day sales were fantastic. The press arrived got their story and took pictures. It had been an outstanding success far beyond Nadine's expectations and she was thrilled. She thanked the group for making it a day to remember. She thanked Jackie for making it possible.

'You did me a favour, Nadine, and I'm thrilled for you. I'd very much like to continue working with this wonderful group if you want me to.'

'What happened to putting your feet up and retiring?' Nadine asked with a smile.

'Never,' Jackie replied. 'This project of yours is so exciting, I can't resist being part of it.'

'In that case, welcome aboard,' Nadine said, shaking hands with Jackie.

'You're very late,' Bill remarked when Nadine got home. 'Would you like some supper?'

'You've changed your tune,' she replied. 'What possessed you to walk out on opening day and what became of, "I'll be behind you in this venture and hope you make a success of it?" The least you owe me is an explanation, Bill. I'm all ears.'

'To be truthful, Nadine, I couldn't believe that you invited those women. To be perfectly honest, I didn't think they were suitable or in keeping with the beautiful shop you have created, and they appeared quite common, for all their efforts in trying to disguise it.'

'It's just as well, then, that the many customers who called today weren't of the same opinion as you,' she declared angrily.

'After all, sales of ten thousand dollars in one day, with a further fifteen thousand dollars in orders, seems to me to speak for itself. They may be common in your eyes, but Claude and I were willing to give them a second chance.'

'Today was obviously a good day, Nadine, but don't come crying to me when you find yourself ripped off. Just think for a minute of the type of associates that these women have come in contact with and, in your naivety, you may be the sufferer in the long run.'

'Well, it's a chance I'm prepared to take. Besides, with Jackie on board I feel very confident.'

'Take no chances, Nadine, because as a business man all my life, I'm wide awake to the con artists and tricksters waiting in the wings. Be warned is what I'm saying.'

Nadine thought long and hard about what Bill had said. She admitted he had a point but she still didn't admire the high moral ground he had taken earlier.

'I felt humiliated and embarrassed by your action,' she told Bill. 'You could at least have waited to be proven wrong.'

'I'm sorry for being so hasty,' he said. 'On the other hand, I'm pleased everything went remarkably well for you. You deserve great credit, Nadine. Consider me well and truly put in my place.'

The Monday morning papers, complete with photographs of the occasion, gave a glowing account of the opening of Nadine's Art Shop. Photos of Nadine and the women from the group, ran alongside an editorial about how she was helping a marginalized group to build up their self-esteem, as well as launching a successful new business. The publicity did wonders for her business. Jackie was inundated with calls from people who wanted to know more about Nadine, and her art classes. Others wanted professional advice and an outlet for their own work.

Bill was keeping a close eye on the publicity. His business colleagues wondered why he had kept so quiet. 'If she needs any advice, look no further,' one business consultant remarked to him. 'Here's my card.' With all this publicity and praise showered on Nadine Bill knew he had to make amends. He booked a table for two at her favourite restaurant and had two-dozen red roses delivered to her shop.

Nadine phoned to thank him. 'Mr Stanhope has just left the building,' his secretary said. 'Would you like to leave a message?'

'Tell him Nadine phoned,' she replied.

'Congratulations! Mrs Stanhope, on the success of the new business. We're all thrilled for you.'

Nadine drove home early to prepare supper. Bill was already at home and smiled gently when she came in carrying the roses.

'I tried to call you earlier to say thanks, but you had gone,' she said, her face the picture of happiness.

He kissed his wife tenderly. 'I've booked us a table, so get your glad rags on, and let's paint the town red.'

'Thank God I haven't to face the kitchen, I'm totally shattered. The phone never stopped ringing all day. Then the roses arrived and changed everything. I love you Bill Stanhope, even when you're grumpy.'

'Nadine, I know I haven't been the most supportive, but I'm really proud of you.' 'Bill, you and I have had a very privileged lifestyle, good jobs, good salaries and holidays every year. Claude has done so well and everything has been trouble free so far. I'm just pleased to be able to give something back.'

Just then, a waiter approached the table. 'Mr Stanhope, there's a phone call for you. Come this way please.'

'Excuse me, Nadine, I'll be right back.'

'Father!'

'Claude!'

'How did the opening go, I meant to ring sooner?

'It went really well, Claude, just wait till you read the papers. Your mother got a brilliant write-up. How are you, son?'

'Okay, you know. Gradually getting used to the way of life and the people. I've met some other medics and volunteers from the various charitable organisations. But I do miss New York and all of you. Is mother there?'

Nadine rushed to the phone. 'Claude, how good to hear your voice.'

'You too, mother. Congratulations! Dad said everything went great. You must be - '

'Hello, hello, Claude, are you there?' Nadine shrugged her shoulders. 'He's gone,' she said.

CHAPTER FOURTEEN

In the run-up to Mary and Dan's wedding, the hectic pace was beginning to tell on Jenny. Mary's arrival back from Peru meant a frenzied round of engagements. From helping her select her going-away outfit to the final fittings for Jenny's own dress, they seemed to spend their time between the dressmaker and boutiques.

'I feel like something the cat dragged in,' Mary remarked to Jenny as they tucked into a pizza after a morning's shopping. Jenny felt exactly the same but assured Mary it was good fun and very exciting. They made use of the lunch break to catch up on all the news.

'Because Dan's Uncle Peter gave us that beautiful house, I've decided not to return to work,' she told Jenny. 'Dan and I have decided to start a family straight away.'

'You have plenty of space in that fine house not to speak of the garden. Did Jake do a good job?'

'Yeah. Dan told me it was a wilderness when he showed it to you, but now it's a prize garden,' Mary replied. 'Thanks for recommending Jake. He even made an M-shaped flowerbed, would you believe.'

'How is he Ralph?'

'He's looking forward to his Easter break,' Mary said, pointing out that he had maintained a gruelling schedule in Lima. 'Aside from my wedding, he's more or less going to take it easy for two weeks with his family. Then the sale of Lincoln Boulevard, and getting the Countess Von Erlich Centre for the homeless built will be his main objective.'

'Has he a site yet?' Jenny asked.

'The old parish hall near Doctor Cain's surgery is to be demolished, along with the other ramshackle buildings around it,' Mary replied. 'He reckons the money he got for the paintings, plus the sale of the house, should just about cover the cost of the building and furnishings. Do you miss living in Lincoln Boulevard?'

'Not really'. When you both left for Peru, things changed. Then when Colin and I were experiencing difficulties, I needed time to think things through.'

'How is Colin now?'

'He's fine. Looking forward to your wedding and to being best man for Dan.'

'Is Claude Stanhope coming? I haven't had a chance to check out all the guests yet.'

'Claude is gone to Africa and will be away for some time,' Jenny replied.

'Do you miss him?' Mary asked, surprised at the news.

'Yes. We became close friends, though he wanted more. I got this letter from him this morning. You may read it if you wish.'

'It's okay, Jenny, I can tell you had to make a tough decision. Claude really went to Africa to try and forget you, but he can't. Am I right?'

'I think so,' Jenny replied. 'It was tough seeing him go, and reading his letter doesn't help either. He is broken-hearted, but looking forward to coming home at Christmas. Please don't mention this to anyone, Mary, I'm desperately trying to make a life with Colin.'

'So Claude still has hopes of finding you when he gets

home. What are you going to do?'

'Fast forward things with Colin,' she replied. 'Despite the hurt he has caused me, I still think we are suited to each other. That is not to say that I didn't care deeply for Claude too. Is it possible to love two men at once?'

'The simple answer is "no", Jenny,' Mary said, realising her cousin had so much to learn. 'From the moment you introduced me to Dan, I knew he was the one. On the other hand, they say that the path of true love is not an easy one.'

'It's certainly true of Colin and I,' she replied.

'Maybe it might be a good idea to sit down and make a definite commitment to each other,' Mary advised. 'Plan ahead, let Colin know you're wishes and expectations. Of course, you've a right to know what's in his mind too, in that regard.'

'That's precisely what I intend to do,' Jenny replied.

'It can't be four p.m. already,' Mary said, jumping to her feet. 'I'm supposed to meet Dan at the hospital in fifteen minutes, and then go to his place to sort out a few things. Could you and Colin join us later for a bite of supper, perhaps?'

'It may be late by the time we get there. I have to meet the Emmanuels to finalise the travel arrangements. They're travelling to Boston with Colin and I on Friday, and I promised Sergio I'd call today.'

'Bring him with you tonight, I'd love to see him and introduce him to Dan,' Mary said.

'He'd enjoy that,' Jenny replied.

The Emmanuel's were in great form when Jenny arrived. Angela made coffee and sat Jenny down in the little front room. 'Wait till I show you my dress for Mary's wedding,' she said, serving the coffee and pastries. Victor smiled and told Jenny how excited they were at going to Boston. 'It's so long since we had a break together that I can't even remember, Jenny.'

Angela returned wearing a multicoloured chiffon knee-length dress, set off with a beaded bag and silver sandals.

'You look stunning', Angela and with Victor at your side, you'll make a very handsome couple indeed.'

'Thank you, Jenny, I'm collecting my hat tomorrow and Victor and Sergio's morning suits, then we're all set,' she said.

Victor beamed at his wife barely able to contain his delight at seeing her so happy. A light knock at the door indicated that Sergio had arrived. He hugged Jenny. 'Glad to see you and thank you for coming,' he said.

'How is school and how is the English course going?' she asked.

'Take a look,' he replied, handing her his report. 'We finished today for Easter.'

Jenny studied the report and was pleased he had done so well, in such a short time.

*

Easter Monday dawned bright and sunny, if not a bit chilly, for Mary and Dan's big day. The wedding cars had arrived at Beacon Hill, to ferry the party to the convent chapel. Helen, Mary Anderson, Mattie and Eleanor were first to depart, followed by Jenny and Colin. The light Spring breeze showered a confetti- like sprinkling of magnolia and apple blossom flowers down on the well- manicured lawn, adding to the romance of the occasion.

Helen's magnificent ensemble of cream silk, complemented by navy accessories was stunning. Dan's parents arrived with the Emmanuels and his sister, Kit. They had all been booked into the same hotel by Helen, and had become well acquainted. Kit had been assigned a special duty, to read one of her Uncle Peter's poems during the reflection of the Mass. It had been written specially by him for Dan and Mary, on the occasion of their wedding. In the peacefulness of the convent chapel vestry, Father Ralph prepared to vest for the ceremony. Sister Bernadine and Angela assisted him. Orchids and lilies filled the church with their perfume while a nervous Dan awaited the arrival of Mary.

Ten minutes past mid-day the organist struck up 'Here Comes The Bride'. Dan smiled gently when Colin wished him 'best of luck.'

The guests stood to attention to welcome the stunning bride on the arm of her uncle, Anthony Lyons. Dan's smile said it all, as he gazed on his beautiful bride, her elegant lace gown and matching headdress, receiving the wow factor from everyone.

Jenny took her bouquet of lily-of-the valley and Father Ralph welcomed his beloved couple at the altar. Colin too smiled approvingly at Jenny, who looked beautiful in a sage green figure-hugging silk gown, complementing her flowing titian hair.

Following the solemn vows of matrimony and Father Ralph's brilliant homily and lovely tributes to Dan and Mary, it was time for Kit to recite Uncle Peter's poem.

She took her stand in the exquisitely carved pulpit of the little convent chapel. Her wide-brimmed white and navy hat topping off an elegant navy and white suit. A faint smile crossed her tanned face as she glanced at her brother and his new wife. Finally she commenced to recite the poem.

April Song

Earth's heart with gladness glows again,
Gone is all wintry gloom;
The sun peeps through my lattice-pane,
And fills my little room
With life divine, and bids me fly
My books and pens awhile,
To wander forth beneath a sky
That wears an April smile.

Old loves at every step I meet,
Sweet fragrance fills the air,
Such songs of praise the birds repeat
As move my soul to prayer;
E'en primrose-clusters on the banks
And violets nestling low,
To Him uplift a look of thanks
From whom all blessings flow.

The hyacinth hangs her languid head
And waits the gentle May,
Now drawing near with noiseless tread
To kiss her tears away

The fields with daisies are besprent
As white as flakes of snow;
And from the whispering woods are sent
Joy-murmurs soft and low.

With love to Dan and Mary on your wedding day
For your health and happiness I'll always pray.

Peter

Dan kissed Mary, when his sister concluded her eloquent rendition of the poem and the guests clapped, and clapped. The convent garden was certainly wearing an April smile, as the wedding party posed for photographs. Every moment of the day was captured on camcorders, ensuring that in the years to come, the great day would be relived and remembered.

*

In the months that followed, Jenny and Colin worked hard and made plans for a future together. During the summer break from college, Colin took several students who needed grinds in mathematics. The money was good and he saved it all with one purpose in mind. He vowed to buy Jenny the best engagement ring he could afford. He even planned secretly the place he would propose to her. When she suggested that he should go home and visit his parents during the summer, he replied.

'I will never ever leave you alone in New York or anyplace else for that matter again.' He sealed his pledge with a kiss and that was that. Frequently they visited Mary and Dan, and shared the long hot sunny evenings, by the pool that Jake had created in the garden.

Dan told them with amusement how he had inveigled his parents to spend a short break in New York along with his sister, Kit.

'You see they never accepted Uncle Peter's invitation when he lived here,' Dan explained. 'They got the impression from his appearance, that he lived in squalor and were totally gobsmacked when they saw this place.'

'It's strange how people like your uncle Peter are often misjudged' Mary remarked. Maybe it's because they're free spirits, poetic, and carefree.

'That's just it,' Dan replied. 'Free-spirited people often don't give a hang about society, and yet, they can be so generous and off-hand as my uncle has proved to be.'

'I only hope some fairy godfather will look favourably on us when our turn comes,' Jenny remarked.

'Are you making any plans?' Mary asked with a twinkle in her eye.

'We have given the matter some serious consideration,' she replied cautiously. 'There are some hurdles to overcome but I think we are both mature enough to handle them well.'

'Such as?' Mary asked, half sorry she did.

'I'd like to continue helping Nadine and Father Ralph for a while longer, then of course there's my job. Colin also has to finish his degree that will set him up for his future. They're the practical considerations, I suppose, that will keep us both grounded.

'You're both still young,' Dan pointed out, reminding them

that in his case it was high time for him to make a move. 'That said, I'm glad I waited and found the wonderful treasure I did.'

'That sounds like a request to go and make some supper,' Mary replied, heading towards the kitchen.

*

Jenny loved receiving letters, especially from Ireland. Usually she looked at the handwriting and decided which one to read first. The honour normally fell to her grandma. Not this time, mainly because she didn't recognise Eleanor O'Driscoll's handwriting. Her curiosity had got the better of her as she quickly opened the envelope.

Eleanor apologised profusely at not having got round to writing sooner but went on to explain, that with preparing her students for Leaving Certificate, and extra tuition, she had been working flat out. Jenny understood and quickly read on. She had taken to Eleanor at Mary's wedding and felt that, this time, Mattie was in the right class, so to speak. Eleanor thanked Jenny for all her kindness to herself and Mattie during her visit to Boston and New York.

It had been the trip of a lifetime for her, she said. She concluded her letter by saying she was looking forward to seeing Jenny and Colin in September. And so do I Jenny thought before making some coffee.

She browsed through the rest of her mail. At the bottom of the pile, she was most surprised to find a letter from Claude Stanhope. He described life in Kigali as tough. He lived in a sort of bungalow with another doctor and two voluntary workers. The hospital was small and he was doing research and helping out in all departments. It was lonely and while he missed New York, his family and friends, he would continue doing what he had set out to do.

'I miss you most of all, Jenny, and often wish I could just see you even for a short while. The other night, for some strange reason, I thought about Joel's, and for a moment, I saw you sitting opposite me in the candlelight. I guess I must have been dreaming but the awakening was a rude one. Please write me a long letter soon. Tell me everything that's happening, no matter how trivial it may seem. Give my regards to Dan and Mary, your aunt Helen and the women's group. I love you, Jenny, and I always will. Claude.'

He was broken-hearted and lonely in Kigali and there was nothing she could do now. To even mention to Colin that she had received a letter would cause major trouble. She decided to reply to Claude just this once. She reminded him of the night in Joel's when he promised to tell her all about his life before they met.

'Now you can write me a long account of your life, Claude. I assure you it will be very therapeutic,' she wrote. 'Take as long as you like and please don't leave out a single thing. Sorry to hear you're so lonely, and of course we all miss you ever so. Love, Jenny.'

The following day she contacted Nadine and arranged to have lunch. She too had received a letter from Claude but it appeared he was in upbeat mood when he wrote to his parents. Jenny told Nadine little about the content of her letter. Nadine didn't pry too much, preferring instead to talk about the shop and the art group.

'Everything is working out really well,' she said, 'and Jackie is proving to be a great asset to all of us. I was thrilled to have had a visit from Father Ralph Melville. He told me of his plans to sell Lincoln Boulevard and how he intended to build a home for homeless people. I'll give him whatever financial help I can.'

'That's very kind of you Nadine he's going to need all the help he can get. Did he give you any indication of when he hopes to start the project?'

'Yes, he hopes to lay the foundation in August and have the work completed by the following spring.'

'So soon.' Jenny was surprised seeing as it was now mid-July. Then she remembered that Mary Jo had said she would have to find new accommodation the following week. Barbara Macy and the Shelton twins had already moved out. Colin had remained on as caretaker of Lincoln Boulevard till the sale was completed.

'Where does the time go?' Jenny remarked to Nadine. 'I mean the summer is nearly over and I'm beginning to feel the need of a holiday. Have you any plans, Nadine?'

'We're waiting to see what move Claude will make. If he goes to Germany or some other part of Europe, we may join him otherwise, we'll probably go to Paris to visit my parents,' she replied. 'Bill has no desire to go to Africa.'

'Look who's here,' Jenny said spotting Father Ralph and Sergio Emmanuel arriving for lunch. She waved cheerily and the two came over.

'The idle rich,' Father Ralph remarked to Sergio, 'nothing to do only swan around all day,' he joked.

Nadine told him it was a working lunch and, anyway, they were discussing business. 'Your business, as it happens.'

'Then you'll be pleased to hear that I've just sold Lincoln Boulevard for a very substantial sum of money,' Father Ralph said excitedly. 'Now I can press on confidently with the project.'

'Why don't I invite you all to dinner in my house?' Nadine suggested. 'This calls for a celebration and please bring Colin too. Would Friday night suit everyone?'

'Do you hear that, Sergio?' Ralph said placing his arm round him. 'I hope you have nothing planned, because to miss a meal in Nadine's house is to miss a real treat.'

Sergio smiled shyly and replied, 'I look forward to coming and thank you, Mrs Stanhope.'

'It's my pleasure, Sergio,' she replied, putting him at ease.

'Does this mean poor Colin is without a roof over his head?' Jenny asked Ralph.

'Certainly not, he's coming to live in my humble gaff,' he replied with a smile.

CHAPTER FIFTEEN

Jenny was busy making sure all loose ends were tidied up before going home to Sliabh na mBan. She completed her reports and handed everything to Mary Jo.

'I'll make sure the place doesn't crumble in your absence,' Mary Jo said. 'I'm going to miss you terribly but I hope you have a lovely time. You sure deserve a break.'

'Thanks,' Jenny replied. 'By the way, how's the new apartment going?'

'Chaotic,' she replied 'I'm lucky to find a stitch to put on my back, and I have neither the energy, nor the inclination, to sort things out. I'll get there eventually, I suppose,' she remarked philosophically.

Jenny knew Mary Jo had a tendency to exaggerate. If a suit jacket was hanging on the wrong hanger, Mary Jo considered it chaos. She was a stickler for order in and out of work. Jenny gave her a big hug and quickly made her way to her apartment. Colin and Father Ralph were waiting to take her to the airport.

'You're early,' she remarked, grabbing her luggage.

'Let me,' Colin said, loading the bags into the jeep. Ralph helped him secure the bags, pointing out that traffic was always heavy on a Friday evening. He was so right.

Eventually they arrived with just enough time to make the flight. Jenny thanked Father Ralph and apologised for not even having time for coffee.

'You guys have a safe journey and give my love to Ireland.'

'We will,' they replied dashing to the boarding gate.

Mattie and Eleanor met them at Shannon Airport with the great news that Clare had her baby the previous day. 'A bouncing baby boy,' Mattie said.

'Johnny's feet haven't touched the ground since his son arrived, he's over the moon with excitement.' Mattie continued.

'Just imagine, Clare is a mother,' Jenny hugged everyone with sheer delight. 'I can't wait to see her and the baby. Could we go straight to the hospital please, Mattie? I promise I'll only stay a few minutes, besides, it's on our way home.'

'Oh very well,' Mattie replied. 'I know I'll get no peace till you have done your cooing and I can't say I blame you.'

'Have you seen him then?' Jenny asked excitedly.

'Eleanor and I peeped in for a brief moment last night. He's gorgeous. Eleanor got to hold him while Clare got ready to change him. Didn't you?'

'It was wonderful,' Eleanor said. 'I think Clare was nervous in case I dropped him.'

Jenny turned to Colin and remarked how she was looking forward to the christening. 'Just imagine, this will be our first godchild. I wonder what they'll call him?'

Mattie spotted a florist. 'Do you want to buy a bunch, Jenny? You may as well add to the sea of flowers already in the room.'

The florist suggested a bouquet of mixed flowers with a nice spray of gypsophila and maiden fern. They smelled divine and Jenny wrote a card with a message from Colin and herself.

'You go first,' Colin suggested, when they arrived at the hospital. 'I'll follow in a few moments.'

'Clare!'

'Jenny!'

For a few moments they hugged, laughed, and cried. Both overcome with joy and emotion. 'Congratulations! How are you feeling Clare and where is the precious bundle?'

'He's just having a bath and should be back any time now,' Clare replied. 'Oh Jenny, it's so good to see you. Welcome home!'

They held hands and waited for the arrival of the baby. Jenny gazed at the new mother, serene in a baby blue nightgown, her glossy hair flowing around her shoulders.

'It must be a wonderful feeling, Clare, to be a mother. How is Johnny?'

'We're both so happy, I can't explain it Jenny. One moment, the pangs of labour grip you, and then it's all forgotten when baby arrives.'

The nurse pushed the little crib in. 'Here is master Vaughan, all cocked and powdered,' she announced, adding it would soon be time to feed him. Jenny gazed at the tiny infant with the pink cheeks and great shock of black spiky hair. She could feel the tears of joy trickling down her cheeks.

'He's a little miracle, Clare, I'm so proud to be his godmother. When is the christening?'

'Sunday week,' Clare replied. 'Would you like to hold him, Jenny?'

'Oh yes, please,' she replied, picking him up and cuddling him close. Colin arrived, smiling broadly. He hugged Clare and congratulated her. 'You look radiant, Clare,' he remarked. 'How is Johnny?'

'He's the doting father, needless to say. Life will never be quite the same,' Clare replied sagely.

Colin turned his attention to the baby. 'He's a fine healthy little chap, I'd say, and by the sounds of it could do with some grub.'

'Well spotted,' Clare replied taking him from a reluctant Jenny.

'We'll be off then, Clare, and thanks for the wonderful surprise. Your timing is perfect,' Jenny said.

'Thanks for the lovely bouquet of flowers. See you soon, eh?'

'Real soon, we promise,' Colin replied.

Mary Anderson was delighted to see Jenny and Colin. 'Sorry we are slightly behind schedule,' Jenny said hugging her grandma. 'We did a little detour and called at the hospital to see Clare and the baby.'

'Well, aren't you the sneaky old things to have got in before me,' she replied with a chuckle. 'I believe he's a bouncer and Clare is in excellent form, according to Alice. '

I'll pop in later today to see them. Meanwhile, sit yourselves down and enjoy the lovely meal Sheila has prepared for you.'

'Lovely to meet you, Sheila,' Jenny said, giving her a big hug. Sheila smiled nervously, taken aback by the friendliness of Jenny. Colin shook hands too. 'We've heard so much about you, Sheila,' Jenny said, taking her seat at the table.

'And it's a whole pack of lies,' Mattie said, causing the poor girl to blush scarlet.

Normally, in Mattie's case, she gave as good as she got but today was different. She had always had a dread of schoolteachers and in the presence of Eleanor decided not to back answer. 'Have you spoken to Alice yet? Jenny asked her grandma.

'She phoned me immediately after the delivery and twice since,' Mary replied. According to Alice Mick and Johnny's father went on the razzle after seeing the baby and the pair were absolutely blotto in Kane's bar.

'What do you make of us queer country folk, Colin,' Mary asked, noticing how amused he was. 'Sure you'd never behave like that in Dublin.'

'I love the country customs,' he replied. 'In fact, I'm going to spend as much time as I can here with Jenny, meeting the old characters and listening to their stories.'

'Then we had better get some rest,' Jenny said, 'before the jet lag takes over.'

'Have you fully recovered after the trip home?' Colin asked Jenny after breakfast on Sunday morning.

'I feel well rested and ready to climb Everest if need be,' she replied. 'Why do you ask?'

'That's good,' he replied. 'Let's get ready and climb Sliabh na mBan. We can bring a packed lunch, make a day of it, and perhaps have dinner in Kane's tonight.'

'Okay. You're on. I only hope that one of us doesn't end up collapsed in a pile halfway up. We're not that fit, you know.'

Having consulted the map, they decided on walk the Number One route. It was a distance of nine kilometres and would take about two-and-a-half hours. They would walk from Kilcash to the summit of Sliabh na mBan by the old dirt track. Jenny had often gone that route before, and indeed had done most of the more taxing routes suggested on the map.

Their chosen route however, was by far the easiest one, but since they were both out of practice, it probably was the safest bet. Armed with walking sticks, knapsacks containing food, binoculars and wearing mountain boots, they started off at eleven a.m.

On a bright September morning, there was nothing more enjoyable, with a south wind blowing the scent of heather and gorse up their nostrils. Dry stock and sheep grazed peacefully on the slopes while the river Anner gurgled gently on its way to join the river Suir.

'Of all the places in this land, this is the most romantic,' Jenny remarked, as they took their first break at the river gorge.

'You're biased,' Colin teased, drawing her close, her heart pounding from the climb.

'Maybe I am, Colin, but in the quiet of the night in New York, I often longed for this place and, dare I say, this moment. I visualised this very spot and longed to see again the native Irish trees. Just look at the birch and rowan swaying in the breeze and the stately oak,' she remarked blithely. 'I heard them in my dreams rustling and calling me. Now I'm here, I want to embrace them in all their beauty. Please tell me everything will be okay in the future.'

'Of course it will,' he replied, reassuring her with a tender kiss. 'I love you with all my heart, and I want to tell the world from the summit of Sliabh na mBan. Now, can we press on so I can make my announcement heard.'

They reached the summit at one forty five p.m. Removing their knapsacks, they sat by an old Megalithic tomb and surveyed the whole countryside. In the shadow of the various mountain ranges lay the fertile valley of Mitchelstown.

Renowned for its cheese and dairy produce, it conjured a peaceful picture today.

'Let's have a picnic,' Jenny suggested, unwrapping her salad sandwiches. Colin had ordered his favourite peanut butter and Sheila had duly obliged.

'Just imagine some of these large cairns we are looking at are about five thousand years old,' Colin remarked to Jenny. People of that era had a strange way of honouring their dead, they thought. 'How on earth did they manage to get them to the top of the mountain?' Colin asked.

'They were mighty men in those days,' Jenny replied remembering some of the poems and stories she had learned, about warriors like Cu Chulainn..

'Their diet was much better than peanut butter sandwiches, I presume,' Colin laughed.

'Wild boar was more up their street,' Jenny replied, rising to her feet.

Colin rose too. At this moment, he had far more important things on his mind, and presently asked Jenny to make a wish. She closed her eyes for a moment. 'Done,' she replied.

Nervously, Colin searched in his pocket. He then dropped on one knee.

'Jenny Anderson, I'm asking you this day on top of Sliabh na mBan to marry me. Please say yes.'

Amid tears of joy, she replied, 'I will marry you, Colin. I love you with all my heart.'

The beautiful solitaire ring fitted perfectly. She admired it again and again. They kissed tenderly, sang and danced with delight.

'This is the most wonderful day of my life Colin. I never want it to end.'

'It's the beginning of a wonderful life together Jenny' Colin said.

Jenny remembered little else of that afternoon. Later in Kane's Hotel, sipping champagne, they promised to keep it a secret till after the christening.

Baby John Michael Finnan was christened the following Sunday at three p.m. Jenny and Colin proudly accepted the duty of godparents. Robed in Mary Anderson's gift, he looked like an angel. Later at a lavish reception attended by all the relations, Jenny and Colin announced their engagement. It was as if the guests somehow expected it.

'I knew my little John Michael would take care of things,' an excited Johnny Finnan said, popping a bottle of Dom P to congratulate them. Clare hugged them both and Mary Anderson wept tears for joy.

'You may have the M.G. to drive to Dublin tomorrow,' Mattie announced. 'Your parents will be thrilled, Colin.'

Vera and John Maloney danced with joy when they arrived.

'When and where?' John and Vera asked, admiring the lovely ring.

'Yesterday on the summit of Sliabh na mBan in the footsteps of Fionn Mac Cumhail and Grainne,' Colin replied.

'How romantic!' Vera said.

*

Back in New York after their hectic holiday, Colin and Jenny had some difficulty settling back into the humdrum of daily life. Friends still wanted to celebrate their good news and weekends meant yet another party. But by mid-October, Colin had to knuckle down to some hard swotting for his degree, with the blessing of Jenny.

'The party has to stop some time,' she remarked to Mary Jo as they faced a gruelling schedule of work, with the inevitable backlog after a holiday. Still they were all delighted with the progress of the Countess Von Erlich centre. It was going up much faster than Father Ralph had expected it would, and thanks to Nadine and Bill Stanhope's friends, money was being donated at a great rate. Sergio Emmanuel was now working full-time with Father Ralph.

Tired after a hard days slog Jenny walked home wondering if her work was having any impact at all. She showered and washed her hair. It felt so good. With a glass of wine and some classical music, it was time to put the feet up. She read Claude Stanhope's letter He had done as she suggested, and given a full account of his life right up to the time they first met.

She smiled gently on reading his account of his childhood and teen years. He adored his grandparents, it seemed. Holidays in Paris and in San Tropez cooling off by the sea were wonderful. He spoke of the big old house by the sea, describing it as quite spooky. In medical school, he was a bit of a Jack-the-lad.

He loved the wild parties but studied hard too. A nice balance was how he put it. He spoke fondly of his parents but wished he had got to know his father better.

'I miss them terribly and I'm so looking forward to Christmas. I miss you too, Jenny. Your photograph is on my bedside locker to keep me company when I'm lonely.'

By way of completing the letter, he made a brief reference to his work and new friends. He had met a Doctor Kelly from Boston who said he knew Dan Flynn. Small world, she thought, folding the letter neatly and putting it safely away in her personal folder.

There would be no further contact with Claude, she told herself firmly. She was now engaged to Colin who disliked Claude intensely. On the one hand it would have been nice to be able to keep in touch with him, but not at the expense of being secretive. Colin must know everything about her life and she about his. They agreed on that.

*

The month of October had passed so quickly, Colin remarked to Jenny, while they prepared for a Halloween party in Dan and Mary's. Earlier, they had walked through Central Park where Mother Nature was wearing her autumn colours with great aplomb. Russets, gold and splendid reds bedecked the trees illuminated by the sun while the leaves danced merrily along the paths. The atmosphere was party-like with children everywhere in fancy dress and painted faces.

'What shall we dress up as?' Colin asked.

'A couple of witches, I suppose,' she replied. 'I have a few old costumes from last year that will do just fine.'

'You're on,' he said, sorting out masks, pointed hats, broomsticks and long black cloaks.

Dan and Mary's house was already full of strange eerie guests. Ghosts, ghouls vampires, pixies and an assortment of other weird and wonderful creatures.

Having welcomed their guests, Mary and Dan announced that there was a prize for the most original costume, and that immediately disqualified Jenny and Colin.

The honour went to Dan's colleague, Dick Evans. Dressed as Jack-o-Lantern, Dick stole the show and he and his lovely wife Emma won the fifty-dollar prize.

When questioned as to the origin of Jack-o-Lantern, it was left to Dan to explain. 'According to legend,' he told his guests 'Jack was unable to enter Heaven because of his miserliness. He couldn't get into hell because he had played jokes on the devil so he had to roam the earth till judgement day.'

Dick quickly divested himself of his costume when he heard the story but was thrilled with his prize. It was an evening of fun and frolics with old favourites such as snap apple, and diving for coins in basins of water being enjoyed by all.

'I have some news for you,' Mary whispered to Jenny as they prepared to serve supper to the guests. 'Can you keep a secret? Promise!'

'I promise,' Jenny replied, crossing her heart.

'I'm pregnant,' Mary said, with a broad smile. 'Dan is so thrilled, we both are, as you can imagine.'

'This is great news Mary I'm thrilled for you. I'll not breathe a word.

Please take it things easy for the time being, you hear.'

'Loud and clear,' Mary replied, placing slices of fresh lemon on the fish platter.

'How are you feeling? I mean, has the dreaded morning sickness set in?'

'I'm only two months gone,' Mary replied, 'and I'm feeling

marvellous. You know how they say you get a special yen for a certain foodstuff when you're pregnant.'

'I have heard you get cravings for chocolate and all kinds of things.'

'Well, I'm hooked on melon,' Mary replied, 'and Dan is carrying Honeydew to me all the time.'

'Seeing as it's mainly water, it can only be good for you,' Jenny said, 'just think of the beautiful skin this baby will have.'

Dan arrived in the kitchen with some friends. 'Are all the trays ready for fetching?' he asked 'There's ghouls, vampires and bats and all sorts of hungry creatures waiting for supper before preparing to haunt the night.'

'Then feed them and set them free,' Mary replied in her most dramatic voice.

Jenny pretended to stir a cauldron. 'Eye of newt, and toe of frog, Wool of bat and tongue of dog; Alders fork, and blind worms sting; Lizards leg, and howlet's wing, I hope as witch that I've catered for all.'

'I'd say you have,' Dan replied, 'now prepare to serve.'

'Just let me cool it with baboon's blood to make the charm firm and good.'

'I loved Shakespeare,' Dan said, 'especially Macbeth. Thanks, dear witch, for that little piece of drama, and now can we please have some real food before we perish.'

All the guests received a veritable banquet of delicious foods and drinks. 'Uncle Peter would have loved this party,' Dan remarked to Mary when the guests had left.

They both wondered how the Serengeti trail had gone since he hadn't been heard of him since March. 'He'll turn up,' Dan said. 'Uncle Peter always does.'

Dan wrestled with sleep and the phone ringing by his bedside. 'Hold on, caller, and I'll take this in another room,' he said, conscious of Mary fast asleep beside him. He sneaked gently out of the room to take the call.

'Kate Gibbs from Massachusetts General, sorry to call you so early, Dan,' the voice on the other end said. He and Kate had known each other fairly well when he worked there.

'What's up, Kate? Has something happened to Helen?'

'No. We have had three men admitted from Africa. They were airlifted with some army personnel and are in very bad shape,' Kate said 'One of them keeps calling Dan and we're wondering if you could help us here. The details of what happened are very sketchy but all of them are seriously ill.'

'It could be a relative of mine who went to Kenya earlier. I'll get the first available flight to Boston. Tell him I'm on my way, Kate, and thanks.'

Dan phoned Dublin. The phone rang out for ages until his irate mother finally answered.

'Dan, why are you calling at this ungodly hour? It's five o'clock in the morning here, for God's sake.'

'Yes Yes I know,' Dan replied impatiently. 'Have you heard anything from Uncle Peter lately?'

'No, I haven't, and you should know by now that Peter was never one for writing or calling,' she replied in a vexed tone. 'Why do you ask?

'Massachusetts General have been on to say a seriously ill patient has been uplifted from Africa and is calling for me.'

'That will probably be Peter alright,' she said 'The old fool probably forgot to get his jabs and is now back with yellow fever, cholera or possibly the plague. What do you intend to do?'

'Get the first available flight,' he replied.

'Let us know how he is and wish him well,' she said, ringing off.

The old man never mattered, it seemed, and nothing had changed with his mother. Why he had bothered ringing her in the first place, he just didn't know. He made some breakfast and took it to Mary

'You're up early, Dan. What's the matter, couldn't sleep?'

'It's Uncle Peter' he's been admitted with some other seriously ill patients. Kate Gibbs phoned earlier. They were airlifted from Africa and he's been calling my name. We have to go to Boston as soon as possible. I'll ask Jenny to come with us, if you don't mind.'

'Poor Uncle Peter,' Mary said, her voice full of sympathy. 'I'm dreading meeting him for the first time under these conditions after all his goodness to us.'

'I know, sweetheart,' Dan said, hugging her in appreciation for her kindness and understanding.

'Have you contacted your mother in Dublin?'

'Yes, but she wasn't very sympathetic. She claims he probably didn't get his jabs before setting out'

'I'll phone Jenny,' Mary said, 'while you make the reservations. I'll phone mother too. Do you want me to mention Uncle Peter?'

'Best not,' he replied. 'I'll drop you ladies at Beacon Hill first and then I'll head to the hospital. Okay?'

'Of course it's okay,' she replied, packing a weekend bag.

Dan arrived at Massachusetts General at two fifteen p.m. Kate Gibbs and the medical team met him.

'They're in isolation, Dan,' she said, handing him his gear. 'We've run some preliminary tests but have nothing conclusive to report just yet.' Dan spoke with other medics and they had little to go on either, except that they had been airlifted from Africa with some injured army personnel who had gone to a military hospital.

They were wearing shorts and vests only when they were found. One of the men told the officer that he was from Boston. The others were too weak to talk. 'We're expecting a spokesman from the army later this afternoon.'

'Can I see the patient?' Dan asked.

'Follow me, Dan,' Kate said. He followed her to the Isolation Unit. Kate introduced him to the nurse on duty. 'Dan is a former colleague of mine, Doctor Gibbs said. 'This patient may in fact be his uncle.'

The nurse glanced at Dan but didn't say a word. Behind a mask, it was difficult to read a person's thoughts. Dan went closer to the patient. Kate and the nurse waited. He studied the man for some time. He was jaundiced and emaciated. His beard was long and wiry and his eyes were closed. An intravenous drip of glucose was in progress and a urine catheter connected to a graduated bottle measured his urinary output. Dan shook his head.

'His not my uncle, that's for sure. Has he called my name recently?'

'About ten minutes ago,' the nurse replied.

'It's just a coincidence,' Dan said, shrugging his shoulders. 'Where are the other two men?'

'Up the corridor,' Kate replied. 'Would like to see them?'

'Please.'

They were both equally emaciated and jaundiced as the first man. One could speak a little. He claimed they were kidnapped, beaten and driven away in a truck for miles. He then lapsed into a semiconscious state.

The army spokesman arrived and asked to speak with Doctor Gibbs. 'Please wait a while, Dan, till I see what this gentleman has to say.'

Dan read the sparse few notes that Kate had written. Several blood tests had been taken including urine samples and a lumbar puncture. Dan talked with the nurse for a while.

'Why did you suppose it was your uncle?' she asked.

'Because he went to Africa in March,' he replied. 'I guess when he called my name, Doctor Gibbs thought there might be a connection.'

'But this is a young man, surely? In fact, the three of them, despite their emaciated conditions, are relatively young.'

'I agree entirely,' Dan said 'Unfortunately I didn't get enough details from her this morning. I could probably have saved myself the trouble.'

Kate returned. 'It seems these men were taken from Rwanda and dumped in Burundi where they were picked up by an Irish patrol,' she told Dan. 'It's all very complicated, I'm afraid, and the authorities are looking into their circumstances. In the meantime, we'll just have to do what we can.'

Something clicked with Dan. 'Do you mind if I take another look at the man who is calling for Dan?'

He did. This time he spoke louder behind the mask.

'This is Dan Flynn, can you hear me?'

The man moved, opened his eyes and a faint smile crossed his dry lips.

'Oh no, it can't be,' Dan said, recognising Claude Stanhope.

'Claude, Claude, what happened to you?'

Kate Gibbs froze. The nurse was crying openly. 'Get me to a phone quickly,' Dan said, beside himself with grief and torment. Kate went with him, afraid to ask any questions.

'He's a colleague from Saint Mary's,' he said to her, dialling New York. Bill Stanhope answered the phone. 'Bill, it's Dan. I'm in Boston and I want you and Nadine to come as soon as possible. Claude has been airlifted from Burundi critically ill. I'm so sorry, Bill, to have to tell you this news. Call me when you've made arrangements and I'll meet you at the airport.'

Kate had coffee arranged for Dan and they sat for a few moments chatting. Dan explained how Claude, with a brilliant future ahead of him as a neurosurgeon, had foregone everything, to research AIDS in Rwanda the previous March.

'We were very close always, although he's younger. He's thirty-five or six,' Dan couldn't remember exactly.

'This is a tragedy of mammoth proportions, Dan. What on earth happened, I wonder?' Kate held little hope for him or the others. Their livers were badly infected and they obviously had been through a terrible ordeal.

'Listen Dan I have some more urgent tests to carry out' please let me know when his parents arrive.'

'Thanks, Kate you've been wonderful, as indeed the entire team have. I have to slip out for a few minutes. My wife is here with me, I'd just like to update her.'

'Of course, Dan.'

Helen was alone in the house when Dan reached Beacon Hill. 'How's your uncle?' she asked.

'Make me some strong coffee, Helen, and we'll talk. Where

is Mary and Jenny?'

'They went down to the convent to see Sister Bernadine and Angela. The nuns wanted to see the wedding photos,' she replied.

Helen poured the coffee and they sat at the kitchen table. 'Helen, the man who was admitted to the hospital is, in fact, Claude Stanhope, and not Uncle Peter.'

Helen swallowed hard. She seemed lost for words and stared incredulously at Dan.

'Yes, I know it's hard to believe that Claude is critically ill, and so too, are the two other young men with him. Kate Gibbs and the team are doing all they can, but the prognosis is hopeless, I imagine.'

'What happened?' Helen asked. 'The last I heard of Claude was that he had gone to Africa to research AIDS sufferers.'

'That was the case. Then he was taking captive with two other men from Rwanda, and dumped in Burundi. He and the two men were found by an Irish patrol obviously days later and airlifted to Boston. According to an army personnel officer, the authorities are examining the case. That's all we know.'

Mary and Jenny came in. 'How is he, Dan?' they asked, anxious to know.

'I'm afraid there's no easy way to break this news,' Dan replied.

'He's dead, isn't he?' Mary asked, the colour draining from her face.

'Sit down a moment and I'll explain,' Dan said. 'Firstly, it's not uncle Peter. It's someone else.'

'Who?'

'Claude Stanhope and two other young men were admitted in a critical condition last night,' Dan said. He then explained what little information he knew in relation to the men.

A deadly silence gripped them. Scenes of utter grief and helplessness followed. Dan held Mary and consoled her, while Helen comforted Jenny.

'I have to see him, Dan,' Jenny said. 'Please take me to him before it's too late.'

Dan glanced at his watch. It was just six p.m. 'Bill and Nadine are on their way from New York, and I'm meeting them at the airport. It might be better if you wait till they have seen him first. I promise I'll be back for you.'

The phone rang. 'Dan, we've decided to take a cab to the hospital,' Bill said. 'Please meet us there.'

'Very well,' Dan replied. 'I'll be there.'

'I have to go,' he said. 'Bill and Nadine are going to need all the support they can get.' He kissed Mary goodbye and promised to be back as soon as he could.

Claude was still drifting in and out of consciousness when he returned. Kate Gibbs had done some more blood tests, the results of which wouldn't be available for some time. 'I had to test for HIV/AIDS, she told Dan. 'In the light of them being attacked and beaten, it could well have been that the attackers used a syringe full of infected blood.'

Dan agreed. 'By the way, his parents phoned,' Kate said. 'They'll be here in fifteen minutes.' It gave Dan enough time to contact his mother in Dublin.

'I've spent the day trying to contact you,' his mother said, 'just to let you know that by a strange coincidence Peter arrived today hale and hearty. Now, tell me what was all the fuss about earlier?'

Nadine and Bill arrived just as Claude's breathing was becoming more laboured. Grief-stricken, they held their son's hand and kissed him, his life slipping slowly away. Jenny joined them.

'I'm sorry we can't do any more,' Doctor Gibbs said. 'I'm afraid pneumonia has set in.'

'Thank you Doctor'. This is terrible, but we are so proud of him.'

'I understand from Dan that he has always worked tirelessly for his patients,' Kate said.

They said goodbye to Claude at ten p.m. His passing was peaceful. Jenny knew her life would never be the same. He had come to her bedside in Saint Mary's, and they had formed a great friendship. At this moment, it was as if he wanted her at his side in the end. She kissed his limp body and left the room. Bill and Nadine linked her to the door.

'Please don't blame me for what's happened,' she said. 'I'm really sorry.'

'Claude loved you, Jenny, and so do we,' they replied gently.

*

The weeks and months that followed were difficult for everyone. Nadine and Bill were overwhelmed by the support of everyone whose lives had been touched by Claude. Professor Manning named his new unit at Saint Mary's after him and had a plaque to his memory erected at the entrance.

For Nadine, it was all the little memories of him growing up that kept her going in her darkest moments. She found herself going through old photo albums and kissing his pictures. Bill too found some consolation in the photographs, but still regretted not having been more involved with his son. They both knew it would take a long time to recover from his death and, in between, there would be moments of calm followed by anger.

There was still no news after three months of what actually happened to the men. The cause of death on Claude's death certificate was pneumonia. Bill and Nadine accepted it.

'I'd like you to have this,' Jenny said to Nadine when she called to the shop one Saturday morning. 'I think you may find it interesting.'

Nadine unwrapped the beautifully bound folder and read the letter addressed to Jenny. 'But this belongs to you, Jenny, I couldn't possibly take it,' Nadine said.

'But I insist, Nadine. I have the original letter for myself and I will always treasure it. He has written about so many precious times in Paris and San Tropez with his grandparents, that I expect will evoke fond memories for you and Bill too.'

'You're right, Jenny, it will. Thank you so much for this, and indeed for being with him in the end. It would have made him so happy. Have you time for a chat?' Nadine asked. 'I just feel the need to share my thoughts with someone.'

'Of course I have,' Jenny replied. 'I know what you must be going through.'

'Am I right in thinking that you and Claude were very close,' Nadine asked. 'He told me he loved you.'

'We were very close, Nadine, but somehow I didn't feel worthy of Claude. 'He was loved by so many people and I always felt that he belonged to them. I could never have shared him Nadine . It's difficult to explain, but one thing I do know, it was a privilege to have been his friend.'

*

There were many moments in the past few months when Colin was glad to be sharing a place with Father Ralph Melville. Since Claude's death, he had felt the need to talk with Ralph quite often. He knew it had a profound impact on Jenny and tried with Ralph's help to get her through her grief.

One evening in particular, while the two of them chatted after supper, Colin admitted that he too felt a sense of loss.

'My loss is based on guilt,' he told Father Ralph. 'Claude was always there for Jenny when she needed him. After her traumatic experience in Lincoln Boulevard, he looked after her in Saint Mary's. And he was with her when she received the Tipperary Person of the Year award. And where was I? Sorting out a murky past, that's where. And yet I hadn't the decency to thank Claude for standing in for me. Instead, I built up hatred against him out of pure jealousy. I never once behaved like a gentleman and now it's too late, Ralph. Furthermore, I was doing Jenny a grave injustice by not trusting her. God knows, she's a beautiful woman, and who could have blamed Claude for falling for her? I'm wondering if I truly deserve her.'

'The past is over, Colin, and a bright future awaits you,' Ralph said. 'You have made your confession and now it's time to move on. You and Jenny have my blessing and I sincerely hope you will be very happy. When is the big day anyway?'

'We haven't set a date yet,' Colin replied. 'I intend to talk to her this week and set definite plans in motion.'

'That's what I like to hear, Colin,' he said. 'Make this the most important week of your life by setting that date and pulling out all the stops.'

'I will, I will,' Colin replied enthusiastically. 'By the way, have you ever been to Ireland, Ralph?'

'No, I'm sorry to say I have not, though many of my Dominican confreres come from the Green Isle,' he replied.

'I'd like to invite you to our wedding, Ralph. The country always looks well in the summer time, especially Sliabh na mBan and the surrounding Tipperary countryside.'

'Nothing would give me greater pleasure, Colin,' he replied with a smile. 'Just as soon as you and Jenny have set a date, let me know. Thank you for inviting me. That will be my summer vacation taken care of for this year.'

Colin arrived at Jenny's apartment the following evening.

'This is a surprise,' she said. 'I thought we had agreed weekends only till after your exams.'

'I know we did,' he replied. 'It's just that Ralph and I got talking last night. After a very enjoyable few hours talking about one thing and another, he asked if we had set a date for the wedding. It got me thinking, I suppose, and that's why I'm here.'

Jenny looked at the calendar. It was April twentieth and they were exactly seven months engaged. 'When have you in mind, Colin?'

'I was thinking in terms of mid-June onwards. By then, I'd have finished my exams and we'd be free to get married. What do you think?'

'I think you're crazy,' she replied angrily. 'You obviously haven't put one ounce of thought into this whole matter. You're treating it far too lightly.'

'What do you mean? I thought you'd be pleased.' Colin poured them a glass of wine.

'Have you any idea of what needs to be done?' she asked. 'There's the priest for starters. Letters of freedom and suitable dates fixed. I mean, there could be several weddings in June and the least we can do is give timely notice.'

'But we can still manage to do everything if we start now,' Colin said. 'Father Ralph has never been to Ireland and he was pleased when I invited him.'

'You invited Ralph? What did he say? I mean, he must have thought it strange getting an invitation at such short notice.'

He said he'd be delighted to come to our wedding. It really made his day,' Colin said.

'Oh, well, that puts a different complexion on everything,' Jenny remarked thoughtfully. 'If Father Ralph is coming, then I guess I better get my skates on. After all he has done for both of us, he deserves a proper 'Cead Mile Failte'.

'And he'll get it,' Colin replied happily. 'Now can we please decide on a date?'

Jenny looked at the calendar. Saturday June thirtieth. We'll wed in Cill Cais church and invite Mattie and Eleanor to be our witnesses. How's that?'

'It's perfect, my darling,' he replied, giving her a kiss. 'Now let's get dialling.'

'First thing in the morning,' she replied 'I know you're in a hurry, Colin, but I don't think they'd appreciate being called at two in the morning.'

'You're right. I am in a hurry to marry the most beautiful woman in the whole world. I want us to wed when June is bursting out all over, especially in Sliabh na mBan.' He refilled their glasses. 'I can't wait to make you my wife and I promise to take care of you always.'

'I suppose I do work better under pressure,' Jenny remarked to Mary the following day. 'Grandma was so thrilled when I phoned this morning that by the end of the conversation, I felt all I had to do was fly home and get married. '

Leave Father Rigney to me," she said. "As for Father Ralph, I'll book him and Sergio along with the Boston and New York guests into Kane's. Just you concentrate on your gown, and let me know what music and flowers you and Colin would like."'

'She's wonderful for a seventy-year-old woman,' Mary remarked. 'I think she thrives on weddings, christenings, and all social occasions.'

'She should definitely be on commission for the number of times she has filled Kane's hotel in recent years. She must be their best customer,' Jenny remarked with satisfaction.

'Are you having the reception there?'

'Yes, it's our local hotel and very well managed.'

'I'd love to be there, but I'll hardly make it in my condition,' Mary smiled. 'Still I promise we'll come as a family next year and spend some time there.'

'It's a deal, Mary.'

With just over nine weeks till her wedding, Jenny furiously wrote hundreds of invitations. Well within the six-week obligatory deadline for sending the invitations, she clapped her hands when she finished. 'Almost the entire population of Sliabh na mBan and Ticknock in Dublin had been invited,' she remarked to Colin.

'The more the merrier,' he replied, checking the New York and Boston invitations.

'We need to think about where to live,' Jenny said.

'Don't worry about it. Mattie can always give us a spare shed if we're stuck.'

'So that's why you were talking to him for so long last night.'

'He's going to be my best man, so why shouldn't we chat.'

'Why not?' she replied with a shrug.

*

The office was buzzing with excited colleagues when Jenny arrived for work the following Monday. 'It's a long way to Tipperary,' they sang, acknowledging the invitations.

'You do work fast,' Mary Jo said, stirring a great mug of freshly brewed coffee. 'Get that down you for now, Jenny, while we arrange a proper hen night.'

'Are you going to live in New York after the honeymoon?' Barbara Macy asked.

'No, I'm not, Barbara,' she replied, 'though to be perfectly honest, I have no idea where I'm going to settle. Asking Colin is like trying to get information out of the secret service.'

'All men ever think about is someone to keep their back warm,' Mary Jo remarked jocosely. 'Please can I have a show of hands of whose in favour of Friday night for the hen party?

Right, Friday, it will be. Is it okay if I arrange the venue this lunchtime and let you all know in the afternoon?' Mary Jo asked.

Everyone agreed.

'Thank you all very much,' Jenny said. 'Now I have to face

328

the music and pay a visit to the head honcho. It's time I let her know of my intentions and tender my resignation.'

*

Bill and Nadine gave a quiet dinner party for Colin and Jenny early in June. It was the first time they had entertained since Claude's death.

'We just wanted to let you know how pleased we are, to hear that you are getting married,' Nadine graciously remarked during the meal. 'Bill and I wish you every happiness in your future life.'

Jenny and Colin thanked them. Nadine tried her best to keep the conversation flowing. They had once been to Ireland, she said, when the aircraft they were travelling to Paris in developed some technical problem. The unscheduled stop meant that they travelled by coach from Shannon to Dublin and stayed in the Gresham Hotel.

'We had a lovely time there and felt honoured because Princess Grace of Monaco was staying there too. I remember our shopping spree in Brown Thomas and other lovely stores on Grafton Street,' she continued.

Colin noticed Bill smiling. 'We nearly missed our flight out of Dublin because Nadine and some of her friends wanted a lunch of Dublin coddle,' he said.

'And very tasty it was too,' she remembered, 'cooked specially for us by a wonderful chef in The Gresham. I'd like to return to Ireland someday and do a proper tour of your lovely country, perhaps next year.' Nadine said.

'Colin and I look forward to meeting you there and to looking after you,' Jenny said.

'I'd like you to have this gift as a token of our friendship,' Nadine said presenting them with Claude Monet's Water Lilies.

They both thanked her and Bill profusely for the lovely gift.

*

Tom Hanley had a meeting with Mary Anderson a few weeks before the wedding.

'I have a few favours to ask of you, Tom,' she said, apologising for giving him such short notice. She poured him a glass of stout and herself a dry sherry. She closed the sitting room door. Have a seat Tom. He wondered what on earth was coming as he crossed his leg and took a long drink of the creamy brew.

'There's a good head on it anyway,' he remarked, taking stock of the glass in front of him.

'You know that old pony's trap that is covered at the end of the big shed,' she said, sipping her sherry.

Tom nodded. 'What about it?'

'I want it taken out varnished and polished and a new set of rugs placed on the floor. Then I want Flan the pony to get a special grooming every day for the next few weeks.'

'Is the President of Ireland coming, or what? Mrs Anderson, this is our busiest time of the year as you are well aware Tom said. I wouldn't want Mattie to see me fiddling around with that sort of thing and he run off his feet.

'Hear me out, Tom,' she said, pouring him another glass of stout. 'It's you who will use the pony and trap when the day comes.'

'What day, for God's sake?'

'Jenny's wedding,' she announced, causing Tom to spurt his drink down his pullover.

'Congratulations,' he said, wiping his mouth with his sleeve. Forgive my bad manners but you've knocked me into a cocked hat with this news.

'I dare say Tom' she replied But I was wondering if you would do me a very big favour. As a respected member of the Anderson staff I'd like you to give Jenny away.

'Me,' Tom said. 'Sure you only have to ask?' 'I'm beside myself with delight and I promise I'll turn up like a Juke for the occasion. Have no worries on that score he said. Tom Hanley can rise to the level of royalty when he has to.'

Mary smiled. 'The demonstration of sleeve to gob a few moments ago didn't conjure a picture of a Juke. However, she knew what he meant.

'Thanks Tom' she said. 'I'd be grateful if you kept this a secret till the day. I want it to be a surprise.'

'My lips are sealed' he said heading off to work.

The floral decorating of the trap could be done the evening before the wedding, Mary decided. A new set of tack for Flan, together with some plumes, and his tail plaited would ensure he would look the business for the occasion.

On the morning of June thirtieth, Jenny gingerly climbed aboard the trap. Eleanor arranged her white lace gown and short train with great care for the short trip to Cill Cais church. She looked a picture as family and friends clicked and videoed her every moment. Flan proudly strutted his stuff the short distance to the church under the guidance of Tom Hanley. The gleaming old trap gaily decorated with garlands, and the colourful plumage of Flan added greatly to the pomp of the day.

Norah Leahy could be heard whispering to Luke 'Will you just look at Tom Hanley, he's like the bloody Lord Mayor.'

Tom Hanley did look impressive. Dressed in a morning coat, grey trousers and grey top hat, he clearly was pleased to give Norah an eye full.

After a moving ceremony conducted by Father Rigney and Ralph Melville, Colin proudly kissed his bride. The massive group of friends posed later for pictures. Aunt Helen, Sergio Emmanuel, Mary Jo, Barbara Macy all smiled broadly. Eleanor caught the bride's bouquet at the end of the lavish banquet. Mattie held her in his arms and whispered, 'Will you marry me?'

'I will,' she replied, without hesitation.

A delighted Mary Anderson, regal in a lemon ensemble, had one important chore left to do.

She handed the keys of a newly refurbished stone cottage belonging to the farm to Jenny and Colin.

'Thanks, grandma,' she whispered. 'It's nice to be home again,' while Colin carried her over the threshold. A delighted Clare and Johnny Finnan with baby John Michael welcomed their new neighbours.

'Which of us will take the first phone call?' Colin asked.

Jenny picked up the receiver and answered the call from New York.

'Dan. What tidings do you bear?'

'Mary has just given me the present of a beautiful baby girl,' he replied joyfully.

'That's just perfect,' said Jenny.